Fun first? Peruge, the Outsider, wondered. **Or business first?**

His hand was slippery with perspiration against the butt of the automatic. God, she was a sexy bitch! Why had she left the Hive and come to his motel room? Had Hellstrom sent her? Should he alert his nightwatch?

And then he decided. **Fun first.**

As though she had read his mind, Fancy unbuttoned the front of her smock and let it fall. She stood there naked, a sensuous pocket Venus that sent his senses racing.

Still without speaking, Fancy approached and clasped both of his bare arms. His left arm tingled and he smelled a sudden, heavy musk. In shocked alarm, he saw a tiny, flesh-colored ampule crushed beneath her forefinger against his skin. He knew he should hurl her away from him, but his muscles remained frozen while the tingling spread through him. His only awareness was of the woman who clung to him.

It was going to be a night to remember—if he lived that long!

HELLSTROM'S HIVE

Frank Herbert

CORGI BOOKS
A DIVISION OF TRANSWORLD PUBLISHERS LTD

HELLSTROM'S HIVE

A CORGI BOOK 0 552 12056 1

First publication in Great Britain

PRINTING HISTORY
Corgi edition published 1982

Copyright © 1972, 1973 by Bantam Books, Inc.

Originally published under the title *Project 40* in *Galaxy Magazine*

This book is set in 10 point Caledonia.

Corgi Books are published by Transworld Publishers Ltd.,
Century House, 61-63 Uxbridge Road, Ealing, London W5 5SA

HELLSTROM'S HIVE

Words of the brood mother, Trova Hellstrom. I welcome the day when I will go into the vats and become one with all of our people.

(Dated October 26, 1896.)

The man with the binoculars squirmed forward on his stomach through the sun-warmed brown grass. There were insects in the grass and he did not like insects, but he ignored them and concentrated on reaching the oak shadows at the hillcrest with minimum disturbance of the growth that concealed him even while it dropped stickers and crawling things on his exposed skin.

His narrow face, swarthy and deeply seamed, betrayed his age—fifty-one years—but the hair, black and oily, that poked from beneath his khaki sun hat belied these years. So did his movements, quick and confident.

At the hillcrest, he drew several deep breaths while dusting the binocular lenses with a clean linen handkerchief. He parted the dry grass then, focused the binoculars, and stared through them at the farm that filled the valley below the hill. The haze of the hot autumn afternoon complicated his examination as did the binoculars, a pair of ten-sixties of special manufacture. He had trained himself to use them the way he fired a rifle: hold breath, concentrate on rapid scanning with only eye movements, keeping immobile the expensive instrument of glass and metal that brought distances into such immediate detail.

It was an oddly isolated farm that met his amplified gaze. The valley was about half a mile long, perhaps five hundred yards wide for most of its length, narrowing at the upper end where a thin trickle of wa-

ter spilled down a black rock face. The farm buildings
occupied cleared ground on the far side of a narrow
stream whose meandering, willow-bordered bed was
only a thin reminder of its spring affluence. Patches of
wavering green moss marked the stream's rocks, and
there were a few shallow pools where water appeared
not to flow at all.

The buildings sat back from the stream—a cluster of weathered boards and blind glass at rustic vari-
ance with the neatness of harvested plantings that ran
in parallel rows within cleanly squared fencelines over
the rest of the valley. There was the house, its basic
unit in the old saltbox pattern, but with two added
wings and a bay window on the wing that pointed toward the creek. To the right of the house there was a
large barn with big doors on the second level and an
upjutting cupola arrangement along its ridgeline: no
windows there, but louvered ventilators were spaced
along its entire length and at the visible end. Up on
the hill behind the barn there stretched a decaying
feed shed; a smaller building on this end that could be
an old outhouse; another small wooden structure higher on the hill behind the farmhouse, possibly an old
pumphouse; and, down by the higher main fence at
the valley's northern end, a squat concrete block about
twenty feet on a side and with flat roof: new pumphouse was the guess, but it looked like a defensive
blockhouse.

The watcher, whose name was Carlos Depeaux,
made a mental note that the valley fitted the descriptions. It was full of default messages: no people stirring about on the land (although a distinctly audible
and irritating machinery hum issued from the barn),
no road coming up from the north gate to the farm
buildings (the nearest road, a one-way track, came up
to the valley from the north but ended at the gate beyond the blockhouse). A footpath with narrow inden-
tations apparently from a wheelbarrow stretched from
the gate to the farmhouse and barn.

The valley's sides were steep farther up and in
places almost craggy with brown rock outcroppings at
the top on the far side. There was a similar rocky up-

thrust about a hundred feet to Depeaux's right. A few animal tracks wound their dusty ribbons through oak and madroña along the valley sides. The black rock of the tiny waterfall closed off the southern end where a thin cinnamon tracery of water spilled into the stream. To the north, the land undulated away out of the valley, widening into pasture meadows and occasional clumps of pine intermingled with oak and madroña. Cattle grazed in the far distance to the north and, although there were no fences immediately outside the farm's barrier, tall grass revealed that the cattle did not venture too near this valley. That, too, accorded with the reports.

Having satisfied himself that the valley still matched its descriptions, Depeaux wriggled backward behind the crest, found a shaded patch beneath an oak. There, he turned onto his back and brought his small knapsack into a position where he could explore its interior. He knew his clothing would blend well with the grass, but he still hesitated to sit up, preferring to wait and listen. The sack contained his binocular case, a well-thumbed copy of *Naming the Birds at a Glance,* a good thirty-five-millimeter camera with a long lens, two thin beef sandwiches wrapped in plastic, an orange, and a plastic bottle of warm water.

He brought out a sandwich, lay for a moment staring up through the oak's branches, his pale gray eyes not really focused on anything in particular. Once, he pulled at the black hairs protruding from his nostrils. This was an extremely odd situation. Here it was mid-October and the Agency still had not been able to observe the farmers in that valley through an entire harvest. The crops had been harvested, however. That was obvious at a glance. Depeaux was not a farmer, but he thought he recognized the stubby remains of corn plantings, although the stalks had been removed.

He wondered why they had cleared away the stalks. Other farms he had seen in the long drive to this valley were still littered with harvest remains. He wasn't sure, but he thought this was another default message in the valley that interested his Agency so much. The uncertainty, the gap in his knowledge, bothered him, however, and he made a note to check on this. Did they burn the stalks?

Presently, sensing no watchers around him, Depeaux sat up with his back against the oak's bole, ate the sandwich, and drank some of the warm water. It was the first food he had allowed himself since before daylight. He decided to save the orange and other sandwich for later. It had been a long, slow approach to this vantage point from the place far back in the pines where he had concealed his bicycle. The van and the stake-out where he had left Tymiena were another half hour's bicycle ride beyond that. He had decided not to venture back before nightfall and knew he was going to be very hungry before he got back to the van. Not the first time on such a job. The peculiar nature of this case had become increasingly obvious the nearer he came to the farm. Well—he'd been warned about that. Stubborn persistence had kept him pressing forward past the imaginary hunger line he knew he'd have to pass on the return. The countryside was much more open and empty of concealment than he'd expected from the aerial photos, although Porter's reports had made specific mention of this. Depeaux had expected to approach from a different direction, however, and find his own cover. But there had been, finally, only the tall brown grass to conceal his stalking climb across a wide pastureland and up to the hill.

The sandwich finished and half his water gone, Depeaux sealed the bottle, restored it and the rest of the food to his pack. For a moment, he peered along his back trail to see if anyone had followed. There was no sign, but he couldn't put down an uneasy feeling that he was watched. The lowering sun was picking up his trail with a shadow line, too. No helping that; the crushed grass represented a track, and it could be traced.

He had driven through the town of Fosterville at 3:00 A.M., curious about the sleeping community where, so he was told, they generally refused to answer questions about the farm. There had been a new motel on the outskirts and Tymiena had suggested they spend a night there before reconnoitering the farm, but Depeaux was playing a hunch on this case. What if there were watchers in the town to report strangers to the farm?

The Farm.
It had been capitalized in all of the Agency's reports for some time, from quite a while before Porter had turned up missing. Depeaux had driven on to a turn-off several miles below the valley and had left Tymiena there shortly before dawn. Now, he was a bird watcher, but there were no birds visible.

Depeaux returned to the gap in the grass and had another look into the valley. There had been a massacre of Indians here in the late 1860's—farmers killing off the remnants of a "wild" tribe to remove a threat to grazing stock. As a marker of that all but forgotten day, the valley had been named "Guarded." According to a historical footnote Depeaux had located, the original name of the valley was Running Water, after the Indian name. Generations of white farming, however, had depleted the water table and now the water did not run year round.

As he studied the valley, Depeaux thought about the record of human nature carried in such names. A casual observer passing this way without doing his homework might think the valley had achieved its name because of its setting. Guarded Valley was a closed-in place with apparently only one real avenue of easy access. The hillsides were steep, a cliff marked the upper end, and only to the north did the valley open out. Appearances could be deceptive, though, Depeaux reminded himself. He had reached his vantage point successfully; his binoculars might just as well be a violent weapon. In a sense, they were: a subtle weapon aimed at the destruction of Guarded Valley.

For Depeaux, that pattern of destruction had begun when Joseph Merrivale, the Agency's operations director, had called him in for an assignment conference. Merrivale, a native of Chicago who affected a heavy English accent, had begun by grinning at Carlos and saying, "You may have to waste a few of your fellow humans on this one."

They all knew, of course, how much Depeaux hated personal violence.

From Hellstrom's Hive Manual. The significant evolutionary achievement of the insects, more than a hundred million years ago, was the reproductive neuter. This fixed the colony as the unit of natural selection and removed all previous limits on the amount of specialization (expressed as caste differences) that a colony could tolerate. It is clear that if we vertebrates can take the same route, our individual members with their vastly larger brains will become incomparably superior specialists. No other species will be able to stand against us, ever—not even the *old* human species from which we will evolve our new humans.

The short man with the deceptively youthful face listened attentively as Merrivale briefed Depeaux. It was early on a Monday morning, not yet nine o'clock, and the short man, Edward Janvert, had been surprised that an assignment conference could be called that early on such brief notice. There was trouble somewhere in the Agency, he suspected.

Janvert, who was called Shorty by most of his associates and who managed to conceal his hatred of the name, was only four feet nine inches tall and had passed as a teen-ager on more than one Agency assignment. The furniture in Merrivale's office was never small enough for him, however, and he was squirming on a big leather chair within a half hour.

It was a subtle case, Janvert observed presently, the type he had learned to distrust. Their target was an entomologist, a Dr. Nils Hellstrom, and it was clear from Merrivale's careful choice of words that Hellstrom had friends in high places. There were always so many toes around to be avoided in this business. You couldn't separate politics from the Agency's version of a traditional security investigation, and these investigations inevitably took on economic overtones.

When he'd called Janvert, Merrivale had said only that it was necessary to keep a second team in reserve for possible assistance in this case. Someone had to be ready to step in on a moment's notice.

They expect casualties, Janvert told himself.

He glanced covertly at Clovis Carr, whose almost boyish figure was dwarfed in another of Merrivale's big wing chairs. Janvert suspected Merrivale had decorated the office to give it the air of an expensive British club, something to go with his bogus accent.

Do they know about Clovis and me? Janvert wondered, his attention wandering under the onslaught of Merrivale's rambling style. To the Agency, *love* was a weapon to be used whenever it was needed. Janvert tried to keep his gaze away from Clovis, but he kept glancing back at her in spite of himself. She was short, only half an inch taller than himself, a wiry brunette with a pert oval face and a pale northern complexion that turned to burn at the drop of a sunbeam. There were times when Janvert felt his love for her as an actual physical pain.

Merrivale was describing what he called "Hellstrom's cover," which turned out to be the making of documentary films about insects.

"Deucedly curious, don't you think?" Merrivale asked.

For not the first time during his four years in the Agency Janvert wished he were out of it. He had come while a third-year law student working the summer as a clerk in the Justice Department. In that capacity, he had found a file folder accidentally left on a table of his division's law library. Curious, he had glanced into the file and found a highly touchy report on a translator in a foreign embassy.

His first reaction to the file's contents had been a kind of sorrowful outrage that governments still resorted to such forms of espionage. Something about the file told him it represented an intricately complex operation of his own government.

Janvert had come up through the "campus unrest" period into the study of law. He had seen the law at first as a possible way out of the world's many dilemmas, but that had proved a will-o'-the-wisp. The law had led him only into that library with its damnable misplaced file folder. One thing had led inevitably to another, just as it always did, without a completely defined cause-and-effect relationship. The immediate thing, however, was that he had been caught reading the file by its owner.

What followed was curiously low key. There had been a period of pressures, some subtle and some not quite subtle, designed to recruit him into the Agency that had produced the file. Janvert came from a good family, they explained. His father was an important businessman (owner-operator of a small-town hardware store). At first, it had been vaguely amusing.

Then the pay offers (plus expenses) had climbed embarrassingly high and he had begun to wonder. There had been startling praise for his abilities and aptitudes, which Janvert had suspected the Agency invented on the spur of the moment because he'd had difficulty seeing himself in their descriptions.

Finally, the gloves had come off. He'd been told pointedly that he might find other government employment difficult to obtain. This had almost put his back up, because it was common knowledge that he'd set his sights on the Justice Department. In the end, he'd said he would try it for a few years if he could continue his law education. By that time, he'd been dealing with the Chief's right-hand man, Dzule Peruge, and Peruge had evinced profound delight at this prospect.

"The Agency needs men with legal training," Peruge said. "We need them desperately at times."

Peruge's next words had startled Janvert.

"Has anyone ever told you that you could pass for a teen-ager? That could be very useful, especially in someone with legal training." This last had come out with all the overtones of an afterthought.

The facts were that Janvert had always been kept too busy to complete his valuable legal training. "Maybe next year, Shorty. You can see for yourself how crucial your present case is. Now, I want you and Clovis—"

That had been how he'd first met Clovis, who also had that *useful* appearance of youth. Sometimes, she'd been his sister; other times they'd been runaway lovers whose parents "didn't understand."

The realization had come rather slowly to Janvert that the file he had found and read was more sensitive than he had imagined and that a probable alternative to his joining the Agency had been a markerless grave in some southern swamp. He had never participated in a "swamping," as Agency old-timers put it, but he knew for a fact that they occurred.

That's how it was in the Agency, he learned.

The Agency.

No one ever called it anything else. The Agency's economic operations, the spying and other forms of espionage only confirmed Janvert's early cynicism. He saw the world without masks, telling himself that the great mass of his fellows had no realization whatsoever that they already lived in what was, for all intents and purposes, a police state. This had been inevitable from the formation of the first police state that achieved any degree of world power. The only apparent way to oppose a police state was by forming another police state. It was a condition that fostered its mimic forces on all sides (so Clovis Carr and Edward Janvert agreed). Everything they saw in the society took on police-state character. Janvert said it. "This is the time of the police states."

They made this a tenet of their pact to leave the Agency together at the first opportunity. That their feelings for each other and the pact thus engendered were dangerous, they had no doubts. To leave the Agency would require new identities and a subsequent life of obscurity whose nature they understood all too well. Agents left the service through death in action or a carefully guarded retirement—or they sometimes just disappeared and, somehow, all of their fellows got the message not to ask questions. The most persistent retirement rumor in the Agency mentioned *the farm;* decidedly not Hellstrom's farm. It was, instead, a carefully supervised rest home that none located with precise geography. Some said northern Minnesota. The story described high fences, guards, dogs, golf, tennis, swimming, splendid fishing on an enclosed lake, posh private cabins for "'guests," even quarters for married couples, but no children. Having children in this business was considered equal to a death sentence.

Both Carr and Janvert agreed they wanted children. Escape would have to occur while they were overseas together, they decided. Forged papers, new faces, money, the requisite language facility—all of the physical necessities were within reach except one: the opportunity. And never once did they suspect adolescent fantasy in such dreams—nor in the work that occupied their lives. They would escape—someday.

Depeaux was objecting to something in Merrivale's briefing now. Janvert tried to pick up the thread: something about a young woman trying to escape from Hellstrom's farm.

"Porter's reasonably certain they didn't kill her," Merrivale said. "They just took her back inside that barn that we are told is the main studio for Hellstrom's movie operation."

From the Agency report on Project 40. The papers were dropped from a folder by a man identified as a Hellstrom aide. The incident occurred in the MIT main library early last March as explained in the covering notes. The label "Project 40" was scribbled at the top of each page. From an examination of the notes and diagrams (see enclosure A), our experts postulate developmental plans for what they describe as "a toroidal field disrupter." This is explained as an electron (or particle) pump capable of influencing physical matter at a distance. The papers are, unfortunately, incomplete. No definite line of development can be determined from them, although our own laboratories are exploring the provocative implications. It seems obvious, however, that someone in the Hell-

strom organization is at work on an operational prototype. We cannot be certain (1) whether it will work or
(2) if it works, to what use it will be put. However, in
view of Dr. Zinstrom's report (see enclosure G) we
must assume the worst. Zinstrom assures us privately
that the theory behind such a development is sound
and that a toroidal field disrupter large enough, amplified enough, and set to the correct resonance could
shatter the earth's crust with disastrous consequences
for all life on our planet.

"This is really a plum of a case we're handing to
Carlos," Merrivale said. He touched his upper lip,
brushing an imaginary mustache.

Carr, who was seated slightly behind Depeaux and
facing Merrivale, noted the flush of sudden red at Depeaux's neck. He didn't like that obvious, pandering
statement. The morning sun was shining in the window to Merrivale's right, reflecting off the desk with a
yellow brown underlight which imparted a saturnine
cast to the operations director's face.

"That movie-company front has got Peruge's wind
up, I must say," Merrivale said. (Depeaux actually
shuddered.)

Carr coughed to conceal a sudden hysterical desire to laugh aloud.

"Under the circumstances, we don't dare go in and
root them out, as I'm sure you can understand," Merrivale said. "Not enough evidence in our kip. Your
job, that. This movie front does offer one of our most
promising points of entry, however."

"What's the subject matter of this film?" Janvert
asked.

They all turned to look at him and Carr wondered
why Eddie had interrupted. He seldom did that sort of
thing casually. Was he fishing for some of the information *behind* Merrivale's briefing?

"I thought I said," Merrivale said. "Insects! They're
making a film about bloody insects. A bit of a surprise,
that, when Peruge first mentioned it. I confess my own
first guess was that they were making unsavory sex

films and—ahhh, blackmailing someone in a sensitive position."

Depeaux, sweating and under a profound aversion to Merrivale's bogus accent and manner, squirmed in his chair, resenting the interruption. Get on with it! he thought.

"I'm not sure I understand the sensitive conditions around Hellstrom's operation," Janvert said. "I'd thought the film would supply a clue."

Merrivale sighed. Bloody nitpicker! He said, "Hellstrom is something of a madman on the subject of ecology. I'm sure you know how politically sensitive *that* subject is. There's also the fact that he is employed as a consultant by several, I repeat, *several* persons of extremely powerful influence. I could name one senator and at least three congressmen. If we were to move frontally against Hellstrom, I'm sure the repercussions would be severe."

"Ecology, eh," Depeaux said, trying to get Merrivale back on track.

"Yes, ecology!" Merrivale made the word sound as though he wanted it to rhyme with sodomy. "The man has access to considerable sums of money, too, and we'd like to know about that."

Depeaux nodded, said, "Let's get back to that valley."

"Yes, yes indeed, Merrivale agreed. "You've all seen the map. This little valley's been in Hellstrom's family since his grandmother's day. Trova Hellstrom, pioneer, widow, that sort of thing."

Janvert rubbed a hand across his eyes. He was sure from Merrivale's description of Trova Hellstrom that the intended picture was of a tiny "widow woman" fighting off attacking redskins from a blazing log cabin, her brats passing a bucket brigade behind her. The man was unbelievable.

"Here's the map," Merrivale said, extracting it from the papers on his desk. "Southeastern Oregon, right here." He touched the map with a finger. "Guarded Valley. The closest civilization is this town here with the unlikely appellation of Fosterville."

Carr wondered: Why an unlikely name? She

glanced covertly at Janvert, but he was examining the palm of his right hand as though he had just found something fascinating in it.

"And they do all of their filming in this valley?" Depeaux asked.

"Oh, no!" Merrivale protested. "My God, Carlos. Didn't you read enclosures R through W?"

"There were no such enclosures in my file," Depeaux said.

"Bloody hell!" Merrivale said. "Sometimes, I wonder how we ever get anything done correctly in this establishment. Very well. I'll give you mine. Briefly, Hellstrom and his camera crews and whatnot have been all over the bloody world: Kenya, Brazil, Southeast Asia, India—it's all in here." He tapped the papers on his desk. "You can see for yourself later."

"And this Project 40?" Depeaux asked.

"That's what attracted our attention," Merrivale explained. "The pertinent papers were copied and the originals returned to where they were found. The Hellstrom aide subsequently returned for his papers, found them where he expected, took, them, and departed. Their significance was not understood at the time. Purely routine. Our man on the library staff was curious, no more, but the curiosity became increasingly intense as the papers were bounced upstairs. Unfortunately, we've not had the opportunity to observe this particular Hellstrom aide since that moment. He apparently is keeping to the farm. It is our belief, however, that Hellstrom is unaware that we know about his little project."

"The speculation seems a little like science fiction, more than a little fantastic," Depeaux said.

Janvert nodded his agreement. Were those explicit suspicions the real reason the Agency was prying into Hellstrom's affair? Or was it possible that Hellstrom was merely developing a product that threatened one of the groups that actually paid most of the Agency's expenses? You never knew in this business.

"Haven't I heard of this Hellstrom before?" Carr asked. "Isn't he the entomologist who came out against DDT when—"

"That's the chap!" Merrivale said. "Pure fanatic. Now, here's the farmstead plan, Carlos."

So much for my question, Carr thought. She curled her legs under her in the wing chair, glanced openly at Janvert, who returned her stare with a grin. He's just been playing with Merrivale, she realized, and he thinks I'm in the game.

Merrivale had a blueprint map on his desk now, unfolding it, indicating features on it with his long, sensitive fingers. "Barn here—outbuildings—main house. We have every reason to believe, as those reports indicate, that the barn is Hellstrom's studio. Curious concrete structure here near the entrance gate. Can't say what purpose it serves. Your job to find out."

"And you don't want us to go right in, nose around," Depeaux said. He frowned at the blueprint map. This decision puzzled him. "The young woman who tried to get away—"

"Yes, that was March 20 last," Merrivale said. "Porter saw her run from the barn. She got as far as the north gate here when she was apprehended by two men who came upon her from beyond the fence. Their point of origin was not determined. They did, however, return her to the barn-studio."

"Porter's account says these people weren't wearing any clothes," Depeaux said. "It seems to me that a report to the authorities giving a description of—"

"And we'd have had to explain why we were there, send our one man up against numerous Hellstrom accomplices, all of this in the presence of the *new morality* that permeates this society."

You damned hypocrite! Carr thought. You know how the Agency uses sex for its own purposes.

Janvert leaned forward in his chair and said, "Merrivale, you're holding something back in this case. I want to know what it is. We have Porter's report, but he's not here to amplify it. Is Porter available?" He sat back. "A simple yes or no will suffice."

That's a dangerous tack to take, Eddie, Carr thought. She watched Merrivale intently to measure his response.

"I can't say I care for your tone, Shorty," Merrivale said.

Depeaux leaned back, put a hand over his eyes.

"And I can't say I care for your secrecy," Janvert said. "We would like to know the things that are not in these reports."

Depeaux dropped his hand, nodded. Yes, there were some things about this case . . .

"Impatience is not seemly in good agents," Merrivale said. "However, I can understand your curiosity, and the need-to-know rule has not been applied in this case. Peruge was specific on that. What has our wind up, as it were, is not just this Project 40 thing, but the accumulation of items, the indications that Hellstrom's film activities are actually (he pronounced it *exshooly*, and once more for emphasis)—*actually* a cover for serious and highly subversive political activities."

Bullshit! Janvert thought.

"How serious?" Carr asked.

"Well—Hellstrom has been nosing around the Nevada atomic-testing area. He conducts entomological researches, as well, you see. His films are offered under the guise of documentary productions. He has had atomic materials for his so-called researches and—"

"Why *so-called?*" Janvert asked. "Isn't it possible he's just what he—"

"Impossible!" Merrivale snorted. "Look, it's really all in the reports here. Observe especially the indications that Hellstrom and his people may be interested in forming some sort of new communal society. It's quite provocative. He and his film crew live that sort of life wherever they go—off to themselves, clubby—and their preoccupation with the emerging African nations, the numerous visits to the Nevada testing area, the ecology thing with its highly inflammatory nature, the—"

"Communist?" Carr interrupted.

"It's—ahhh—possible."

Janvert said, "Where's Porter?"

"That—ahh—" Merrivale pulled at his chin. "That's a bit sticky. I'm sure you understand the delicacy of our position in all of—"

"I don't understand it," Janvert said. "What's happened to Porter?"

"That's one of the things we hope Carlos can ascertain," Merrivale said.

Depeaux turned a speculative look on Janvert, returned his attention to Merrivale, who had sunk back into apparent concentration on the blueprint map.

"Porter's missing?" Depeaux asked.

"Somewhere around this farm," Merrivale said. He looked up as though just noticing Depeaux. "Presumably."

From recorded comments of brood mother Trova Hellstrom. Some threat is good for a species. It tends to stimulate breeding, to raise the level of awareness. Too much, however, can have a stupefying effect. It is one of the tasks of Hive leadership to adjust the level of stimulating threat.

As the sun moved lower behind him on the hill above Guarded Valley, Depeaux took care that the light did not outline him. There were both advantages and disadvantages in such light. It tended to throw some details of the farm into relief—the fencelines, the paths on the opposite hillside, the weathered boards on the barn's western face.

There still had not been one sign of human activity outside the buildings and no sure indication of humans within them. The irritating hum continued to issue from the barn and Depeaux had exhausted his speculations on what it might be. He had opted tentatively for air conditioning and wished he could enjoy that relief from the hot afternoon in the dusty grass.

A long, cold drink, that's what I need, he told himself.

The fact that the farm fitted all of the reports and the descriptions (including Porter's) did not really say anything for it.

Depeaux scanned the valley once more through

his binoculars. There was a peculiar *waiting* air to the
emptiness of the place, as though forces were being
marshaled to fill the farm with life.

Depeaux wondered what Hellstrom did with his
farm's products. Why was the entire area so devoid of
human activity? There'd been no vacationers or picnickers on the dirt road to the valley—although the
area seemed attractive enough. Why were the Fosterville residents so closemouthed about Hellstrom's farm?
Porter had been intrigued by this, too. This was a hunting area, but Depeaux had seen no deer sign and not
one hunter. The stream obviously held no attraction for
fishermen, but still . . .

A Steller's jay flapped into the tree behind Depeaux, called once with its raucous voice, then flew
across the valley into the trees of the far slope.

Depeaux watched the bird's flight with peculiar
interest, realizing it was the first higher life form he'd
seen in Hellstrom's valley. One damned jay! That was
some record for a day's work. But he was supposed to
be a bird watcher, wasn't he? Just a simple little old
vacationer, a traveling salesman for the Blue Devil
Fireworks Corporation of Baltimore, Maryland. He
sighed, worked his way back to the oak's shade. He
had studied the maps, the aerial photographs, Porter's
descriptions, all of the accumulated reports. Every detail had been committed to memory. He scanned his
back trail with the binoculars. Nothing moved in the
tall grass of the open area or in the trees beyond it.
Nothing. The oddity of this became increasingly demanding of his attention.

One damned jay?

It had been a thing long inserting itself into his
awareness, but now he focused on it to the exclusion
of all other considerations. One bird. It was as though
animal life had been swept away from the region
around Guarded Valley. Why hadn't Porter mentioned
that? And the grazing cattle down there to the north
toward Fosterville. No fence kept them from approaching the farm, but they kept their distance.

Why?

In that instant, Depeaux recognized what it was

that had made the farm's fields appear so strange to him.

They were clean.

Those fields had not been harvested. They had been swept clean of every stalk, every leaf, every twig. An orchard occupied the upper reaches of the valley and Depeaux crawled back to study it through the binoculars. There were no bits of rotten fruit on the ground, no culls, no leaves or limbs—nothing.

Clean.

But the tall grass remained all around on the perimeter hills.

Hellstrom's own addenda to the dietary notes. The key workers must, of course, take the supplemental leader foods without fail, but it is equally important that they keep up their intake from the vats. It is here that we get the markers that maintain our awareness of mutual identity. Without the chemical sameness provided by the vats, we will become like those Outside: isolated, alone, drifting without purpose.

By late afternoon, Depeaux had become almost obsessed with the desire to find something animal and alive in the valley. But nothing stirred there and the sun had moved several long notches toward the horizon.

Perhaps another vantage point, he thought.

The longer he stayed on the hill above the farm, the less he liked his cover story. Bird watcher, indeed! Why hadn't Porter mentioned the absence of animal life? Insects, of course: the grass was alive with them, crawling, buzzing, flitting.

Depeaux slid and crawled away from the crest, got to his knees. His back ached from all of the unnatural movement. Grass burrs had invaded his collar, under his belt, under his stocking, up his sleeves. He managed a smile, half grimace, at his own discomfort; he could almost hear Merrivale commenting, *Part of*

*the price you pay for engaging in this line of work, old
bean.*

Son of a bitch!

Porter's careful reports had indicated no guards
posted outside the farm's perimeter, but that was just
one man's account. Depeaux asked himself how he felt
about his position in the open under the oak. You
stayed alive in this business by trusting only your own
senses ultimately—and Porter was missing. That represented an important piece of information. It could
be innocent or ominous, but it was safer to believe the
worst. At the worst, Porter was dead and the people of
Hellstrom's farm were responsible. Merrivale believed
this. He'd made that clear, and the secretive bastard
could have information to confirm it without any of
his agents being the wiser.

"You will proceed with the utmost caution, keeping in mind at every juncture our need to determine
precisely what has happened to Porter."

The son of a bitch probably already knows, Depeaux told himself.

Something about the emptiness of the region
spoke of hidden dangers. Depeaux reminded himself
that agents who leaned too heavily on the reports of
others often ended up dead, sometimes in painful and
ugly fashion. What was it about this place?

He swept his gaze around his back trail, saw no
sign of movement or watching eyes. A glance at his
watch told him he had slightly more than two hours
before sunset. Time to get to the head of the valley
then and scan the length of it.

Bending low at the waist, Depeaux got to his feet
and, in a crouching trot, moved swiftly toward the
south below the concealing ridge. His breathing deepened easily with the effort and he thought for a moment that he wasn't in such bad condition for a man of
fifty-one. Swimming and long walks weren't the worst
recipe in the world, and he wished he were swimming
that instant. It was dry and hot under the ridge, the
grass full of nose-tickling dust. Desire for a swim did
not bother him greatly. Such wishes had come often in
the sixteen years since he'd moved up from an office

clerk in the Agency. He usually passed off the fleeting desire to be elsewhere as an unconscious recognition of danger, but sometimes it could be attributed to no more than bodily discomfort.

When he'd been a mere clerk in the Baltimore office, Depeaux had enjoyed his daydreams about working as an agent. He'd filed final reports on agents "wasted in action" and had told himself that if he ever got to be an agent, he would be extremely cautious. That had not been a hard promise to keep. He was, by nature, careful and painstaking—"The perfect clerk," some of his fellows carped. But it was painstaking care that had led him to commit the farm and its surroundings to memory, to note possible cover (little enough of that!), and the game trails through the tall grass indicated on aerial photos.

Game trails but no visible game sign, he reminded himself. What kind of game ran these paths? It was another note added to his increasing sense of caution.

Depeaux had once overheard Merrivale commenting to another agent, "The trouble with Carlos is he plays for survival."

As though old *Jolly*vale didn't do the same! Depeaux told himself. The man hadn't reached his present eminence as operations director without an eye for the main line.

Depeaux could hear the faint trickling of the waterfall. A clump of madroñas stood at the invisible line on Depeaux's mental map, marking the northernmost reach of Hellstrom's valley. Depeaux paused in the shade of the madroñas and made another survey of his surroundings, paying special attention to his own back trail. Something about that open area—nothing moved in it, but Depeaux made a decision then and there to wait for darkness to cover his return across that space.

Thus far, it had not been too bad a go, he told himself. Just that faintly disquieting sense of an unknown danger. The second examination of the valley from this upper vantage point should not take too long. Perhaps he might reconsider and go back by daylight to the bicycle and an early check-in with Tymiena at the van. Perhaps. That first sense of decision to wait for darkness had gone deeply into him, though.

Play it safe, he reminded himself. Play for survival.

He turned left briskly, unslung his binoculars, and slipped up through a stand of oak and madroña to a clump of oily green bushes behind the rock face of the valley's upper limit. The tinkling waterfall was quite noisy off through the undergrowth. At the bushes, Depeaux dropped to all fours, tucking the binoculars under his shirt and cinching the pack tightly against his right side. He went through the now-familiar stalking crawl, turning partly onto his left side to protect the binoculars and keep the pack off the ground. The bushes ended presently in a short rock lip which exposed a lengthwise view of Guarded Valley.

As he brought out the binoculars, Depeaux wondered idly where the "wild" Indians had been slaughtered. The noise of the waterfall was quite loud about fifty feet to his right. He rested on his elbows, brought up the binoculars.

The farm buildings were farther away from him this time and the large barn-studio concealed all but the western wing of the house. A crooked stretch of stream was clearly visible from this new vantage. Its surface remained mirror calm, as though stagnant, reflecting the trees and brush at its verge. The view opened up at the valley's far end, revealing the rolling grasslands and clumps of trees, the patches of distant cattle.

Why wouldn't the cattle venture nearer into the rich grass closer to the end of the valley? There was nothing visible to keep them away: no fence, no ditch —nothing.

Depeaux became aware of a vehicle moving in a dust cloud far off beyond the cattle. That was the narrow track he and Tymiena had taken. Who was coming down there? Would they see the van-camper? Tym would be out there with her paints drawing pictures of the stupid landscape, of course, but still . . . Depeaux focused his binoculars on the dust, made out presently a large covered truck. It was following the crazy meander track toward the valley and moving fast. He tried to locate Tymiena, but the hill to his left blocked off that vista, and they'd taken the camper into tree shade along a side road. The oncoming truck might not come close enough to see her. It made no difference, anyway, he told himself. A strange excitement gripped him.

He brought his attention back to the farm buildings. Surely, someone would come out and greet the truck. He would get his first look at the occupants of this odd place. He studied the scene intently.

Nothing moved within the valley.

They must hear the truck. He could hear it himself even from this greater distance and above the waterfall's intrusion.

Where were the farm's occupants?

The binoculars had collected dust again. Depeaux paused to reflect on the situation while he applied the linen cloth once more to the lenses. He knew it might appear ridiculous, but the absence of surface activity in the presence of so much evidence that people carried on an active life here filled him with disquiet. It wasn't natural! Everything was so damned *motionless* in the valley. He experienced the skin-creeping sensation of being watched by countless eyes. When he rolled over and peered backward through the brush, he could see not one moving thing. Why did he expect trouble from these conditions? He did, though, and his inability to explain the expectation filled him with irritation. What were they hiding here?

Despite Merrivale's attempts to present this case as a plum for the chosen agent, Depeaux had tasted the sourness of it from the beginning. Shorty Janvert obviously had shared that sense of something profoundly wrong. This thing was sour! And it was not the sourness of green fruit and easy pickings. It was a prickling of the senses that came from knowledge of something overripe and rotten, something stewed too long in its own sour juices.

The truck was just beyond the valley now, making its final climb up the easy slope to the north fence. Depeaux brought his binoculars to bear on it once more, saw two white-clad figures in the cab. They were visible only dimly through sun reflections on the windshield.

And still, no one came from the farm buildings.

The truck turned close to the north fence, revealing large words on its flat white side: *N. Hellstrom, Inc.* The machine made a wide turn until it was heading away from the farm, stopped then, and backed up to the gate. Two blond young men emerged from the cab. They trotted briskly to the rear, dropped the gate that extended to a ramp on rollers. They clambered up into the open cave of the bed, slid a tall yellow and gray box from the shadows there. The box appeared heavy from the way they strained. They tipped it onto the gate's rollers, let it slide swiftly to a jolting, dusty stop on the ground.

What the hell was in that box? It was big enough for a coffin.

The men hopped down, strained against the box until they brought it teetering upright. They walked it then to a position clear of the tail gate, closed up the truck, got back into the cab, and drove away.

The box remained about ten feet outside the north gate.

Depeaux examined the surface of the box through his binoculars. It was taller than the men from the truck and it was heavy. It appeared to be made of wood and was bound by what seemed to be flat metal straps that ran around it from the top to the bottom.

A delivery, Depeaux mused. What in hell could be delivered to this farm in a box that shape?

Hellstrom had his own truck to bring things to the farm, but he didn't worry about his deliveries waiting in the sun outside his gate. There might be nothing unusual about that, on the surface of it. The Agency's dossier carried considerable information about Hellstrom's film company. That was the N. Hellstrom, Inc. Hellstrom was both owner and manager. He made documentary films about insects. Sometimes, Hellstrom's film efforts were incorporated into quite substantial productions which were distributed through other companies in Hollywood and New York. It was all easily explained until you sat on this hillside and

watched the operation, as Depeaux was doing now
and as Porter had done before him. What had become
of Porter? And why wouldn't Merrivale permit a
straightforward missing-person investigation?

There was something else about Hellstrom's operation.

His nonoperation.

From the Hive Manual. The relationship between
ecology and evolution is extremely close, deeply impli-
cated in organic changes among a given animal population, and profoundly sensitive to the density of numbers within a given habitat. Our adaptations aim to
increase the population tolerance, to permit a human
density ten to twelve times greater than is currently
considered possible. Out of this, we will get our survival variations.

The conference room held an air of detached
waiting as Dzule Peruge strode in and took the Chief's
chair at the head of the long table. He glanced at his
wristwatch as he put his briefcase on the table: 5:14
P.M. In spite of it being Sunday, they were all present,
all of the important men and the one woman who
shared responsibility for the Agency.

Without any of the usual preparations, Peruge sat
down and said, "I've had an extremely trying day. To
cap it, the Chief called me just two hours ago and told
me I would have to deliver his report to you. He had
to take care of some questions from upstairs. That, of
course, took priority."

He swept his gaze around the room. It was a
quiet and cushioned place, this penthouse board room.
Gray curtains covered the double windows on the
north side, giving the sun's afternoon rays a feeling of
cool, underwater light as they filtered through to the
dark, polished wood of the tabletop.

There were some impatient coughs around the table, but they took the replacement without objection.
. Peruge squared the briefcase in front of him, ex-

tracted its contents—three thin folders. He said, "You've all seen the Hellstrom file. The Chief tells me he circulated it three weeks ago. You will be glad to know that we have now cracked the code on page 17 of the original papers. It was a rather interesting code based on a four-unit configuration that our people tell me was derived from the DNA code. Very ingenious."

He cleared his throat, pulled one thin sheet from the top folder, scanned it. "Again, this refers to Project 40, but this time distinctly in terms of a weapon. The exact words are 'a sting that will make our workers supreme over the entire world.' Very suggestive."

A man down the table on Peruge's left said, "Poppycock! This Hellstrom produces movies. That could be a dramatic piece of business for a film."

"There is more," Peruge said. "It includes partial instructions for an exchange circuit which our man at Westinghouse assures us is real. He was quite excited by the implications. He called it 'another key to the puzzle.' He concedes that it is an incomplete key; where the circuit would fit in the larger scheme is not indicated. However, there was one more item in the coded section."

Peruge paused for effect, glanced once around the table. "The message is quite direct. It instructs the bearer of the subject papers to transmit his future reports through a man in Washington, D.C. The man is named. He is the senator whose activities we have come to question."

Peruge wanted to laugh. Their reaction was precisely what the Chief had said it would be. He had their undivided attention, a thing seldom granted in this room of giants.

The man directly at his left said, "No doubt of that?"

"None whatsoever."

From Dzule Peruge's original report on Joseph Merrivale. Subject has no detectable inhibiting emotions of warmth toward his fellows, but he counterfeits these reactions quite well. His administrative abilities are adequate for the necessary tasks, but he lacks qualities of initiative and daring. He is exactly what we had in mind, a man who can keep his division running smoothly and can, if directed, send his people to their deaths without a qualm. Promotion recommended.

As he left the conference, Peruge allowed himself a small sense of triumph. There had been a few touchy moments with that bitch, but he had managed them well, all things considered. He still could not understand why they had ever allowed a woman onto that board.

It was raining when he reached the street, freshening the evening air, but also imparting a smell of wetted dust that Peruge particularly disliked. He hailed a cab.

The driver, as luck would have it, was a woman. Peruge settled back into the seat with a sigh of resignation and said, "Take me to the Statler."

There was no telling where women would intrude next, he thought. They were essentially frail things and should not be allowed into these occupations. He had that judgment from observations of his mother who had gone through life torn by conflicting attitudes toward her ancestry and toward the demands of her sex. That she knew about, she had black, Cherokee, Portuguese, and Cajun ancestors. Sometimes, she had been proud of her progenitors. "Never forget, boy, that your ancestors were here before the first white thief set foot on these shores." Other times, she would remind him, "We were sailors under Henry the Navigator when most sailors never came back from a long voyage." But she could temper these outbursts of bitter pride with cautious warnings: "Dzule, you look white enough for nobody ever to know about the niggers in our blood. Play the white game, boy; that's the only way to win in this world."

And he had won the field this day, no doubt about that. The bitch of the board room had tried to cross-examine him about Hellstrom's corporate activities, trying to catch him in a contradiction. The Chief had warned him about that. "They'll try to take advantage of you and check up on the Agency. I'm trusting you to give them blow for blow." That was the Chief for you: like a father to those he trusted.

Peruge had never known his own father, who had been only the first in a long line of men who partook of Juanita Peruge's favors. Her family name had been Brown, a commonplace easily discarded for the more mysterious Peruge. The father had stayed with Juanita long enough to name the infant Dzule for a half-remembered uncle, then he had gone commercial fishing on a voyage that would have satisfied the Navigator's worst fears. His boat was lost in a storm off Campiche.

Tragedy had been the firming cement of Juanita's character. It offered her the splendor of a lifelong search to replace a love that time made ever more romantic and unattainable. And for Dzule, she created a myth of the mighty John (originally Juan) Peruge: tall, bronzed, capable of any great deed he might envision. A jealous God had taken him, which said something pertinent about gods.

It was this tragedy, seen through his mother's fantasies, that made Dzule forgive any of her offenses against morality. His earliest and strongest image of women told him that they could not withstand life's crueler torments except by seeking the pleasures of the bed. That was just the way they were and one had to accept it. Others might deny this, but obviously they were hiding identical behavior in their own women.

The Agency had been a natural place for Dzule Peruge to find himself. Here, the strong sought their place in life. Here, those who took the blinders from their eyes naturally gravitated. And most important, it was a last outpost of swashbuckling. In the Agency, no dream was too remote, provided that you recognized most humans as essentially frail—especially women.

The bitch of the board was no exception. There was a weakness in her; had to be. She was clever, though, with her own brand of driving ruthlessness.

Peruge stared out of the taxi's window at the rain-washed streets, reviewing the encounter in the board room. She had opened the attack by bringing

out her own copy of the Hellstrom file. She had found
the entries she wanted, referred to them, and said,
"You tell us Hellstrom's company is private, incorporated in 1958; one chief stockholder, himself, and
three officers—Hellstrom, a Miss Fancy Kalotermi,
and a Miss Mimeca Tichenum." She'd put down the
file and stared down the long table at him. "The disturbing thing to many of us is that, although two wom-
en signed their names to these incorporation documents in front of witnesses, duly notarized, you show
no other record of them."

Peruge's response, he thought, had suited the attack. He shrugged and said, "That's correct. We don't
know where they came from, where educated, nothing.
They both sound foreign, but the notary in Fosterville
was satisfied with their identities, and the attorney saw
no objection to their being officers in a corporation
doing business in this country. Mimeca could be an ori-
ental name, as some of you have indicated, and the
other one does sound Greek; we just do not know.
This is not a page we intend to keep in its present
blank state. We are exploring this avenue."

"Do they live at Hellstrom's farm?" she asked.

"Apparently."

"Any description of them?"

"Vague: dark hair, possessed of general female
characteristics."

"General female characteristics," she mused. "I
wonder how you'd describe me. Well, no matter. What
is their relationship to Hellstrom?"

Peruge had taken his time with the response. He
knew how he appeared to women. He was tall, six feet
four inches, and imposing, 221 pounds. His sandy
hair held a distinct touch of red which his eyebrows
carried to a darker tone. His eyes were that dark
brown often mistaken for black, deeply socketed
above a rather abbreviated nose, wide mouth, and
square chin. The whole effect was dominantly masculine. He sent this machismo message down the table
with a sudden grin.

"Madame, I would not describe you to anyone,
not even to myself. Such is my responsibility to the

Agency that you remain nameless and faceless. As to
these *other* women, Hellstrom trusted them sufficiently
to want them as officers of his corporation, which
makes us extremely curious about them. We intend to
satisfy that curiosity. You'll note the documents list
the Kalotermi woman as vice-president and the other
one as secretary-treasurer, yet each has but a one percent interest in the corporation."

"How old are they?" she asked, glowering at him.

"Adult."

"Do they travel with Hellstrom?"

"We have no record of that."

"And you don't even know whether these women
have husbands or male attachments of any other nature?" she pressed.

Peruge's heavy brows tended to draw down in
thought or anger, and he brought them into this position, holding his voice flat and level to betray no upset
at his present ignorance. "We don't know this; no."

She suspected his distress, though, because she
moved to the same attack on Hellstrom. "And Hellstrom, is he married or otherwise entangled?"

"Not that we know. The reports tell you all that
we have at this time."

"All?" she sneered. "How old is Hellstrom?"

"We're guessing at thirty-four. That's farm and
ranching country and he was educated at home for the
first seven years. His grandmother, Trova Hellstrom,
was an accredited teacher."

"I've done my homework," she said, tapping the
file. "Only thirty-four. I raise that question to suggest
that he's fairly young to have caused so many waves."

"Old enough."

"You say he lectures and does an occasional
seminar or colloquium, and he's been on the faculties
of several universities. How does he get these *dangerous* assignments?"

"Oh his reputation."

"Hmmmph! What do we know of his other associates?"

"His technical people, business connections—you've
seen the file."

"And he banks in Switzerland. Interesting. Any indication of his worth?"

"Only what's in the file."

"Have you considered making discreet inquiries of his lawyers?"

"Do you take us for cretins?" Peruge asked.

She stared at him silently for a moment. "I said *discreet.*"

"His legal counsel, as you've seen there, is a native of Fosterville, which is a *small* town," Peruge explained carefully. "A liaison between two dogs cannot be undertaken discreetly in such a setting."

"Hmmmph."

Peruge looked down at the folders in front of him. She knew, of course, as did the rest of them, that he was not telling the full story. That was expected, but she had no way of guessing the actuality. She had nothing but her suspicions.

"Have any of our people ever met this Hellstrom?" she asked.

Peruge looked up, wondering: Why are they letting her be their spokesman? Most unusual. "As you perhaps know, the Chief has connections to a vice-president of the bank that handles financial matters for the film company that usually markets Hellstrom's productions. This vice-president has met Hellstrom socially and we have his report, which will be in your hands shortly."

"This bank does not work for Hellstrom's own company?"

"No."

"Have we made overtures through our Swiss connections?"

"There's no provable fraud involved and we cannot, therefore, gain open access to the Swiss records. We are still pursuing this, however."

"What is the vice-president's impression of Hellstrom?"

"A capable man in his own fields, rather quiet, with occasional bursts of concentrated energy where his own interests are concerned—specifically, when the subject of ecology arises."

"What salaries does Hellstrom pay his employees?"

"Union scale where that's indicated, guild scale, but we have no tax returns for some of them."

"The two women on his corporation records?"

"Apparently they serve him for something other than money. We believe they live on the farm, but they have declared no income. It has been suggested that Hellstrom is less than generous or that fraud is involved. We cannot say as yet. Such records as we've seen indicate that his film company makes no profit. All of the income appears to be taken by ongoing activities of an apparently legal, that is to say, educational nature."

"Could that farm be some sort of subversive school?"

"Some of the younger people allegedly stay there for an education in film making and in ecology. That's detailed in the file."

"Detailed," she said, her voice flat. "Can we presume his installations have been inspected, building inspectors and that sort? Oregon must have laws about such things."

"He was inspected by local people, and the accuracy of information based on those inspections remains in question. We will update your files as we are able."

"Hellstrom's technical people, cameramen and such, are they all recognized in the industry?"

"They have done work that has attracted praise."

"But the people themselves, are they admired?"

"One could say so."

"What would *you* say?"

"The question has little meaning except as an indicator for further investigations. It is our opinion that successful people in that industry tend to achieve a surface admiration from their fellows, but this surface attitude conceals an often quite profound hostility. Admiration in the usual sense has little to do with the situation except as it may indicate competence or income."

"How much traveling has Hellstrom done since the report in our hands?"

"One trip to Kenya and two days at Stanford."

"Is he away at the moment?"

"Possibly. I would have to consult our most recent reports to be sure. We have just fielded a new team, as you know. You will be informed, of course."

"Your previous reports show him staying away from his farm for two weeks to a month at a time. Who minds the store while he's away?"

"We do not as yet know."

"How thorough have our investigations of him been during his more vulnerable travel periods?"

"We've had his luggage searched and found only cameras, film, technical works, papers, that sort of thing. The most common subject matter for any written material in his possession has been insects. He appears most thorough where his specialty is concerned. We have found nothing incriminating."

"What about planting something on him?"

"It is contraindicated because of his stature in education. Too many would believe his protestations."

She sat back then, quiet for a moment. Presently, she said, "You will inform the Chief that there must be a profit in this somewhere. We are not satisfied."

Not satisfied! Peruge thought, tapping his finger impatiently on the taxi's black plastic seat. But they were afraid, and that was enough for the time being. If the actual material of the Project 40 file panned out, if it developed along the lines he and the Chief had purposely not reported, there would be profits enough for all, including Dzule Peruge. It would never be a weapon, of course. The thing created too much heat in its own circuits. But at low temperatures, that heat might be translated into an induced heat for metal and plastic products. At the very least, it would transform metallurgy, reducing present costs by a breathtaking factor. There'd be *profit* in that!

Brood instructions for selected workers. We use the language of the Outside, but with our own meanings.

It is important that the key distinctions not be confused. The practices of concealment demand this. Because we are virtually defenseless against the best forces of the Outside, our major defense remains in their never learning that we live among them, patterning ourselves after Hive creatures.

As the afternoon above Hellstrom's valley wore on, Depeaux began reflecting on the briefing sessions with Merrivale. It was a matter of emphasis, but he began to wonder just how many agents had been *wasted* on this project. Merrivale was a very queer duck —that damned affected British accent and all. There had been times when he gave off the distinct impression that he admired Hellstrom. It was Merrivale's pattern to admire only success, but it was an admiration always tinged with fear. The closer to Merrivale the success occurred, the greater his fear.

The isolated valley continued to bake in the hot autumn sun. Depeaux grew somnolent and there were moments when his eyelids drooped.

He forced himself to concentrate on the farm buildings. If the last reports were to be believed, Hellstrom himself was somewhere down there in one of those buildings. Nothing showed itself to confirm this assumption, however.

Why would Merrivale admire Hellstrom?

An abrupt slamming sound shocked Depeaux into full awareness. He saw movement at the far-left corner of the barn-studio. A wheeled cart came into view. It was an odd vehicle, reminiscent of an old-fashioned railway baggage cart, the hand-pulled kind used in stations. It had high slat sides and big spoked wheels. A high-pitched voice called out a command from somewhere behind the building, but Depeaux could not make out the words. It had sounded like "work a load." That made no sense, though.

A young woman strode from behind the barn to the front of the cart and, at first, Depeaux thought she was nude. The binoculars revealed skin-colored briefs, but she wore no bra, no blouse. Her feet were tucked into sandals.

The powerful glasses put Depeaux right up next to the young woman as she lowered a steering bar that had been caught upright at the front of the cart. She had firm breasts with dark nipples. He was so intent on watching her that he almost missed the approach of another young woman clad the same way, noticing her only when a strange third hand entered his field of vision. The young women were enough alike to be sisters, but they didn't fit the descriptions he had of the women who served as officers of Hellstrom's corporation. Their hair was light gold.

The young women took the steering bar and, pulling on it, trundled the cart toward the north gate. They moved with a bouncing urgency Depeaux found inconsistent with the long wait that box had enjoyed outside the gate. He saw no other reason for the cart. They were going to get the box. What was in that damned thing? And why were they almost nude? He recalled how the two deliverymen had strained in moving the box, wondered if the two women were expected to get that heavy object onto their cart. Surely, others would come out and help.

With increasing amazement, he watched the women open the gate, wheel the cart into position, drop its end, and tip the box into the cart's bed. They lifted the heavy box with a muscular ease that astonished him, displaying a far easier time with it than had the men who delivered it. Briskly, they closed the end of the cart and trotted back toward the barn with the same sense of urgency they'd shown on the outward trip. In far less time than he'd expected, they were at the barn and out of sight behind it. Again, there came that abrupt slamming sound. A door?

Depeaux estimated the whole incident had taken no more than five minutes. Astonishing! They were amazons! Yet, they'd appeared at first to be no more than well-developed, nubile young females. Was Hellstrom's farm a hideout for health nuts, a kind of inland muscle beach? The nudity argued for some such answer as that. Depeaux didn't like that answer, though.

Everything about the women had been too casually businesslike. They weren't muscle fanatics. They'd just been two workers going about a job and it had been a job they knew well enough not to need excess words or motions in executing it. Why women for that kind of work?

It was another goddamned default message!

Depeaux glanced at his watch: less than an hour to sunset. The valley and farm had settled back into its disturbing surface tranquillity. The place had been rendered even more empty by the brief spurt of human energy from the young women.

What the hell was in that box?

The low sun washed across the ridgetop to his left, shadowing the valley's depths now, but light reflected from golden grass and leaves on the opposite hillside kept the shadows lucent. Depeaux knew he was in good cover under the dark bushes, but valley and countryside once more had taken on that sense of ominous quiet. He took a deep breath and reaffirmed his decision to wait for night before leaving. This place had all of the atmosphere of a trap. He squirmed backward, deeper into shadows, peered left at the open countryside he would have to cross. The long, low light bathed the field in a golden glow touched with orange. The light cast a definite shadow along the path of crushed grass that marked his trail.

I was a fool to come up that way, he thought.

And perversely: *What was Porter's mistake?*

A sense of desperate immobility overcame him. The unexpected muscularity of those seminude young women, the persistent irritating hum from the barn-studio, the unspoken warnings in Merrivale's briefings and the reports, that internalized vacuum of a valley set against the distant movement of cattle far outside it (why so far?)—everything told him to wait for darkness. He lay for almost an hour, watching, stewing in his own premonitions.

The light dimmned. Low in the west, the sky took on a purple streaming against incandescent orange. The slopes of the valley drifted into a dusky almost blackness where it was difficult to determine if he actually saw details or was remembering them. No lights showed from the farmhouse or the barn. Visibility dropped to only a few feet, but when he crept out from under the bushes there were stars and a far aura of light on the northern horizon. That would be Fosterville, he knew. Still no lights from the farm.

Another default message.

Depeaux felt around him to make sure he was free of the bushes, got to his feet. There was a tension ache in his back. He groped in his knapsack, took out the sandwich in a rattling of paper, unwrapped it, and ate it while he regained his sense of direction. Fosterville's glow was a good landmark. The sandwich restored him and he took a long swallow of water and secured his pack.

The sense of danger remained.

The illogic of it dominated his consciousness, but he had learned to trust that sense. It was a message contained in everything he had studied about this place—all he had heard and all he had seen—a message, as well, of things not seen and not heard. The combined default message said *danger*.

Get the hell out of here, he told himself.

He twisted his watchband to bring the luminous dial of its companion compass into view, sighted along it, and set off across the field. As he moved out of the trees, his vision improved and he gained a sense of the long, sloping expanse of dried grass through which he had crept earlier.

The ground was uneven under the grass and he stumbled often. He kicked up dust unavoidably and several times he stopped to repress a sneeze. His passage through the grass seemed to him abnormally loud in the night silence, but there was a faint breeze and, when he stopped, he could hear it soughing in the trees ahead of him. There was a similarity between the two sounds that he tried to improve upon by slowing his pace. He had accumulated more grass burrs and they rasped his skin. Slow movement irritated him, too. He found himself unconsciously picking up speed. Something inside him said *hurry*.

The luminous dial of his compass and the glowing sky oriented him well, though. He found he could see the occasional trees in the field and avoided them easily. The dark line of thicker trees through which he had come stood out plainly. There would be the game trail to follow through there. He expected to encounter the trail long before his feet actually felt the hard, grassless surface. He crouched then to feel the surface with his hands, tracing the almost worn-down hoof-marks in the dirt. No deer had passed this way in a long while. Those were very old marks; he had noted this earlier, but now it compounded the total message of this place.

Depeaux started to straighten and strike out along the trail when he became aware of a distant swishing in the field behind him. He tipped his head to listen. The swishing sounded neither like someone walking through the grass nor like the wind. It had no definite position—just somewhere back there. Starlight showed nothing but distant shadows which could be trees, the configuration of the land. The sound was growing louder and he felt menace in it. There was something more akin to a susurrant humming in it now than to swishing. He straightened, turned away from the sound, and began trotting along the trail. He found he could make out the track if he peered down at a sharp angle.

Soon, he was at the line of thicker trees, the witch-spread of madroñas, and the heavier spacing of pines. The trees reduced the faint assistance of the starlight, and he was forced to slow his pace to a walk. Several times he lost the trail and had to grope for it with his feet. He longed to take out the small flashlight in his pack, but that odd sound had grown even louder behind him. It was a definite hissing-humming now. What made that sound? The noise of countless hoop-skirts dragging through grass would not be as mechanical. The image of hoopskirts amused him for a moment, though, until he thought of the seminude young amazons at the farm. Somehow, they were not amusing, even when clad in his imaginary hoopskirts.

He had hidden the bicycle in bushes where the game trail crossed a narrow dirt road. That road led around a low hill and down a long slope to the country road where he had parked the van. The bicycle had a handlebar light and he promised himself he would use that light and ride like hell.

Was that sound behind him louder? What the hell could make such a sound? Was it something natural? Birds, perhaps? The susurrant intrusion now reached out into the grass on both sides of him, as though he were being drawn into the wings of an advancing army. Depeaux had the auditory impression of many creatures moving in a wide fan to enclose him. He tried to increase his speed, but it was too dark; he kept running into trees.

What *was* that sound?

His body was wet with perspiration, fear tight in his chest.

Again, he tried to quicken his pace, tripped and fell full length. The susurrant pursuit stopped. Depeaux lay quietly waiting for a moment, probing with his ears. Nothing. What the hell! The absence of sound was as frightening as its presence had been. Slowly, he got to his feet and, immediately, the noise started again. It was on both sides and behind him. Terrified now, Depeaux stumbled forward, tripping, lurching, crashing through trees, on the trail sometimes and sometimes off it.

Where was that goddamned road where he'd hidden the bike?

The horns of enclosing noise were ahead of him now, on both sides and ahead. Depeaux, panting, stumbling, groped for the flashlight in his pack, found it. Why hadn't he brought a gun? An automatic even? Something small, like the one Tymiena carried. Damn! What was that noise? He wondered if he dared turn on the flashlight and sweep its beam around him. He couldn't bring even a little gun! No! His bird-watcher cover ruled against it! He was panting and gasping now. His legs ached.

The road was under his feet before he realized it. He stumbled to a halt, tried to get his bearings in the dark. Had he left the trail just back there? He didn't believe he could be far from the bushes where he'd hidden the damned bike. It had to be nearby. Did he dare use the flashlight? The hissing-hum enclosed him now. The bike had to be just to his right. It had to be. He groped toward blacker shadows among shadows, stumbled over a bush, and landed in the frame of the bicycle.

Cursing under his breath, Depeaux got to his feet, pulled the bicycle upright, and leaned against it. He could see the road better now: a separation of lightness in the dark, and he thought suddenly how good it would be just to get on the bicycle and coast back to the van and Tymiena. But the hissing-hums had grown louder, closing in on him! The hell with them! He yanked the flashlight from the pack, depressed the switch. A beam of light stabbed out into the trees. It revealed three young women clad as the amazons at the farm had been, tight briefs and sandals, but their eyes and noses were hidden behind glossy dark shields the shape of diving masks. Each of them carried a long wand with a whiplike twinned end. The wands made him think of some odd antenna system, but their doubled ends were pointed directly at him and there was no mistaking the menace.

From Nils Hellstrom's diary. Sometimes, I realize my name isn't important. It could be any other grouping of sounds and I'd still be me. Names are *not* important. This is a good thought. It is precisely as my brood mother and my first teachers said. The name I use represents an accident. It is not the name that might have been given to me had I been born into an Outsider family with all of their usual self-centered individualism. Their consciousness is not my consciousness; their timeline is not my timeline. We of the Hive will do away with names someday. My brood mother's words convey a deep sense of reassurance in this. Our perfect society cannot allow permanent individual names. They are labels, at best, are names. They are useful only in a transient way. Perhaps we will carry different labels at different stages in our lives. Or numbers. Somehow, numbers feel more in keeping with the intent my brood mother expressed so well.

It was 2:40 A.M. and for almost ten minutes now Clovis had been watching Eddie pace back and forth in the tiny living room of her apartment. The telephone had awakened them from deep sleep and Eddie had answered it. He had come openly to her apartment. The Agency didn't mind that. It expected certain sexual antics from its people and appreciated it when this activity was kept intramural. Nothing deep and demanding in this sex; just good, energetic bodily enjoyment.

All Eddie had said after hanging up was, "That was DT. Merrivale told him to call. They've lost contact with Carlos and Tymiena."

"Oh, my God!"

She'd gotten out of bed then, draped a robe about her body. Eddie had gone directly into the living room.

"I should've answered the phone," she said now, hoping this would break him out of his deep reverie.

"Why? DT was looking for me."

"Here?"

"Yes."

"How did he know you were here?"

"He tried my place and nobody answered."

"Eddie, I don't like that."

"Shit!"

"Eddie, what's the rest of it? What'd DT say?"

He stopped in front of her and stared down at her feet which she had pulled partly under her body when flopping into a chair. "He says we've gotta play brother and sister again. Nick Myerlie is going to be our daddy and we're going on a nice vacation way out in Oregon!"

From Nils Hellstrom's diary. Fancy is showing sure signs of unhappiness about her life in the Hive. I wonder if she has, somehow, become conditioned to prefer life Outside. We've always worried about that and it does appear to happen sometimes. I'm afraid she'll try to run away. If she does, I think I will opt for stumping her, rather than putting her in the vats. Her first-born, Saldo, is everything we had hoped. I do not want the Hive to lose that breeding potential. It's too bad she's so good with the insects. We will have to keep close watch on her until the present film is finished. Whatever happens, we cannot send her on any more Outside assignments until we're sure of her. Perhaps we should give her more internal responsibility for the film. She might grow to share my vision of the film then and be cured of this instability. This film is so very necessary to us. It is a new beginning. With it, and the ones to come, we will prepare the world for our answer to human survival. I know that Fancy shares the schismatic belief. She believes the insects will outlast us. Even my brood mother feared this, but her answer and my refinement of that answer must be developed. We must become more intensely like those upon whom we pattern our lives.

"Does that shock you?" Hellstrom asked.

He was a blond man of medium build, whose appearance suggested no more than the thirty-four years Depeaux knew the Agency's records credited to him. There was a great sense of internal dignity about Hellstrom, a sense of purpose that revealed itself in the way his blue eyes held a direct stare on anything or anyone of interest to him. There was a feeling about him that he contained more energy than he released.

Hellstrom stood in a laboratory confronting his captive, who had been tied into a plastic chair. The laboratory was a place of polished metal and gleaming white surfaces, of glass and instrument dials illuminated by a flat milky light that came from a coving completely around the ceiling's edge.

Depeaux had awakened here. He did not know how long he had been unconscious, but his mind was still fogged. Hellstrom stood in front of him, and two

completely naked women guarded him. He knew he
was paying too much attention to the women, another
pair of amazons, but he couldn't help it.

"I see it shocks you," Hellstrom said.

"Guess it does at that," Depeaux admitted. "I'm
not used to seeing so much naked female flesh around
me."

"Female flesh," Hellstrom said and clucked his
tongue.

"Don't they mind us talking about them this
way?" Depeaux asked.

"They do not understand us," Hellstrom said.
"Even if they did, they would not understand your attitude. It is a typical Outsider attitude, but I never fail
to find it strange."

Depeaux tried a cautious testing pull at the bindings that held him to the chair. He had awakened with
his head throbbing, and it still ached. There was a
pain right behind his eyes and he had no idea of how
much time had passed. He recalled starting to speak to
the three young women his flashlight had revealed,
then he'd been startled into silence by the sudden
awareness that many more similar figures filled the
darkness all around him. A confused welter of memories clouded that recollection. God, his mind still felt
so thick. He remembered speaking, an innocuous and
stupid response brought about by fear and shock.
"This is where I left my bicycle."

Christ! He'd been standing there, holding the
damned bicycle, but those opaque diving masks had
daunted him. They gave no clue to the eyes behind
them or to intentions. The wavering double wands aimed
at him could only mean threat. He had no idea what
those wands were, but a weapon was a weapon was a
weapon. The double wands branched from short handles
which the young women gripped with a firm sense of
competence. The tips of the instruments emitted a low
hum that he could hear when he held his breath, wondering if he dared try to break through the circle. As
he wondered, a night bird swooped toward the influt-
tering insects attracted by his flashlight. As the bird
swept past him, a figure in the dim area beyond the

light raised her double wand. There came a sudden
dry hissing, the same sound he had heard all around
him crossing the fields. The bird collapsed in the air
and plummeted to the ground. A woman scrambled
forward, stuffed the bird into a sack at her shoulder.
He saw then that many of the women carried such
sacks and that the sacks bulged.

"I—I hope I'm not trespassing," Depeaux ventured. "I was told this was a good area for my hobby.
I like—to watch birds." As he spoke, he thought how
stupid that sounded.

What in hell were those wands? That bird hadn't
even flopped once. Hiss-bang! Merrivale hadn't said
anything about this. Could this be Project 40, for
God's sake? Why didn't the crazy broads around him
say something? It was as though they hadn't heard him
—or didn't understand him. Did they speak another
language?

"Look," he said, "my name is—"

And that was all he could remember, except for
another brief burst of that odd hissing-hum off to his
left and, yes, the painful sensation that his head had
exploded. He remembered that now: explosive pain
within his skull. His head still ached as he stared up at
Hellstrom. Those wands had done it; no doubt of that.
The two women standing guard behind him carried
the same weapons, although they weren't wearing the
masks of the group that had encircled him.

I'm in the soup, he thought. Nothing to do but
brazen it out. "Why do you have me tied up?" he
asked.

"Don't waste our time with the ingenuous approach," Hellstrom said. "We must keep you secured
until we decide how to dispose of you."

Depeaux, his throat painfully dry, his heart suddenly pounding, said, "That's a nasty word, that *dispose.* I don't like that word."

Hellstrom sighed. Yes, it had been a poor choice
of words. He was tired and it had been a long night
and it wasn't over yet. Damn these Outside intruders!
What did they really want? He said, "My apologies. I
don't mean to cause you needless worry or discomfort.

But you are not the first person we have caught here in similar circumstances."

Depeaux experienced an abrupt sensation of déjà vu. He felt that he was reliving something half-remembered because it had not been his own experience, but something that had happened to someone close to him. Porter? He hadn't been all that close to Porter, but . . .

"And you *disposed* of these others, too?" Depeaux asked.

Hellstrom ignored the question. This was all so distasteful. He said, "Your credentials identify you as a salesman for a fireworks company. One of the others who intruded here worked for this identical company. Isn't that strange?"

Depeaux forced his words through a dry mouth. "If his name was Porter, there's nothing strange about it at all. He told me about this place."

"No doubt a fellow bird watcher," Hellstrom said. He turned his back on Depeaux. Was there no other way to meet this threat?

Depeaux recalled the bird the woman had knocked from the night sky. What was that weapon? Was it the answer to the mystery of Project 40? He decided to try another tack. "I saw some of your women friends kill a bird last night. They shouldn't do that. Birds are an important part of—"

"Oh, be still!" Hellstrom spoke without turning. "Of course they killed a bird—and insects, rabbits, mice, and quite a few other creatures as well. We couldn't waste the night sweep just picking you up."

Depeaux shook his head. *Night sweep?* "Why do they do that?" he asked.

"For food, naturally."

Hellstrom glanced back at his captive. "I must have time to consider the problem raised by your presence. I don't suppose you'll drop your subterfuges and tell me the whole story?"

"I don't even know what you're talking about," Depeaux protested, but he was sweating profusely and knew Hellstrom could read that sign.

"I see," Hellstrom said. He sounded sad. "Do not try to escape. The two workers there know they must

kill you if you try to get away. There's no sense trying
to talk to them. They don't speak. They're also quite
jumpy; they can smell your difference. You are an
Outsider in our midst and they've been trained to dispose of such intruders. Now, if you'll excuse me."

Hellstrom strode from the room, pushing aside a
sliding door. Before it closed, Depeaux glimpsed a
wide corridor filled with milky light and thronging
with humans—males and females, and all completely
nude. Two of them passed the door as Hellstrom left,
causing him to hesitate. The two, both women, carried
what appeared to be a naked male body, the head and
arms flopping, swaying.

From Nils Hellstrom's diary. It is a conceit that makes
me write these lines, trying to imagine the specialists
who will read them. Are you really there in some future time, or are you just creatures of my imagination?
I know the Hive will need the abilities of readers for a
long time, perhaps forever. But that's an even longer
time and it dwarfs my small utterances. You who may
be reading these words, then, if you share my ques-
tionings, must realize that your talents as a reader may
be abandoned eventually. It is a real question whether
this specialty serves an infinite purpose. There may
come a time when these words remain, but there will
be no one to read them. In a practical sense, that is
unlikely, too, because the material on which my words
are recorded would then be recognized as useful stuff
to be employed for other purposes. It must be a conceit then that I address myself to anyone. That I do so
at all must be attributed to an instinct for short-term
purpose. I support my brood mother's solution to the
Outsider problem. We must never merely oppose the
Outsiders, but should work with compromise and constant pressure to absorb them into our unity. This is
what we do now at my direction and, if you have
changed that, I tell myself that helping you understand
me may be useful in your planning for the future.

Hellstrom had been awakened from his daysleep by a young female watchworker. Her observation screen had revealed the Outsider intruding on Hive territory. Hellstrom's cell had been closed off for the privacy that a key worker could enjoy, and the young watchworker had come personally to Hellstrom, shaking his shoulder gently to awaken him. She had given him the information in the swift and silent gesture-language of the Hive.

The intruder could be observed on the hill above the Hive-head buildings. He was using binoculars to study the area. His approach had been noted far out by sensors in a perimeter tunnel. He had left a companion with a vehicle near the road to Fosterville.

The entire message took three seconds.

With a sigh, Hellstrom slid from the foam-and-down warmth of his bed, flashed a hand signal indicating that he understood. The watchworker left the cell. Hellstrom crossed the floor's smooth tiles, their coolness helping to awaken him, and he activated the bank of repeaters that gave him contact with the Hive's security system sensors. He focused on the section the watchworker had indicated.

At first, Hellstrom had difficulty locating the Outside intruder in the tall grass. The light was always bad in that direction at this hour of the afternoon. He wondered if the watchworker could have been mistaken about the correct screen. The watchworkers got sensitive and twitchy at times, but he had yet to find one turning in a false alarm or making a major error.

Hellstrom studied the tall brown grass carefully. The panorama of dry grass in the hot afternoon light appeared unbroken. Abruptly, something moved in the grass at the ridgecrest. As though movement had created a new scene, he saw the intruder: the Outsider was a male clothed to match the grass so closely that it surely could not be accidental. More than seventy years of living the Hive life had made the necessity for concealment a reflex with Hellstrom. He had possessed the sense of caution long before he'd assumed a false age and moved out of the Hive to build an Outsider identity. Now, seeing the prying intruder, he moved briskly, slipped his feet into sandals, and draped a white lab smock over his body. As he moved, he glanced at the crystal-driven clock on his wall: 2:59 P.M. The clock, accurate to four seconds in a year, had been built by a brood mate whose breeding and training had sent her into the laboratories for life.

Hellstrom thought about the intruder. If this one waited as the others had, he could be taken in the dark. Hellstrom made a mental note to get the night sweep started early and with special preparations for this possibility. The Hive had to learn why these Outsiders were prying.

Before leaving his cell, Hellstrom studied the Hive's outer perimeter on his repeaters and saw, far down in the valley, a van-camper with a woman seated beside it sketching on a tablet in her lap. He magnified the view, saw nervous tension in the woman's shoulder muscles, an involuntary movement of the head that drew her gaze up the slopes leading to the Hive. She would have to be picked up, too. Why were they suspicious of the *farm?* Who was behind this? There was something professional about this intrusion which made Hellstrom's heartbeat quicken.

He chewed thoughtfully on his lower lip while he searched inwardly for an instinct with which to meet this threat. The Hive was strong and hidden in a way that did not invite attention, but he knew how vulnerable it was, how little that strength would count against the shocked awareness of the Outsiders.

His gaze moved absently around his cell. It was one of the larger cubicles in the complex warren beneath the farm and the surrounding hills. It had been one of the first constructed by the original colonists who had brought their centuries-long migrations here under his brood mother's guidance.

"It is time to stop running, my beloved workers. We, who have lived furtive double lives among the Outsiders for more than three hundred years, dissembling, always ready to move at the slightest suspicion, have come to the place that will shelter us and make us strong."

She had claimed a vision guided her, a visit in her dreams from the blessed Mendel "whose words told us that the way we had always known was the true way."

Hellstrom's earliest education, the one he'd received before going Outside as a counterfeit teen-ager sent at last to get his "book learning," had been filled with the thoughts of his brood mother.

"The best must breed with the best. In that way we produce the disparate workers we need for every task our Hive can confront."

On that cold April day in 1876, when they had begun to dig out from the natural caverns beneath the farm, building their first Hive, she had told them, *"We will perfect our way and thus become the 'meek' whose earth will one day welcome them."*

This cell he now occupied dated from the first digging, although the diggers and his brood mother had long ago gone into the vats. The cell was sixteen feet wide and twenty-two feet long, eight feet from floor to ceiling. It was not quite square at the rear to accommodate an arm of the original natural cavern. The cell could have had a door in that arm, but the decision had been made to put service conduits, piping, and other ducts there. From the original limestone labyrinth, the Hive had been extended downward more than a mile, reaching outward in a circle almost two miles in diameter below the three-thousand-foot level. It was a teeming warren of nearly fifty thousand workers (far beyond his brood mother's hopes), closely integrated with their own factories, hydroponics gardens, laboratories, breeding centers, even an underground river that helped produce the power they required. No wall of the original cavern could be seen now. All walls were a uniform smooth gray of their own mucilaginous prestressed concrete.

In Hellstrom's own cell, over the years, the tough gray wall space had been covered with various plans and sketches involved in the Hive's growth. He had never taken them down, a wasteful idiosyncrasy the Hive tolerated in very few workers. His walls were now thick with pasted-over records of the Hive's vitality.

Although he had more cell space than others, his furnishings were otherwise Hive-standard: a bed formed of the mucilage slabs with rawhide lacing under a foam pad, chairs of similar construction, a desk of mucilage supports for a ceramic top in rich glass-green, twelve metal filing cabinets of Outsider manufacture (Hive cabinets were sturdier, but he fancied these for their reminder value), the repeater console with its screens and direct line into the central computer. A wardrobe with Outsider clothing in one corner marked him as one of the key workers who fronted for the Hive in that threatening world beyond their perimeters. Except for two adjustable lamps, one over the desk and the other over the repeater console, the room was illuminated by coved radiating tubes along the intersection of ceiling and walls, a standard practice in all of the galleries, tunnels, and cells of the Hive.

He could have had one of the newer and more sophisticated cells in the lower levels, but Hellstrom preferred this place that he had occupied since the day his brood mother had gone to the vats—"becoming one with us all."

Hellstrom strode back and forth on the tiles of his floor now, worrying about the intruder. Whom did that man represent? Certainly, he was not there out of casual curiosity. Hellstrom sensed a powerful Outside force slowly turning its deadly attention toward the Hive.

He knew he could not delay his response longer. The watchworkers would be irritably restless. They needed commands and a feeling that proper action was being taken. Hellstrom bent to his console, coded his instructions, and sent them into the relay system. Those instructions would be transmitted throughout the warren. Key workers would take preassigned actions. Every worker selected by the relay system through the Hive's central computer would see gesture signals on a screen. The silent language of the Hive would bind them into a common defense.

In common with many of the key workers who would unite thus, Hellstrom knew how thin the Hive's defenses really were. The knowledge sent fear through him now and he longed for the mental oblivion of the common worker who had few concerns beyond immediate tasks.

Driven by his fear, Hellstrom opened a filing drawer, extracted a folder tagged "Julius Porter." The ordinary vat mark had been stamped on the outside of the folder to tell what had happened to Porter's flesh, as though he had been discarded breeding stock whose records were kept as commentary on offspring, but Porter had no offspring in the Hive. He had merely brought a sense of mysterious threat which he had left largely unanswered. Something about the new intruder made Hellstrom think of Porter. Hellstrom trusted such instincts. He glanced through the closely spaced lines of information inscribed in Hive code. Porter had carried credentials identifying him as an employee of the Blue Devil Fireworks Corporation of Baltimore. He had babbled something finally about "the agency." This agency had represented in his terrified mind something that would revenge him.

Agency.

Hellstrom regretted now that they had sent Porter so soon into the vats. That had been callous and careless.

The idea of *using* the pain of a fellow creature, however, went against Hive sensitivities. Pain was a recognizable phenomenon. When it occurred in a worker and could not be eased, that worker might go to the vats. Outsiders did not behave this way, though. This was a Hive peculiarity. One killed to eat, to survive. The killing might cause pain, but that was quickly ended. One did not prolong it. Ohhh—survival might dictate another course, but the Hive had avoided those ways.

Presently, Hellstrom put the folder aside, depressed a key at his repeater station. He asked for one of the security overseers in the aerie watchroom of the barn-studio. The instrument that carried his voice was of Hive construction and he admired its flat functionalism as he waited for a response. Presently, Old Harvey came on the Screen above the instrument. His voice quavered slightly. Old Harvey would have to go into the vats before long, Hellstrom reflected, but that could be delayed because this man had talents that the Hive required, and never more desperately than right now. Old Harvey had been one of the first breeders. His seed was all through the Hive. But he was also knowledgeable in the ways of the Outside and an imaginative guardian of Hive security.

They spoke openly on the internal circuit. There wasn't even the remotest chance that the Outsiders possessed instruments that could penetrate the Hive's electronic barriers. In this field, Hive specialists already had moved far ahead of Outsiders.

"You know about the intruder, of course," Hellstrom said.

"Yes."

"You've been watching him personally?"

"Yes. I sent the watchworker to call you."

"What's he been doing?"

"Just watching. With binoculars mostly."

"Do we have anyone out?"

"No."

"Any exterior activity scheduled?"

"Only a delivery—diamond bits for our level-fifty-one drills."

"Don't pick it up until you clear with me."

"Right."

"Is there any chance he's carrying relay instruments that could monitor his activities from a distance?"

"Porter carried no such instruments."

Hellstrom suppressed a feeling of irritation, but noted that Old Harvey had also made that unconscious connection. "I mean, have we checked?" Hellstrom asked.

"Not completely; we're still in process of checking."

"Ahh, you're being thorough," Hellstrom said.

"Of course."

"Tell me as soon as you're sure."

"Yes."

"What about aircraft?" Hellstrom asked. "Anything?"

"Two jets very high more than an hour ago."

"Any indication of probes from the jets?"

"Nothing. They were commercial transports. Clean."

"Does the intruder look as though he's settled in for a long stay?"

"He has a knapsack and lunch. We think he'll wait for nightfall before leaving. We've been hitting him with an occasional low-frequency burst to keep him jumpy."

"Excellent." Hellstrom nodded to himself. "Keep up the subsonics. If he's nervous, he'll make mistakes. But don't use too much; you could drive him off before dark."

"I understand," Old Harvey said.

"Now, as to that woman waiting by the vehicle out near our perimeter: what do you make of her?"

"We're keeping her under close surveillance. The intruder came from her direction. We think they're associated." He cleared his throat, a loud and rasping sound which said something distinct about his age. Hellstrom was made acutely aware that Old Harvey must be more than two hundred years old and that was *very* old for first colonists who'd not had the benefit of an entire lifetime under Hive regimen.

"Undoubtedly they're associated," Hellstrom said.

"Could they be innocent intruders?" Old Harvey asked.

"Do you really entertain that idea?" Hellstrom asked.

There was a long pause. "Not likely, but possible."

"I think they come from the same source as Porter," Hellstrom said.

"Should we have our people in the East look into the Blue Devil Fireworks Corporation?" Old Harvey asked.

"No. That might betray the extent of our influence. I think extreme caution is indicated—especially if this pair has come to find out what happened to Porter."

"Perhaps we acted too hastily with that one."

"I've had my own misgivings on that score," Hellstrom admitted.

"What is this agency that Porter represented?"

Hellstrom reflected on this question. It contained his own unease. Porter had talked profusely at the end. It had been disgusting and had hastened his transit into the choppers and the vats. Yet, the necessities of that incident could have clouded its content. No member of the Hive would ever have behaved that way, not even an ordinary worker, although they could speak no language intelligible Outside. Porter had said the agency would get them. The agency was all-powerful. "We know about you now! We'll get you!" Porter had been the first adult Outsider ever to see the inner workings of the Hive, and his hysterical revulsion at the ordinary things necessary for Hive life had shaken Hellstrom.

I responded to his hysteria with a hysteria of my own, Hellstrom thought. *I must never do that again.*

"We will question this pair more carefully," Hellstrom said. "Perhaps they can tell us about this agency."

"You think it wise to capture them?" Old Harvey asked.

"I think it necessary."

"Perhaps other responses should be considered first."

"What are you suggesting?" Hellstrom asked.

"Discreet inquiry by our people in the East, while we dissemble for these new intruders. Why should we not invite them in and let them watch our surface activities. They surely cannot prove we are responsible for the disappearance of their fellow."

"We don't know that for certain," Hellstrom said.

"Surely, their reaction would've been different if they knew we were responsible."

"They know," Hellstrom said. "They just don't know how or why. No amount of dissembling now will put them off. They'll keep worrying at us like ants at a carcass. We must dissemble, yes, but we must keep them off balance at the same time. I am keeping our people Outside informed, but my instructions remain that we exercise the utmost restraint and caution there. Better to sacrifice the Hive than to lose all."

"In your considerations, please note that I disagree," Old Harvey said.

"Your exception is noted and will not be ignored."

"They are sure to send others," Old Harvey said.

"I agree."

"Each new team is likely to be more skilled, Nils."

"No doubt of that. But great skill, as we've learned from our own specialists, tends to narrow the vision. I doubt very much that these first probes involve the central element of this agency that wishes to know about us. Soon, however, they will send someone who knows all of the things we wish to know about those who come prying into our affairs."

Old Harvey's hesitation betrayed that he had not considered this possibility. Presently, he said, "You will try to capture and control such a one?"

"We must."

"That's a dangerous gambit, Nils."

"Circumstances dictate the risk."

"I disagree even more," Old Harvey said. "I have lived Outside, Nils. I know them. This is an extremely perilous course you plot."

"Do you have an alternative with a lower potential risk?" Hellstrom asked. "Extend your plotline before answering. You must think of the ultimate consequences along the sequence of events dictated by our present response. We made a mistake with Porter. We thought him the kind of Outsider we have previously taken and consigned to the vats. It was the wisdom of the sweep leader that brought him to my close attention after his capture. The mistake at that point was mine, but the consequences involve us all. My own regrets do not change the situation one whit. Our problem is complicated by the fact that we cannot erase all of the back tracks that led Porter to us. We have been able to do that before without exception. Our previous successes lulled me into a false complacency. A long history of success does not insure correct decisions. I knew this and yet failed. I will entertain an action to depose me, but I will not change my present decision on a course of action, a course of action that includes knowledge of my past mistake."

"Nils, I'm not suggesting that we depose—"

"Then obey my instructions," Hellstrom said. "Although I am a male, I am chief in the Hive at my brood mother's command. She reckoned the importance of that choice and, thus far, her vision has remained close to actual events. While you're putting the sonic probes on that woman and her vehicle, check it for the possibility that she may have a child inside."

Old Harvey sounded hurt. "I'm aware of our constant need for new blood, Nils. Your orders will be obeyed at once."

Hellstrom released the communications key and Old Harvey's face disappeared from the screen. Old Harvey might be *very* old, with a Hive awareness dulled by that early history of Outside life, but he knew how to obey against the dictates of his most basic fears. In this respect, he was completely trustworthy —more than could be said for most of the human species that had evolved Outside, conditioned as they were by the sharp limitations prevailing in what the Hive thought of as "wild societies." Old Harvey was a good worker.

Hellstrom sighed, aware of the burden he carried: almost fifty thousand dependent workers going about their activities in the Hive warren. He listened with his whole being for a moment, probing for the sense that told him all remained normal in the Hive. It was like the low humming of harvesting bees on a hot afternoon. There was a restful sense to this normalcy and he needed it at times to restore him. But the Hive gave him back no such reassurance now. He felt he could actually sense the disquiet of his own commands spreading through the Hive and reflecting back onto himself. All was *not* well here.

The need for caution had always been a constant

pressure on the Hive and every one of its inhabitants. He had his own fair share of this inbred caution, finely tuned by his brood mother and the ones she'd chosen to educate him. He had been against making the documentary movies at first. That was getting a bit close to home. But the Hive aphorism "Who could know more about insects than the Hive-born?" had overcome his objections and, finally, even he had entered the spirit of the film enterprise without reservations. The Hive always needed that ubiquitous energy symbol, money. The films brought a great deal of money to their Swiss accounts. That money focused on the Hive's remaining needs for Outside resources—the diamond bits for their drills, for instance. Unlike the wild societies, however, the Hive sought a harmony with its environment, cooperating to serve that environment, thus purchasing the environment's service to the Hive. Surely, that profound internal relationship that had always supported the Hive in the past would support them now. The films are not a mistake! he told himself. There was about them even a sense of something poetically amusing: to frighten Outsiders in this guise, to show them reality in the form of films about the world's multi-farious insect populations, while a much deeper reality out of that insect mold would feed on the fears it had helped augment.

He reminded himself of the lines he had insisted be written into the script of their most recent film effort. "In the perfect society, there is neither emotion nor mercy; precious space cannot be wasted on those who have outlived their usefulness."

This new Outsider intrusion made Hellstrom think now, however, of the bee wolf, whose predatory raids must be met with every resource a hive could muster. In the cooperative society, the fate of each could be the destiny of all.

I must go topside immediately, he told himself. I must take personal command at the center of our protective efforts.

Moving briskly, he went out to a nearby communal bath-washroom, showered along with several chemically neutered female workers, used a Hive-made depilatory on his face, and returned to his cell. There, he dressed in heavier Outside garments: tan trousers, a white cotton shirt and dark gray sweater, a light brown jacket over that. He put on socks and a pair of Hive-made leather shoes. As an afterthought, he took a small foreign pistol from a desk drawer and slipped it into his pocket. The Outsider weapon had greater range than a stunwand and would be familiar to the intruders, recognizable by them if a threat were needed.

He went out then, down the familiar galleries and corridors with their hum of Hive activities. The level's hydroponics rooms were on his way, their doors open to permit easy access for harvesters. He glanced in as he passed, noted now swiftly the routine was progressing. Hide baskets were being filled with soybeans, two workers to a basket. An Outsider might have interpreted the scene as one of confusion, but there was no squabbling, no conversation, no colliding workers, no spilled baskets. Filled baskets were being slid smoothly into the dumbwaiter slots in the far wall, there to go up to processing. Any necessary signals were conveyed by silent hand motions. When examined in the light of Hive awareness, the giant rooms were a collection of evidence, all of which pointed to supremely efficient organization. These were chemically conditioned workers, effectively neutered, none of them hungry (feeding conveyors were only a few steps away down the main gallery), and they worked in the certain awareness that what they did was vital for the entire Hive.

Hellstrom's own progress past the harvesting became a kind of elegant dance through entering and emerging workers. No precise scheduling of crews was required here. Workers left when hungry or overcome by fatigue. Others entered to fill the gaps. All knew what was required of them.

At the elevator—one of the older, upper-level models visibly jerking past the open doorways—he was delayed a moment while a planting crew filed past him, headed for the hydroponics rooms with selected seed stock for replanting. There must be no delay in maintenance of the food cycle which lay at the very base of their survival.

Hellstrom stepped into the open gap of the elevator doorway when space appeared on an upbound car. The heavy animal odor of the Hive, which the scrubbing systems erased from vented air exchanged Outside, was strong in the elevator, a sign that leaks were developing far down in the shaft and would have to be repaired. Maintenance was a constant drain on them and could not be ignored even now. He made a mental note to inquire about shaft maintainance. Within two minutes, he was in the subbasement of the barn-studio, his attention concentrated once more on the immediate emergency.

We must not consign these new intruders to the vats too soon, he told himself.

From Nils Hellstrom's diary. In the oral tradition that spanned more than a hundred years before our progenitors began their first written records, it was said that the refusal to waste any colony protein dated from our earliest beginnings. I have come to doubt this. Outsider reactions indicate this is no more than a pleasant myth. My brood mother likened this to the openness that we of the Hive have with each other. The vats were for her a beautiful metaphor of the uninhibited internal communication and, as she often said, "In this way, when one dies, no secret dies with her; whatever each has learned will be contributed to the success of the whole." Nothing in the more than two hundred years of our written records calls the original myth into question, and I will not do so now in our open councils. Thus, I conceal something in the name of a myth which strengthens us. Perhaps, this is how religions begin.

In the Hive-head subbasement, caution became a visible thing. A ladder of Hive steel was anchored in one corner of the open area beneath the baffles and sound dampers of the floor supports. The ladder led

upward through the baffles to a concealed trapdoor
that emerged in a cubicle of a communal toilet in the
barn's basement. A concealed screen at the top of the
ladder slid into position when a worker climbed to that
point. The screen revealed whether the cubicle was occupied. A remote locking system secured the cubicle's
door when a worker from below was emerging.

There were secondary monitoring screens at the
base of the ladder with a watchworker on duty there.
The worker waved Hellstrom ahead, signaling that no
Outsiders were in the studio area. The ladder was attached to a wall of one of the giant ventilation ducts
that emerged in the barn roof. He felt the subtle vibra-
tions as he climbed. He emerged from the cubicle
presently and into an empty washroom, which gave
him passage into the studio's actual basement, a space
of wardrobe stores, film stores, editing and processing
facilities for film, dressing rooms and makeup areas,
and props. By Outsider standards, it was all very normal. Workers were going about their activities in the
area, but they ignored him. Ordinary stairs at the end
of a long hallway gave entrance through a sound-baffle
system into a double-doored lock passage and thence
to the main studio which took up most of the barn's
cavernous interior.

From the permanent minutes of the Hive Council.
Present computations indicate that the Hive will begin
to feel swarming pressures when it passes a population
of sixty thousand. Without some protections, as Project 40 would offer, we cannot permit such a swarming to occur. For all of the ingenuity provided us by
our specialist, we are helpless before the combined
might of the Outside, whose killing machines would
crush us. The total dedication of our workers would
make them fall by the thousands in the suicidal attempt to insure the future of our kind. But we are few
and the Outsiders are many. The unreasoning brutality
of nature's underlying plan must be stayed for this
time of preparation. Someday, given the potency of a
weapon such as Project 40, we will be able to emerge,

and, if our workers die on that day, they will die with reason—through selflessness, not through greed.

"They are, as usual, firm and polite, but evasive," Janvert said, turning from the telephone.

It was daylight outside Clovis's apartment now, and she had dressed in preparation for the specific summons they both knew would come soon.

"They told you to be patient," Clovis said. She had returned to her favorite position on the long couch and sat with her feet tucked under her.

"And one thing more," Janvert said. "Peruge himself *definitely* is going to head this team. Old Jollyvale doesn't like that one bit."

"You think he wanted this one himself?"

"God, no! But he is operations director. With Peruge in the field, Jollyvale can't give orders. He's effectively no longer operations director. Now *that*, he doesn't like."

"It's definite about Peruge?"

"No doubt."

"That explains why they're not being very informative."

"I suppose so." Janvert crossed to the couch and sat beside her, taking her hand in his and rubbing the warm skin absently. "I'm scared," he said. "I'm really scared for the first time in this shitty business. I've always known they didn't give one particle of a damn about us, but Peruge—" Janvert swallowed convulsively, "I think he takes a positive pride in how many people he can waste, and he doesn't care whose people they are, ours or theirs."

"Don't let him know how you feel, for God's sake," Clovis said.

"Oh, I won't. I'll be the usual happy-go-lucky Shorty, always ready with a quip and a smile."

"Do you think we'll be going out today?"

"Tonight at the latest."

"I've often wondered about Peruge," she said. "I've wondered who he actually is. That funny damned name and everything."

"At least he has a name," Janvert said. "The Chief, now—"

"Don't even think it," she warned.

"Haven't you ever wondered if we really work for the government?" he asked. "Or—whether our bosses represent an overgovernment behind the visible one."

"If you talking about what I think you're talking about, I don't want to know anything about it," she said.

"That's a good, safe attitude," he said. He dropped her hand, stood up, and returned to his restless pacing.

Clovis was right, of course. This place was bugged. They'd known precisely where to call for him. No helping that: when you worked to make the world a fishbowl, you lived in a fishbowl. The trick was to become one of the fish watchers.

From the Hive Manual. In the selection of workers, breeders, and the various specialists, in the development of a Hive consciousness through all of the chemical and manipulative devices at our disposal, the blueprint of our cooperative society is etched with a potential for permanence that must be monitored with the greatest caution. Here, each generation comes into this world as a continuation of the previous ones, each individual a mere extension of the rest. It is in the consequences of that extension that we must build our eventual place in the universe.

As Hellstrom emerged into the open cavern of the studio that occupied most of the north half of the barn, a young woman production assistant, who had been working with a glass-enclosed beehive nearby, saw him and waved to attract his attention. Hellstrom hesitated, torn by the desire to go immediately up to the command post aerie and the recognition of a need to maintain an air of unbroken continuity in Hive-supportive work. He recognized the young woman, of course: one of the lesser crew who could front on occasion for limited contact with the Outsiders who came to look into the film work for legitimate reasons. She was one of the Niles-8 genetic line: poor eyesight in that line which would have to be corrected in the breeding processes. They were also susceptible to Outsider tastes, as was the FANCY line.

He noted that members of the second film crew were standing around the glassed beehive with their arms folded. Everything about the scene spelled a delay. That could be costly. Hellstrom weighed his various problems. Old Harvey could be trusted to obey his orders. The money represented by this film equaled a vital resource. Hellstrom shifted direction in mid-stride, headed toward the production assistant and her idle crew. She had a plain face not helped by large granny glasses and blonde hair pulled back in a severe chignon. But she had a full figure and was obviously fertile. Hellstrom wondered idly if she had been examined yet for her personal breeding potential.

Using her Outsider name, he spoke as he came up to her. "What is it, Stella?"

"We're having some unexpected trouble with this beehive and I wanted to call Fancy in for assistance, but I was told you have her on another assignment from which she cannot be released."

"That's true," Hellstrom said, realizing that someone had taken him literally in his private instructions to keep Fancy under close surveillance. "What's happening with your bees?"

"They're balling on the queen every time we try to get her exposed for photographing. The last time that happened, Fancy told us to call her and she might be able to help."

"Did she give you an alternative to calling her?"

"She said to try a tranquilizer in their feeder and in their air."

"Have you done this?"

"We'd like to have them more active."

"I see. Did Fancy tell you what might be causing this?"

"She thinks it's something in the air—maybe atmospheric electricity or a chemical emitted by our own bodies."

"Can we shoot around these bees for now?"

"Ed thinks we can. He wanted to call you earlier and see if you'd be available for one of the lab sequences in which you appear."

"When would he want to shoot it?"

"Tonight, probably by around eight o'clock."

Hellstrom fell silent, considering all of his manifest problems. "I think I can be ready for that shooting by eight. Tell Ed to set up for it. I've had my day-sleep and can work all night if need be." He turned away; that should keep things here on an even keel, but he saw the bees at once as a metaphor of his own Hive. If the Hive became too upset, things could get out of hand. Workers might take action on their own. He signaled to a boom operator in the center of the studio, pointed to himself and to the loft that gave entrance to the command aerie.

The boom cage on its long arm swung down to the studio floor with all of the silent grace of a mantis reaching for its prey. Hellstrom stepped into the cage and it wafted him upward, swung in a wide arc, and deposited him at the edge of the loft floor. As he stepped out of the cage, Hellstrom reflected on how admirably this device served the needs of both security and cover. No one could get up to the loft without the help of a trusted boom operator, yet it was the most natural thing to think of a boom as an elevator and to use that as an excuse for leaving no other access into the security section.

The loft had been set up with a central well running for half the length of the barn. The other half concealed the outlets for ventilators, with a bypass for visual examination of the valley's upper reaches. Slide ropes had been coiled neatly at even spacing along the edge of the loft floor, each rope secured to one of the stanchions of the guardrail. The ropes, which the Hive's workers had practiced on, but had never been forced to use, offered emergency access to the studio floor. Neither the ropes, nor the inner wall behind the

walkway, nor the doors into the various security stations were visible from the studio floor.

Hellstrom walked along the open area, noting a
slight smell of dust that alerted him to remind the
cleaning crews that the studio must be kept free of
dust. The catwalk, with its view of the multiple activities in the studio below, led him along the sound-
proofed wall to an end door with both sound and light
baffles.

He let himself into Old Harvey's station through
the dark passage of the baffle. It was gloomy inside
and filled with the smells of Outside that came in
through open louvers at the end. An arc of green-
glowing repeater screens had been installed along the
inner wall against a thermite-bomb destruction system
that could burn out the entire barn right down to the
noninflammable mucilaginous quick-plugs that could
be triggered to seal off the Hive head. The present
emergency made Hellstrom acutely conscious of all
these preparations which had been a part of Hive
awareness for so many years.

Old Harvey looked up from the console as Hellstrom entered. The old man was gray haired, with a
big, forward-thrust face like a Saint Bernard. He even
had dewlaps at the edges of his jawline to accent the
likeness. His eyes were widely spaced, brown and deceptively mild. Hellstrom had once seen Old Harvey
behead a hysterical worker with one sweep of a meat
cleaver—but that had been long ago in his own childhood and that hysterical line had been weeded out of
the Hive's breeding stock.

"Where's our Outsider?" Hellstrom asked.

"He had something to eat a while back, then
crawled off the hilltop," Old Harvey said. "He's working his way toward the upper end of the valley now. If
he stations himself where I think he will, we'll be able
to look out the louvers at the other end and watch him
directly with binoculars. We're keeping all the lights
off inside, of course, to reduce the chance that he'll
notice activity up here."

Good, cautious thinking. "Have you reviewed the
Porter material? I noticed earlier that you—"

"I've reviewed it."

"What's your opinion?" Hellstrom asked.

"Same sort of approach, clothing designed to give him concealment in the grass. Want to bet his cover is he's a bird watcher?"

"I think you'd win."

"Too much professionalism about him, though." He studied one of the console screens over an observer's shoulder, pointed, and said. "There he is, just as I expected."

The screen showed the intruder crawling under a stand of bushes to get a view down the length of the valley.

"Is he carrying a weapon?" Hellstrom asked.

"Our sensors indicate not. I think he has a flashlight and a pocketknife in addition to those binoculars. Look at that: there are ants up there on the ledge and he doesn't like them. See how he's brushing them off his arm."

"Ants? How long since we've swept that area?"

"A month or so. Do you want it checked?"

"No. Just have it noted that it may be time for another sweep there by a small crew. We need several nests in the newer hydroponics sections."

"Right." Old Harvey nodded and turned to relay instructions by hand signal to one of his assistants. Presently, he turned back and spoke musingly. "That Porter was a strange one. I've been reviewing what he said. He told us quite a bit, really."

"He was in the wrong business," Hellstrom agreed dryly.

"What do you think they're after?" Old Harvey asked.

"We've somehow attracted the attention of an official agency," Hellstrom said. "They don't have to be after anything except satisfaction for their own brand of paranoia."

Old Harvey grimaced, shuddered. "I don't like the feeling of this, Nils."

"Nor I."

"Are you sure you've made the right decision?"

"To the best of my ability. Our first step must be

to pick up this pair. One of them must know more
than the late Mr. Porter."

"I sure hope you're right, Nils."

From Nils Hellstrom's diary. Three of our younger ge-
neticists were in among the fertile females again today,
and some of the older colonists in genetics complained. I had to explain to them once more that it
was unimportant. The breeding impulse cannot be
suppressed in active key workers who require the full
functioning of their mental abilities. I have been
known to indulge myself thus from time to time and
the older genetics specialists know this very well. They
were really complaining about me, of course. When
will they ever understand that genetic manipulation
has very severe limits, given our present stage of development? Luckily, the older ones are dying out. Our
own truism applies here. *"Into the vats old, out of the
vats new."* Any offspring from this latest foray will be
watched closely, of course. Talent is where you find it.
We all know how desperately the Hive needs new talent.

Merrivale did not like the tone of voice Peruge
was using over the telephone, but he managed to conceal this fact under an even flow of reasonable responses.
Peruge was angry and was not attempting to conceal
it. To Merrivale, Peruge represented the one major
obstacle between himself and another promotion. Merrivale thought he understood Peruge very well, but felt
offended by those reactions in Peruge that spoke of the
other man's superior position in the Agency.

Merrivale had been called away from the early
afternoon briefing session they had set up for the new
teams being sent out to Oregon. He had left the session reluctantly, but without delay. One did not keep
Peruge waiting. Peruge was one of the chosen few who
had daily face-to-face contact with the Chief. He
might even know the Chief's real identity.

There was a letterknife in the form of a cavalry

saber on the smooth gray blotter of Merrivale's desk. He picked it up, pricked at the blotter with the sharp tip while he listened, gouging deeply when the conversation took a painful turn.

"That was earlier in the month, Dzule," Merrivale said, knowing the explanation was insufficient, "and we did not know as much then as we know now."

"What do we know now?" The question was biting and accusatory.

"We know there's someone out there who does not hesitate to make our people just—disappear."

"We already knew that!"

"But we had not gauged the extent of our opposition's determination to defy us."

"Do we have so many people that we can just waste them finding out such important facts?" Peruge demanded.

The hypocrite! Merrivale thought. *Nobody has wasted more agents than Peruge! He gave me the explicit orders that cost us these teams!*

Merrivale dug a deep gouge in the blotter, frowned at the disfiguration of the surface. He reminded himself to have the blotter replaced as soon as this call was completed. "Dzule, none of our agents believes this business is safe. They know the chances they take."

"But do they know the chances *you* take with them?"

"That's unfair," Merrivale blurted, and he wondered what Peruge was doing. *Why this abrupt attack? Was there trouble farther upstairs?*

"You're a fool, Merrivale," Peruge said. "You've lost us three good people."

"My orders were explicit and you know it," Merrivale said.

"And given those orders, you did what you thought best."

"Naturally." Merrivale could feel sweat collecting under his collar and he rubbed a finger around against his skin there. "We had no way of knowing precisely what had happened to Porter. You told me to send him in alone. Those were your very words."

"And when Porter—just vanished?"

"You said yourself that he could've had personal reasons for disappearing!"

"What personal reasons? Porter's record was one of the best."

"But you said he'd quarreled with his—wife."

"Did I say that? I don't remember that at all."

So that's the way it is, Merrivale thought. His stomach felt painfully knotted. "You *know* you offered that as a possible reason for sending in a double team, but with identical orders for them."

"I don't know anything of the kind, Merrivale. You've sent Depeaux and Grinelli down that Oregon rathole and you sit there making excuses. When Porter was missed, you should've originated an official inquiry for a *vacationer* believed to be missing in that region."

So that's going to be our new approach, Merrivale thought. And if it succeeds, Peruge gets the credit. If it fails, I get the blame. How neat!

Merrivale said, "I presume that's the line of attack you'll take when you get out to Oregon."

"You know damned well it is!"

The Chief himself is probably listening to this, Merrivale thought. Oh, God! Why did I ever get into this business?

"Have you told the new teams that I'll be leading them personally?" Peruge asked.

"I was briefing them when you called."

"Very well. I'll be leaving within the hour and I'll meet the new teams in Portland."

"I'll tell them." Merrivale spoke with weary resignation.

"And tell them this: tell them I want it emphasized that this new operation must be handled with the utmost discretion. There will be no grandstand plays, understood? Hellstrom has powerful friends and I don't mind telling you that this ecology issue is explosive. Hellstrom has said all the right things to the right people and they think he's some kind of ecological messiah. Luckily, there are others who realize he's a fanatic madman, and I'm sure we'll prevail. Understand me?"

"Perfectly." Merrivale did not try to conceal his bitterness now. The Chief was listening to Peruge. No doubt of that. The whole thing was a staged performance: preparation of the sacrificial goat. The goat's name was, of course, Merrivale.

"I doubt very much that you understand me perfectly," Peruge said, "but it's likely that you understand me well enough to follow the orders I've just given you without any more disgusting errors. See to it at once."

There was a sharp click on the line.

Merrivale sighed, replaced the receiver in its cradle on the elaborate scrambling phone. The signs were clear. He must juggle his own hot potato. And if he dropped it, or if anyone else dropped it, fingers would point in only one direction. Well, he had been in this position before, just as he had placed others in the identical position. There was only one safe response. He must delegate authority, but do it so subtly that everything still appeared to be in his own hands. The logical candidate was Shorty Janvert. As a first step, Shorty would be named as number two on this project, right under Dzule Peruge himself. Peruge had not specified who he wanted as number two. That had been a mistake on his part. If Peruge changed this assignment, a thing he might very well do, then he would be responsible for the actions of his new second. Shorty was a logical choice. Peruge had made it clear on several occasions that he didn't fully trust Janvert. But the little man was imaginative and resourceful. The choice could be defended.

From the Hive Manual. The neutered worker is the true source of freedom in any society. Even the wild society has its neutered workers, the neutering being maintained behind a mask of actual fertility from which real offspring come. But such offspring have no share in the free creative life of the wild society and thus are effectively neutered. Such workers can always be recognized. They are not burdened with intellect, with unrestricted emotion, or with individual identity. They are lost in a mass of creatures like themselves. In this, neither our Hive nor the insects are giving the universe anything new. What the insects have and what we are copying is a society formed in such a way that its workers toil together to create the illusive Utopia—the perfect society.

It took Hellstrom's number-two camera crew almost six hours to shoot the new lab sequence with mice and wasps. Even then, Hellstrom was not satisfied that they had the proper effect on film. He had become very sensitive to the artistic merit of what they created. He expected the rushes to be far short of what he had hoped for in this sequence. The demands for excellence he was making now went far beyond the implicit knowledge that quality brought more income to the Hive. He wanted quality for the thing itself, just as he wanted it for every aspect of the Hive.

Quality of specialists, quality of life, quality of creations—all were interrelated.

Hellstrom had the boom lift him to the aerie after they finished shooting, trying to conceal his worries over the latest reports on the night sweep. Because he had been in this sequence, he had been tied to the set during the most important part of the sweep. It was still many hours to dawn and the problem had not been solved: the female who had accompanied their captive intruder remained at large.

One of the Hive's chief concerns had always been to produce workers who could "front" for them with the Outside, incorruptible workers who would not betray even by chance what lay beneath Guarded Valley and its surrounding hills. Hellstrom wondered now if they might not have uncovered a breeding defect somewhere in the personnel charged with the sweeps. The male intruder had been picked up easily beyond the bordering trees of the west meadow. A sweep detail had enveloped the van-camper almost immediately afterward, but somehow they had missed the female.

It didn't seem possible that she could escape, but none of the sweep-workers had even smelled her trail.

Many key security workers were in the aerie command post when Hellstrom entered. They noted his entrance, but stayed at their jobs. Hellstrom scanned the dimly lighted room with its arc of repeater screens, its little clutches of workers discussing the problem. Saldo was there, dark in the manner of his breeder mother, Fancy, but with the harsh hawk features of his Outsider father. (That was one thing Fancy did well, Hellstrom reminded himself. She bred Outside at every opportunity and the resultant new genes were prized by the Hive.) Old Harvey's post at the security console had been taken over by a younger male of Fancy's line. He took the name of Timothy Hannsen in his Outside guise. Hannsen had been chosen as a front because of penetrating good looks that tended to overpower the conscious balance of Outsider females. He also had a sharply incisive mind which made him particularly valuable in a crisis. That was true of many in Fancy's line, but particularly so of Saldo. Hellstrom had high hopes for Saldo, who had been taken on as a special educational charge by Old Harvey.

Hellstrom paused inside the door to gauge conditions in the aerie. Should he take over? They would defer to him at the slightest indication that he was assuming command. Brood mother Trova's decision had never been really questioned. They always sensed how much more potent was his commitment to the Hive, how much more effective his decisions. They might disagree at times, and occasionally even prevail over him, but there remained a subtle air of deference even when they voted him down in the Council. And when, as often happened, his view later proved to have been the correct one, his hold on them became even stronger. It was a situation toward which Hellstrom maintained a constant mistrust.

No worker is perfect, he told himself. The Hive itself must be supreme in all things.

Old Harvey stood against the wall at Hellstrom's left, arms folded, his face underlighted by the glowing screens, giving the illusion that he had been cast from green stone. There was movement in his eyes, though. Old Harvey was watching the room critically. Hellstrom crossed to his side, glanced once at the dewlapped old face, then at the consoles. "Any sign of her yet?"

"No."

"Didn't we have her under constant infrasurveillance?"

"Radar and sonics, too," Old Harvey muttered.

"Did she have instruments to detect us?"

"She tried to use her radio, but we jammed it."

"That alerted her, then?"

"Probably." Old Harvey sounded tired and displeased.

"But no other instruments?"

"The vehicle had a small radar-type speed-trap warning device. I think she may have detected our surveillance that way, too."

"But how could she slip through our sweep?"

"They're reviewing the tapes again. They think she could've gone searching for her companion and been lost in the general confusion our sweep created on the instruments."

"The sweep would've picked her up despite that."

Old Harvey turned, looked directly at him. "So I told them."

"And they overruled you."

Old Harvey nodded.

"What do they believe happened?" Hellstrom asked.

"She took a calculated risk and went right into the midst of our searchers."

"Her smell would've given her away!"

"So I said, and they agreed. They then suggested she slipped away from the truck to the north, using it as a shield. Their thought is that she walked softly to hide her movements in the background static. There *was* a time gap between darkness and when our sweep reached her vicinity. She could've done it. She had two choices: get away or slip up on us from another direction. They think she's out there stalking us."

"And you don't agree with that?" Hellstrom asked.

"Not that one," Old Harvey said.

"Why?"

"She wouldn't slip up on us."

"But why?"

"We hit her hard with the low frequency. She was twitchy and nervous all afternoon, much too nervous to come for us."

"How do you know what her reserves of courage might be?"

"Not that one, Nils. I watched her."

"She didn't look like your type, Harvey."

"Make your joke, Nils. I watched her most of the afternoon."

"So this is no more than your opinion from personal observation?"

"Yes."

"Why aren't you pressing that opinion?"

"I did."

"Given your choice, what action would you take?"

"You really want to know?"

"I do, or I wouldn't ask."

"First, I think she's slipped down to the northeast among those cattle in the pasture. I'm guessing that she knows cattle. There was something about her—" He wet his lips with his tongue. "If she knows cattle, she could move among them with no problems. They'd mask her smell; they'd provide all the cover she needs."

"No one here agrees with you?"

"They say those are range cattle and they'd have spooked at the first smell of her. We'd have detected that."

"And your response?"

"A lot of spooking depends on whether a cow can smell your fear. We know that. We do it ourselves. If she wasn't afraid of them and moved softly —well, we can't just close our eyes to that possibility."

"They don't want to search among the cattle, though?"

"They're bothered by the complications of a sweep down there. If we send workers, they're sure to get out of hand and kill a few cows. Then we have local problems, just the way we have every time that happens."

"You still haven't told me what you'd do."

"I'd send some of us. We're trained to deal with the Outside. Some of us have lived out there. We have better control over the hunt response during a sweep."

Hellstrom nodded, spoke his thoughts aloud. "If she's up here close to us, she hasn't a rabbit's chance of getting away. But if she's down there among those cows—"

"You see what I mean," Old Harvey said.

"I'm astonished that the others don't see it, too," Hellstrom said. "Will you lead the search party, Harvey?"

"Sure. I see you're not calling it a sweep."

"I'd just as soon you went out and brought back only one thing."

"Alive?"

"If at all possible. We're not getting much from that other one."

"That's what I heard. I was down there when they first started questioning him, but—well, that sort of thing bothers me. I guess I lived too long Outside."

"I have the same reaction," Hellstrom said. "This is something better left to the younger workers who don't even know the concept of mercy."

"Sure wish there was some other way," Old Harvey said. He took a deep breath. "I'd best get about the—search."

"Choose your men and see to it."

Hellstrom watched the old man move out into the room, and he thought about the often sheer perversity of the young. The old possessed a special value for the Hive, a kind of balance that could not be denied. This incident was a sure demonstration of their value. Old Harvey had known what to do. The young workers had not wanted to venture out into the night themselves, though, as common workers did, and they'd decided it was unnecessary.

Several of the younger male and female apprentices and the security workers of middle years had heard Hellstrom's conversation with Old Harvey. They made a shamefaced show now of volunteering for the search.

Old Harvey picked some of them, instructed them briefly. He made a special point of naming Saldo as his second-in-command. That was good. Saldo displayed a devoted respect for Old Harvey and it was surprising that the younger worker had not taken his teacher's side. This came out in the briefing when Saldo said, "I knew he was right, but you wouldn't believe me, either." Apparently Saldo *had* sided with his teacher, but the others had lumped them both in one bag. Ever conscious of his role as educator, Old Harvey chided Saldo for this remark. "If you thought that, you should've given your own arguments, not mine."

The troop filed out of the room properly chastened.

Hellstrom smiled to himself. They were good stock and learned quickly. One had only to give them the correct example. "In age is balance," as his brood mother had been fond of saying. Youth, to her, represented an extenuating circumstance which had always to be taken into account.

The words of Nils Hellstrom. Of the billions of living things on earth, only man ponders his existence. His questions lead to torment; for he is unable to accept, as the insects do, that life's only purpose is life itself.

Tymiena Grinelli had not liked this assignment from the beginning. She hadn't objected so much to working with Carlos (they'd combined forces many times in the past) as she did to the time she would spend with him when they were not working. Carlos had been flashingly handsome in his youth and had never accustomed himself to the gradual wearing away of his compelling attraction to women.

She had known that the off-duty association would be a constant bout of sortie and repartee. Gri-

nelli didn't fancy herself as a femme fatale, but she
knew from experience her own magnetism. She had a
long face that might have been taken as ugly were it
not for the personality behind it. This shone through
overlarge and startlingly green eyes. Her body was
slender, the skin pale, and there was about her an air
of profound sensitivity that fascinated many men, Carlos among them. Her hair was a dark red-auburn and
she tended to keep it confined in tight hats or berets.

   Tymiena was a family name and its original Slav-
ic meaning had been "a secret." The name described
her manner. She held herself in constant reserve.

   Merrivale had alerted her sense of danger originally by assigning only the two of them to the case.
She had not liked what she had read in Porter's accounts and in the reports accumulated under the label
of "The Hellstrom File." Too many of these reports had
been second or third hand. Too many of them were
semiofficial. They smacked of amateurism. Amateurs
were a deadly indulgence in this business.

   "Only two of us?" she'd objected. "What about
the local police? We could file a missing-person report
and—"

   "The Chief does not want that," Merrivale had
said.

   "Did he say so specifically?"

   Merrivale's face darkened slightly at any reference to his well-known propensity for *personalized* interpretation of orders. "He made himself abundantly
clear! This is to be handled with the utmost discretion."

   "A discreet local inquiry sounds to me well within that requirement. Porter was in that area. He's
missing. These reports in the file indicate others may
have disappeared there. This family of picnickers with
the twin babies, for instance, they—"

   "A logical explanation has been accepted for every such occurrence, Tymiena," Merrivale interrupted.
"Unfortunately, logic and actuality do not always co-
incide. Our concern is for the actuality and, in our
pursuit of it, we shall utilize our own tested resources."

"I don't like their logical explanations," Tymiena said. "I don't give one particle of a damn what explanations local dumbheads may have accepted."

"Our own resources only," Merrivale repeated.

"Which means we put our lives on the line again," she said. "What does Carlos say about this case?"

"Why don't you ask him? I've arranged for a briefing at 1100 hours. Janvert and Carr will be here, as well."

"Are they in this?"

"They're in reserve."

"I don't like that, either. Where's Carlos?"

"I believe he's in Archives. You have almost an hour to explore this matter with him."

"*Merde!*" she said and swept from the room.

Carlos was no more helpful than Merrivale. The assignment had struck him as "routine." But then, assignments tended to strike Carlos as cast in some familiar mold. His response was a universal, clerkish thoroughness of preparation: read all of the material, study all of the plans. It had not surprised her that Carlos was in Archives. He had an Archives mind.

The trip to Oregon and the cozy journey in the van-camper had been everything she'd expected. Crawling hands and a crawling mind. She had finally told Carlos that she'd contracted a serious venereal disease on her previous assignment. He refused to believe her. Quite calmly, she'd told him then that if he persisted, she would put a bullet in him. She had displayed the small Belgian automatic she always wore in its wrist holster. Something about the clear calmness of her manner told him to believe this. But he had taken the rebuff in muttering bad grace.

The job was another matter, though, and she'd wished him luck when he took off in his ridiculous bird-watching clothes. All through the long day then, when she'd been fulfilling her part of the cover by painting, she had grown increasingly nervous. There had been no particular thing on which to focus her uneasiness, nothing concrete to explain it. The whole scene bothered her. It reeked of trouble. Carlos had

been predictably imprecise about his estimate of return time. It all depended on what he saw in his preliminary scan of the farm.

"Shortly after dark at the latest," he'd said. "You
be a good wife and paint your pretty pictures while I
go look for birds. When I come back, I'll teach you all
about the birds and the bees."

"Carlos!"

"Ahhh, my love, someday I shall teach you to
say that exquisite name with true passion." And the
bastard had chucked her under the chin as he took his
leave.

Tymiena had watched him zigzag his way up the
grass-brown slope into the trees. The day was already
warm and filled with that special kind of insect-singing
stillness that spoke of more heat to come. Sighing, she
had taken out her watercolor materials. She actually
was quite a good watercolorist and, occasionally, during the long day she had experienced real involvement
in capturing the essence of the autumn fields. The
golden browns were particularly warm and inviting.

Shortly after midday, she put her painting aside
temporarily and fixed herself a light lunch of sliced
hard-boiled eggs and yogurt cold from the camper's
icebox. During the break, although the camper's interior was oven hot, she stayed inside to check over the
instruments. To her surprise, the speed-trap warning,
which could be turned on its base and had a null indicator, showed radar activity in the direction of the
farm. There was a clear signal aimed at the camper.

Radar surveillance of her from the farm?

She interpreted this as a danger sign and thought
of going after Carlos to call him back. An alternative
was to warm up the radio and report this development
to headquarters. She knew with a sure instinct that
headquarters would make light of it. And Carlos had
ordered her to stay with the camper. In the end, she
opted for neither course. Her own indecision added a
frustrating accent to the nervousness that afflicted her
throughout the afternoon. The sense of danger accumulated. She felt that something was warning her to

get out of there. Leave the camper and get out of there! The camper was a big, fat target.

In the half-light of dusk, she folded up her painting tablet, dropped it and her paints on the cab seat, and slipped into the seat. It took a moment to warm up the radio and she checked the signal monitor, found a search resonance fanning across her own frequency. When she keyed her transmitter, the search resonance homed on her signal and jammed it. The monitor howled with the interference. She slapped the off switch, stared up the dusky hillside toward the farm. The place was not visible from this parking spot, but she felt it out there as a malevolent presence.

There was still no sign of Carlos.

Darkness would be on her within minutes. She felt nervously for the little automatic in its wrist holster.

What the hell was delaying Carlos?

She turned off all of the camper's lights, sat in the settling darkness. Radar from the farm's direction. They jammed her radio. This case had turned nasty. She stood up, moved softly to the rear door, slipped out on the side opposite the farm. The van itself would shield her from that searching beam. She dropped to all fours and worked her way swiftly into the tall grass. She had seen cows far down in the pasture below her and she headed for them with a sure instinct. She had grown up on a Wyoming cattle ranch and, although she preferred approaching cattle on horseback, she felt no threat from them. The threat was behind her, somewhere up at Hellstrom's farm. The cows would offer her a masking confusion, concealment from that radar sweep. If Carlos returned, he'd turn on the camper's lights. She would see that from a safe distance in the pastureland. Somehow, she did not expect Carlos to return. This whole situation did not make sense, and it had not made sense from the beginning, but she trusted her own instinct for self-preservation.

The words of Nils Hellstrom. This primeval planet Earth is an arena of continual contest where only the most versatile and resourceful endure. On this testing ground where the mighty dinosaur staggered and fell, one silent witness hangs on. This witness remains our guide to human survival. This witness, the insect, has a three-hundred-million-year head start on mankind, but we will overtake him. He dominates our earth today and exploits his dominion well. With each new generation come new experiments in shape and function, transforming him into specters as limitless as the imagination of the insane. Yet, what this witness can do, we of the Hive can do because we are witness of him.

Old Harvey led his troop from a concealed perimeter exit at the northern edge of the Hive. Sod rolled back, a stump with a mucilage-sealed earth plug folded outward on a silent hinge, and the troop emerged into the night. They were lightly clad in dark gray and the night was cold, but they ignored the chill. Each carried a stunwand and wore a night-vision mask with a powerful infrared emitter (of Hive manufacture) around its rim. They looked like a troop of skin divers and the wands were like strange double-ended spears.

The stump-plug was seated securely before they left it, all sign of their passage removed.

They fanned out over the field and moved northward.

Old Harvey had chosen twenty-three of the key workers, mostly aggressive males, and he had seen to it that the females received hormones to hype them before he'd issued his careful instructions.

They wanted this Outsider female alive. Nils needed the information she carried. She was probably down among the cows. The cows could be frightened off with a low stun, but none were to be killed. This was not a sweep; it was a search. Only the Outsider female would go eventually into the vats from this venture, but that would come after she had given up the necessary information.

It had been a long time since Old Harvey had participated in a hunt and he felt the excitement of it pumping in his veins. There was life in this old worker yet!

He signaled for Saldo to take the left flank and moved out to the right himself. The night air tasted of many scents in his nostrils. There were the cattle, the dust in the tall grass, the raw earth, and the subtle esters of insects, a touch of tree resin. It was all there in his sensitive nostrils, but he could not separate out an odor that said the Outsider female was ahead of him. If she were there, the nightsight would reveal her.

Saldo had moved immediately to his assigned position and Old Harvey relaxed on that score. The young man was green, but his potential was enormous. The regular reports to Hellstrom pleased them both mightily. Saldo was among the twenty or so who might someday step into Hellstrom's sandals. He was one of the smaller, energy-saving new breed, dark and slim, filled with a nervous energy and willingness to please, but with his own mind showing more strongly each day. He would be a power in the Hive someday, or he might even take a swarm of his own out to start a new hive.

The searchers had spread into a wide fan, walking openly down into the pastureland. Old Harvey noted that it was a good night for this search. Clouds were beginning to cover the sky, obscuring the late-rising waning moon. The cattle could be seen easily in the nightsight reflection. He kept his eyes on the scattered clumps of trees, however, ignoring the cattle for the moment. They passed one small herd with minimal disturbance of the animals, although the warm smell of the cows excited the hunter drive in the entire troop. Saldo and two others searched through the herd, making sure the animals screened no Outsider.

Hunt excitement could not be denied, though. It was evidenced by an increasing nervousness in the troop and an outflow of external hormones that began to spook the cattle. More and more, individual cows and then whole groups of them snorted and ran off with a panicked thumping.

Old Harvey began to regret that he had not included a selective hormone suppressant in his preparations. The subtle chemical signals that one animal could send to another had their uses at times, but they introduced complexities now. He kept his attention on the trees, however, leaving the cattle for Saldo and the others to scan. Nightsight gave his surroundings a faint silver cast, as though the light came from within every object he saw.

She will hear us coming and she will try to hide in a tree, he told himself. It's her style.

He couldn't say why or how he knew this from just one afternoon's observation, but he felt certain of it. She would hide in a tree.

Old Harvey heard a night bird call from far off to his right and felt his heartbeat quicken. He was not too old for the sweeps. Perhaps it would be a good thing to go out occasionally with the workers.

The words of Nils Hellstrom. Unlike other creatures who struggled against their environment, the insect learned early to seek its protective embrace. He created an endless wardrobe of camouflage. He and his environment became one. When predators came, he was nowhere to be found. So artistic were his methods of deception that predators could crawl upon his body in their search for prey. He did not choose merely one means of escape, but countless means. Not for him speed or the treetops, but both of these, and more.

Tymiena saw one flank of the sweep just as the first searchers saw her, confirming Old Harvey's prediction. Early in her flight, she had tripped in a rabbit hole and sprained her left ankle. The pain had forced her to make the climb into a low oak where she had braced herself in a notch and taken off the shoe on the injured foot. She sat wedged in the notch about twenty feet up, the little automatic held firmly in her right hand now. A powerful little pen-size flashlight was in her left hand, her thumb on its switch.

The ankle throbbed with a fiery pain that made thought difficult. She wondered if she had broken a bone.

Running cattle gave her the first indication of trouble. She heard them snorting above the pounding of their hooves as they passed. Then came a mysterious swish-swish hissing. This sound grew louder until it circled her tree and stopped. She could just make out the darker shadows of the hunters in the blackness. They had formed a rough circle all around her.

In panic, she thumbed the flashlight switch, swept its beam in a short arc around the part of the circle that faced her. At first sight of the nightmasks and stunwands, she gasped, recognizing deadly menace. Without thinking, she began shooting.

The words of Nils Hellstrom. Perhaps, in time we will become fully functional as are those we copy. We will develop faces without expression; only eyes and mouth; just enough to keep the rest of the body alive. No muscles to smile with, or frown with, or in any way to betray what's lurking beneath the surface.

The little automatic erupted as a monstrous surprise to the Hive's hunters. Five of them were dead before Tymiena was brought tumbling from the tree by a concentration of stuns. Old Harvey was among those killed, his nightmask shattered and a bullet in his brain. Saldo suffered a bullet burn on his jaw, but his shouted command brought order to the frightened workers. They had been full of "hunt juice," as the old-timers put it, and the Outsider female's attack had raised them to a deadly pitch. They leaped in to finish her off with their hands, but Saldo's cry stopped them. In the end, it was Hive discipline that kept them off her.

Saldo moved up to the unconscious female, issued swift orders. Someone must run to inform Nils. The dead must be returned to the vats. That was what good workers deserved. Thus, they became one with all. "Into the vats old, out of the vats new."

When his orders were being obeyed, he knelt to examine the unconscious female. Her flashlight still glowed in the grass. He pushed his nightmask back onto his head, used the flashlight to help his examination. Yes, she was still alive. It was difficult to conduct the examination calmly. He felt hate filling him. This one had harmed the Hive. Nils needed her, though. The Hive needed her. Saldo managed a kind of calm as he continued his examination. She appeared to have no broken bones. A painful ankle, obviously. It was swelling and discolored. Workers had suffered much worse, though, and gone on with their tasks. He directed that her weapon be found and returned to the Hive.

Old Harvey's death neither saddened nor gladdened him. Such things occurred. It would have been better had it not happened, but the reality could not be avoided. The reality had placed him in command of the search troop and he was required to give correct orders. That was how Old Harvey had taught him to behave.

There was the Outsider female to be sure of first. He judged that she could be revived for questioning. That would please Nils. It pleased Saldo now. He began to sense a greater interest in this female. She was possessor of fascinating odors. There were alien Outsider soaps and perfumes over faint, but familiar, musks. He bent close to sniff at her, the first Outsider female he'd ever encountered alone in the wild. Beneath the dominant acridity of her fear there were exciting odors. He slipped a hand under her blouse, felt a breast, found it full and firm under a restraining garment. He knew about such garments from his training for key worker roles. It was called a bra and was fastened with metal hooks at the back. She was a true female, apparently no different from females of the Hive, and the available evidence said she was fertile. How odd these wild Outsiders were. He moved his hand down under her waistband, explored the pubic hairs and genitals, brought the hand out and smelled it. Yes, fertile. So it was true that Outsider females wandered around when they were fertile. Did they go on a mating hunt of some kind as a brood mother was supposed to do? The books, the films, and the lectures of his education had not prepared him for the actuality, although he could rattle off the facts readily enough. She excited him and he wondered if Nils would entertain a suggestion that she be kept for breeding. It would be interesting to breed with her.

A female in his band snarled at him then, a wordless sound of deep menace. Another said, "This Outsider female isn't a breeder! What are you doing with her?"

"I investigate," Saldo said. "She is fertile."

The one who had snarled at him found her voice, "Many of these wild ones are fertile."

The other said, "She killed five of us. She's fit only for the vats."

"Where she probably will go when we have finished questioning her," Saldo said. He spoke without trying to conceal an abrupt feeling of sadness. This Outsider female would be destroyed by the questioning; no doubt of it. That was happening to the captive male and it could be no different for the female. Such a waste. Her flesh would be good for nothing but the vats.

He arose, restored his nightmask to its position over his nose, and said, "Bind her and carry her to the Hive. See that she does not escape. Two of you go to her vehicle. Bring it in for salvaging. Erase its tracks. There must be no sign remaining that this female and her companion were in our vicinity. See to it."

The orders came from his mouth as Harvey had taught him, but Saldo felt a form of despair that such commands were necessary. The responsibilities of leadership had fallen upon him so abruptly. A remote part of his awareness realized that Harvey's choice of so young a worker as second-in-command on this search had been a training gesture. A promising young worker needed this experience. Another part of Saldo's awareness rested securely in his sense of competence. He was a specialist in Hive security. He trusted

his own responses. Despite his youth, he felt perfectly
fitted for the task at hand, as though the entire Hive
were reacting through his person. Harvey had lived
beyond his day, had paid for a mistake with his life. It
was a serious loss to the Hive. Nils would have the
news of it by now and there would be concern, but for
the moment, Saldo knew he must proceed alone. His
was the seat of command.

"Those of you without other tasks," he said, "see
that no sign of our activities remains here. I do not
know all of your talents as Old Harvey did, but *you*
know them. Divide yourselves according to your abilities. No one of you is to return to the Hive until it is
done. I will remain until the last to inspect the job."

He stooped, recovered the flashlight he had left
beside the Outsider female, extinguished it, put it in
his pocket. Workers already had bound the female and
were ready to take her back to the Hive. It saddened
Saldo that he would never see her again. He didn't
think he wanted to watch the questioning. A sudden
anger at Outsider stupidity shook him. They were such
fools! Whatever happened to her, she deserved it.

Saldo glanced around at his troop. They were busy
obeying his orders and they appeared content on the
surface, but he sensed an air of uncertainty underneath. They knew how young and untried he was.
They obeyed out of habit. In truth, they were still obeying Harvey. But Harvey had made a fatal mistake.
Saldo promised himself that he would not make such a
mistake.

"Get down on your hands and knees and be thorough," he said. "Two of the nightmasks were shattered. There will be splinters to recover. Get them
all."

Saldo wandered up through the tall grass toward
the place where he knew two of his troop were ready-
ing the vehicle for removal to the Hive. She had come
down this way, that Outsider female. How odd it was
that they wandered around freely when they were fertile, as though they had no concern whatsoever about
selecting the best male for breeding. In truth, they
were not like a brood mother at all. They were merely

wild, fertile females. Perhaps someday, when there were many hives, such wild animals would be captured and put to proper breeding, or they would be neutered and employed in useful work.

Some of the cattle that had fled the scene of disturbance had returned, drawn by curiosity, no doubt. They were bunching up in the open below the place where his troop worked, and they were facing the troop. The smell of blood and the noise had left them on edge, but they offered no threat. The cattle could not see his workers, but his workers could see the cattle. Saldo held his stunwand at the ready and moved to place himself between the cattle and his troop. A good imagination could guard against the unexpected. If the cattle charged, they would be knocked down by one sweep of his stunwand.

As he moved, Saldo stared off across the rangeland toward the distant glow of the town, a dim reflection on clouds. It wasn't likely anyone that far away had heard the shooting, but even if they had, they would be sensible. Townsmen had learned to be reticent and cautious about Guarded Valley. The Hive possessed a buffer there, too, in the person of the district deputy sheriff, Lincoln Kraft. He was Hive-born and one of the most successful fronts they'd ever produced. Other Hive observers moved as ordinary Outsiders in the town, as well. There were even more important fronts in the Outside world. Saldo had seen two of them when they visited the Hive: a senator and a judge. They filled dangerous posts that someday would not be needed.

The sounds of his troop busily carrying out his orders pleased Saldo. He sniffed at the night air, detected a smell of gunpowder. Only the Hive-trained would be likely to recognize that now. It was but a faint trace among many other odors.

The cattle began to quiet down and a few left the bunched herds to graze. This annoyed Saldo. Bunched up, the cows did not offer temptation, but he knew how disturbed his workers were. One of them could conceivably take a lone cow. That must be prevented. This would be Hive land someday, and they might even have their own cattle. But for now, such protein cost too much in plant energy. Such wastefulness must be left to the profligate Outsiders and their cattle must not be molested on this night. Nothing to attract unwanted attention must occur here.

Saldo returned to his workers, moved among them, speaking in a low voice. They must not take any cattle. There must be time for this earth to conceal marks that were not erased. No suspicious Outsiders must appear here for as long as possible.

Someday, Saldo told himself, there would be other hives, many of them sprung from this one parent he served which now must conceal all trace of itself from the Outsiders. For now, they must be cautious and guard their future. They owed this to generations of countless workers as yet unborn.

The words of Nils Hellstrom. Our main breeding lines must be designed with the utmost attention to Hive necessities. In this, we walk a much tighter edge than do the insects who provide us with our model for survival. Their life begins as ours, with fertilization of a single cell, but the miracle of creation differs for us from that point onward. In the time it takes a single human embryo to develop, an insect can produce over four hundred billion of his own kind. We can increase our Hive birthrate many times over, but never can we hope to match this proliferation.

A worker came down the beaten-grass path from the Hive, waving to attract Saldo's attention. There was still no sign of dawnlight, but it had turned colder as it often did here just before daybreak. The worker stopped in front of Saldo and spoke in a low voice. "Someone's coming from the Hive."

"Who?"

"I think it is Nils himself."

Saldo turned his attention in the direction indicated by the worker, recognized the oncoming figure by his gait. Yes, it was Nils. He wore a nightmask, but carried no wand. Saldo put down a sense of relief tempered by a surge of displeasure. His decisions had been the correct ones, but Hellstrom chose to come personally. Immediately, Saldo chided himself. He could almost hear the reprimand in Harvey's aging voice: *Isn't that what you would do?* The leader of the Hive could do no less. This thought restored Saldo's feeling of calm competence. He greeted Hellstrom casually.

Hellstrom stopped a few paces from Saldo, examined the scene before speaking. He had seen Saldo at the instant the younger worker had identified him. The recognition had been obvious in Saldo's movements. The loss of Old Harvey touched Hellstrom deeply, but he noted with approval that Saldo was doing all the necessary things. Saldo had the instincts of a good protector.

"Tell me what has happened and what you have done," Hellstrom said.

"Have you had no report from the ones I sent to you?"

"They reported, but I would prefer that the leader of this search troop give me his own assessment. Sometimes, workers miss important things."

Saldo nodded. Yes, that was wise. He told Hellstrom of the discovery of the Outsider female, the shooting, left out no detail, even to the wound on his own jaw.

"Should your wound be treated?" Hellstrom asked, peering at it. What devilish bad luck if they lost Saldo, too!

"It's a minor wound," Saldo said. "No worse than a small burn."

"Take care of it as soon as you return."

Saldo heard concern for him in Hellstrom's voice, was warmed by it.

"I heard Old Harvey choose you as his second-in-command," Hellstrom said.

"I was his choice." Saldo spoke with calm confidence.

"Have any of the others displayed evidence of resenting this?"

"Nothing serious."

Hellstrom liked that answer. It said Saldo was

aware of incipient challenges but felt able to deal with
them. He no doubt could deal with them, too. Saldo
carried himself well. He possessed a sure sense of
rightness. There was about him that unspoken air of
dominance. It must be tempered, though.

"Did you enjoy it when you were chosen by Old
Harvey?" Hellstrom asked, keeping his voice flat.

Saldo swallowed. Had he done something wrong?
There'd been a prying coldness about that question.
Had he put the Hive in peril? But Hellstrom was smiling faintly, a thin movement of his mouth beneath the
nightmask.

"I enjoyed it," Saldo admitted, but there was uncertainty in his tone.

Hellstrom heard that self-questioning quality in
the younger man's voice, and he nodded. Uncertainty
bred caution. One could go from liking authority into
a gambler's stance: overconfident. Hellstrom explained this now in a quiet voice that carried only between them. When he'd finished, Hellstrom said, "Tell
me everything you have ordered here."

Saldo thought for a moment, then took up his account where he had left off. He spoke with noticeable
hesitation, questing in his own mind for possible errors, for needed corrections.

Hellstrom interrupted to ask, "Who was first to
see the Outsider female?"

"Harvey," Saldo said, recalling the motion of the
old man's hand, the upthrust pointing finger to denote
his discovery. A trickle of perspiration ran down Saldo's cheek. He wiped at it irritatedly and the action
burned his wound.

"What orders did he give then?" Hellstrom asked.

"He had told us earlier that we were to circle her
when we found her. We carried that out without orders."

"What did Harvey do then?"

"He had no chance to do anything. The female
turned on her light and immediately began shooting."

Hellstrom looked down at the ground between
them, glanced around. Several nearby workers had left
their tasks out of curiosity and had moved closer to

listen. "Why aren't you workers doing as your leader ordered?" Hellstrom demanded. "Your leader gave you specific instructions. Carry them out." He turned back to Saldo.

"They are tired," Saldo said, defending his workers. "I will make a personal inspection of their work before leaving."

This one is a jewel, Hellstrom thought. He defends his people, but not too much. And he takes personal responsibility without hesitation.

"Exactly where were you when she began shooting?" Hellstrom asked.

"I was at the other end of the sweep from Harvey. When we closed the loop, I found myself beside him."

"Who knocked her out of the tree?"

"The workers across from us where her light did not reach. The rest of us were dodging."

"And Harvey gave no more commands?"

"I believe he was the first one hit. I heard her first shot and—" he hesitated, shrugged, "for just an instant, I froze. Then I was hit and we were all rushing about. I saw Harvey go down and I started toward him. There were more shots and suddenly it was all over. She fell out of the tree."

"Your confusion is understandable because you were wounded," Hellstrom said. "I notice, however, that you kept your sense of balance sufficiently to prevent the killing of the captive. You have lived up to my expectations. But always remember what happened here. You have had a good lesson. The hunting of an Outsider is never the same as the hunting of any other animal. Do you understand that now?"

Saldo knew he had been both praised and censured. His attention went to the tree in which the female had concealed herself, then, reluctantly, back to Hellstrom. Presently, Saldo saw the slight lift of Hellstrom's mouth that denoted pleasure. Sure enough, Hellstrom said, "You caught the female alive and that's the important thing." He pursed his lips. "She carried a weapon and Harvey should have anticipated that. He should've brought her down the instant he saw her. He was within range. Do you know how to use such Outsider weapons, Saldo?"

"Yes—yes, I know. Harvey trained me himself."

"Learn to use them well. The Hive could have need of such abilities. Let's see, you're thirty-two years old, isn't that correct?"

"Yes."

"You still could pass for a youth among Outsiders. It may be that we will send you out to one of their schools before long. We have ways of doing such things. You know about this."

"I have not spent much time Outside," Saldo said.

"I know. What experiences have you had?"

"Only with others, never alone. About a month in all. I spent a week in the town once."

"Work or training?"

"Training for myself and others."

"Would you like to go Outside alone?"

"I don't think I'm ready for it."

Hellstrom nodded, pleased with the candor of that answer. Saldo would make a superb security specialist. He already was far and away the most intuitively accurate among the new breed. Give him a bit more experience and there would be none to compare with him. He possessed that beautiful Hive candor. He wouldn't lie, not even about himself. He was a leader to be preserved and nurtured. Hive conventions demanded this and the present circumstances required that Hellstrom begin that nurturing.

"You are doing very well," Hellstrom said, speaking loud enough for the others to hear. "When the present crisis is over, we'll make arrangements to send you Outside for further education. For now, report to me when you've finished out here." He turned slowly, strolled back toward the Hive, pausing occasionally to glance around. Every movement said he was satisfied to leave matters in Saldo's hands.

For a moment, Saldo watched Hellstrom go. The Hive's first counselor, leader in every crisis, the prime male, the one to whom all others turned when in doubt—even those who guided breeding and food pro-

duction and tool fabrication—the chief worker among
them all had come out on a fact-finding expedition
and had approved what he found. Saldo returned to
overseeing the cleanup with a new sense of elation
strongly tempered by a deeper respect for his own limitations. That, he realized, had been a major purpose
of Hellstrom's visit.

Minutes of the Hive Council. Interview with Philosopher-Specialist Harl (translated from Hive-sign):
Again, Philosopher Harl, we must disappoint you by
telling you we have not come to take you to the
blessed vats. Your great age, greater than that of any
other worker in the Hive, the artificial means we must
use to keep life burning within you, and all the other
things your wisdom uses in its arguments that we give
you the release of the vats, all of this is difficult to re-
fute. We respectfully request that you cease these arguments and recall the Hive's great need for your wisdom. We come again to ask your advice on how the
Hive should employ the results of a successful Project
40. We can anticipate your first question and must answer it by saying that Project 40 is not yet fruitful.
The specialists charged with the project say, however,
they can assure us of success. They say it is only a
matter of time.
The words of Philosopher-Specialist Harl: Possession of an ultimate weapon, of an ultimate threat to
all of the life that shares this planet, brings with it no
guarantee of supremacy. The very act of threatening
to use such a weapon, based on certain conditions,
puts control of that weapon into the hands of all those
who control the conditions. You face the problem of
what to do when these others say to you, "So use your
weapon!" In this manner, many will have the weapon.
Even more to the point, anyone able to threaten the
possessor of such a weapon also possesses it. Thus, an
ultimate weapon is useless unless those who control it
can temper the weapon's violence. The weapon must
have degrees of application that are less than ultimate.
Take your lesson from the defense mechanisms every-

where visible in the insects who provide us with our pattern for survival. The spikes and prickles, the stingers and thorns, the burning chemicals and poisoned spears that jut angrily into the air, all of these are, first, defense mechanisms. They say, "Don't threaten me."

Tymiena realized quite slowly that her hands were bound behind her and that she was fastened securely into a chair of some kind. The chair's surface was hard and she could feel the cold smoothness of its back against her arms. The most central part of her mind focused on her ankle, which throbbed painfully where she had sprained it. Fighting a deep reluctance, she opened her eyes, but she found only an impenetrable darkness, thick and ominous. For a moment, she feared she might be blind, but a faint glow insinuated itself into her awareness. The glow existed at an indeterminate distance directly in front of her. It moved.

"Ahhh, you're awake, I see."

It was a deep, masculine voice from somewhere above the moving glow. Something about the echo quality of the voice told her she was in a room, quite a large room.

She put down her terror with difficulty, forced a false nonchalance into her voice, and said, "How can you see? It's pitch dark."

Hellstrom, seated in a corner of the laboratory where he could watch the glowing instruments that told him the female's reactions, could only admire her courage. They often were so very brave, these wild ones.

"I can see," he said.

"My ankle hurts like hell," he said.

"I truly regret that. We will give you something for that presently. Try to be patient."

She found an oddly reassuring sincerity in the voice. It was a man's voice, ranging from low to tenor. Exquisite control.

"I hope it won't be very long," she said.

She must be brought into some semblance of calmness, Hellstrom told himself. The nightmask was irritating where it pressed against his nose and fore-

head. He did not like the way it limned the female in a
silvery glow. The irritation came from fatigue, he
knew. Sometimes the Hive demanded too much of
him. But this Outsider female must be questioned, and
he found himself reluctant to turn her over to the merciless youngsters who waited so eagerly for the opportunity to prove themselves. He told himself that he delayed with this female because he did not trust what
the others had wrenched from Depeaux. How could
the Outsiders know about Project 40? One of the in-
terrogators must have mentioned it! That was it, of
course. Well, it could be tested with this female.

"First, I must ask you a few questions," he said.

"Why're you keeping it so dark?" she asked.

"So you cannot see me."

Sudden, wild elation filled her. If they didn't
want her to see someone, that meant she would have
an opportunity to describe her captors. It could only
mean they meant to release her!

Hellstrom read her reaction on his instruments
and said, "You were very hysterical out there. Did you
think we were going to harm you?"

She wondered what he meant by that question.
They had her tied up like a Christmas turkey, which
didn't indicate the best of intentions. "I was terrified,"
she said. "Did—did I hurt anyone?"

"You killed five of our people and injured two
others," Hellstrom said.

She had not expected such a coldly candid answer
and it shocked her. Five dead? Could they actually
release her after that?

"I—I felt trapped," she said. "My—my husband
was not back and I was—alone. I was terribly afraid.
What've you done to Carlos?"

"He is suffering no pain," Hellstrom said. And that
was true, he told himself. It was difficult to lie outright,
even to a wild Outsider. His statement was true. Depeaux
had been blissfully unconscious when his torn body had
been slipped into the choppers and thence to the dis-
solving fluids of the vats. He had suffered no pain there,
and surely death had overcome him before any glim-

mering return to consciousness. The choppers were quick.

"Why do you have me tied this way?" she asked.

"To keep you in one place while I ask my questions. Tell me your name."

They would have her cover identification papers, she thought. "My name's Tymiena—Tymiena Depeaux."

"Tell me about this government agency for which you work."

Her heart skipped a beat, but she managed a semblance of masked response. "Gov—I don't work for any government agency! We were on vacation. My husband sells fireworks."

Hellstrom smiled sadly at what his instruments revealed. It was true, then. Both of them worked for a government agency and that agency was curious. Although he had been opaque to most of their probings, Porter had revealed as much. But Porter had not said anything about Project 40. Would this female impart such information? He felt a quickening of his pulse. This was the kind of danger the Hive had always feared, but there was something in it that aroused his hunt juices.

"Is your agency the CIA?" Hellstrom asked.

"I'm just a housewife!" she protested. "Where's Carlos? What've you done with my husband?"

Hellstrom sighed. It was not the CIA, then—provided her responses could be trusted, and provided she even knew the connections behind her employment. It was possible she did not know. Such agencies had a proclivity for putting covers on covers on covers. "Do not worry about your husband," he said. "You will be with him soon. We know, however, that you are not a simple housewife. Simple housewives do not carry such weapons as you had in your possession. They certainly do not demonstrate the proficiency you displayed with such a weapon."

"I don't believe I killed anyone," she said.

"But you did."

"Carlos insisted I have that gun. He taught me how to shoot it."

Another lie, Hellstrom observed. He felt cheated.

Why was she continuing to hide? Surely, she must know by now that she had been exposed by her accomplice. His questions could not conceal this. Hellstrom had forced himself to read the Depeaux interrogation account, avoiding nothing. What the merciless youngsters did, they did in the name of all the Hive. He wondered if he dared put her through a chemical reduction of personality. The youngsters argued against it. The method was painless, but uncertain. It had reduced Porter to slavering imbecility. The heroic totality of such an effort tended to erase memories as it exposed them. He did not want the Porter effort repeated and decided not to listen to his own inner revulsions. What must be, must be. He would continue with present methods, however, as long as she did not suspect her emotions were being monitored and as long as information was being gathered. The tapes were spinning to record everything that occurred here. They could be subjected to full analysis later. Even the Hive's central computer might be helpful in the analysis, although Hellstrom tended to distrust computers. They had no emotions. Having no emotions, they failed when confronted by human problems.

"Why do you lie?" he asked.

"I'm not lying!"

"Is the agency that employs you an arm of the U.S. State Department?"

"If you won't believe me, there's no sense answering. I just don't understand what's going on here. You chase me, knock me out, tie me up, and all for—"

"And you killed five of my friends," he reminded her. "Why?"

"I don't believe you. You'd better let me go. Carlos is a very important man in his company. There are people who'll come looking for us if I don't call them."

"If you don't report in?" Hellstrom studied his instruments. She'd been telling the truth there, for once.

"It's not like that!"

So she was supposed to report in, probably at regular intervals, Hellstrom thought. The eager youngsters had not elicited that from Depeaux. But then they hadn't asked.

"Why were you sent here?" he asked.

"I wasn't sent!"

"Then what were you doing here?"

She seized this opportunity to elaborate on her cover story: the long hours Carlos usually worked, the rare vacations, his interest in birds, her own interest in landscape painting. There was a certain delicate practicality about her account, a sense of domesticity she found herself almost wishing were true. Carlos hadn't been such a bad sort in spite of . . . She broke off her account as this thought intruded. It confused her. There was internal significance in such a thought. Why would she think about Carlos in the past tense? Carlos was dead! She felt certain of this. What had that character over there in the dark said to give her this feeling of certainty? She trusted her instincts and felt fear rising like a tide of bile.

Hellstrom saw the emotion on his instruments, tried to divert her. "Are you hungry?" he asked.

She found it difficult to speak at first, then responded in spite of a dry mouth. "No, but my ankle hurts terribly."

"We'll take care of that pretty soon," he reassured her. "Tell me, Mrs. Depeaux, if you were frightened, why did you not drive down to Fosterville in your camper?"

That's what I should've done! she told herself. But she suspected this character and his friends had been prepared for such an attempt and that wouldn't have succeeded, either. She said, "I must've done something wrong. It wouldn't start."

"That's odd," he said. "It started immediately for us."

So they had the camper, too! All evidence of Depeaux and Grinelli would be gone by now. Carlos and Tymiena, both dead. A tear trickled down the edge of her left cheek.

"Are you a communist agent?" she husked.

In spite of himself, Hellstrom chuckled. "What an odd question from a simple housewife!"

His amusement filled her with bracing anger. "You're the one who keeps talking about agents and the State Department!" she flared. "What's going on here?"

"You are not what you appear to be, Mrs. Depeaux," Hellstrom said. "There is even some doubt in my mind as to whether you actually are Mrs. Depeaux." Ahhh, that hit a nerve! he noted. So they were just working together and not married. "I suspect you did—do not even care much for Carlos."

Did not care! she thought. That's what he was going to say! He caught himself. The lie came out!

She began to think back over this unseen man's every reference to Carlos. The dead felt no pain. There was a sense of over-and-done-with about every mention of Carlos. She revised her assessment of her own situation. Darkness could have more significance than hiding the identity of her interrogator. It could be a deliberate ploy to confuse her, lower her defenses. She began exploring her bindings, straining against them. They were damnably tight!

"You do not answer me," Hellstrom said.

"Why should I? I think you're awful!"

"Is your agency an arm of the government's executive branch?"

"No!"

He read otherwise in her responses, but it was a tempered reading. The answer probably was that she believed this to be the case but harbored her own doubts. He noted she was twisting frantically, trying to escape her bonds. Didn't she believe he could see her?

"Why does the government investigate us?" he asked.

She refused to answer. The bindings were deceptive. They felt like leather and appeared to give when she strained against them, but when she stopped struggling even for an instant, they felt as tight as ever.

"You work for an agency associated with the executive arm of government," he said. "It is a matter of curiosity that such an agency should pry into our affairs. What interest could the government have in us?"

"You're going to kill me, aren't you?" she asked.

She gave up struggling, felt completely exhausted. Her mind teetered on the edge of hysteria. They were going to kill her. They'd killed Carlos and were going to kill her. Something had gone very sour. It was the very thing she'd sensed in this assignment from the first. That damn fool, Merrivale! He never got anything right! And Carlos—the dope of dopes! Carlos had probably walked right into a trap. They'd caught him and he'd spilled his guts. That was obvious. This questioner knew too many things already. Carlos had babbled and they'd killed him anyway.

Hellstrom's instruments revealed her approach to hysteria. The fear disturbed him. He knew it was partly his own sensitivity to her subtle bodily excretions. She was broadcasting terror for anyone Hive-trained to receive. No worker could escape such awareness. He didn't even need his instruments. This room would have to be flushed out later. They'd had to do the same thing after interrogating Depeaux. Any workers who encountered such emissions would be disturbed. He still had his duty to the Hive, though. Perhaps in her fear she would reveal what he most wanted to know.

"You work for the government," he said. "We know this. You were sent here to pry into our affairs. What did you expect to find?"

"I wasn't!" she screamed. "I wasn't! I wasn't! I wasn't! Carlos just told me we were going on vacation. What've you done with Carlos?"

"You're lying," he said. "I know you are lying and you certainly must realize by now that your lies are not working with me. It will go better with you if you tell me the truth."

"You're going to kill me anyway," she whispered.

Damn! Hellstrom thought.

His brood mother had warned him that this crisis within a crisis might come in his lifetime. His workers had tortured a wild human. It had been done far outside the concept of mercy. Such a concept had not even entered the workers' awareness as they went about their business of extracting information necessary for the Hive's survival. But such actions left their mark on the entire Hive. There were no more innocents anywhere in the Hive. We've moved a step closer to the insects we mimic, he thought. And he wondered why the thought saddened him. He suspected that any life form that inflicted unnecessary pain tended to find its consciousness eroding. Without consciousness to reflect back upon life, all life might lose its sense of purpose.

In sudden anger, he snarled, "Tell me about Project 40!"

She gasped. They knew everything! What did they do to Carlos to make him tell everything? She felt icy with terror.

"Tell me!" he barked.

"I—I don't know what you're talking about."

The instruments told him what he needed to know. "It will go very badly with you if you do not tell me," he explained. "I wish to spare you that. Tell me about Project 40."

"But I don't know anything about it," she moaned.

The instruments accorded this the value of an almost truth. "You know some things about it," he said. "Tell me those things."

"Why don't you just go ahead and kill me?" she asked.

Hellstrom found himself working through a haze of deep sadness, almost despair. Powerful wild humans Outside knew about Project 40! How could that be? What did they know? This female was little more than a pawn in a larger game, but she might yet provide a valuable clue.

"You must tell me what you know," he said. "If you do, I promise to treat you gently."

"I don't trust you," she said.

"You have no one else to trust."

"They'll come looking for me!"

"But they will not find you. Now, tell me what you know about Project 40."

"It's just a name," she said, wilting. What was the use? They knew everything else.

"Where did you encounter this name?"

"There were papers. They were left on a table at MIT and one of our people copied them."

Stunned, Hellstrom closed his eyes. "What was in those papers?" he asked.

"Some figures and formulas and things that didn't make much sense. But one of our people suggested they could be part of a design for a weapon."

"Did he say what kind of weapon?"

"I think they said a particle pump or something like that. They said such a weapon could resonate matter at a distance, break glass, that sort of thing." She sighed deeply, wondered why she was talking. They were going to kill her anyway. What did anything matter?

"Are—your people attempting to make such a weapon from these papers?"

"They're trying, but I heard that the papers they found were incomplete. They're not sure about a lot of things and there's an argument over whether it's really a weapon."

"They do not agree that it's a weapon?"

"I don't think so." Again she sighed. "Is it a weapon?"

"It is a weapon," he said.

"Are you going to kill me now?" she asked.

The plaintive, pleading note in her voice sent rage erupting in him. The fools! The utter fools! He groped for his stunwand which he'd dropped to the floor beside the instruments, found it, and brought it up, setting for full charge. Those wild idiots Outside had to be stopped. He thrust the wand toward her as though he wanted to penetrate her flesh with it, let her have the full charge. The force of it resonating in the insulated confines of the laboratory stunned him for an instant and when he had recovered he saw that all of the needles on his instruments had dropped to zero. He turned on the lab's coved lights, got to his feet slowly, and crossed to the female form sagging in the chair. She lay slumped to her right, held by the bindings. She was utterly still. He knew she was dead before he bent and confirmed it. She had taken a charge strong enough to kill a steer. There would be no more questioning of Tymiena whatever her name was.

Why did I do that? he wondered. Had it been the memory of Depeaux's shattered flesh going into the vats? Was it some higher demand from his Hive awareness? Or had it been a peculiar personal quirk? He had acted in reflex, not thinking. It was done; no calling it back. But his own behavior troubled him.

Still in the grip of anger, he strode from the lab. When the eager youngsters in the outer room crowded around, he waved them aside, told them the captive female was dead. He answered their protests with curt gestures, saying only that he had learned what he needed to learn. When one of the youngsters asked if they should take the carcass to the vats or try for a sexual stump, he paused for only the briefest reflection before agreeing that they should try for a stump. Perhaps some of that female flesh could be revived and preserved. If her womb could be maintained, she might yet serve the Hive. It would be interesting to see a child of that flesh.

Other problems dominated his thoughts, however. He stalked from the lab area, still angry with himself. Outsiders knew about Project 40! A Hive worker had been destructively careless. How had such papers been allowed out of the Hive? Who had done this? How? Papers at MIT? Who had done the research there? The Hive must learn the extent of this disaster and take quick action that nothing of this sort ever happened again.

He hoped the breeder labs succeeded in making a sexual stump of Tymiena. She had served the Hive already and she deserved to have her genes preserved.

General memo from Joseph Merrivale. Whether Porter, Depeaux, and Grinelli are actually dead is unimportant for these present considerations. Although we presume they are dead, nothing is changed if they are only missing. We have learned that Hellstrom will not hesitate to act against us. In view of his frequent overseas trips, ostensibly in connection with his insect films, a renewed effort to assess his foreign contacts is indicated. His ruthless actions bear a certain familiar stamp. On the home front, the problem is more complex. Because we cannot admit the purposes that prompted our investigation, we cannot now proceed through ordinary channels. Suggestions on alternate procedures will be welcomed. Destroy this message immediately after reading. This is mandatory. Do it now.

Appended comment by Dzule Peruge with cover: For the Chief's eyes only! *Nuts! I'm opening several straightforward inquiries. I want an examination of that film company along every avenue we can open. My approach in Oregon will be to launch a missing-person inquiry through every agency I can reach. FBI assistance will be solicited. Your help there would be appreciated.*—Dzule

Janvert did not bring up the subject of their companions in this project until they were on the plane headed west. He had chosen seats for Clovis and himself well forward of the others and on the left side. The window beside him gave a good view of a sensational sunset over the left wing, but he ignored it.

As expected, he and Clovis had been ordered to assume teen-age guise, and Nick Myerlie, whom both of them considered to be an ineffectual ass, had been named to cover as their father. What none of them had expected was that Janvert would be selected for the number-two spot.

He and Clovis held their heads close together, speaking in barely audible whispers.

"I don't like it," Janvert said. "Peruge will hit the ceiling and choose someone else in the field."

"What good would that do him?"

"I don't know, but you wait and see. Tomorrow at the latest."

"It could be recognition of your sterling qualities."

"Shit!"

"Don't you want the second spot?"

"Not on this merry-go-round." His lips set in a stubborn line. "This one's a nasty."

"You think they're looking for a scapegoat?"

"Don't you?"

"It's possible. How do you get along with Peruge?"

"Not badly, considering."

"Considering what?"

"The fact that he doesn't trust me."

"Eddie!"

One of their teammates took this moment to wander past, headed for the forward toilets. The teammate was an ex-door gunner from the Vietnam War (he called it "Nam") named Daniel Thomas Alden, and everyone called him DT. Janvert remained silent while DT passed, noting the hard, youthful face, the square and deeply tanned line of jaw. There was a white scar in the shape of an inverted V at the bridge of his nose, and he affected a flight cap with transparent green visor which imparted a dark green cast to his face. Janvert suspected DT of being a spy for the brass. Rumor had it he was shacking up with Tymiena, and Janvert found himself suddenly wondering what the younger man must be thinking now.

As he passed, DT glanced at them, but there was no sign he recognized them or even noticed them.

When he had passed, Janvert whispered, "Do you suppose DT enjoys this work?"

"Why?"

"You'd think he would find it a bit more constraining than an actual war; not as many chances to kill people."

"Sometimes, you're too damned bitter."

"And you shouldn't be in this business at all, honey," Janvert said. "Why didn't you beg off sick or something?"

"I thought you might need someone to defend you."

"The way you did last night?"

She ignored him and said, "Have you heard the talk about DT and Tymiena?"

"Yes. I almost feel sorry for him."

"You think she's—"

"I don't want to think about it, but yes, I do."

"But why? Couldn't they all just be—"

"You can smell it in a case like this one. They were the shock troops. You expect casualties with shock troops."

"What are we then?"

"With Peruge along, I don't know. I'll tell you when I find out how he deploys us."

"Front line or rear."

"Right."

"Aren't they going to serve dinner on this flight?" she asked.

"Those stewardi are too interested in getting our *elders* drunk."

"That's one of the things I hate about playing this kiddy role," she whispered. "I can't ask for a drink."

"I hate the makeup," he said. "I'll bet they don't feed us before Nebraska."

"This is a bean-and-cod special," she said. "They'll give us fish balls and haricot. Are you still feeling low?"

"Honey, forget some of the things I said last night. I was feeling like the very end."

"To be strictly accurate, there were two of us in that mood. It's probably the phase of the moon."

"I still don't know a good reason why I was named number two on this case, do you?"

"None I'm sure of." And almost as an after-thought, "The others are pretty old."

"All the more reason—I mean, why would they want a younger agent in command?"

"Youth must have its day," she whispered, and she bent close to nibble his ear. "Knock it off, darling. The old goat right behind me is trying to eavesdrop."

Janvert knew better than to glance back at once, but he straightened presently and glanced around at the crowded aircraft. The lights were on now and it was dark outside, each window a patch of black with occasional stars. The white-haired old man behind Clovis had his light on and was reading *Time* magazine while drinking a whiskey over ice. He looked up as Janvert turned around, but immediately went back to his magazine and drink. Janvert could not recall ever having seen the old man before, but you never knew in this business. He could be someone sent to keep tabs on them.

Angrily, Janvert sank back into his seat, bent close to Clovis. "Honey, we've got to break away from this racket. We've just got to. There must be a country somewhere that would be safe for us. There must be someplace where the Agency can't reach us."

"The other side?"

"You know what that'd be—more of the same only in a foreign language. No—we need a nice tidy little foreign country where we can blend into the population without being noticed. It has to exist somewhere on this dirty planet."

"You're thinking about DT and Tymiena."

"I'm thinking about you and me."

"He's listening again," she whispered.

Janvert folded his arms and sank into sullen silence. It was going to be a bitch of a flight all the way to Portland. He resigned himself to it.

Later, when Nick Myerlie came past and bent over them to ask, "You kids getting along okay?" Janvert just growled at him.

Inter-Hive memo: Project 40. The heat problem remains severe. Our latest model melted before becoming fully operational. Secondary resonance was measurable, however, and it was climbing toward the expected peaks. If the proposed new cooling techniques are successful, we should get our first fully operational tests within the month. The test is sure to cause manifestations that will be noticeable Outside. At the minimum, you can expect a new island to appear in the Pacific Ocean somewhere off Japan.

Peruge caught a late flight out of Dulles and was forced to accept coach, compounding his annoyance over the conference with Merrivale. The Chief had insisted on that meeting, however, and Peruge had seen no good way to avoid it. He had driven over to Operations after preparing the way with a call, and they'd met in Merrivale's office. The gloves had been off right from the beginning.

Merrivale had glanced up at the intrusion without change of expression as Peruge strode into the office. There was a pinched, frightened look around Merrivale's eyes, and Peruge thought: He knows he's been nominated for patsy.

Peruge seated himself across from Merrivale in one of the hokey leather chairs and indicated a folder on the desk. "You're reviewing the reports, I see. Any holes in them?"

Obviously, Merrivale thought this put him at a disadvantage because he immediately tried to recapture control of the situation. "My reports are precisely fitted to the circumstances for which they were made."

The pompous bastard!

Peruge was well aware that his presence annoyed Merrivale. It always did. Peruge was such a damned big man. They all said he'd be gross if he ever let himself go to fat. But he possessed a softly sinister grace that never failed to irritate Merrivale.

"The Chief wanted me to ask you why you seconded that little shrimp Janvert," Peruge said.

"Because he's long overdue for responsibility."

"He's not trustworthy."

"Nonsense!"

"Why didn't you delay and let me appoint my own second?"

"No sense in delay. The briefing had to proceed."

"So you rushed into another mistake," Peruge said. His voice conveyed a sense of calm, superior knowledge. That mention of the Chief had been telling.

Merrivale could feel his own chances of ever reaching a higher status in the Agency dwindling away to zero. His face darkened.

"Why are you going out to Oregon yourself?"

"It's indicated by the circumstances," Peruge said.

"What circumstances?"

"Three of our best people lost."

Merrivale nodded. "You spoke of something important to discuss with me. What is it?"

"Several things. First, that memo you circulated indicating that we were unsure of our next step in this case. The Chief was rather upset by that."

Merrivale actually paled. "We—the circumstances—"

Peruge interrupted as though he hadn't heard Merrivale. "Second, we are concerned about the instructions you gave those three agents. It seems strange to us that—"

"I followed my bloody orders to the letter!" Merrivale said, slamming a hand onto the folder.

The story of his life, Peruge thought. He said, "There are rumors that Tymiena didn't like this assignment."

Merrivale sniffed, managed to look unimpressed. "They always object and then talk about it behind my back. What good are rumors?"

"I got enough hints to convince me she may have had a valid objection to the way things were being handled. Did she talk about specific objections?"

"We talked, yes. She thought we should go in openly after Porter, a more official approach."

"Why?"

"It was just a feeling she had, nothing more." Merrivale made *feeling* sound like a peculiar female foible.

"Just a feeling, nothing specific?"

"That's all it was."

"That feeling appears to have been accurate. You should have listened to her."

"She was always having those crazy feelings," Merrivale objected. "She didn't like working with Carlos, for one thing."

"So she did have specific objections. Why did she object to Carlos?"

"I'm only guessing, but I presume he'd made offensive advances to her at some time. At any rate, it wasn't the kind of quibble we tolerate in the Agency.

They know the work they're called on to do and what it may entail."

Peruge just stared at him.

Merrivale's face was an open page, his thoughts written across it for anyone to read: They're blaming me for these losses. Why are they blaming me? I only did what they told me to do.

Before Merrivale could begin giving voice to these thoughts, Peruge said, "There is pressure from farther up the line and we're going to have some explaining to do. Your part in this comes in for particular questioning."

Merrivale could get the whole picture now: pressure from higher up and someone was being prepared as sacrificial goat. That goat was named Joseph Merrivale. The fact that he had protected himself this way on many occasions would not ease the pain of finding himself today's target.

"This is not fair," Merrivale husked. "It is simply not fair."

"I'd like you to recount as much as you remember of your last conversation with Tymiena," Peruge said. "Everything."

Merrivale took a moment to regain his composure. "Everything?"

"Everything."

"Very well." Merrivale had a neatly organized mind which could reproduce most conversations from memory. He was hampered this time, however, by the necessity of screening every scrap through a self-protective analysis. Unconsciously, he lost his fake British accent as he proceeded. Peruge found this amusing.

Presently, Peruge interrupted, "So she went looking for Carlos."

"Yes. Carlos was in Archives, I believe." Merrivale wiped perspiration from his forehead.

"It's too bad we don't have her here to question," Peruge said.

"I've told you everything!" Merrivale protested.

"Oh, I believe you," Peruge said. He shook his head. "But—still there was something. She'd read the reports and—" He shrugged.

"Agents do die in the line of duty," Merrivale argued.

"Of course, of course," Peruge said. "It's perfectly ordinary."

Merrivale scowled, obviously thinking the facts were being twisted to damn him.

"Carlos had no similar objections?" Peruge asked.

"None whatsoever."

Peruge pursed his lips in thought. Damnable business! So the little clerk had finally bought it. His legendary caution had failed him at last. Unless that caution had somehow pulled him through. Carlos might still be alive. Somehow, Peruge did not give much weight to that possibility. The first pawn had been taken, then the second and the third. Now, it was time for a more powerful piece. He said, "Did Carlos and Tymiena quarrel about this job?"

"Perhaps."

"What does that mean?"

"They were always snapping at each other. Who noticed after a while?"

"And we don't have them here to ask," Peruge mused.

"I don't need reminders of that."

"Do you recall what Carlos said when you last saw him?"

"Certainly; he told me he'd report within forty-eight hours of his arrival on the scene."

"That long? Did they have radio?"

"There was one in the van they picked up in Portland."

"And no reports from them after that?"

"They called in to check the equipment. That was from Klamath Falls. Portland relayed."

"Forty-eight hours," Peruge muttered. "Why?"

"He wanted time to get set up on the scene, to reconnoiter the area, choose his observation site."

"Yes, but—"

"That was not an unreasonable delay."

"But Carlos was always so cautious."

"This speaks of caution," Merrivale objected.

"Why didn't you order him to make more frequent periodic calls?"

"It did not seem indicated."

Peruge shook his head from side to side. It was diabolic. A pack of amateurs would not have left this many loose ends and blunders behind them. Merrivale would admit no mistakes, though. And the man had those explicit orders to fall back on. Embarrassing. He would have to be shunted aside, though. He'd have to be stored somewhere, ready for the axe to fall. Merrivale was a miserable incompetent. There was no excuse for him. He was just the kind of man they needed right now, someone to point to when the really embarrassing questions were asked.

With angry abruptness, Peruge pushed himself out of the chair, stood glowering down at Merrivale, who appeared thoroughly cowed.

"You're a fool, Merrivale," Peruge said in a cold, hard voice. "You've always been a fool and always will be. We have a full report from DT on Tymiena's objections. She wanted a backup team. She wanted frequent radio contact. You specifically told her not to bother Portland-relay unless it was something vital. You told her she was to take her orders from Carlos and not to question them. You ordered her not to mount any official inquiry into Porter. Under no circumstances was she to move out from under her cover. Those were your instructions—" Peruge pointed to the folder on Merrivale's desk, "and you had read that!"

Merrivale sat in shocked silence at the outburst. For one horrible moment, he appeared about to cry. His eyes glistened with unshed tears. Shocked awareness of that possibility cooled him, though, and he managed to respond with a semblance of his accent intact.

"I say! You don't leave your opinions in any doubt!"

Later, on the telephone from the airport, Peruge said, "I suppose we ought to be grateful to him. There's no doubt now of the situation we're in."

"What do you mean by that?" the Chief asked, his voice hoarsely disgruntled.

"I mean, we went in not knowing Hellstrom's situation. Now, we know it. He's willing to play for high stakes."

"As though we weren't."

"Well, I've settled with Merrivale, at any rate. I ordered him to stand by for reassignment."

"He won't do anything stupid?"

"Hasn't he done enough stupid things already?"

"You know what I mean, dammit!"

"I think he'll obey his orders to the letter," Peruge said.

"But you upset him badly." It was a statement, not a question.

"No doubt of it." This was an unfamiliar tack, and Peruge hesitated, staring thoughtfully at his scrambler cap on the telephone.

"He's been on the phone to me," the Chief said. "He complained about you bitterly. Then he said he was putting our written instructions to him *in a safe place*. He also made a point of telling me he had given Janvert the special Signal Corps number and code letters, as per our instructions for supervising agents. He even quoted the section to me from some set of orders we gave him years ago."

After a long silence, Peruge said, "We might have to take stronger measures with him."

"Yes, there's always that," the Chief said.

The words of Nils Hellstrom. Unlike man, whose physical limitations are dictated from the moment of his birth, the insect is born with the ability to actually improve upon his body. When the insect reaches the limits of his capability, he miraculously transforms into an entirely new being. In this metamorphosis, I find the most basic pattern for my understanding of the Hive. To me, the Hive is a cocoon from which the new human will emerge.

Hellstrom sat thinking in his cell. His eyes were absently aware of the charts and diagrams pasted on the walls, the reassuring standby-blink of his repeater console. But he was not actually seeing these things. They'll send in the first team now, he thought. They were just probing before. Now, we'll get the real experts and from them we may learn enough to save ourselves.

It had been a long night and a longer day. He had managed to get a two-hour nap, but the Hive was tense and twanging with crisis awareness. Body chemistry told the workers what was happening if nothing else told them.

When he'd returned to the cell a little more than two hours before, Hellstrom had been so tired he had tossed his Outsider jacket onto a chair and flopped on the bed in his clothes. Something heavy in a pocket of the jacket had dragged the jacket into a mound on the floor beside the chair. He could see the lump of the heavy object in his pocket and wondered idly what he'd left there. Abruptly, he remembered the Outsider pistol he'd picked up before leaving his cell—how long ago? It seemed not only another lifetime ago, but in another universe. Everything had changed. Powerful Outside forces had developed an interest in something that was sure to lead them to the Hive.

Project 40.

The source of the leak appeared so innocent on the surface that Hellstrom shivered when he thought about it. Jerry, as one of the cameramen, had been assigned to the MIT sequences and, as part of that assignment, had been charged to do a special research project in the library. He remembered leaving the papers on a table "no more than a half hour." They'd been in the same place when he'd returned and he'd collected them, thinking no more about it. How innocent! But that had been all the Outsiders needed. It was as though they were possessed of a malevolent genie who watched out to take advantage of such casual slips.

Jerry was heartsick. He felt he had betrayed his

beloved Hive. And he had. But it was bound to happen someday. The miracle was that they had endured so long. How could they expect to go forever undetected? The peace of anonymity had its own life cycle, apparently. Peace at any price never quite worked out the way one hoped. There was always a higher price to pay.

Feeling nervous and irritable—emotions he knew his body would transmit like an invisible trail all along the way—but somehow not caring, Hellstrom arose suddenly, went down to check on Project 40. They had to speed things up down there. They had to!

Coded memo from Peruge. For the time being, I will not change Janvert's assignment. We must consider the delicate problem of a replacement for Merrivale. Certain aspects of Janvert's enrollment in the Agency appeal to me in this regard. Our hold on him could be made very firm. There appears to be no doubt of our observation that a strong attachment has developed between Janvert and Clovis Carr. This could be worked to our advantage. To be on the safe side, I have commissioned D. T. Alden to keep a special watch on both of them. A copy of his report will be forwarded to you.

Peruge dumped his suitcase on the bed of the motel room on the outskirts of Fosterville. He had allowed himself only one small bag and a camera case with his communications gear. He draped the camera case over a chair arm. It was the way he liked to travel: bags under the airplane seat, no airport fuss, in and out of an area with as little attention called to himself as possible. In spite of his six feet four inches, he knew he tended not to attract second glances. Long ago he had learned a self-effacing diffidence which he could adopt when he needed it. When traveling, he tended to put this manner on like a garment.

It had taken all morning to get the backup teams positioned in the mountains north of town where they could operate line-of-sight communication to both his motel room and the farm. He was hungry for lunch, but there were things to be done first. He glanced around the room. It had been furnished in Grand Rapids western—dark wood with imitation brand burns, a heavy-wear fabric for all upholstery. The place reeked of expense-account minimums. He sighed, dropped into a chair that creaked under his 220-plus pounds. One big hand found the telephone on the lamp table and he dialed the motel office.

Yes, they knew the number for the office of the local deputy sheriff. Was there trouble?

Peruge explained that he had been asked by his company to make a missing-persons inquiry. Just routine. He had to listen to an involved explanation then about the local office having only one deputy, who was a local man, but a good one, mind you. The sheriff's office was actually over at the county seat. Presently, by answering all of the probing, curious questions with monosyllabic grunts, Peruge got the number he wanted and the motel office made the connection for him. Two minutes later he was discussing his problem with Deputy Lincoln Kraft, a man with a flat, almost characterless voice.

"We're reasonably sure they're missing," Peruge insisted. "Carlos was supposed to be back at work Monday and today's Friday. That's not like him. Very punctual, our Carlos."

"His wife, too, eh?" Kraft made this sound accusatory.

"Men often take their wives with them on vacation," Peruge said. He wondered then if that had been too flip for the local law.

Kraft apparently missed the sarcasm. He said, "Yes, I guess they do at that. Seems kind of strange your company would send you looking for these people, though."

"Carlos has one of our most important routes," Peruge explained. "We can't let that sort of thing go by default. The competition moves right in on you, you know."

"Guess that's right. What line of work did you say you were in?"

"I'm vice-president of the Blue Devil Fireworks Corporation of Baltimore. It's one of the biggest in the country. Carlos was one of our best salesmen."

"Was?" Kraft asked. "You got reasons you haven't told me that make you believe he's in real bad trouble?"

"Nothing specific," Peruge lied. "It's just that it isn't like him not to show up when he's supposed to."

"I see. Probably some real ordinary explanation behind this, but I'll see what I can do. What makes you think he's missing in this area?"

"I received a letter from him. It mentioned a valley near Fosterville where he was going to look for scaled quail."

"For what?"

"Scaled quail. It's a bird that lives in arid land."

"He a hunter? He might've had a hunting accident and not been able to—"

"He didn't hunt birds to kill them. He liked to watch them and study them, sort of an amateur ornithologist."

"Ohh, one of those." Kraft made it sound faintly disreputable, perhaps reflecting on the man's sex habits. "What's the name of this valley?"

"Guarded Valley. Do you know where it is?"

Such a long silence ensued that Peruge became impatient. "You still there, Mr. Kraft?" he asked.

"Yeah, I'm still here."

"Do you know this valley?"

"Yeah. That's Hellstrom's place."

"Whose place?" Peruge rather liked the fine air of misunderstanding he managed to impart to this question.

"That's Doc Hellstrom's place. He owns that valley. Been in his family for years."

"I see. Well, perhaps this medical gentleman won't mind if we make inquiries in his neighborhood."

"He's not a hospital doctor," Kraft said. "He's a bug doctor. He studies bugs. Makes moving pictures about 'em."

"That shouldn't make any difference," Peruge said. "Will you see to the inquiries, Mr. Kraft?"

"You gotta come in and sign a formal request," Kraft said. "Missing-persons report. I got one of the forms around here someplace. We haven't had a missing person since the Angelus kid got herself lost in the Steens Mountain. That wasn't the same thing as your problem, of course. Didn't need a missing-person report for that."

Peruge considered this response, beginning to wonder about the deputy. The Agency's files showed quite a number of missing persons in the area going back over a period of some fifty years. They all had *reasonable* explanations, but still . . . He decided that Kraft sounded nervous under the flat voice. Perhaps a little fishing would be in order. Peruge said, "I hope this doctor's place isn't dangerous. He doesn't have poisonous insects around, does he?"

"Might have a scorpion or two," Kraft said, his voice brightening. "They can be mighty bad sometimes. You got pictures of these missing persons?"

"I have the photograph of Carlos and his wife that he kept on his desk," Peruge said.

"That's fine. Bring that along with you. Did you say they were in a camper?"

"They had one of those big van-campers, a Dodge. Carlos was very proud of it."

"Doesn't seem a thing like that could just disappear," Kraft said.

Peruge agreed with him and asked how to find the deputy's office.

"You got a car?" Kraft asked.

"I rented a car in Klamath Falls."

"This Carlos fellow must be pretty important to your company."

"I've already told you he is," Peruge said, allowing just a trace of testiness to appear in his voice.

"They fly you all the way out here from Baltimore just to inquire about him?"

Peruge took the phone away from his ear, stared at it. What gave with this country cop? Peruge put the phone back to his ear and said, "Carlos covered the whole West Coast for us. It's important that we find out about him as soon as possible. If something's happened to him, we have to replace him immediately. The buying season is about to begin. I've already talked to the Stage Patrol in Salem. They told me to contact the authorities here."

"Thought you said you got a car in Klamath Falls," Kraft said.

"I went that far by chartered plane," Peruge said and waited with increasing interest for Kraft's response.

"Chartered plane? My, my. You coulda flown right into here and landed on our little dirt strip if you wanted. Why didn't you do that?"

So both of us are fishing, Peruge thought. Good. He wondered what Kraft's response would be if the explanation included an account of how Peruge had missed connections in Portland and had been forced to rendezvous with his people in Klamath Falls.

"I don't like these little country landing fields," Peruge said.

"Can't say I blame you much for that, but this is a nice enough little field. You file a report with the State Police in Salem?" Kraft's tone was alert and probing.

Good interrogation technique, Peruge thought. This country cop was no simpleton.

"Yes, I did. Carlos had his van shipped to Portland for this vacation and took it from there. The State Police are making inquiries along the way. They have copies of the photograph."

"I see. Fireworks must be big business," Kraft said. "You people are spending a lot of money—chartered airplanes and everything."

Peruge considered this, decided a barb was called for. He said, "We look after our people and hang the cost, Mr. Kraft. I hope you'll start your inquiries as soon as possible. Now, how do I get to your office?"

"You're at the motel, eh?"

"Yes."

Kraft told him to come out of his motel parking lot, turn right "like you were going to Lakeview" and come out to County Road 14. "Hang a left there and come up to the new shopping center. You can see it from the highway. I got a little office on the second floor. Everybody knows where it's at."

"I'll be right over," Peruge said.

"Just a minute, Mr. Peruge," Kraft said. "You carrying any skyrockets or firecrackers, things like that?"

"Of course not!" Peruge managed to sound properly shocked while noting that Kraft had his name down correctly and was obviously on the official offensive. Did they think him unaware of state laws on fireworks? He said, "We ship only through legal channels, *Deputy* Kraft. Our people carry photographs and order lists. If we broke laws we wouldn't be in business very long. I find your question interesting, however."

"Just want to be sure you know our law," Kraft explained. "We don't take it kindly when people come around saying one of our folks may have caused harm to a visitor. You gotta be mighty—"

"I didn't even suggest that," Peruge interrupted. "I take it as very interesting that you suggest it, however, Deputy Kraft. You can expect me in your office in just a few minutes."

Silence, then, "Okay. Don't forget that picture."

"I wouldn't think of it."

Peruge sat staring at the telphone for a moment after hanging up. Presently, he placed a call to Salem and told the State Patrol he had talked by telephone with Deputy Sheriff Lincoln Kraft and asked if the patrol had anything to report. They had nothing. He called the Baltimore switchboard next and asked them to contact the FBI. This had been agreed upon as a code signal that he distrusted the local authorities and his office was to firm up the request for FBI assistance.

He depressed the stem on his wristwatch transmitter then and felt the faint throbbing against his skin that told him the teams at the Steens Mountain campsites were on the job and monitoring his signal. Everything was in order. Time to begin bearding Hellstrom in his den.

The words of Nils Hellstrom. The living prototype of
the computer was designed by nature long before man
ever set foot on earth. It is nothing more nor less than
the termite mound, one of the first experiments in social order. It is a living reminder that all may not be as
man would wish it to be among the life forms that
share this planet with him. We all *know,* of course,
that compared with man, the insect does not display
what we could describe as intelligence. But why
should we feel proud about that? Where there is no
intelligence, there may be no stupidity. And the termite mound stands there as a living accusation, a finger pointed at our pride. A computer is a mechanism
programmed with a thousand tiny bits of information.
It operates by juggling information into a form of logic. Think about it. Is a beautifully functioning society
not a form of logic? I say that the creatures of such a
mound, each a *bit* of the whole, move through their
hidden circuits, a thousand tiny particles of information organizing themselves into an indisputable form
of logic. Their source of power is a brood mother, a
queen. She represents a great throbbing mass of energy, motivating all around her with insatiable need.
Thus, our Hive rests firmly on its breeding chambers.
Within the queen's pulsating body lies the future of the
mound. Within our breeding chambers lies our future
and, in truth, the future of humankind.

Kraft called the farm as soon as Peruge had broken the connection. He had Hellstrom on the line
within a minute.

"Nils, there's a fellow at the motel named Peruge. Says he's from the Blue Devil Fireworks Corporation and he's looking for a missing salesman and the
salesman's wife. Missing in *your* area. Says he has a
letter from the salesman which mentions Guarded
Valley. Should we know anything about that?"

"I told you to expect this," Hellstrom said.

"I know, but this fellow sounds *very* sharp. He's

already talked to the State Patrol and I wouldn't be a bit surprised if he called in the FBI."

"Don't you think you can handle him?"

"I may've made him suspicious."

"How?"

"I kept probing for some kind of admission from him that this wasn't an ordinary missing-persons case. He's on his way over here right now. Says he has a photograph of the missing couple. State Patrol has a copy, too. FBI is sure to get another one. Somebody's bound to've seen this pair, and they're going to center them right here."

"They won't find anything at the farm," Hellstrom said. He sounded sad and tired, and Kraft felt the first twinge of a deeper concern.

"I sure hope you're right. What should I do?"

"Do? Cooperate with him in every way. Take the photograph. Come up here to inquire."

"Nils, I don't like this. I hope you're—"

"I'm trying to keep the interface of our conflict as small as possible, Linc. That is my most urgent concern."

"Yes, but what if he asks to tag along?"

"I hope he does."

"But—"

"Bring him!"

"Nils—if I bring him up there with me, I hope he's coming back with me."

"That is our concern, Linc."

"Nils—I'm real worried. If he—"

"I'll handle it myself, Linc. We'll have everything smooth and ordinary when you arrive."

"I sure hope so."

"How did he get to Fosterville, Linc?"

"Rented car."

"Is he alone?"

"I don't think so. There's several new campers up on the mountain."

"We noted the activity. Rented car, hmmm?"

"Look, Nils, this guy had better not have an accident in that car. I got a funny feeling about this one. He's big trouble."

"No doubt of it," Hellstrom agreed. "They've sent in the first team."

From the Hive breeding record. This new group must be watched with extreme care. This includes all of the breeding batch designated Fractionated Actinomycin Nucleotide Complex Y (FANCY) series. Although they offer us a great potential in several specializations desperately needed by the Hive, they may harbor a strain of instability. This instability may be evidenced in a heightened breeding drive, in which case it can be diverted to the Hive's advantage. However, other symptoms may crop up and should be reported to Breeding Central immediately.

Hellstrom sat in reflective silence after the emergency meeting of his Council. He felt that the entire Hive had become something of what he imagined a hunted submarine to be: rigged for silent running. All power systems, including ventilation, were operating at minimums; water interchange with the deep underground river that ran their turbines and was their major water source had been put under special special observation to prevent anything from entering it that might arouse Outside suspicions when that water reached the Snake River system.

Hellstrom wondered how much Peruge and his cohorts knew about Project 40. It had been a question left unanswered by the Council meeting. The Outsiders could not know everything about Project 40, nor was it likely they knew anything about the Hive as yet. Hellstrom felt confident of this. At the barest suspicion that something like the Hive existed, they would be in here with an army. Some accommodation had to be reached with these Outsiders before they learned too much. The deaths were regrettable, but they had followed as an inevitable consequence of Porter's death. That had been an error.

We have lived too long in the security of our camouflage, he thought. We have become too bold.

Making films did that, and all the necessary intimate arrangements with Outsiders that grew out of the films. We have underestimated the Outsiders.

Hellstrom suppressed a weary sigh. He missed Old Harvey. The present security team was a good one, but Old Harvey had possessed a special ability, a balancing wisdom. The Hive needed him now more than ever, and all they had of Old Harvey's legacy was his favorite protégé, Saldo. Was Saldo that which came out of the vats new? Saldo had undergone a profound maturing since the night of the hunt. The transformation appeared to Hellstrom in some ways like a metamorphosis. It was as though, on that fatal night, Saldo had really inherited Old Harvey's wide experience and wisdom. Hellstrom knew he was leaning on Saldo for the same kinds of support he had learned to expect from Old Harvey. Whether Saldo could bear up to these demands remained to be seen. Thus far, he had shown bursts of brilliance and imagination, but still . . . Hellstrom shook his head. It was difficult to lean on a young and untried member of the new breed in a crisis such as this one. But who else did he have?

The Council meeting had started at noon in a screening room that occupied one entire corner of the barn-studio. It was a room of outwardly conventional appearance: oval table flanked by massive chairs, Hive-made of heavy extrusion plastic to counterfeit teak. A pulldown screen filled one end of the room, a speaker on each side of it against the ceiling corners, and a small double-glass window at the other end leading into the projection room. The walls were baffled and hung with loosely draped heavy fabric to dampen random sounds.

Saldo had remained behind the others at Hellstrom's request. The bullet scar along his jawline had not completely healed. It stood out whitely against his dark skin. The hawkish features remained relaxed now, but there was a steady alertness in his brown eyes. Hellstrom recalled now that Saldo was also of the S_2a-1 series on the female side. That made him one of Hellstrom's cousins. The younger man had been picked from prime stock and subjected to all of the proper chemical reinforcements. And now, Saldo represented a nice convergence of the functional traits upon which the Hive relied so heavily.

"We must be prepared at every level to respond quickly and thoroughly if anything goes wrong," Hellstrom said, looking up and starting the conversation as though Saldo had shared the preceding reverie. "I have sent messages to all of our special fronts Outside that they must be prepared to proceed on their own if we are lost. All records alluding to such fronts have been made ready for demolition."

"But have we anticipated every contingency?" Saldo asked.

"The question I've been asking myself."

"I know." And Saldo thought: Our prime male is too tired. He needs rest and we cannot give him that rest. Saldo felt in this moment extremely protective toward Hellstrom.

"You were right to suggest that Peruge probably will be carrying special electronic equipment," Hellstrom said. "At the very least, he'll be transmitting his position and condition to monitors Outside. I'm sure of it."

"Those people on the mountain."

"To them, yes. We must know the nature of his equipment as soon as possible."

"I've made all the preparations for that," Saldo said. "Nils, shouldn't you get some rest?"

"No time. Peruge is on his way and he's just the tip of the iceberg."

"The what?"

Hellstrom explained the allusion, then, "How many people do you think he has on the mountain?"

"There are at least ten people camping up there. They could all be his."

"That many?" Hellstrom shook his head.

Saldo nodded, sharing Hellstrom's disquiet. The idea of at least ten people snooping into the Hive's affairs created a profound disturbance of his inbred caution and conditioning.

"Does Linc have anyone he can send up the

mountain to play camper with those others?" Saldo
asked.

"He's looking into it."

"Linc is bringing this Peruge personally, isn't
he?"

"Yes. But we mustn't assume that Peruge trusts
Linc."

"Linc was no match for Peruge, that's obvious,"
Saldo said. "I heard his account."

"Learn from that," Hellstrom said. "It's good to
have our own Outside fronts, including a deputy sheriff, but each one creates its own problems. The more
we expose ourselves, even in seeming secrecy, the
more danger we're in."

Saldo tucked this lesson into his memory. One
did not put out agents with complete impunity. The
very existence of an agent carried its own message
when that agent was exposed. If Peruge suspected Lincoln Kraft, that revealed something about the Hive.
Saldo vowed to remember this when the present crisis
was past. He had no doubt that they would surmount
present difficulties. His trust in the prime male, Hellstrom, was profound.

"Peruge may possess a device to reveal that we're
probing for his equipment," Hellstrom said.

"I have given instructions to monitor for that,"
Saldo said.

Hellstrom nodded, pleased. Thus far, Saldo had
anticipated every contingency that had arisen in Hellstrom's own mind—and some that had not. Prime
breeding stock always showed its worth in the crunch.
Saldo possessed a penetrating intelligence. The younger male would be of inestimable value to the Hive
when he had been tempered and fully trained.

"What excuse have you prepared if he detects
our probes?" Hellstrom asked.

"I want to discuss that with you. Suppose, for the
film in progress, we are making a sound track with a
great deal of complex mixing. It would be perfectly
explainable electronic activity. The visit of this Peruge
surely could not be expected to interrupt that. We

have a schedule to keep. Any interference with Peruge's equipment could be explained by this work."

Hellstrom nodded thoughtfully. "Excellent. And I ask him when he arrives if he has a radio, because—"

"A radio would interfere with our equipment," Saldo completed for him.

"See to the cover preparations," Hellstrom said.

Saldo arose, stood with his fingertips touching the table, hesitating.

"Yes?" Hellstrom asked.

"Nils, are we sure the others didn't have such equipment? I've been reviewing the tapes and records and—" He shrugged, obviously loath to criticize.

"We searched them. There was nothing."

"That seems odd—the fact that they didn't carry such equipment."

"They weren't considered important enough," Hellstrom said. "They were sent in to see if they would be killed."

"Ahhhhh—" Saldo's expression betrayed both understanding and shock.

"We should've understood that about Outsiders," Hellstrom said. "They are not very good humans, the wild ones. They commonly waste their workers this way. The ones who intruded here were expendable stock. I know now that it would have been far wiser for us to confuse them and send them away with a believable story."

"It was a mistake to kill them?"

"A mistake to make it necessary to kill them."

Saldo nodded his understanding of the fine distinction. "We made a mistake," he said.

"I made a mistake," Hellstrom corrected him. "Too much success made me careless. We must always keep that possibility in mind: any of us can err."

The words of brood mother Trova Hellstrom. Let me introduce a word about the quality that we call caution. Where we say we have been and where we say the Hive is headed—somewhere in that mysterious future—are by necessity somewhat removed from what we imagine are facts. Our own interpretation always intervenes. What we say we are doing is inevitably modified by our own understanding and by the limits of our comprehension. First, we are partisan. We see everything in terms of Hive survival. Second, the universe has a way of appearing to be one thing when it is actually something else. In this light, *caution* becomes a reliance upon our deepest collective energies. We must trust the Hive itself to possess wisdom and to manifest that wisdom through us, its cells.

When they reached that point on the lower road where Peruge could get his first look at Hellstrom's farm, he asked Kraft to stop. The deputy brought his green and white station wagon to a skidding, dusty halt and peered questioningly at his passenger.

"Something wrong, Mr. Peruge?"

Peruge merely tightened his lips. Kraft interested him. The deputy could have been typecast for the role he played. It was almost as though someone had looked at him and said, "Now, this one, we'll make him the deputy." Kraft had a sunburned, western appearance, thick nose and beetling brows, pale yellow hair topped by a wide-brimmed western hat. His blocky features surmounted a blocky body that moved with a stiff-legged horseman's walk. Peruge had seen several people on Fosterville's one main street who looked vaguely like Lincoln Kraft.

Kraft accepted Peruge's silent appraisal without qualms, secure in the knowledge that he was a Hive hybrid whose appearance could not possibly excite questions about alien background. Kraft's father had been a local rancher seduced in a gene-foray by a breeding female. Many Fosterville locals had remarked Kraft's resemblance to the father.

Now, Kraft cleared his throat. "Mr. Peruge, I said—"

"I know what you said."

Peruge glanced at his wristwatch: a quarter to three. Every delay imaginable had been thrown in the way of this excursion: telephone calls, careful exami-

nation of the missing-persons report, a lengthy study
of the photograph, question after question and a labo-
rious assemblage of answers on paper, all executed in
a slow and meticulous longhand. But here they were,
finally, in sight of Hellstrom's farm. Peruge felt his
pulse quicken. The air carried a dry, cloying silence.
Even the insects were still. Peruge sensed something
out of character about the stillness. He grew aware
slowly of the absence of insect sounds and asked Kraft
about this.

Kraft pushed his hat back, rubbed a sleeve across
his forehead. "I expect someone's used a spray."

"Really? Does Hellstrom do that sort of thing? I
thought all the environmentalists were against sprays."

"How'd you know the doc was into ecology?"

Sharp! Sharp! Peruge reminded himself. He said,
"I didn't know it. I just assumed an entomologist would
have that as one of his concerns."

"Yeah? Well, maybe the doc isn't spraying. This
is rangeland right here."

"Somebody else could be doing it?"

"Maybe. Or the doc could be doing something
else. Did you have me stop just so you could listen?"

"No. I want to get out and scout around the area
and see if I can spot any sign of Carlos's camper."

"Not much sense in that." Kraft spoke quickly
with an undertone of sharpness.

"Oh? Why?"

"If we decide he's really been around here, we'll
do a thorough search."

"I thought I told you," Peruge said. "I've already
decided he was around here. I'd like to get out and
have a little look at the area."

"Doc don't like people wandering around his
place!"

"But you said this was rangeland. Does he control it?"

"Not exactly, but—"

"Then let's have a look." Peruge put a hand on
the door.

"You just wait a minute!" Kraft ordered.

Peruge nodded silently. He'd found out what he

wanted to know: Kraft was here to block *any* investigation by strangers.

"All right," Peruge said. "Does Hellstrom know we're coming?"

Kraft had put the station wagon in gear, prepared to resume their lurching progress toward the farm, but now he hesitated. Peruge's demand that they stop had shocked him. The first thought had been that the Outsider had seen something suspicious, something overlooked by the Hive's cleanup workers. Peruge's attempts to get out and search the area had done nothing to ease that initial disquiet. Now, it occurred to Kraft that Peruge or his people might have tapped the telephone to the farm. But Hive Security was always wary of that; surely they'd have detected such intrusion.

"Matter of fact, he does know," Kraft said. "I called to make sure the doc was here himself. Sometimes he goes gadding off to mighty strange places. And I wanted to clear it that we were coming. You know how these scientists are."

"No. How are they?"

"They do experiments sometimes. Outsiders go blundering in and upset everything."

"Is that why you don't want me to get out here?"

Kraft spoke with obvious relief. "Sure it is. Besides, the doc makes movies up here all the time. He gets a bit testy if you ruin his pictures. We try to be good neighbors."

"You'd think he'd put out guards or something."

"No-o-o. The locals all know about his work. We steer clear of his place."

"How testy does he get if one ruins his experiments or his movies?" Peruge asked. "Does he—ahhh, shoot?"

"Nothing like that! Doc wouldn't really hurt anybody. But he can be mighty rough mouthed when he wants. He's got important friends, too. Pays to be on his good side."

That he has, Peruge thought. And that could explain the strange behavior of the local law. Kraft's job must be a sinecure. He'd be careful not to lose it.

Peruge said, "Okay. Let's go see if we can find Dr. Hellstrom's *good* side."

"Yes, sir!"

Kraft got the car moving, made a special effort to act casual and unconcerned. Hellstrom's orders had been explicit: this was a routine investigation into some missing persons. All cooperation would be extended.

Peruge admired the farm buildings as they approached the north fence. The farm had been built in a time when materials were squandered without any worries about the supply. There wasn't a knot in any of the lumber visible on this side of the farmhouse or the barn, although the wood had that dark gray of long weathering and probably could have used a coat of paint. Peruge wondered idly why the farm wasn't painted.

Kraft stopped parallel to the fence, just clear of the gate. "We walk from here. Doc doesn't like us bringing cars up to the buildings."

"Why's that?"

"Something to do with his work, I expect."

"The place could use a coat of paint," Peruge said as he got out of the car.

Kraft got out, closed the door, and spoke across the roof of the car. "I heard tell Doc used some kind of wood preservative on his buildings. They just *look* weathered. Kind of pretty when you think about it."

"Oh?" Peruge walked to the gate, waited for Kraft. "What's that concrete building over there?" He pointed to the low structure inside the fence to the left of the gate.

"Might be a pumphouse. About the right size for a big one. Or it could be something to do with the doc's work. I never asked." Kraft watched Peruge carefully. The concrete structure housed an emergency ventilation system which could be opened by explosives and was linked to standby pumping. There were several more such installations scattered around the area, but the others were camouflaged.

"Is Hellstrom married?" Peruge asked.

Kraft opened the gate before answering. "I don't

rightly know." He stood aside to let Peruge enter, closed the gate. "Doc has lots of pretty gals around here sometimes. For his movies, I s'pose. Maybe he thinks there's no sense buying a cow when milk's free." Kraft chuckled at his own hairy witticism and added, "Let's get along up to the farm."

Peruge shuddered as he fell into step with the deputy. That humor had been a little heavy. This deputy was neither pure western, pure yokel, nor pure anything else. Kraft tried too hard to appear the semi-rustic of earthy origins. The trying was so obvious at times that it dominated every other action. Peruge had decided earlier to watch the deputy carefully, but now he put an extra note of caution on his resolve.

"Place looks kind of shabby," Peruge said, hurrying to keep pace with Kraft's long-legged stride. Despite the stiffness of his gait, the deputy moved with a no-loitering directness that suggested he didn't want Peruge to take too close a look at the surroundings.

"I thought it looked pretty good here," Kraft said. "They keep the farm area pretty neat."

"Do they do much farming?"

"Not much anymore. His folks used to keep a lot more crops. Some of the kids the doc has here plant corn and things in the spring, but they're just playing at farming, seems to me. City people, most of them. They come up here from Hollywood or out from New York and gawk at us natives and play farmer."

"Hellstrom has a lot of visitors?" Peruge kicked at a dusty clump of grass as he spoke. The dry, hot air of the place bothered him. There was an irritant humming sound in the background, and an underlying animal smell that made him think of a zoo. This odor had not been apparent outside the fence, but it became stronger the deeper they went into the little valley. What he could see of the creek on his right showed only a thin trickle of water. It was mostly pools and puddles connected by narrow rills of green algae that waved in weak currents. There appeared to be a small waterfall at the upper end of the valley, however.

"Visitors?" Kraft asked after a long pause.

"Sometimes the place is crawling with 'em. Can't spit without hitting someone. Other times, he probably doesn't have more'n ten or twelve people here."

"What's that smell?" Peruge demanded.

"What smell?" Kraft asked, then realized Peruge meant the Hive odor, most of which was washed from the vented air but was always detectable here in the valley. Kraft rather enjoyed the odor. It reminded him of his childhood.

"That animal smell!" Peruge said.

"Oh, that. Probably something to do with the doc's work. He keeps mice and things in cages up there. I saw them once. Regular menagerie."

"Oh. Is that a year-round waterfall?"

"Yep. It's pretty, isn't it?"

"If you like that sort of thing. What happens to all the water? The creek seems rather small down here." Peruge stopped as Kraft looked directly at him, forcing the deputy to come to a halt, also.

"I expect the ground soaks it up," Kraft said. He appeared impatient to continue, but unable to think of a good argument. "The doc may take part of it up there for irrigation or cooling or something. I dunno. Let's get on up, eh?"

"Just a minute," Peruge said. "I thought you said Hellstrom didn't do much farming."

"Doesn't! But what he does still takes some water. Why you so curious about his creek?"

"I'm curious about everything on this place," Peruge said. "There's something *wrong* about it. No insects. I don't even see any birds."

Kraft made a swallowing motion in a dry throat. Obviously, there'd been a very thorough night sweep recently. Trust this Peruge to notice the absence of local faunal. "Birds often hide where it's cool in the hot part of the day," he ventured.

"Is that right?"

"Didn't your bird-watching friend ever tell you that?"

"No." Peruge glanced around him, peering carefully at everything in sight. It was a quick and intense motion of head and eyes which alarmed Kraft. "What he did say, once," Peruge continued, "was that there was an animal or a bird for every time of day or night. I don't believe the birds are hiding; you can't hear them. There are no birds here and no insects."

"Then what was your friend doing here?" Kraft asked. "If there are no birds, what was he watching?"

Ahhh, my friend, not so fast, Peruge thought. We aren't ready yet to take off the gloves. He was convinced now that Kraft was in league with Hellstrom. "Carlos would've noticed the absence of birds and he might've gone hunting for an explanation. If he found an explanation that could cause trouble for someone, that might explain why he's missing."

"You sure got a suspicious mind," Kraft said.

"Haven't you?" Peruge asked. He moved into willow shadows at a bend in the creek, forced Kraft to follow. "What's this Hellstrom really like, Deputy?"

Kraft didn't care for being called *Deputy* in that tone of voice, but he kept his manner casual. "Ohhh, he's just a plain, ordinary, run-of-the-mill scientist type."

Peruge noted how Kraft's voice came out flat and reasonable, but something in the set of his body, especially in the watchful turn of head and eyes, put the lie to this mask. Peruge nodded, as though he understood this, silently urging Kraft to continue.

"They're all crazy, of course," Kraft said, "but not dangerous."

"I've never really agreed with that harmless, crazy scientist picture," Peruge said. "I don't think they're all innocent and harmless. To me, no atomic physicist is completely responsible and trustworthy."

"Ohh, come now, Mr. Peruge." Kraft was making a valiant attempt to sound jovial and hearty. "The doc makes movies about bugs. Educational. I expect the worst thing he's ever done is bring some pretty girls up here for some moonlight nooky."

"Not even dope?" Peruge pressed.

"You believe all that stuff you read about Hollywood types?" Kraft asked.

"Some of it."

"I'd bet my bottom dollar that the doc is clean," Kraft said.

"Would you?" Peruge asked. "How many missing-persons cases have you really had in his area over, say, the past twenty-five years?"

With a sinking feeling, Kraft thought: He's seen all of the old records! Nils had been right about this one without even seeing him. The Outsiders had sent a sharp and prying mind this time. Peruge was aware of all the old mistakes the Hive had made. Bad, bad, bad. To hide his reaction, Kraft turned away, resumed his progress toward the farm buildings, now less than fifty yards ahead. "Depends on what you call a missing person," he said. And, as he noted that Peruge still stood in the willow shadow, "Come on! We can't keep the doc waiting."

Peruge followed, suppressing a smile. The deputy really was so transparent. Kraft had been shaken by the missing-persons barb. This was not just a plain, ordinary, run-of-the-mill deputy. Things were beginning to jell in Peruge's mind. Three agents had been wasted here, chasing a suspicion. Discovery of a deputy-who-wasn't-a-deputy gave those suspicions a new dimension. Something had been learned, after all. And Peruge thought: Hellstrom's learned what we're willing to pay for access to his Project 40. Now, we find out what he's willing to pay.

"I always thought a missing person was a missing person," Peruge said, addressing Kraft's blocky back.

Kraft spoke without turning. "That all depends. Some people want to be missing. Guy runs out on his wife, or his job—I guess he's technically missing. But that's not what you're saying about your man. When I say 'missing person,' I generally mean someone who's in real trouble."

"And you don't think any real trouble could happen here?"

"This isn't the Old West anymore," Kraft said. "This area is tamer than a lot of your cities. People don't even lock their doors most places around here. Too damn much trouble fishing around for the keys." He grinned back over his shoulder in what he hoped was a disarming gesture. "Besides, we wear our pants kind of tight. Don't leave much room in our pockets."

They were passing the farmhouse now. The barn loomed before them across a bare stretch of dirt perhaps sixty feet wide. An old fence divided the open area, but only the posts remained. The wire had been removed. There were yellowed curtains on the bay window of the farmhouse wing that jutted toward the creek, but the place held an oddly vacant air. Kraft wondered about that house. Empty? Why? Houses were supposed to be occupied. Did Hellstrom and his crew live there? Did they eat there? Why wasn't someone inside rattling pots and pans and things? He recalled Porter's reference to "negative signs." A very penetrating observation. It wasn't so much what you could see around Hellstrom's farm as what you couldn't see.

There was another positive sign now, though—an acid odor. He thought first of photo chemicals, then rejected that answer. The smell was much more penetrating and biting. Something to do with Hellstrom's insects, perhaps?

A swinging door had been set into the old sliding door of the barn. The smaller door opened as Kraft and Peruge approached. Hellstrom himself stepped out. Peruge recognized the man from the photographs in the Agency's files. Hellstrom wore a white turtleneck shirt and gray trousers. His feet were tucked into open sandals. His rather sparse light hair appeared as though it had been tangled by the wind and then pushed into a semblance of order by hurried fingers.

"Hi, Linc," Hellstrom called.

"Hi there, Doc."

Kraft strode right up to Hellstrom, shook hands. Peruge, following close behind, received the odd impression of a rehearsed action. They shook hands with such a perfunctory sense of unfamiliarity.

Peruge moved to one side, choosing a position that gave him a view of the barn door Hellstrom had left standing partly open. Nothing was visible except darkness in the small gap remaining.

The action appeared to amuse Hellstrom. He

grinned as Kraft introduced him to Peruge. Peruge found Hellstrom's hand cool, but rather dry. There was a sense of forced relaxation about the man, but no sign of excess perspiration in the palm. He had himself well under control, then.

"Are you interested in our studio?" Hellstrom asked, nodding toward the door and the direction of Peruge's gaze.

Peruge thought: Now, aren't you the cool one! He said, "I've never seen a movie studio."

"Linc told me on the phone that you were looking for one of your employees who might be missing in our area," Hellstrom said.

"Ahhh, yes." Peruge wondered why he couldn't see anything beyond that open door. He'd seen Hollywood studios and remembered a sense of organized confusion: bright lights, dollies, cameras, people bustling about, then that frozen stillness of the moments when they were filming.

"Have you seen anyone nosing around here, Doc?" Kraft asked.

"Nothing but our own people," Hellstrom said. "No strangers, at least recently. When did these people turn up missing?"

"About a week ago," Peruge said, returning his attention to Hellstrom.

"That recently!" Hellstrom said. "My. Are you sure they aren't just extending their vacation without notice?"

"I'm just as sure as a man could be," Peruge said.

"You're welcome to look around," Hellstrom said. "We've been pretty busy in the studio lately, but we'd have noticed any strangers in the area. We keep a pretty close watch to see that no one bursts in on our work unexpectedly. I don't think you're going to find any sign of your people in our area."

Kraft visibly relaxed, thinking: If Nils thinks they've cleaned up well enough, then it's clean.

"Oh?" Peruge pursed his lips. It came to him abruptly that there were several levels to this conversation. He and Hellstrom knew it. Most likely the deputy did, too. The various parts of the interleaved message were distinct. Peruge was welcome to pry around, but he'd find nothing incriminating. No strangers could come upon Hellstrom's farm without being seen. Hellstrom remained confident that his *powerful connections* would keep the real contest submerged. Peruge, for his own part, had revealed to Hellstrom an awareness that people were missing in the immediate vicinity of the farm. In a way, Hellstrom had not denied this, but had merely pointed out how useless it would be to look for the missing people. How, then, were the real stakes to be introduced into the game?

Hellstrom said, "Deputy Kraft tells me you work for some kind of fireworks company."

Ahhh, Peruge thought with delight. "We have diversified interests in my firm, Mr. Hellstrom. We're also interested in metallurgy, especially new processes for exploitation. We're always on the hunt for potentially valuable inventions."

Hellstrom stared at him for a moment. "Would you like to come in and see the studio? We're very busy right now, behind schedule on our latest epic." He started to turn, hesitated as though at an afterthought. "Oh, I hope you're not carrying any radio or something of that kind. We use short-range radio in part of our mixing circuitry for the sound tracks. Other equipment can play hob with our work."

You son of a bitch! Peruge thought. He folded his hands casually in front of him, left wrist in right palm, turned off the tiny wristwatch transmitter. And he thought: If you think you're going to keep me out of your little playpen, baby, you think again. I'm going in there and I may see more than you expect.

Helstrom, noting the movement of Peruge's hands, and suspecting the reason, still found himself wondering at the man's curious statement about diversified interests, metallurgy, and new inventions. What could that have to do with Project 40?

The words of Trova Hellstrom. Whatever we do in breeding for the specialists we require, we must always include the human being in our processes, preferring this to the intrusion of surgical instruments. The sexual stump can be condoned only as long as we include the body's original genetic materials in the practice. Anything that smacks of genetic surgery or engineering must be looked upon with the gravest misgivings. We are, first and foremost, human beings, and we must never loose ourselves from our animal ancestry. Whatever we are, we are not gods. And whatever this universe may be, it obviously rests heavily in dependence upon the accidental.

"He's not transmitting," Janvert said, moving the control dials on his instruments. He sat in the curtained shadows of their van's interior, the receiver mounted in front of him on a shelf originally intended as part of the camper's kitchen. Nick Myerlie's bluff and sweaty body was leaning over him, one red-knuckled hand on the counter beside the radio. The big man's heavy features carried a frown of deep concern.

"What do you think's happened to him?" Myerlie asked.

"I think he turned his transmitter off deliberately."

"For God's sake! Why?"

"The last thing I received," he tapped the tape recorder over the radio, "was Hellstrom saying something about not bringing any radio equipment into their studio."

"That's risky damned business, turning off his transmitter," said Myerlie.

"I'd have done the same," Janvert said. "He has to get inside that studio."

"But still—"

"Oh, shut up! Is Clovis still outside with her telescope?"

"Yes." Myerlie sounded hurt. He knew Janvert was second-in-command on this case, but it was irritating to take such short-tempered treatment from a runt.

"See if she's seen anything."

"That thing's only twenty-power and it's still pretty misty out there."

"Go find out anyway. Tell her what's happened."

"Right."

The camper creaked and moved as Myerlie took his big body out the door.

Janvert, who had lifted one earphone away from his right ear to talk to Myerlie, replaced it now and stared at the receiver. What had Peruge meant by that last odd conversation? Metallurgy? New inventions?

The words of Trova Hellstrom. Our future lies in an ultimate form of human domestication. All outside patterns of humankind must be seen, then, as wild forms. In our domestication process, we will necessarily introduce a multiplicity of diverse human types into our social scheme. No matter how much diversity this brings, the mutual interdependence and consequent sense of respect for our essential oneness must never be lost. Brood mother and prime male are different only in surface features from the lowliest worker. If the most exalted among us have any prayer, it must be one of thanksgiving that there are workers. It is salutary, when seeing a common worker, to think, there, but for leader foods and training, am I.

Entering the studio through a double-door system that explained why he had not been able to see inside the building from the yard, Peruge sensed something odd about the sounds and movements. That fetid animal smell was very strong in here, too. He ascribed it to a glass-fronted structure off to his left, behind which he could discern animals in cages. He identified mice, guinea pigs, and monkeys.

In all of the film companies Peruge had seen before, he had observed a special quality of silence while group energies flowed up a mysterious channel into the camera lens. This place was different, though. No one tiptoed. Those who moved about walked with a casual silence that said they found this normal. The door baffles had eliminated that incessant humming so irritatingly noticeable outside, but in here there was a faint susurration to replace it.

Only one camera crew appeared to be working. They were set up in a corner to his right and were working very close to a glass container about three feet on a side. The glass reflected hot shards of light.

Hellstrom had warned Peruge not to talk until given permission, but Peruge pointed to the camera crew in the corner, lifted his eyebrows in a silent question.

Bending close, Hellstrom whispered, "We're capturing the articulation of insect body parts in a new way. Magnified views. The lens is actually inside that glass case which maintains a special climate for the subject insect."

Peruge nodded, wondering why they must remain silent for that. Would they be doing sound-on-film for such a sequence? It didn't seem likely, but his acquaintance with film making was perfunctory at best, hurriedly augmented for this assignment, and he knew better than to speak his question aloud. Hellstrom would be delighted to have an excuse to throw him out. The man's nervousness had become increasingly obvious as they entered the studio.

Hellstrom leading and Kraft bringing up the rear, they struck out diagonally across the center of the studio area. As always when an Outsider was this close to the workings of the Hive head, Hellstrom found himself unable to suppress completely feelings of disquiet. The Hive's territorial conditioning went too deep. And Peruge reeked of Outsider smells. He did *not* belong in this place. Kraft, behind them, would be having an even worse time of it. He had never before accompanied an Outsider into these precincts. The working crews were behaving with outward normalcy, however. They would *feel* this Outsider's presence as a constant rasping on their awareness, but front training dominated their reactions. All proceeded smoothly.

Peruge noticed the movement of people around them: across their diagonal path, beside them, off in the corners of the cavernous studio. Everyone appeared to be on normal business and none gave more than a casual glance to the trio crossing the open area, but Peruge could not avoid feeling that he was under the closest scrutiny. He looked upward. The bright lights being used in the lower part of the studio left the upper regions in deep shadows that his vision could not penetrate. Was that deliberate? Were they hiding something up above him?

As he watched, the swinging descent of a cage on the end of a boom caught his attention and he stumbled over a coil of cables. He would have fallen if Kraft had not leaped forward to catch his arm. The deputy restored Peruge to balance, put a finger to lips for silence. Kraft released Peruge's arm reluctantly. It felt more secure to have a controlling arm on this intruder. Kraft found himself torn by tormenting worries. Nils was playing with fire! There were voiceless workers out there on the studio floor. Naturally, they'd been conditioned for the menial tasks here, but their presence posed an explosive danger. What if one of them reacted to Peruge's Outsider chemistry? The man's smell was offensive!

Peruge, seeing his path clear for a few paces, glanced back at the descending boom cage. It had swung from the gloomy mystery of the upper reaches and was moving in oiled silence down to the camera setup in the corner. A woman in a white smock occupied the cage. She had startlingly pale skin accented by ebony hair tied at the neck in a simple chignon. The fluttering of her smock in the wind of the boom's movement suggested that she wore nothing under it.

Kraft pushed Peruge's arm, urging him to move faster. Reluctantly, Peruge picked up his pace. There had been something magnetically attractive about that pale-skinned woman and he could not get her image out of his mind. Her face had been a madonna oval beneath that black cap of hair. The arms protruding from the smock's short sleeves had been almost too fat, but suggesting sensuous softness rather than obesity.

Hellstrom stood now at a door in a structure that had been erected as a separate, flat-roofed building in-

side the studio. A wall climbed to the upper areas behind the flat roof. Peruge estimated that the wall split
the barn in half lengthwise and wondered what lay behind it. He followed Hellstrom into a dimly lighted
room where there was heavy glass from waist height to
ceiling across two of the inner walls. One glass parti-
tion gave a view into a smaller studio where insects
were flitting openly back and forth through blue light
—pale, big-winged moths by their appearance The
other window framed a shadowy room where men and
women worked at a long, curved bank of electronic instruments with small screens directly in front of each
operator showing lilliputian movements. It reminded
Peruge of a television control booth.

Kraft closed the door behind them and moved
three paces into the room. He stood there now, arms
folded across his breast as though guarding the entrance. There was another door in the far-right corner,
Peruge noted, but that led into the shadowy room of
electronic instruments. Again, Peruge felt that the entire setup did not quite fit his picture of a movie studio.

There was a small oblong wooden table with four
chairs around it in the room and Hellstrom took a
chair on the far side and spoke in a calm voice. "The
men you're watching in there, Mr. Peruge, are mixing
several sound sources for a combined track. It's rather
delicate work."

Peruge studied the people in the shadowy room,
unable to pinpoint what struck him odd about them.
Abruptly, he realized that of the six men at the arc of
instruments and three women standing on the far side
of the arc, all but one looked enough alike to be from
the same family. Again, he scanned the face illuminated by the low, wavering light. Five of the men and
three of the women were alike, not only in the uniform
white smocks, but in short blond hair and rather
pinched faces dominated by large eyes. The women
were distinguished only by rather obvious breasts and
a slight softening of the features. The lone male who
differed from the others was also blond and reminded

Peruge of someone. He realized then that the odd man
out looked like Hellstrom.

As all this flashed through Peruge's mind, the
outer door opened behind Kraft and the young women
he had seen on the boom entered. At least, Peruge
cautioned himself, she appeared to be that same young
woman, but the people in the next-door booth made
him wonder.

"Fancy," Hellstrom said, speaking quickly in
alarm. Why was she here? he asked himself. He hadn't
sent for her and he didn't like the stalking feline expression on her face.

Kraft stepped aside grudgingly to allow her to
pass.

Peruge watched her, noting the oval face, almost
doll-like, the extremely sexy body that she moved with
full awareness of its contours showing through the thin
smock. She kept her attention on Hellstrom while
speaking, but there was no dcubt she was playing to
Peruge.

"Ed sent me over," she said. "He wants you to
know that we have to reshoot that mosquito sequence.
You're in it, you know. I told you we'd have to reshoot. The mosquitoes were disturbed, but you
wouldn't listen to me."

Abruptly, she appeared to notice Peruge, moved
up to within a pace of him, and asked, "Who's this?"

"This is Mr. Peruge," Hellstrom said, a deep
note of caution in his voice. What was Fancy doing?

"Hello, Mr. Peruge," she said, her voice lilting.
She moved even closer to him. "I'm Fancy."

Hellstrom watched her closely. What *was* she
doing? He inhaled a deep breath through his nose, half
anger, half probing, and detected that Fancy had shot
herself up with breeding hypes. She was trying to
arouse Peruge! Why? She was having an effect, too.
Peruge was attracted to Fancy and unable to explain
the sudden magnetism. No wild Outsider could understand the simple chemistry of the situation. Kraft, too,
was caught momentarily by her powerful sexuality,
but Hellstrom flashed a hand signal which alerted him.
Kraft, long out of the Hive's daily contacts and con-

stant reinforcements, took a few seconds to recover. Peruge, however, was not recovering.

Hellstrom wondered if he should let this continue. She was playing a dangerous game and acting without instructions. Granted, it would be desirable to have Peruge's genes in the Hive stocks, but . . .

Peruge stood in semishock. He could not recall ever being caught up in sexual excitement this swiftly and this thoroughly. The woman felt it, too. She was panting for him. He wondered distantly if these people had done something to him, but rejected that immediately. This was that oddly random chemistry one heard about. He realized, catching up with her words, that Fancy was asking if he were going to stay the night.

With an effort, Peruge said, "I'm staying in town."

She glanced at Hellstrom. "Nils, why don't you invite Mr. Peruge to stay with us?"

"Mr. Peruge is here on business," Hellstrom said. "I imagine he'd prefer staying in his own quarters."

Peruge wanted nothing more than to stay the night with this compelling woman, but he began to sense inner alarm signals.

"You're just being stuffy," Fancy said to Hellstrom. Again, she looked up into Peruge's eyes. "Are you in films, Mr. Peruge?"

He tried to fight free of that enveloping aura of sexuality, tried to think. "No. I'm—I'm, ah, looking for some friends, an employee and his wife, really, who're missing around here someplace."

"Oh, I hope nothing's happened to them," she said.

Hellstrom rose from the table, crossed to Peruge's side. "Fancy, we *do* have a schedule to keep."

Peruge tried to wet his lips with his tongue; his mouth felt dry, his body trembled. The delectable little witch! Was she told to make a play for him?

Hellstrom glanced at Kraft, wondered if they should do something physical to get Fancy out of the room. She'd really shot herself up, the crazy female! What was she doing? He spoke to her in a reasonable, but commanding tone. "Fancy, you'd better get back to the crew. Tell Saldo I want special attention paid to the most urgent problems first and tell Ed I'll be ready to reshoot the mosquito sequence tonight."

Fancy drew back a step, relaxed. She had this Peruge on a string and she knew it. The man almost followed her as she moved away from him. He would keep. She said, "All you ever think about is work. Anybody would think you were just a plain old, common everyday worker."

Hellstrom realized she was taunting him.

Fancy obeyed, though, her Hive training dominant. She turned slowly, went to the door with only a flicking glance at Kraft, opened the door, and paused in the doorway to look back at Peruge. She smiled at the Outsider then, sly and inviting, raised her eyebrows in another silent taunt directed at Hellstrom, and went out, closing the door softly behind her.

Peruge cleared his throat.

Hellstrom studied Peruge. The man was having trouble recovering, not surprising in view of how Fancy had armed herself for that attack. It had been an attack, Hellstrom realized. Pure attack. She was out to get Peruge, to breed him.

"That's a—very attractive woman," Peruge said, his voice husky.

"Would you like to go over to the house for a cup of coffee?" Hellstrom asked, feeling a sudden sympathy for Peruge. The poor wild creature had no idea what had happened to him.

"That's very kind of you," Peruge said, "but I thought we were going to look at your studio."

"Didn't you see the studio out there?"

"Is that all there is to it?"

"Oh, we have the usual support facilities," Hellstrom said. "Some of it's too technical for the casual visitor to understand, but we have a wardrobe section and one of the best editing labs in the business. Our collection of rare insects is without equal anywhere in the world. We could also screen some of our film for you if you'd like, just to show you what we do here, but not today, I'm afraid. The schedule is pretty tight. I hope you understand."

Kraft took up his cue. "Are we delaying you, Doc? I know how important your work is. We just came up to find out if any of your people had seen Mr. Peruge's friends."

"I'll certainly inquire about that," Hellstrom said. "Why don't you come back and take lunch with us tomorrow, Mr. Peruge? Maybe I'll have something to report by then."

"I'd like to do that," Peruge said. "What time?"

"Would eleven be all right?"

"That'd be fine. Maybe some of your people would like to hear about my company then, too. We *do* have an intense interest in metallurgy and new inventions."

There he goes again! Hellstrom thought. He said, "If you get here by eleven, that'll give you about an hour before lunch. I'll have some one show you around—editing, wardrobe, the insects." He smiled pleasantly.

Will my guide be Fancy? Peruge wondered, feeling his heartbeat quicken. "I'll be looking forward to that. In the meantime, I hope you won't mind if I call in some help and have a look around the area myself?"

Hellstrom noted how Kraft's muscles tightened, and he spoke quickly. "Not right here on the farm, I hope, Mr. Peruge. We're getting ready to shoot some outside footage as long as this weather holds. It doesn't help much when people stumble over our setups and delay us. I hope you understand how costly such delays can be."

"Oh, yes, I understand," Peruge said. "I was thinking only of having a look at some of the range area around your farm. Carlos's letter made it clear that he was in this area. I thought we might see if we could turn up something."

Aware of Hellstrom's mounting alarm, Kraft said, "We don't want you interfering with the official investigation, Mr. Peruge. Amateurs can completely destroy evidence without—"

"Oh, I'll have only the best professional help," Peruge said. "You can count on that. They won't interfere. one bit with the *official* investigation. And I'll make sure they don't bother Mr. Hellstrom at his movie making. You'll have nothing but admiration for the quality of professional help I'm calling in, Mr. Kraft."

"Guess you don't care how much money you spend," Kraft muttered.

"Expense is no object," Peruge agreed. He was enjoying this suddenly. This pair was on the hook. They knew it, too. "We're going to find out what happened to our people."

That challenge is plain enough, Hellstrom thought. "Of course, we sympathize with your concern. Our own immediate problems tend to dominate our attention. We can be pretty single-minded when our schedule is threatened."

Peruge felt himself beginning to come down from the lift Fancy had given him and, now, alarm and anger began to take over. They'd tried to catch him with a little pussy! He said, "I understand how things are, Hellstrom. I'm going to tell my home office to employ all the professional manpower we can spare"

Kraft stared at Hellstrom, seeking a cue.

Hellstrom spoke evenly, though. "We understand each other, I think, Mr. Peruge." He glanced at Kraft. "You just keep intruders from interfering with us, eh, Linc?"

Kraft nodded. What did Nils mean? How could he stop an army of investigators? This Peruge was going to call in the FBI. The bastard had done everything but use their name!

"Until tomorrow, then," Peruge said.

"Linc knows the way out," Hellstrom said. "I hope you will forgive me if I don't see you out. I really must get on with my work."

"Of course," Peruge said. "I've already noticed how well Deputy Kraft knows his way around your farm."

Hellstrom's eyes glittered as he shot a restraining signal at Kraft. "Local officials have never been barred from our land," Hellstrom said. "We will see you tomorrow, Mr. Peruge."

"You certainly will."

Peruge moved ahead of Kraft to the door, opened it, and stepped out into a full collision with Fancy, who appeared to be returning. He caught an arm around her to keep her from falling. There was no doubt that she wore nothing under the smock. She ground into him as he jerked his arm away in shock.

Kraft pulled her away. "You all right, Fancy?"

"*I'm* fine," she said, grinning at Peruge.

"That was clumsy of me," Peruge said. "I'm sorry."

"You needn't be," she said.

Hellstrom spoke from behind them. "We've had enough commotion out here, Linc. Would you see Mr. Peruge out?"

They left hurriedly, Peruge in considerable confusion. He'd received the unmistakable impression that Fancy had been ready to flop him down and screw him right then and there!

Hellstrom waited until the outer door closed behind Kraft and Peruge, then turned an inquiring stare on Fancy.

"He's in the bag," she said.

"Fancy, what *are* you doing?"

"I'm doing my homework."

Hellstrom suddenly noted the thickening of Fancy's cheeks, the way her upper arms stretched the fabric of the smock. He said, "Fancy, do you see yourself as a brood mother?"

"We haven't had one since Trova," she said.

"And you know why!"

"All that nonsense about a brood mother exciting the swarming drive!"

"It's not nonsense and you know it!"

"Some of us think it is. We think the Hive may swarm without a brood mother and that might be disastrous."

"Fancy, don't you think we know our jobs? The Hive will have to produce at least ten thousand more workers before swarming pressures become apparent."

"They're apparent right now," she said. She rubbed her arms. "Some of us can feel them."

Comment on the current film. The film sequence shows an insect cell, the development of the egg, and, finally, the caterpillar emerging. How striking is this metaphor. We emerge from the parent body, those wild creatures who call themselves humankind. The message of this metaphor goes much deeper, however. It says we must prepare for our emergence. We are immature at this stage, our needs dominated by preparations for adulthood. When we emerge, it will be to take dominion over the surface of the earth. When we have achieved our adult form, we will eat to live rather than to grow.

Peruge heard the telephone ringing for a long time before the Chief answered. Peruge had been sitting on the edge of his motel bed after returning from lunch with Hellstrom. It had been an extremely disappointing lunch: no sign of Fancy, everything very formal and shallow in the dining room of the old farmhouse, and absolutely no rise to his bait about new inventions. The Chief was not going to like this report.

The Chief's voice came on the phone presently, alert and responsive despite the long delay in answering. The old man had not been asleep, then, but doing something he refused to interrupt even to answer what he often referred to as "that instrument from hell."

"I told you I'd call as soon as I got back," Peruge said.

"Where are you calling from?" the Chief asked.

"The motel, why?"

"Are you *sure* that phone's clean?"

"It's clean. I checked."

"Let's scramble anyway."

Peruge sighed, got out his equipment. Presently, he had the Chief's voice in his ear with that distant flatness the scrambler imposed.

"Now, tell me what you found out," the Chief ordered.

"They refuse to respond to any overture about metallurgy or new inventions."

"Did you quote an offer?"

"I said I knew someone who'd pay up to a million for a promising new invention in that field."

"That didn't tip them?"

"Nothing."

"The board is beginning to pressure me," the Chief said. "We're going to have to act soon, one way or another."

"Hellstrom must have some price!" Peruge said.

"You think if you up the ante, he may bite?"

"I don't know for sure. What I'd like to do is send Janvert and probably Myerlie around to the south of Hellstrom's valley and look for signs of Carlos and Tymiena. I have a hunch they may have approached from the south. Lots of trees that way and you know how cautious Carlos was."

"You send no one."

"Chief, if we—"

"No."

"But if we could put that kind of pressure on Hellstrom we might get him for much less. We could have this thing all sewed up and ready to move before the board gets—well, you know how they can be when they get suspicious."

"You would teach your grandfather to suck eggs. I said *no!*"

Peruge began to sense complications. "Then what do you want me to do?"

"Tell me what you saw at Hellstrom's place."

"Not much more than I saw yesterday."

"Be specific."

"In one sense, it's ordinary; very ordinary. Almost too ordinary. No laughter, smiles, relaxation; everything very serious and, well, *dedicated*. That's the word that kept occurring to me: dedicated. *That* is not ordinary. They put me in mind of a Chicom farm commune laboring to meet its harvest quota."

"I don't think we're going to find a red in this woodpile," the Chief said, "but that's something to keep in mind if we need to cover ourselves with glory. However, the matter is much more serious than you realize."

"Oh?" Peruge was suddenly alert, intensely concentrated on the voice coming to him over the phone.

"I had a call from upstairs today," the Chief said. "A special assistant to the Man. They wanted to know if we were the ones poking into Hellstrom's affairs."

"Oh—oh!" Peruge nodded. That explained why Hellstrom had appeared so confidently in command of the situation. How did this little bug doctor get that kind of clout?

"What did you do?" Peruge asked.

"I lied," the Chief said, his voice bland. "I said it must be somebody else because I hadn't heard about it. However, I promised to check because sometimes my people get a bit overzealous."

Peruge stared at the wall in silence for a moment. Who was being set up here? He said, "We have Merrivale set up if we need a patsy."

"That was one of the things I considered."

One of the things! Peruge thought.

The Chief interrupted his development of that worry, asking, "Now, tell me what they're doing on that farm."

"They're making movies about insects."

"You told me that yesterday. Is that *all?*"

"I'm not sure what else they're doing, but I have some ideas about *where* they may be doing it. There's a basement in that barn-studio: wardrobe and some other crap down there, all disgustingly normal in appearance. But there's a tunnel from the barn to the house. They took me through it and we had lunch in the house. There were some very strange dames to wait on us, too, I tell you. Beautiful dolls, all four of them, but they don't talk—not even when you speak directly to them."

"What?"

"They don't speak. They just serve table and go away. Hellstrom said it's because they're perfecting special accents and have been ordered by their voice coach not to say *anything* unless the coach is there to listen and correct them."

"That sounds reasonable."

"Does it? It struck me as odd."

"Were you transmitting to Janvert and the others?"

"No. It was the same as yesterday. They were very nice about it and so-o-o reasonable. Radio for their sound tracks and so on. Would I please not cause problems?"

"I still don't like you going in there without radio. If something—maybe you'd better replace Janvert with Myerlie or DT as your second."

"Relax. They as much as told me that I'd be all right if I played it cool."

"How'd they do that?"

"Hellstrom explained in detail how angry he gets when people cause setbacks in their schedule. I was told to stick close to my guide and not stray."

"Who was your guide?"

"Some little guy named Saldo, no bigger than Shorty Janvert. Very closemouthed. There was no sign of the dame they threw at me yesterday."

"Dzule, are you sure you're not imagining—"

"I'm sure. Look, we're stymied. I need help. I want the highway patrol, the FBI, and anyone else we can dragoon into it crawling over those hills around Hellstrom's farm."

"Dzule! Didn't you hear me when I told you about my call from upstairs?"

Peruge tried to swallow in a suddenly dry throat. The Chief could be very abrupt and final when his voice took on that calm, reasonable tone of correction. So there was more to that call from upstairs than just reported. The troops were stirred up.

"You cannot ask for help on a project that doesn't exist," the Chief said.

Peruge said, "Did you know I'd transmitted a request through Signals for FBI help?"

"I intercepted that and cut it off. That request no longer exists."

"Is there any way we could get an overflight to inspect that farm?"

"Why?"

"It's what I was starting to explain. There's this tunnel from the barn to the house. I'd like to know if there are more such tunnels under that area. Geological Survey has techniques to detect that kind of thing."

"I don't think I could ask for that without tipping our hand. I'll look into it, though. There may be some other way. You're suggesting they may have laboratories and such under the barn in tunnels?"

"Yes."

"It's an idea. I've a couple of friends in the oil industry who owe us favors."

"The board—"

"Dzule!" There was a warning note in that voice. It said, don't question my intelligence!

"I'm sorry, Chief," Peruge said. "It's just that—well, I'm very uneasy about this thing. All afternoon, I kept wanting to get the hell out of there. There's a stinking animal smell about the place and—it's a very creepy place. The trouble is, I can't pin down a single thing to make me uneasy except the blatant facts of Porter and company."

The Chief's voice took on a patronizing, fatherly tone. "Dzule, my boy, don't go inventing trouble. If we can't get our hands on Hellstrom's invention and control the metallurgical process, this becomes a very straightforward case. I can discover that some of my *overzealous* boys have uncovered a hornet's nest of subversion. To do that, however, we need much more than we already possess."

"Porter and—"

"They don't exist. You forget that my signature was on the orders."

"Ahhh—yes, of course."

"I can go upstairs and say we have this bit of a file, little more than a memorandum, really, that one of our boys found at the MIT library. I can *do* that, but only if I'm ready to defend the argument that it involves a private development of a major weapon system."

"Unless we have more information, they'll make the same kinds of guesses we did."

"Precisely!" the Chief said.

"I see. Then you want me to take this to an open negotiation with Hellstrom?"

"Indeed I do. Is there any reason why you think you cannot do that?"

"I can attempt it. I have a date to go back there tomorrow. I led them to believe I'll have an army of professional help to conduct a search of the area within a day or so, and they—"

"What are your preparations?"

"Janvert and his teams will be using line of sight to follow my movements while I'm outside the buildings. When I get inside, I most likely will be incommunicado. We will, of course, probe for a soft spot—a window or something that could act as a microphone for our laser pickup. However, I don't believe I should wait for that kind of contact before opening—"

"How do you propose to open the negotiations?"

"First, I'll lay it on heavily about the reserves I can call up. I'll admit that I represent a powerful agency in the government, but I won't identify us, naturally. After that—"

"No."

"But—"

"We have three agents probably dead and they—"

"They don't exist. You said it yourself."

"Except to us, Dzule. No. You will merely tell them that you represent people who are interested in Project 40. Let them worry about what reserves you may have. They've probably killed three people; that, or they're holding prisoners and—"

"Should I look into that possibility?"

"For God's sake! Of course not! But the chances are high they'll be more fearful of what they suspect than of what they know. For all they know, you could have the army, the navy and the Marine Corps standing by with the FBI in reserve. If you need leverage, mention our *missing* friends, but don't appear anxious to get them back. Refuse to negotiate on that score. We want Project 40, nothing else. We don't want murderers or kidnappers or missing people. Is that clear?"

"Very." And, an empty feeling growing within him, Peruge thought: What if I turn up missing? He thought he knew the answer to this question and he didn't like it.

"I'll get those oil people to do what they can," the Chief said, "but only if it can be done without tipping our hand. Finding out *where* Hellstrom's people work doesn't strike me as too helpful at this point."

"What if he refuses to negotiate?" Peruge asked.

"Don't provoke a showdown on it. We still have the board and its forces in reserve."

"But they'd—"

"They'd take the whole thing and throw us a bone, yes. But a bone is better than nothing."

"Project 40 could be entirely innocent."

"You don't believe that," the Chief said. "And it's your job to prove what we both *know* in this case." The Chief cleared his throat, a loud, hacking noise over the scrambler. "As long as we have no proof, we don't have a damn thing. They could have the secret of the end of the world down there, as we led the board to believe, but we can't move unless we prove it. How many times do I have to say that?"

Peruge rubbed his left knee where he had bumped it against a lightstand in Hellstrom's studio. It wasn't like the Chief to repeat a point that many times. What was happening back there in the office? Was the Chief trying to send a subtle message that he couldn't speak openly.

"Do you want me to find a good excuse for us to pull out of this?" Peruge asked.

There was open relief in the Chief's voice. "Only if it seems the *right* thing to do, my boy."

Somebody's with him, Peruge realized. It had to be someone accorded a degree of trust, somebody important, but someone who could not be told everything. Try as he might, Peruge could not fit anyone he knew into this description. It should be perfectly obvious to the Chief that his agent in the field had no intention of pulling out. *But he was fishing for that suggestion from me.* Which meant the someone in the Chief's office was hearing both ends of the conversation. The cryptic nature of the hidden message in this conversation bespoke extreme caution at headquarters. A call from *upstairs*. How powerful a man was this Hellstrom?

"Can you say anything about the kinds of toes we may be stepping on?" Peruge asked.

"No."

Isn't it even possible to find out whether Hellstrom's influence has a purely political base—big contributions to the party, that sort of thing—or whether it's possible, for instance, that we're nosing into the affairs of another agency?"

"You're beginning to understand the problem as I now see it," the Chief said.

So it's somebody from another agency with him now, Peruge thought. That could only mean it was one of the Chief's own people who'd been infiltrated into the other agency. It could mean there were two agencies interested in Hellstrom, or it could mean Hellstrom's Project 40 was the product of another agency. Investigators could be tripping over each other if this thing were stirred up enough.

"I get the message," Peruge said.

"When you meet Hellstrom," the Chief said, "don't introduce this other possibility yourself. Leave that up to him."

"I understand."

"I certainly hope you do—for your own sake as well as mine."

"Shall I call you back later today?"

"Not unless you have something new to report. Call me immediately after you've seen Hellstrom, however. I'll be waiting."

Peruge heard the connection close at the other end. He disconnected his scrambler, replaced the telephone on its stand. For the first time in his life, Peruge began to sense what his field agents felt. It'll all very well for him to sit back there all safe and tidy, but I've got to go out and risk my neck and he won't lift a finger if I get chopped!

The words of Trova Hellstrom. At all cost, we must avoid falling into what we have come to understand as "the termite trap." We must not become too much like the termite. Such insects, which give us our pattern for survival, have their ways and we have ours. We learn from them, but not slavishly. Termites, never able to leave the protective walls of their mound, come into a world that is completely self-sufficient. And thus it must be with us. The entire termite society is guarded by soldiers. And thus it must be with us. When the mound comes under attack, the soldiers know they can be abandoned outside the mound, left to die buying time for others to make the mound impregnable. And thus it must be with us. But the mound dies if the queen dies. We cannot be that vulnerable. If the mound dies, that is the end of them. We cannot be that vulnerable. The small seeds of our continuation have been planted Outside. They must be prepared to go on alone if our *mound* dies.

As he returned to the Hive down the long slope of the first gallery, Hellstrom listened for some sound or other message to reassure him that all was well here. No such message came to him. The Hive remained an entity; it still functioned, but the sense of profound disturbance reached all through it. That was the Hive's nature: touch one part of it and all of its cells responded. The chemistry of their internal communication could not be denied. Key workers, driven by the urgency of their situation, emitted subtle pheromones, external hormones that spread through the common air. The Hive's filters had been reduced to a minimum to conserve power. The pheromone signals remained for all to inhale and for all to share the common disturbance. Already, signs could be detected that said this situation could not continue without profound and possibly permanent effect on the totality.

His brood mother had warned him once, "Nils, the Hive can learn just as you learn. The totality can learn. If you fail to understand what the Hive learns, this could bring about destruction for us all."

What was the Hive learning now? Hellstrom wondered.

Fancy's behavior suggested something demanded by the Hive in its deepest needs. She spoke of swarming. Was that it? They had been working for more than forty years to delay swarming. Had that been a mistake? He was worried about Fancy and had just tried unsuccessfully to find her. She was supposed to be with the shotting crew, but she hadn't been at her station and Ed had not known where to find her. Saldo had assured him that Fancy was under constant surveillance now, but still Hellstrom worried. Could the Hive create a *natural* brood mother? Fancy might be a logical choice for this role. What could the Council do if that happened? Should they send Fancy to the vats rather than risk an early swarming? He hated the thought of losing Fancy—that superb bloodline that had produced so many useful specialists. If they could only breed out the instability!

Provided it *was* instability.

Hellstrom came to the concrete arch that opened into the second-level feeding station and saw that Saldo awaited him there as ordered. Saldo could be depended on. This reassured Hellstrom. He realized how much he had come to depend on the younger male. Without speaking, Hellstrom moved to Saldo's side. They entered the feeding station and fed together at the conveyor, drinking deeply of the common broth from the vats. Hellstrom always found a deep satisfaction from eating the food of the common workers. It was a satisfaction that the supplemental leader foods never gave him. The leader foods might double the expected Hive lifetime, but they lacked that one ingredient Hellstrom identified as "unifying force."

Sometimes we need a lowest common denominator, he thought. This was never more apparent than in a time of crisis.

Saldo signaled that he was anxious to report, but Hellstrom gave the sign for patience, recognizing his own unwillingness to hear that report. While eating, Hellstrom had felt himself overcome by the realization of how fragile the Hive was. The domesticated world they sought for humankind seemed now no more than a thin-shelled egg about to be crushed. It was all so clear and sturdy in the Hive Manual, but so shimmering and weak in the execution. Although his mind searched for a clue, he could see no help in the manual . . .

"The Hive moves toward a nonverbal base for human existence. It is a major purpose of the Hive to find that base, then to build a new language fitted to our needs. First, in the light of that plain message from the insect world, we shed the errors of the past."

They had not shed the errors of the past. They might never shed them. The path loomed so long, so exacting in its demands. No one had really imagined how long it might require, or how many pitfalls they might have to surmount. At first, three hundred or more years ago, back in the oral-tradition times, they had assumed "a hundred years or so." How swiftly that error of the past had made itself known! The new *truth* had arisen, then: the Hive might have to endure for a thousand years or more, unless a dramatic death convulsion overcame the Outsiders. A thousand years until the earth lay domesticated under their dominion.

Hellstrom recalled thinking how the familiar Hive walls around him might crumble and be repaired hundreds of times before the Hive came into its own and the workers took control of the planet surface.

What a fantasy! These walls might endure no more than another few hours and *never* be rebuilt.

The necessity of breathing confidence into the Hive had never seemed so difficult. Reluctantly, Hellstrom signaled for Saldo to speak, noting with a sense of revulsion how obvious it was that the younger man thought a few words with the prime male would solve all problems.

"Fancy got the breeding hypes from Hive stores by stealing them," Saldo said. "There's no record of an official—"

"But *why* did she take them?" Hellstrom asked.

"To defy you, the Council, and the Hive," Saldo said. He obviously thought the question demented.

"We must not be too quick to judge," Hellstrom said.

"But she's dangerous! She should—"

"She must be allowed to continue without inter-ference," Hellstrom said. "Perhaps the entire Hive actually speaks through her."

"Trying to breed with this Peruge?"

"Why not? We've used that method of getting Outside blood many times. Peruge has been preselected for us by the wild Outside. He is living evidence of success."

"Success at what price?"

"However we get the strong ones, you know we must get them. Perhaps Fancy knows better than any of us how to deal with this threat."

"I don't believe it! I think she's using this talk of a swarm as an excuse to leave the Hive. You *know* how fond she is of Outsider foods and comforts."

"There is that possibility," Hellstrom agreed. "But *why* does she want to leave? I think your explanation too glib."

Saldo appeared more abashed by the implied rebuke than it had warranted. He was silent for a moment. "Nils, I don't understand what you're saying."

"I do not understand it clearly myself, but Fancy's behavior may not be as simple as you imagine."

Saldo stared questioningly at Hellstrom's face as though some line or flicker there might provide enlightenment. What did the prime male know that others did not? Hellstrom was an offspring of the elders, the first colonists of this, the first true Hive. Had he received special instructions from that mysterious source of wisdom—what to do in this kind of crisis? Saldo's attention was caught by the activity to his left: the bowls of broth were moving on the conveyor as someone took a bowl from the end. Workers were feeding around them, taking no particular notice of the two superior specialists. It was natural that no special notice be taken. Common chemistry told the workers who belonged here and who did not. Bring in an Outsider, though, and unless the workers could see that the Outsider was under the control of their fellows, or unless the alien's chemistry had been sufficiently masked, the intruder would go immediately into the vats carried there by unspeaking workers who

cared only that a dangerous mass of protein be removed. The workers' responses now appeared all very
normal, but Saldo began to experience in this moment
some of Hellstrom's sense that the Hive had been
deeply wounded. There was a jerky stiffness to some
of the movement, a belligerent thrust about the stride.

"Is there something wrong of which I am unaware?" Saldo asked.

Ahhh, the wisdom of this young male! Hellstrom
thought, pride suffusing him.

"That may well be," Hellstrom said. He turned,
signaled for Saldo to follow, led the way out into the
gallery. They took the first side ramp and the next lat-
eral passage. They proceeded briskly to Hel 'rom's
own cell. Inside, Hellstrom indicated a chair for Saldo, but stretched his own body on the bed. Ahhh!
Blessed brood, but he was tired!

Obediently, Saldo sat down, glanced around. He
had been in this cell before, but present circumstances
made the place appear vaguely strange. A disturbing
difference clamored for his attention, but he could not
pinpoint it. Presently, he realized the difference was
the reduced noise from the service tunnel behind the
rear wall of the cell. The hushed minimum of Hive operation could not be excaped in this place. Perhaps
that was why Hellstrom refused to move to better
quarters. Subtle odors of disturbance could be detected in the air, too. All the messages of crisis came to
focus here.

"Yes, there are things wrong that *none* of us
know about," Hellstrom said, picking up the conversation with an answer to the question Saldo had asked at
the feeding station. "That is our problem, Saldo.
Things will happen to alarm us and we must be prepared to deal with those things on their own terms. As
the Outsiders say, we must hang loose. Do you understand?"

"No." Saldo shook his head. "What kind of
things do you mean?"

"If I could describe them, they would not fit the
description of *unknowns*," Hellstrom said, his voice
sad. Moving only his eyes, keeping his hands clasped

behind his head, Hellstrom glanced across at Saldo. The young male suddenly appeared as fragile as the Hive. What could Saldo's imaginative resourcefulness really do to avert the disaster building around them? Saldo was only thirty-four years old. Hive education gave those years a specious sophistication, a false worldliness of a kind never seen Outside. Saldo's naiveté was Hive naiveté. He did not know the kinds of liberties he might exercise Outside. He did not know what it was to be truly wild. Except vicariously through books and all the other trappings of Hive education, Saldo had little experience of the wild randomness that prevailed beyond the confines of the Hive. Given time, Saldo might gain that experience as Hellstrom had. The young male was the very type the Hive must send into the tempering caldron of wild humankind. But much of what he learned from his Outside ventures would bring him nightmares. He would, as every front specialist did, encyst those nightmares in a special unconscious core at the depths of his being.

Just as I have walled up my own worst experiences, Hellstrom thought.

There could be no complete and permanent denial of such memories short of the vats, though. They came stealing out through unexpected cracks in one's defenses.

Taking Hellstrom's long silence as rebuke, Saldo lowered his gaze. "We do not know all the kinds of things that may happen to us, but we must be prepared anyway. I see that now."

Hellstrom felt like crying out: *I am not perfect! I am not invincible!*

Instead, he asked, "How is Project 40 coming?"

"How did you know I'd just inquired of it?" Saldo asked, awe in his tone. "I didn't mention it."

"All of us who carry the extra burden of awareness are inquiring regularly into Project 40," Hellstrom chided. "What did you find?"

"Nothing new—really. Oh, they are building the new test model swiftly and it will—"

"Have they changed their opinion about its prospects?"

"They are raising new arguments about the generation of extremely high heat."

"Is there more?"

Saldo lifted his gaze, studied Hellstrom. Despite the prime male's obvious fatigue, there remained one more matter that could not be avoided.

"A band of hydroponics harvesters was found wandering in the upper levels about an hour ago," Saldo said. "As nearly as we can determine, they were expressing a need to go to the surface."

Hellstrom sat upright on the bed, shock suppressing his fatigue. "Why wasn't I told immediately?"

"We handled it," Saldo said. "It was blamed on the general disturbance. They've all been chemically adjusted and are back at work. I've instituted patrols in all of the galleries to prevent a recurrence. Have I done wrong?"

"No." Hellstrom lay back on the bed.

Patrols! Of course, that was all they could do now. But this told how deeply disturbed the entire Hive had become. Fancy was right: the predictions about the swarming urge had not taken into account a crisis such as this one.

"Were there breeders among them?" Hellstrom asked.

"A few potentials, but they—"

"They were swarming," Hellstrom said.

"Nils! Just a few workers from—"

"Nevertheless, they were swarming. It is in the calculations of our earliest written records. You *know* this. We have watched for it and tried to predict it from the first. And without our leadership being able to set the exact moment, we have reached a critical condition."

"Nils, the—"

"You were going to speak about numbers. This is not a mere consequence of numbers. Total population in a given space figures in our calculations, but this is something else. Young workers and potential breeders, at the very least, find themselves driven to leave the Hive. They were striking out on their own. That is swarming."

"How can we prevent a—"

"Perhaps we cannot."

"But we can't allow it now!"

"No. We must do our best to delay the swarming. To let them go now would destroy us. Have the filters turned back to maximum for a few hours and then adjust them to optimum."

"Nils, a suspicious Outsider in our midst might—"

"We cannot do otherwise. Desperate measures are required. A quiet weeding of population may be indicated if this—"

"The vats?"

"Yes, if the pressure becomes too great."

"The hydroponics workers who—"

"Watch them carefully," Hellstrom said. "And the breeders—even Fancy and her sisters. A swarm will need breeders."

Peruge's private instruction to Daniel Thomas (DT) Alden. Janvert has come into possession of the special Signal Corps number and code required to call the president. If you see any attempt by Janvert to make such a call, any secretive attempt to use a telephone, you are to stop him, using whatever force you find necessary.

Peruge tuned in a symphony concert on the motel room's radio under the mistaken idea that it might distract him. Time and again, he found himself returning to contemplation of that disturbing woman at Hellstrom's farm.

Fancy.

What an odd name that was.

This motel had been chosen because it provided him with a room whose rear windows gave line-of-sight communication with the Steens Mountain camps where his backup teams had stationed themselves in the guise of vacationers. Peruge knew he had but to signal out that rear window and he could be in direct touch with any one of the three teams. The laser transceiver would catch their voices as clearly as if they stood in the room with him.

It bothered Peruge that he had allowed Shorty Janvert to remain in charge of the teams on the mountain. Damn that slimy-minded Merrivale!

This was not a reassuring situation and, as night gathered over the brown countryside beyond his room, Peruge reviewed his instructions and his preparations.

Had it been wise to restrict Janvert by the explicit order, "You're to report everything to headquarters before initiating nonspecified movements during those periods when I'm out of communication on that farm."

The *specified* movements were extremely few and limited in scope: trips to Fosterville for groceries and visual check on Lincoln Kraft; shift of campsite to meet necessities of protecting the overall cover; visits between camps to transfer the watch and maintain constant surveillance . . .

Thus far, Janvert had given no overt indication of untrustworthiness. His communications fitted all of the reliability requirements.

"Does the Chief know you're going in there without communications?"

"Yes."

"I don't like that."

"I'm the one to worry about that, not you," Peruge had countered. Who did Janvert think he was?

"I'd like to see inside that place myself," Janvert said.

"You're not to make any such attempt without specific advice from headquarters and then only if I have been out of communication beyond a preset time limit."

"I don't doubt your capabilities," Janvert said, his tone remarkably conciliatory. "I'm just worried about all the things we don't know in this case. Hellstrom displays a remarkable lack of respect for our persons."

Peruge suspected Janvert of trying to fabricate a tone of real concern where none existed; he felt impatient with such embroidery.

"The farm is my problem," Peruge said. "Your problem is to observe and report."

"Fat chance we get to observe while you're in there without a transmitter."

"You still can't find a weak spot in their armor?"

"I'd have told you first thing if I had!"

"Don't get upset about it. I know you're trying."

"There's not a sound behind those walls. They must have a sophisticated damper system of some kind. Plenty of odd sounds in the valley, but nothing we can really identify. Machinery, mostly, and it sounds like heavy machinery. I suspect they have equipment sufficient to've spotted our probes. Sampson and Rio are moving their rig to grid position G-6 some time tonight. They did most of the probing."

"You're staying put?"

"Yes."

Janvert was taking all of the right precautions. Peruge thought: Why do I distrust him? Would the little runt always live under the cloud generated by his reluctant recruitment? Peruge felt angry with himself. It was disloyal to entertain the thoughts flowing through his mind. What was the Chief really doing?

The magnetic woman at Hellstrom's farm—was she just teasing him? Some women considered him handsome and his big body exuded a sense of animal power that might explain most of what had happened up there.

Nuts! Hellstrom put her up to it!

Did the Chief consider Dzule Peruge just another of the many expendables?

"You still there?" Janvert asked.

"Yes!" Voice angry and sharp.

"What gave you the idea there might be more people on that farm than we can see? The tunnel?"

"That—yes, but there's more that you can't put your finger on. Record this for transmission, Shorty. I want a watch put on the ordinary supplies going into that place. How much food, that sort of thing? Be discreet, but pry."

"I'll take care of it. Do you want DT assigned to that?"

"No. Send Nick. I want an estimate on how many people would match the normal food orders."

"Right. Did the Chief tell you about the diamond bits for well drills?"

"Yes. They would've been delivered just about the time Carlos and Tymiena were supposed to be there."

"Weird, isn't it?"

"It fits an odd kind of pattern," Peruge said. "We just haven't found the precise nature of that pattern." He cast about in his mind, wondering at the reason for diamond drill bits in a movie company. There was just no explaining it and no sense wondering without more evidence. More likely to come up with a wrong answer than a right one, and, either way, he couldn't be certain.

"I agree," Janvert said. "Anything more for this report?"

"Nothing." Peruge signed off, replaced the equipment in its cover packaging, stored it in his shaving kit.

Janvert had been more talkative than usual, and the surface attempts to be pleasant couldn't be anything but false from that feisty little bastard.

Peruge thought about this as he lay in the quiet darkness of his motel bed. He knew he had been cut off. He was alone, removed even from the protection of the Chief, and he wondered why he went on.

Because I want to be rich, he thought. *Richer than the bitch of the board. I will be, too, if I can get my hands on Hellstrom's Project 40.*

Script consultation, Nils Hellstrom speaking. On the screen, the audience will see a butterfly emerging from its cocoon. We will see much more and, in a deeper sense, we want the audience to see what we see, unconsciously. The butterfly personifies our own long struggle. It is the long darkness of humankind when the wild ones imagined they talked, one to another. It is the metamorphosis, the transformation of our Hive into the salvation of the human species. It fore-shad-

ows the day when we will emerge and show our beauty
to the admiring universe.

"The transmitter is in his wristwatch," Saldo said.
"We caught it just before he turned the thing off."

"Good work," Hellstrom said.

They stood in the electronic gloom of the barn
aerie, the security command post, workers going about
their jobs quietly all around, a sense of determination
in every movement. Nothing would get through this
guard.

"Those probes we detected came from Steens
Mountain," Saldo said. "We've located the position on
the chart."

"Excellent. Is their lack of success igniting a renewed effort or are they quiet now?"

"Quiet. I've arranged to send a picnic party into
the area tomorrow. They'll play and enjoy themselves
and report back tomorrow night. The party will be
composed only of extremely experienced fronts."

"Don't count on them learning much."

Saldo nodded agreement.

Hellstrom closed his eyes tightly in distress and
fatigue. He couldn't seem to get enough rest and what
little he got failed to restore him. What they needed
and would never find was a way to send Peruge packing, a way to answer all of his questions without answering them. Those mysterious, probing questions
about metallurgy and new inventions irritated Hellstrom. What could that possibly have to do with Project
40? New invention—yes, possibly. But metallurgy? He
decided to communicate his question to the lab at the
earliest opportunity.

Saying of the Hive specialists. How primitive and far
behind us are the behaviorists of the wild Outside!

Peruge heard the scratching at his door as part of
a dream. It was a dog from his childhood calling him

to get up for breakfast. Good old Danny. Peruge could see the wide, ugly face, the dripping jowls, in his dream. He actually felt the fact that he was in bed, clad only in pajama bottoms as had always been usual for him. Abruptly, circuits closed in his memory. That dog had been dead for years! He was awake instantly, silent and probing with all of his senses for evidence of danger.

The scratching continued.

He slipped his heavy automatic from under his pillow, arose, and went to the door. The floor was cold against his bare feet. Standing at one side with the weapon ready, he jerked the door open on its chain.

There was a night light outside his door. It cast a yellow glow on Fancy, who stood there wrapped in something furry, dark, and bulky. She supported a bicycle with her left hand.

Peruge closed the door, released the chain, swung the door wide. He knew he appeared strange standing there in his pajama bottoms with a big man-killer automatic in his hand, but he sensed the urgent need to get her out of sight into his room.

He felt a surge of elation. They'd sent this little pussy to compromise him, eh? But *he* had one of them outside their goddamned farm!

Fancy entered without speaking, wheeling her bicycle. She leaned the bicycle against the wall as Peruge closed and locked the door. When he turned toward her, she was facing him and removing her outer garment, a long fur coat. She threw the coat over the bicycle's handlebars, stood there in the thin white smock she'd worn when he'd last seen her. Her eyes were focused intently on his with a smoky, mocking look.

Fun first? Peruge wondered. Or business first? His hand was slippery with perspiration against the butt of the atuomatic. God, she was a sexy bitch!

He went to the window beside the door, slipped back the draperies, peered out. He could see no watchers. He crossed to the rear window, looked out over the parking lot toward the mountain. No prying strangers visible there, either. Nobody. What time was it, for Christ's sake? And why wasn't the bitch talking?

He crossed to the nightstand, lifted his wristwatch: 1:28 A.M.

Fancy watched all of this activity, a half-smile on her lips. Outsiders were such strange creatures. This one appeared even stranger than usual. Their bodies told them what they should do and they constantly disobeyed. Well, she had come prepared.

Peruge glanced at her from his position by the nightstand. Her hands were clenched into fists, but she appeared to be carrying no weapon. He slipped his gun into a drawer of the stand. Was she being quiet because this room had been bugged? That couldn't be! He'd made certain the room was clean. He moved carefully, being sure not to turn his back on her. Why had she come on a bicycle? And in a fur coat, for the love of God! He wondered if he should alert the night watch on the mountain. Not yet. Fun first.

Fancy reached up with her left hand as though she had read his mind, unbuttoned the front of her smock, shrugged out of it, and let it fall. She stood there naked, a sensuous pocket-venus body that sent his pulse racing. There were open sandals on her feet. She kicked them off, stirring up dust from her ride into town.

Peruge, his eyes glittering, wet his lips with his tongue, and said, "Aren't you something!"

Still without speaking, Fancy approached him, reached up, and clasped both of his bare arms. His left arm tingled as she touched it and he smelled a sudden, heavy musk. His gaze jerked toward the tingling in shocked alarm and he saw a tiny, flesh-colored ampule crushed beneath her forefinger against his skin, a fleck of his own blood there. In panic, he knew he should hurl her away from him, call for help from his night watch, but his muscles remained frozen while that tingling spread through his body. His gaze slipped from the ampule on his arm to Fancy's firm breasts, the dark nipples protruding with sensual tension.

As though a fog was creeping up from his loins, Peruge felt his will dissolve until his only awareness was of the woman who was now clinging to him, pressing against him with surprising strength, forcing him backward onto the bed.

Now, Fancy spoke. "You want to breed with me? That's good."

From the Hive Manual. A basic aim of the socializing process should be to create the widest possible tolerance of diversity among the society's components.

"Fancy's missing!" Saldo said.

He had come to Hellstrom's quarters, racing down the corridors and galleries that were never lacking activity, ignoring the upset his running passage created among the workers.

Hellstrom sat upright in his bed, rubbing sleep from his eyes, shaking his head to wake himself. He had been in deep sleep, his first in days, praying for a good rest before tomorrow's certain confrontation with Peruge and whomever Peruge added to the pressure on the Hive.

Fancy missing!

He peered up at Saldo's frightened face in the cell glow. "Alone?"

"Yes."

Hellstrom exhaled a sigh of relief. "How did she get out of the Hive? Where is she?"

"She used that faulty emergency ventilator in the rock at the north perimeter. She had a bicycle."

"Weren't there guards?"

"She stunned them with de-hype."

"But the security watch!"

"They missed it," Saldo confessed. "She's obviously used this route before. She went into the trees and avoided every one of our detectors."

Of course, Hellstrom thought. A bicycle. Why a bicycle? Where had she gone? "How did she get a bicycle?" he asked.

"It's the one we took from the Outsider, Depeaux."

"What was that still doing around? Why wasn't it reduced for salvage?"

"Some of the engineers were playing with it. They were thinking of manufacturing our own model to speed up delivery service in the lower galleries."

"Which direction did she go?" Hellstrom levered himself out of the bed. What time was it? He glanced at the crystal clock on his wall: 3:51 A.M.

"She apparently went across the Palmer Bridge. There are tracks."

Toward town then. Why?

"The guards she stunned say she was wearing Outsider garments," Saldo said. "Wardrobe reports a fur coat missing. She was into Hive stores again, too. We haven't yet determined what she took."

"How long has she been gone?" Hellstrom asked. He slipped his feet into Hive sandals, groped for a robe. It was cold, but he knew that was only his own lowered metabolism.

"Almost four hours," Saldo said. "Guards were unconscious for a long time." He rubbed at the healing wound on his jaw. "I'm sure she's gone into town. Two chemical trackers went as far along her trail as they dared. She was still headed for town when they broke off."

"Peruge," Hellstrom said.

"What?"

"She's gone to breed with Peruge."

"Of course! Shall I call Linc and have him—"

"No." Hellstrom shook his head from side to side.

Saldo trembled with impatience. "But that bicycle belonged to one of Peruge's agents!"

"Who identifies bicycles? They're not likely to make the connection. Fancy won't tell him where that machine came from."

"Are you sure?"

"I'm sure. Fancy has a one-track mind where breeding is concerned. I should've realized that when I saw her go on the attack with Peruge as target."

"That man is clever! She could tell him something without even realizing it."

"A possibility we'll have to investigate. But for now, you will alert Linc. Tell him where she is and see that he makes certain they don't take her away for interrogation. Peruge is sure to have his friends watching him. We don't want any more activity around that motel than absolutely necessary."

Saldo stared at Hellstrom in shocked silence. He had expected Hellstrom to call up all of the Hive's defensive resources. This was not an adequate response!

"Any more indications of swarming pressure?" Hellstrom asked.

"No. The—the ventilation appears to have helped."

"Fancy is fertile," Hellstrom said. "Getting her pregnant by an Outsider will help, too. She becomes quite tractable while producing a child."

"Ahhhhh—" Saldo stood in admiration of Hellstrom's wisdom.

"I know what she took from stores," Hellstrom said. "She will have a male sex-fraction in an ampule to hype up Peruge. She wants to breed with him, that's all. Let her. Outsiders have extremely odd reactions to this natural form of human behavior."

"So it is said," Saldo murmured. "I've studied the behavioral precautions for work Outside."

"Depend on it," Hellstrom said, smiling. "I have seen this happen many times. Peruge will show up here tomorrow the figure of contrition. He will be with Fancy and very defensive. He will feel guilty. That will make him vulnerable to us. Yes—I believe I know how to handle this situation now, thanks to Fancy. Bless her."

"What are you saying?"

"The wild Outsiders aren't all that different from us, chemically. It took Fancy to remind me of this. The same techniques we use to make our workers tractable, domesticated, and yielding to the Hive's needs will work on Outsiders."

"In their food?"

"Or their water or even their air."

"Are you sure Fancy will return?" Saldo could not keep down the niggling doubt.

"I'm sure."

"But the bicycle—"

"Do you really think they'll identify it?"

"We cannot risk it!"

"If it makes you feel better, warn Linc about this possibility. I think Peruge's senses will be so dulled after a night of hyped-up breeding with Fancy that he wouldn't even recognize a bicycle when he saw it."

Saldo frowned. There was a manic note to Hellstrom's manner and voice which was deeply disturbing. "I don't like this, Nils."

"You will," Hellstrom assured him. "Trust me. Tell Linc you are sending in a special security team. I want their instructions to be explicit, no misunderstandings. Go over them with the utmost care. They are not to interfere tonight. Their major task is to insure that Fancy is not removed from that motel. She must spend an uninterrupted night with Peruge. In the morning, they are to collect her at the first opportunity and bring her to me. I wish to thank her in person. The Hive *does* learn; it *does* react to danger as a single organism. It is just as I have always suspected."

"I agree we should make sure she gets back here," Saldo said, "but thank her?"

"Naturally."

"For what?"

"For reminding us that Outsiders share our chemistry."

Wisdom of the Hive. The superior specialist, bred to the demands of our most basic needs, will win for us in the end.

Peruge awoke in the gray dawn gloom, swimming up to consciousness from some faraway energy-drained place. He turned his head to see the tangled confusion of his bed, came to the slow realization that he was alone in the bed and this should be important information. A bicycle with a coat thrown over the handlebars stood against the wall beside the door.

There was a crumpled white garment on the floor between bed and door. He stared at the bicycle, wondering why he felt that a bicycle should be so important.

A bicycle?

Water splashed in the bathroom. Someone was humming.

Fancy!

He pushed himself to a sitting position, his mind as muddled as the bed. Fancy! For the love of God! What had she used on him? He had a foggy remembrance of what he though were eighteen orgasms. An aphrodisiac? If so, it was more potent than anything in his wildest fantasies.

Water still splashed in the bathroom. She was taking a shower. God! How could she move?

He tried to reassemble the night in his memory, met only the wildest confusion, a recurrent image of writhing flesh. He thought: *That was me! For God's sake! That was me!* What was that stuff Fancy had given him? Could that be Project 40, for the love of heaven? He wanted to laugh hysterically, but couldn't summon the strength. The sound of splashing water came to an abrupt stop. His attention moved to the bathroom door. Movement there, the voice humming. Where did she get the strength?

The door opened and Fancy emerged, a towel wrapped around her loins, another towel in her hands with which she was drying her hair.

"Good morning, lover," she said. And she thought: He looks completely used up.

He stared at her without speaking, memory searching.

"Didn't you like breeding with me?" she asked.

That was it! That had been the thing he had tried to remember but couldn't until she spoke. Breed with her? Could she be one of those kooky, turned-on members of the new generation: sex for procreation only?

"What'd you do to me?" he asked. His voice came out in a husky croaking which shocked him.

"Do? I just—"

He lifted his left arm to expose the area where

she had injected him with that mysterious musky substance. Faint discoloration there revealed a subcutaneous bruise.

"Oh, that," she said. "Didn't you like it when you were hyped up?"

He levered himself back against the bed's headrest, adjusted a pillow behind him. God, he was tired. "Hyped," he said. "So you shot me with some kind of dope."

"I only gave you an additional store of what every male has when he's ready to breed," she said, knowing her tone betrayed her own puzzlement. Outsiders were so strange about breeding.

Peruge's head ached and he felt that her words increased the pain. Slowly, he turned, looked squarely at her. God! What a voluptuous body! He spoke painfully, but clearly, "What's this breeding crap?"

"I know you use other words for what we did," she explained, trying to sound reasonable, "but that's what we like to call it—breeding."

"We?"

"My—friends and I."

"You *breed* with them?"

"Sometimes."

Crazy communal hopheads! Could that be what Hellstrom was hiding: sex orgies and aphrodisiac drugs? Peruge felt a deep and sudden prurient envy. Suppose that was what these crazies did! Suppose they had regular parties such as the one he'd experienced with Fancy. It was wrong, of course. But what a hold an experience like that could get on a man! On a woman, too, no doubt.

It was criminal to do such things, but. . .

Fancy dropped her towels, began putting on her smock, seemingly with no more concern about her nudity than she'd experienced the night before.

Despite his headache and profound lassitude, Peruge marveled at her sensuous grace. She was all woman!

As she dressed, Fancy admitted to herself that she felt hungry and she wondered if Peruge had money to buy breakfast. She enjoyed the thought of exotic

Outsider food, but she had not prepared herself with money from Hive stores before sneaking out. A warm coat, the male breeding hype, and the bicycle, but no money.

I was in a hurry, she thought, and she could not suppress a joyful giggle. The wild Outsider males were such fun when one hyped them, as though their suppressed breeding energies had been stored up for just such an occasion.

As he watched Fancy dress, Peruge found his original worries returning. What had driven her to his bed? Breeding? What nonsense! She had come into possession of an undoubted aphrodisiac, though. He couldn't deny this. His own behavior in the night gave ample testimony to this.

Eighteen times!

Something was very sick up there at that farm. *Breeding!*

"Have you had any babies?" he asked.

"Oh, several," she said, then realized it had been wrong to admit this. Her own training in Outsider sex inhibitions had been explicit on that score. Her personal experiences had reinforced the training. Now, it was a potentially dangerous admission. Peruge had no way of knowing how old she was. Old enough to be his mother, no doubt. That Hive difference between appearance and age was one of the things that could never be shared with Outsiders. She felt an abrupt resurgence of Hive caution.

Her answer astonished him. "Several? Where are they?"

"Oh—with friends." She tried to act casual and unconcerned, but now she was fully alert. Peruge must be diverted. "You want to breed some more?" she asked.

But Peruge was not to be shunted from this fascinating disclosure. "Don't you have a husband?"

"Oh, no."

"Who fathered your *several* children?" he asked, then realized he probably should have asked about fathers, plural.

His questions increased her nervousness. "I don't

want to talk about it." Admitting that she'd borne children had been a mistake. Hive consciousness restored other memories of the night with Peruge, as well. The Outsider had made interesting admissions while in the throes of breeding ecstasy. There had been, for a time, a level of his deepest awareness completely open to her. Moving with an elaborate show of casualness, she crossed to the bicycle, took up the long fur coat, held it over her arm.

"Where are you going?" he demanded. He forced his legs off the edge of the bed, let them fall to the cold floor, which restored some of his energy. His head whirled with fatigue and there was now an aching in his chest. What the hell had been in that shot? She'd really used him up.

"I'm hungry," she explained. "Can I leave the bicycle while I go out and eat? Maybe we can breed some more later."

"Eat?" His stomach rebelled at the thought.

"There's a café just down the street," she said. "I'm very hungry—" she giggled, "after last night."

She at least has to come back and get her damned bicycle, he thought. And he realized he was no match for her in his present weakened condition. He'd have a reception committee ready for her when she did return, though. They were going to unravel the mystery of Nils Hellstrom, and the beginning of the thread was named *Fancy*.

"Just down to the café," he said, as though he were explaining it to himself. He recalled seeing the neon sign.

"I like an—breakfast," she said and swallowed in a sudden chill. Nervousness had almost tripped her into saying an "Outsider" breakfast. *Outsider* was a word one did not use with Outsiders. She covered her slip, asking, "Do you have any money? I sneaked out in such a hurry last night I didn't bring any."

Peruge missed her stumbling phrase, gestured to his trousers on a chair across the room. "Hip pocket. Wallet." He put his head in his hands. The effort of sitting up had taken a frightening amount of his reserves, and the chest pain and headache left him confused. He realized it was going to require a tremendous will to stand up. Maybe a cold shower would help. He heard Fancy fumbling for the money, couldn't bring himself to look at her. Take it all! Damned bitch!

"I'm taking five dollars," she said. "Is that all right?"

I often pay more, he thought. But she obviously was no regular whore, or she'd have taken more.

"Sure, anything you need."

"Should I bring you coffee or something?" she asked. He really did look sick. She found herself worrying about him.

Peruge swallowed an upsurge of nausea, gestured weakly. "No—I, uh—I'll get something later."

"You're sure?"

"I'm sure."

"All right, then." His appearance worried her, but she reached for the door handle to let herself out. Perhaps he just needed a little more rest. She called cheerfully as she opened the door, "I'll be right back."

"Wait," he said. He dropped his hands from his face, lifted his head with an application of conscious effort.

"Did you change your mind about my bringing you something?" she asked.

"No. I—just—wondered. So we *bred*. Do you expect to have a baby by me?"

"I certainly hope so. I'm right at the top of my fertility." She smiled disarmingly and added, "I'm going to go eat now. I'll be back before you know it. Everybody says I'm a fast eater."

She went out, closing the door briskly behind her.

Fast breeder, too, he thought. Her answer only added to his confusion. What the hell had he run into? A baby? Was this what Carlos had discovered? He had a sudden vision of the dapper Carlos Depeaux held in some subterranean bondage by Fancy and her friends, a continual hyped-up orgy with that mysterious aphrodisiac for as long as it lasted. Or for as long as Carlos lasted. It'd be a continual orgy of *breeding*, babies on an assembly line. Somehow, he could not imagine Carlos in that role. Certainly, he couldn't see Tymiena in it or even Porter. Tymiena had never struck him as the motherly type. And dry-as-dust Porter ran from intimate encounters with women.

Hellstrom was involved in something to do with sex, though, and it was probably dirty as hell.

Peruge rubbed a hand across his forehead. The motel had provided an in-room coffee maker with paper packets of instant brew. He lurched to his feet, found the equipment in the closet alcove beside the bathroom door, heated water, and made two cups. He drank it much too hot. His mouth felt scalded, but it gave him a lift and reduced the throbbing in his head. He could think a bit more clearly now. He put the front door on the chain latch and got out his transceiver.

The second signal burst at the mountains brought contact with Janvert. Peruge's hands were unsteady, but he pulled a chair up to the window, rested the equipment on the sill, and set himself grimly to the task of reporting. They exchanged code-recognition signals and Peruge launched himself into the whole story of his night with Fancy, sparing nothing.

"Eighteen times?" Janvert sounded unbelieving.

"As nearly as I can remember."

"You must've had some time." The beam transceiver failed to mask Janvert's tone of cynical amusement.

"Don't give me any crap," Peruge growled. "She shot me full of something, an aphrodisiac or something, and I was just a big, eager bundle of flesh. See if you can keep this on a professional level, will you? We have to find out what it was that she gave me." He glanced down at the bruise on his arm.

"How do you propose doing that?"

"I'm going up there today. I may brace Hellstrom about it."

"That might not be too wise. Have you checked with HQ?"

"The Chief wants—I've checked!" Christ! It was too difficult to explain that the Chief had ordered direct negotiations. This development couldn't change that. It only added to the things to be introduced in the negotiations.

"You play it cool," Janvert said. "Remember, we've three people missing already."

Did Janvert take him for an idiot, for Christ's sake?

Peruge massaged his right temple. God, his head felt empty, as empty as his body. She'd really drained him.

"How'd this dame get down from the farm?" Janvert asked. "Nightwatch didn't report any car headlights out that way."

"She rode a bicycle, for Christ's sake! Didn't I already tell you that?"

"No, you didn't. Are you sure you're feeling all right?"

"I'm just a little tired."

"That I can understand." There he went with the goddamned humor again! "So she rode a bicycle. You know, that's interesting."

"What's interesting?"

"Carlos was a bicycle nut. The Portland office said he took a bike with him in the van. Remember?"

Peruge glanced back at the bicycle leaning against the wall. He *did* remember now that Shorty mentioned it. A bicycle. Was that possible? By any stretch of good fortune, could that set of flimsy wheels be linked to Depeaux? "Do we have a serial number or anything else to identify Carlos's bicycle?" he asked.

"Maybe. There might even be fingerprints. Where's this bicycle now?"

"Right here in the room with me. I'm bike-sitting while she gets breakfast." He recalled his original resolve, then. Christ Almighty! His mind was going! "Shorty," he barked, some of his old strength returning for a moment, "you get a team down here as soon as you can. Collect this bicycle, yes, but we have to get our hands on Fancy for a long and thorough interrogation."

"That's more like it," Janvert said. "DT is right here listening to us and he's all hot to go."

"No!" DT had to stay there and keep an eye on Janvert. The Chief had been explicit about that. "Send Sampson's team."

"DT is seeing to it. They'll be on their way in just a minute."

"Tell them to hurry, will you? I only know one way of delaying this dame and, after last night, I'm really not up to it."

The words of Nils Hellstrom. I remember my childhood in the Hive as the happiest period, the happiest experience a human could ever enjoy. Nothing I really needed was denied me. I knew that all around me were people who would protect me with their lives. It came to me only gradually that I owed these people the same full measure of payment were it ever demanded of me. What a profound thing the insects have taught us! How different it is from the wild Outside opinions about insects. Hollywood, for instance, has long contended that the mere threat of having an insect crawl on one's face is enough to make a grown man beg for mercy and tell every secret he ever knew. Philosopher Harl, the wisest of his specialty among us, tells me that from childhood nightmares to adult psychosis, the insect is a common horror fixation in the Outsider's mind. How strange it is that Outsiders cannot look beyond the insect's great strength and efficient face to see the lesson embodied there for us all. Lesson one, of course, is that the insect is never afraid to die for his brethren.

"How could they let those—those *Outsiders* get away with that bicycle?" Hellstrom stormed.

He stood almost in the center of Hive Central Security, a chamber deep within the Hive that could tap into and repeat the data collected from any of its internal and external sensors. The room lacked only the positive direct visual backup of the barn aerie to make it the most important security post in the Hive. Hellstrom often preferred this backup post to the aerie. The sense of bustling workers whose activities spread outward all around gave him a feeling of protection that he believed helped his thought processes.

Saldo, who had made the report, shuddered under the combined weight of Hellstrom's wrath and of complex personal knowledge not only of the danger this development brought, but of the judgment error that went directly back to the prime male. Saldo was shaken in his innermost being. If only Hellstrom had heeded the words of warning. If only . . . But it would not be wise to remind Hellstrom of this as yet.

"Our surveillance workers did not know what was happening until it was too late," Saldo explained. "Fancy had emerged earlier and they were lulled into a sense of complacency. A closed truck drove up. Four men went into Peruge's room and two of them emerged with the bicycle. They were driving away before our people could get across the street and try to stop them. We pursued, but they were prepared for that and we were not. Another truck blocked our pursuit and let them get away. They were at the airport and the bicycle was gone before we could catch up."

Hellstrom closed his eyes. His mind felt clotted with foreboding. He opened his eyes and said, "And all this time, Fancy was down the street at the restaurant eating Outsider foods."

"We've always known how she is about that," Saldo said. "It's a defect." He made the vat sign, eyebrows raised questioningly.

"No." Hellstrom shook his head. "Don't be too quick to discount her value to us. Fancy's not yet ready for the vats. Where is she right now?"

"Still at the restaurant."

"I thought I ordered her brought in."

Saldo shrugged.

Of course, Hellstrom thought. The workers were fond of Fancy and many of them knew about her defect. What harm was there in letting her finish a meal of exotic Outsider food? Fondness could be a defect, too. "Have her picked up and brought back immediately," he ordered.

"I should've ordered that myself at once," Saldo

admitted. "No excuse. I was at my station monitoring our communications with town when—no excuse. All I thought of was hurrying down the gallery to you."

"I understand." Hellstrom indicated a communications console ahead of him.

Saldo moved to the station quickly, relayed Hellstrom's order. It felt good to be taking positive action, but his deeper disturbance was not eased. What did Hellstrom mean with his mysterious allusions to Fancy's value? How could she possibly help save the Hive with such behavior? But the older ones often *did* know things denied to the younger. Most of the Hive's workers knew this. It did not seem possible that Fancy was helping, but the possibility could not be denied in the face of Hellstrom's positive assertion.

The words of Nils Hellstrom. There is another respect in which we must guard against becoming too much like the insects upon whom we pattern our design for human survival. The insect has been called a walking digestive tract. This is not without reason. To support his own life, an insect will consume as much as a hundred times his own weight each day—which to each of us would be like eating an entire cow, a herd of thirty each month. And as the insect population grows, each individual naturally needs more. To those who have witnessed the insect's profligate display of appetite, the outcome is clear. If allowed to continue on his reproductive rampage, the insect would defoliate the earth. Thus, with our lesson from the insect, comes a clear warning. If the race for food is to be the deciding conflict, let no one say it came without this warning. From the beginning of time, wild humans have stood helpless, watching the very soil they nurtured give birth to a competitor that could outeat them. Just as we must not let our teacher the insect consume what we require for survival, we must not launch a similar rampage of our own. The pace of our planet's growing cycle cannot be denied. It is possible for insects or for man to destroy in a single week what could have fed millions for an entire year.

"We lifted all of the prints we could enroute and put everything on a chartered plane to Portland," Janvert said over the laser transceiver. "The preliminary report says some of the prints match those of the dame's that we lifted in your room. Have our boys picked her up yet?"

"She got away," Peruge growled.

Clad only in a light robe, he sat in the front of the window, looking out at the morning light on the mountain and trying to keep his mind focused on the report. It was becoming increasingly difficult. His chest ached with a demanding persistence, and every movement took so much energy he wondered each time if there would be any reserves left.

"What happened?" Janvert asked. "Did our team slip up?"

"No. I should've sent them to the café. We saw her come out and head back here, but three men drove up and intercepted her."

"They grabbed her?"

"There was no struggle. Fancy just jumped into the car with them and they drove off. Our people just weren't in place. The delay van that helped us get away with the bike wasn't back yet. Sampson ran out when we saw what was happening, but it all happened too quickly."

"Back at the farm, eh?"

"I'm sure of it," said Peruge.

"Did you get a license number?"

"Too far away, but it makes little difference."

"So she just went along with them?"

"That's how it looked from here. Sampson thought she looked unhappy about it, but she didn't argue."

"Probably unhappy that she couldn't come back and play with you some more," Janvert said.

"Stuff that!" Peruge snapped, then put a hand to his head. His brain felt blocked off, not working at all the way it should. There were so many details, and he could feel things slipping away from him. He really needed to take a cold shower, snap out of this fog, and get ready to return to the farm.

"I've been referring to the files," Janvert said. "This Fancy fits the description of the Fancy Kalotermi who's an officer of Hellstrom's corporation."

"I know, I know," Peruge sighed.

"You feeling all right?" Janvert asked. "You're sounding a little off your feed. Maybe that shot she gave you—"

"I'm okay!"

"You don't sound like it. We don't know what was in that stuff she used to charge you up last night. Maybe you'd better go out for a physical and we send in the second team."

"Meaning you," Peruge growled.

"Why should you have all the fun?" Janvert asked.

"I told you to stuff that! I'm all right. I'll take a shower and get ready to go pretty soon. We have to find out how she did that."

"I want to be the first to know," Janvert quipped.

That fool! Peruge raged, rubbing his head. God, how his head ached—and his chest. He had to go out on a job as touchy as this one, and nothing but that fool up there to back him! It was too late to change that now. Peruge felt his hand tremble against his forehead.

"You still there?" Janvert asked.

Peruge winced at the sound. "I'm here."

"Wouldn't it be a gas if this Project 40 turned out to be an aphrodisiac?"

Shorty was impossible! He was like some perfect antithesis of everything Peruge needed right now. There was no doubt of the malice in Janvert's responses, no doubt of the man's unreliability. What could be done to change that now, though? The teams were scattered all over the area. And he had to be up at that damned farm in a couple of hours. He didn't know how he was going to do that, but it had to be done. For just a moment, he tried to consider whether Janvert's cynical banter might contain a small seed of good sense. What had that shot contained? Christ! If he could get a corner on that, it'd make more than ten

metallurgical processes! Make a fortune under the
counter.

"You're taking an awful long time between answers," Janvert said. "I'm going to send Clovis down
to have a look at you. She's had some nursing experience and—"

"She stays right there with you! That's an order."

"That dame could've done a helluva lot more
than just charge you up as a bed partner," Janvert
argued.

"That's all it was, dammit!" But Shorty's words
carried the seeds of panic. The night with Fancy had
distorted his perceptions of many things, including his
idea of *woman*. The uninhibited little cunt!

"I don't like the way you sound at all," Janvert
said. "Is Sampson still around?"

"I sent him back to you."

"The backup van isn't here yet. What if we—"

"You contact them the way I told you and you
get them up there! You hear me, Shorty?"

"But that would leave you in town alone. They'd
have a team there and we wouldn't."

"They don't dare attack me!"

"I think you're wrong. I think they may already
have attacked you. That town could be completely in
their hands. The deputy sure as hell is!"

"I'm ordering you to stay up there with all of
your teams," Peruge said.

"We could have you at a clinic in Portland within
two hours," Janvert said. "I'm going to call for—"

"I am ordering you not to contact headquarters,"
Peruge said.

"I think you're out of your mind. A clinic might
be able to examine you and tell us what was in that
shot."

"Not likely. Christ! She said it was—a hormone
or something."

"You believe that?"

"It's probably true. Sign off now and do what I
told you." He dropped a hand onto his own cutoff
switch, heard the blip as the transceiver went dead.

Damn! Everything took so damned much energy.

Willing every movement, he put away the transceiver, went into the bathroom. A cold shower. That was what he needed. If he could get fully awake. The bathroom still showed the scattered wetness of Fancy's ablutions. He stepped into the tub, supported himself with a hand on the showerhead while he groped for the faucet. Cold water. He turned it on full. At the first shock of the chilling stream, he felt a sharp band of pain tighten on his forehead and chest. He staggered from the tub, trying to breathe, left the water running. He stumbled from the bathroom, dripping, knocked the remains of his coffee making from the counter as he passed, but didn't even hear it. The bed! He needed the bed. He flopped his wet body on the bed, rolled onto his back. His chest was on fire, his skin trembling with a deep chill. It was so cold! He arched his back, tried to pull the bedding around himself, but his fingers lost their grip and his suddenly outflung hand fell over the edge of the bed. He was dead before his relaxing fingers touched the floor.

The words of Nils Hellstrom. In the sense popularly believed Outside, it is not possible to fight back against any aspect of nature. What must be understood is that we fit ourselves *into* existing patterns, adapting as our influence on those processes brings about inevitable change. The way the wild Outsiders *fight* insects is particularly enlightening. By opposing themselves to a powerful aspect of existing processes, the wild ones unwittingly add fuel to the defenses of those they oppose. The Outsiders' poisons bring instant death to most insects. But the few who survive will develop an immunity—a tolerance to ingest the poison with no harmful effect. Returning to the womb of the earth, these survivors pass on this immunity to new generations of billions.

The Hive was always so neat, efficient, and reas-

suring after the Outside, Fancy thought. She admired
the way her fellow workers moved about their tasks
without fuss, with that quiet, purposeful air of knowing what they did. Even the escort taking her down the
familiar galleries, down the relays of elevators, gave
off this same air. She did not think of her escort as
captors. They were fellow workers. It was good to get
out of the Hive occasionally, but so much better to
come back. Especially with the almost certain knowledge that she had added to the Hive's gene store by
last night's foray. The Hive comforted her mind and
body now just by its presence around her.

Outsiders could be great sport, too; especially the
randy wild males. In her fifty-eight years, Fancy had
brought nine Outsider-fathered babies into the Hive,
each concealed in the mysterious fecundity of her
body. That was a great contribution to the gene pool.
She understood gene pools just as she understood insects. She was a specialist. Outsider males and ants
were her favorites.

Sometimes as she watched an ant colony in the
lab, Fancy felt that there might be a way for her to
move right into the colony with her charges, perhaps
even become their brood mother. It might just require
a period of chemical acclimatization for her charges to
accept her as one of their own. In her fantasy, she
could imagine the escort that now took her deep into
the Hive as her own queen's guard. She would be the
ant queen. And the strange thing was that ants did
tend to accept her. Ants, mosquitoes, many different
kinds of insects showed no disturbance at Fancy's in-
trusions. When she recognized this and had these fantasies, it was easy to imagine the Hive as her own colony.

So firmly had imagination taken hold of Fancy's
consciousness that when the escort brought her into
Hellstrom's presence, she looked upon him at first
with queenly condescension, and she failed to observe
the state he was in.

Hellstrom noted that she still wore the fur coat
she'd taken from wardrobe and she appeared mighty
proud of herself. He nodded to dismiss the guards.

They retreated into the background, but remained alert and observing. Saldo's orders had been explicit about that. Many security workers were growing to recognize that Saldo possessed qualities that demanded obedience. In this room of the Hive's inner security processes, at least half of the workers harbored such divided loyalties.

"Well, Fancy," Hellstrom said, his voice tired but carefully neutral.

There was a desk beside Hellstrom and she perched now on a corner of it, grinning at him.

Hellstrom took the chair behind the desk and sank into it with a feeling of gratitude. He looked up at her. "Fancy, would you try to explain to me what you thought you were doing in last night's escapade?"

"I just spent the night breeding with your dangerous Mr. Peruge," she said. "He was about as dangerous as any other Outsider male I've ever met."

"You took things from Hive stores," Hellstrom said. "Tell me about that."

"Just this coat and a shot of our own male breeding hormones," she said. "I hyped him up."

"Did he respond?"

"Just like always."

"You've done this before?"

"Lots of times," she said. Hellstrom was acting so strangely.

Hellstrom nodded to himself, tried to read another message into Fancy's responses, something to confirm his suspicion that she was acting out of an awareness of the Hive's most fundamental needs. Additions to the gene pool were beneficial, yes; and Peruge's genes would be most welcome. But she had taken a prized Hive secret Outside, risked Outsider discovery that the Hive possessed a profound knowledge of the workings of human hormones. By her present admission, she had done this more than once. If Outsiders learned some of the things the Hive could do in manipulation of human chemistry. . .

"Did you ever discuss this with anyone?" Hellstrom asked. Surely, there must be some circumstance to explain such behavior.

"I've talked about it with lots of the breeder females," she said. What possibly could be bothering old Nils? She saw now that he was working against deep tensions.

"With breeder females," he said.

"Certainly. Lots of us use the hormones when we go Outside."

Shocked, Hellstrom shook his head silently. *Blessed brood mother!* And none of the Hive's ruling specialists had ever once suspected! What other unsuspected things might be going on here in the Hive?

"Peruge's friends have the bicycle," Hellstrom said.

She looked at him, not understanding.

"The bicycle you took when you sneaked into town," Hellstrom explained.

"Ohhh! The workers who picked me up were so insistent they made me forget all about it."

"By taking that bicycle, you've created a crisis," Hellstrom said.

"How could that be?"

"Don't you recall where we got that bicycle?"

She put a hand over her mouth in sudden comprehension. All she'd been thinking about when she'd borrowed the machine was a quick way to get into town. There'd been a certain amount of pride in the action, too. She was one of the few workers who'd learned how to manage a bicycle. She'd demonstrated her ability for the engineers during the preceding week, even taught one of them to ride it. Her ingrained Hive-protective sense was fully aroused now, though. If that bicycle could be traced to the couple they'd thrown into the vats. . .

"What can I do to get it back?" she asked.

This is the Fancy I can work with and admire, Hellstrom thought, responding to her sudden alertness. "I don't know yet," he said.

"Peruge is coming to see you today," she said. "Can I demand that he return it to me?"

"Too late for that. They've sent it away in an airplane. That must mean they suspect."

She nodded. Fingerprints—serial numbers. She knew about such things.

"Our best move may be to deny that we ever had that bicycle," she said.

"No telling who may've seen you on it," Hellstrom said.

And he thought sadly: Our best move may be to deny that Fancy exists. We have others with a close enough resemblance to her face and body. Were her fingerprints likely to be on any of the documents she'd signed as Fancy Kalotermi? Not likely after this length of time.

"I've done wrong, haven't I?" Fancy asked, beginning to grasp the extent of the problem she had created.

"It was wrong for you and other females to take Hive stores Outside. It was wrong to take that bicycle."

"The bicycle—I see that now," she admitted. "But the breeding hypes only insured fertilization."

Even as she spoke, Hive honesty forced Fancy to admit to herself that this didn't explain fully why she and the others used Hive stores this way. It had been an experiment at first, then a delightful discovery of how susceptible Outsider males were. She'd shared the discovery with a few sisters. They'd made up their own stories to explain to Outsider males who became curious. This was a *very expensive* new drug they had stolen. They might not be able to get more of it. Better use it while they had it.

"You must name all of the females who shared your little trick," Hellstrom said.

"Oh, Nils!"

"You must and you know it. All of you will give us detailed accounts concerning the reactions of Outsider males, how curious any of them may have been, who they were, how many times you've raided Hive stores this way—everything."

She nodded dejectedly. It would have to be done, of course. The fun was ended.

"On the basis of our review, we may conduct some experiments Outside, fully controlled and observed," Hellstrom said. "For that reason, be explicitly detailed in your account. Anything you recall could be valuable."

"Yes, Nils." She felt contrite now, but secretly elated. Perhaps the fun wasn't ended. Controlled experiments meant further use of Hive methods on Outsiders. Who better qualified for such a project than those experienced in such tactics?

"Fancy, Fancy," Hellstrom said, shaking his head. "The Hive has never been in greater peril and you continue to play your games."

She clasped her arms around her body, hugging herself.

"Why?" he asked. "Why?"

She remained wordless.

"We could even be forced to send you to the vats," Hellstrom said.

Her eyes went wide in alarm. She slipped off the desk, stood facing Hellstrom. The vats! But she was still young. She had many years of breeding service ahead of her. They needed her talents with the insects, too. Nobody was better than she was with the insects! She began to voice these arguments, but Hellstrom cut her short.

"Fancy! The Hive comes first!"

His words shocked her and she recalled suddenly the thing she had reminded herself to tell Hellstrom. Certainly, the Hive came first! Did he think her a moral reject?

"I have something else to report," she said. "It may be important."

"Oh?"

"The hype hit Peruge very hard. He thought I was asking him questions at one point. I wasn't, but when I recognized what he was doing, I did ask questions. He wasn't fully awake, just reacting. I think he spoke the truth."

"What did he say? Out with it!"

"He said he'd come to make a deal with you. He said their study of the papers they'd found—about Project 40, you understand—led them to believe you were developing a new way to shape metals. Steel, that sort of metal. He said a metallurgical breakthrough could be worth billions. It didn't always make sense, what he said, but that's the gist of it."

Hellstrom felt such elation at her words he wanted to get up and hug her. The Hive *had* been working through her!

Saldo came into the room as these feelings coursed through Hellstrom, and Hellstrom almost called the young male over to explain. Fancy's discovery gave them a way out. It was a commercial invasion! This confirmed his deepest instinct about Hive learning. The lab would have to be told immediately. This might even help them in their own research. The wild Outsiders sometimes came up with rare insights.

"Have I helped?" Fancy asked.

"Indeed you have!"

Saldo, who had stopped for a few words with one of the observers at the banks of instruments, glanced across at Hellstrom and shook his head. Peruge was not yet on his way, then. Saldo had been instructed to give word at the first sign.

Hellstrom wanted Peruge to come now.

Metallurgy! Inventions! All those mysterious allusions now made sense, a remarkable degree of sense.

Fancy still stood at the desk watching Hellstrom.

"Did Peruge say anything else?" Hellstrom asked.

"No." She shook her head.

"Nothing about the agency that sent him, the government agency?"

"Well, he did say something about somebody named Chief. He hates Chief. He cursed horribly."

"You have helped enormously," Hellstrom said, "but you must go into hiding now."

"Hiding?"

"Yes. You've helped in many ways. I don't even mind it any longer that you stole Hive stores. You've reminded us that we share the same body chemistry with Outsiders. We've changed somewhat in three hundred years, of course, because we've bred for that, but—" He gave her a brilliant smile. "Fancy, you must do nothing else now without consulting us."

"I won't. I really won't."

"Very good. Was Mimeca one of the breeder females you shared this little trick with?"

"Yes."

"Excellent. I want you—" He hesitated, taking in her pale face, the expectant expression. "Is there any chance that last night's excapade was successful, that you're impregnated?"

"A very good chance." She brightened. "I'm right at peak fertility. I've become pretty good at judging it."

"See if the gestation lab can confirm that," he said. "If it's positive, your period of hiding should be pleasant enough. If you've been impregnated, turn yourself in at Worker Gestation Prime. Tell them it's at my instructions. Don't go on dormancy, though, until we've sent someone down to interrogate you on your use of the breeding hype with Outsiders."

"I won't, Nils. I'll go down to the lab right away."

She turned, hurried across the chamber, several workers looking up at her passage. She probably still trailed some of the hype. Hellstrom had been too busy to notice. She was really a ridiculous female, he thought. What had they bred in this FANCY line?

Saldo approached Hellstrom's alcove now, glancing back until Fancy left the chamber.

Hellstrom rubbed his chin. He kept himself on hair suppressants during most of his Hive days, but the beard insisted on growing anyway. He needed a shave and would have to get one before meeting Peruge. Appearance was important with Outsiders.

So it was metallurgy and inventions, was it?

As Saldo stopped just inside the alcove, Hellstrom asked absently, "What do you want?"

"I listened while you were talking to Fancy," Saldo said.

"You heard what she said about Peruge?"

"Yes."

"Do you still think you were at fault in letting her out of the Hive?" Hellstrom asked.

"I—" He shrugged.

"It was the Hive working this out in spite of us,"

Hellstrom said. "The whole Hive can react as a single organism or it can react delicately through any one of us. Remember that."

"If you say so," Saldo said. He didn't sound as though he believed it, however.

"I say so. Oh, and when you interrogate Fancy, I want you to be gentle with her."

"Gentle? She endangered the—"

"She did not! She gave us our escape hatch. You will be gentle with her. And with the other females, too, the ones she names."

"Yes, Nils." Saldo felt that these orders · went against reason, but he could not bring himself to outright disobedience of the prime male.

Hellstrom arose, moved around the desk, and headed out of the chamber.

"Will you be in your cell if I need you?" Saldo asked.

"Yes. Have me called the instant Peruge is sighted."

The wisdom of Harl. By the stance you take *against* the universe, it is possible to destroy yourself.

Instead of going directly to his cell, Hellstrom turned left into the main gallery outside the security chamber, turned left again down a side ramp and, at the ramp's end, when a car appeared, he entered the open gap of an express elevator. He jumped out of the moving car at level fifty-one into another wide gallery, but this one showed less activity than the upper chambers and conveyed a deep sense of cushioned stillness even in the activity it did possess. Here, those workers who moved about on supportive tasks went with cat-footed softness and a sense of silent importance.

Hellstrom weaved his way through them and it wasn't until he was actually walking through the widely arched entrance to the Project 40 lab that he began to review what he would tell the specialists.

Outsiders think this is an invention dealing with

*the making and forming of such metals as steel. They
obtained this impression from studying only pages 17
through 41 of Report TRZ-88ₐ. They obviously are
aware of the heat problem from knowing about only
this tiny part of your work.*

That should do it. Brief enough to satisfy the
physical researchers' characteristic impatience with all
interruptions, but containing the essential information
plus his own primary observation.

Hellstrom stopped just inside the doorway of the
cavernous domed lab to await a break in the activities
that would allow his interruption. One did not intrude
here except on the most urgent matters. These specialists were notoriously short-tempered.

Although he was sufficiently accustomed to
working with the Hive's physical researchers not to
react to their strangeness, Hellstrom often thought
about the stir this breed would create if they were
loosed among the wild Outsiders.

There were twenty of them at work on a massive,
tubular object in the brilliantly floodlighted center of
the lab, each researcher attended by a muscular symbiote. These physical researchers were precious to the
Hive and so difficult to bring into being, so difficult to
maintain even then. Their gigantic heads (fifteen inches from a snowy hairline to the bottom of a hairless
chin, eleven inches across the brow above bulging blue
eyes that stood out with a startling glitter in their black
skins) dictated Caesarean birth for each of them. No
female had ever borne more than three, in breeding
further complicated by many natural abortions in early pregnancy. Death of the mother at birth was common with these prized specialists, but the Hive paid
that price willingly. They had proved their worth
countless times and were a major reason the first colonists had ended their centuries of secretive migrations.
These researchers must be concealed from Outsider
eyes at all costs. Their work must be hidden, as well; it
stamped the Hive-born with another kind of strangeness. The stunwand, of which Project 40 was an out-
growth, was only one of their creations. They had giv-
en the Hive's electronic instruments a marked edge in

reliability, subtlety, and power. They had produced the newest refinements in food additives to set the neutered worker into a more secure niche.

The physical researchers were instantly recognizable. In addition to the magnificent braincase, the gene line that produced them carried characteristics that could not be separated from the sought-after specialization and marked them as even further differentiated from the original wild form. Their legs were stunted stumps, and each specialist required the constant attendance of a pale, muscular, chemically neutered worker bred especially for brawn and a pliable disposition. Because of the useless legs, they were moved about on spidery wheeled carts or in the attendants' arms. Although the researchers' arms were not stunted, they were spindly and weak, with hands that bore long, delicate fingers. These specialists were genetically sterile as well, each one a single creation ending in its own flesh. Since their driving need for full intellect meant they could not have their emotions chemically tempered, they tended to a touchy irrascibility in their dealings with all other workers. Even their symbiote attendants came in for such attacks. However, they were gentle and showed a high degree of mutual consideration with their own fellow specialists, a characteristic the Hive had managed to breed into them after a series of conflicts had reduced the usefulness of the first of the breed.

One of the busily working specialists finally stopped and peered across the lab at Hellstrom. The worker signaled in Hive-sign, fingers shaping a "hurry-up" symbol against the tubular construction in a way that, in a flashing instant, said plainly, "Don't delay this." In the same movement of hand and fingers, the specialist pressed the symbol against a dark forehead, saying just as plainly, "Your interruptive presence delays my thinking."

Hellstrom hurried across the room. He recognized the specialist as one of the elders in this breed, a female whose skin bore numerous ropy scars from experiments gone awry. She was attended by a pale, bent-shouldered neuter-male whose arms and torso bulged with muscles. The attendant watched in cowed diffidence as Hellstrom flashed his report in abbreviated Hive-sign.

"What do we care what Outsiders believe?" she demanded.

"They were able to detect the heat problem from just these few pages," Hellstrom signaled.

She spoke aloud then, knowing that voice could convey more of her angry irritation. "You think Outsiders can teach us?"

"We often learn from their mistakes," Hellstrom said, refusing to respond to her anger.

"Be still a moment," she ordered and closed her eyes.

Hellstrom knew those reference pages would be flashing in her mind, the data being correlated with their present work and Peruge's mistaken belief.

Presently, she opened her eyes and said, "Go away."

"Does this help you?" Hellstrom asked.

"It helps," she said. Dragging the admission out in a grudging growl, she added with a return of her former irritability, "Apparently your type can learn an occasional thing of value—when you have a lucky accident!"

Hellstrom managed to restrain a grin until he had turned away and was headed back across the lab. The sound of the work here seemed no different to him as he moved, but when he glanced back from the doorway, he saw several of the specialists clustered into a busily communicative group, their hands darting and flashing in Hive-sign. He caught the symbol for "heat" several times, but most of the other symbols escaped him. The researchers had developed their own language for use among themselves, he knew. They would have this new data all sorted out and introduced into their project in a very short time.

Privately circulated memo to the Agency board. DE-STROY THIS IMMEDIATELY AFTER READING. There is more to the Hellstrom file than we have been shown. They are holding out on us. Our *other* source says the MIT papers contained at least three additional pages. These indicate that Project 40 involves a new and *far cheaper* process of manufacturing and forming steel and that it is not a weapon at all. As I have told you all time and again, I knew this pair would try something like this on their own someday. They are through as of now!

Mimeca Tichenum's report on Outside use of Hive stores. Within a few seconds after injection of our breeder formula, the skin of the Outsider male becomes warm to the touch and somewhat flushed. This is similar to the reaction of Hive males, but more pronounced, also more rapid. The reaction takes no more than five to ten seconds. The dissimilarities then become quite pronounced. The Outsider male sometimes displays an initial muscle rigidity, almost like shock, which holds him virtually immobile until the major breeder transformations have occurred. This is not consistent with all Outsider males. Almost immediately after the skin response and sometimes simultaneously, the male undergoes an extremely rigid erection which is never subdued by a single orgasm. A six-orgasm reaction is not unusual. On one occasion, I noted thirty-one. Concurrently, the male emits a bitter-smelling perspiration that appears to be characteristic in all cases and which I find extremely exciting. It appears to accelerate and heighten the full spectrum of female breeding responses. This bitter smell may represent a hormone in the same class as our XB5 formula which, you will recall, elicits a similar female response, although not as extreme as what I am describing. The smell is particularly noticeable around the male nipples which, in every case I have observed, have become swollen, very tense, and firm. Occasionally, I have noted severe trembling of the male's thigh, neck, and shoulder muscles. This appears to be autonomic and often coincides with grimaces of the face interspersed with what appear to be random head movements, moans, and groans. In general, I would say that those elements of the usual Hive breeding responses, conscious initially among our males, tend with Outsider males to be involuntary when subjects are injected with our male breeding hormones. My personal reaction (in which my sisters concur) is to find these Outsider responses immensely more stimulating than the usual Hive breeding responses.

It was twenty minutes to twelve and for the past half hour Hellstrom had been pacing the farmhouse dining room wondering if his preparations were adequate. The dining room had been decorated originally as a front showpiece, a place to entertain the occasional Outside business contact. Dining room and living room could be seen through a dark wood archway. A long imitation Jacobean table occupied the center of the dining room with ten matching chairs around it. A newly polished glass chandelier glittered over the table. A break-front china cabinet stacked with heavy blue crockery occupied almost all of one wall opposite the arch to the living room. Tall, many-paned bay windows with faded lace curtains drawn back from them opened at the end of the room into a view of willows along the creekbank and bits of brown grass beyond looking hot and dusty in the bright sunlight. A swinging door opened in a corner of the opposite wall, with a tiny glass inset near the top to give glimpses into the kitchen where specially trained workers busily prepared for an Outsider's visit.

Four places had been set at the kitchen end of the table—with the heavy blue ware and bone-handled utensils.

Adequate preparations! Hellstrom sneered at himself. Not superb and sure, but adequate.

The closer to the hour of Peruge's arrival, the more Hellstrom's earlier elation had worn thin and, now, Peruge was late.

Mimeca was helping in the kitchen. From time to time, Hellstrom glimpsed her through the glass inset in the door. She was enough like Fancy to be a gene sister, but Mimeca was from a parallel breeding strain, not the FANCY line. There was something about that dark hair and pale, faintly rosy skin that had linked itself genetically to other characteristics sought by the Hive: high fertility, independence of imagination, drive to succeed, Hive loyalty, intelligence . . .

Hellstrom glanced at the old-fashioned pendulum clock beside the door to the kitchen. A quarter to twelve and still no sign of Peruge. Why would he be late? He'd not been late before. What if he had decided not to come, but to take some other action? Could they already have discovered something incriminating about that damned bicycle? Peruge was perfectly capable of showing up with the FBI. But with Mimeca playing the role of Fancy, they might yet confound the hunters. Fingerprints would not match. She had not been bred recently, and that could be proved by medical examination. He would insist on an Outside medical examination. That would serve the double purpose of getting every one of the intruders away from here.

He heard the outer door to the front hall open.

Could that be Peruge at last?

Hellstrom swiveled, strode through the archway into the living room with all of its early twentieth-century furnishings and carefully maintained musty smells. As quickly as he went, he was only halfway across the living room when a stranger entered two steps ahead of Saldo. The stranger was a diminutive male, an inch or so shorter than Saldo, with wind-blown brown hair and a cautiously reserved manner behind the eyes. There were dark lines around his eyes and deep creases in his forehead. He appeared to be in his early twenties except for the lines, but Hellstrom had sometimes found age difficult to determine with small Outsiders. The stranger wore tan work pants, heavy boots, a white turtleneck shirt of some light fabric that allowed reddish chest hairs to poke through. A brown buckram jacket with slash pockets had been pulled over this. The right-side pocket bulged as though it concealed a gun. Pale yellow grass seeds could be seen sticking in his trouser cuffs.

He stopped short when he saw Hellstrom and barked, "You're Hellstrom?"

Saldo, a pace behind the stranger, flashed a warning signal in Hive-sign.

Hellstrom felt his heartbeat quicken at the demanding, official tone in the man's voice, but before he could respond, Saldo spoke up. "Dr. Hellstrom, this is Mr. Janvert, an associate of Mr. Peruge's. Mr. Janvert parked his car down by the old sawmill turn and walked in across the meadow."

Janvert kept his face grim, his manner probing. Things had moved very rapidly since Peruge's body had been discovered. There had been a necessary call to headquarters and the Chief himself had come on the line as soon as the word was passed. *The Chief himself!* Janvert could not suppress a puffed-up feeling at that conversation. "Mr. Janvert, we are all depending on you. This is the last straw!" *Mr.* Janvert, not Shorty. The Chief's instructions had been brief, explicit, commanding.

Walked in? Hellstrom wondered. Reference to that route across the meadow bothered him. That was the path Depeaux had taken.

Saldo moved up to stand on Janvert's right, again flashed a warning signal, then said, "Mr. Janvert has shocking news. He tells me that Mr. Peruge is dead."

The information momentarily stunned Hellstrom. He tried to assess this, his mind racing. Fancy? No, she'd said nothing about . . . He saw that some response was expected, allowed his surprise to come out naturally. "Dead? But—I was—" Hellstrom gestured toward the dining room, "expecting—I mean, we'd made another date for—what happened? How did he die?"

"We're still trying to find out," Janvert said. "Your deputy tried to prevent us from taking the body, but we got a court order from a federal judge in Salem. Peruge's body is on its way to the University of Oregon Medical School in Portland."

Janvert tried now to assess Hellstrom's response. That had to be genuine surprise—unless he was a consummate actor. He *was* a maker of movies.

"We'll have an autopsy report very soon," Janvert said, as though Hellstrom had not made the logical connection.

Hellstrom pursed his lips. He didn't like the way this Janvert said "*your* deputy." What had Linc done? Were there more mistakes to contend with now?

"If Deputy Kraft interfered, that's regrettable," Hellstrom said, "but that certainly has nothing to do with me. He is not *our* deputy."

"Let's stop the bullshit," Janvert said. "One of your dames spent last night with Peruge and she shot him full of some kind of dope. There was a bruise on his arm as big as a dollar. We're going to find out what that was. We're going to bring in the FBI, the Alcohol Tax people—they deal with narcotics crimes, you know—and we're going to open your farm up like a can of rotten worms!"

"Just a minute now!" Hellstrom said, trying to suppress his panic. Open up the farm! "What's this about someone spending the night with Mr. Peruge? Narcotics? What're you saying?"

"A hot little doll from your outfit by the name of Fancy," Janvert said. "Fancy Kalotermi, I think her full name is. She spent last night with Peruge and she shot him full of—"

"This is nonsense!" Hellstrom interrupted. "Are you saying one of—Fancy? That she had some sort of sexual liaison with Mr. Peruge?"

"Did she ever! Peruge told me the whole story. She shot him full of dope and we're betting that's what killed him. We're going to question your Miss Kalotermi and the rest of your people. We're going to get to the bottom of this."

Saldo cleared his throat, trying to distract Janvert, to give Hellstrom time to think. These words pointed in profoundly disturbing directions. Saldo felt all of his Hive defense reactions coming to full-alarm state. He had to restrain himself consciously from launching a physical attack on Janvert.

Janvert spared only a glance for Saldo. "You got something to add?"

Before Saldo could respond, Hellstrom said, "Who is this *we* you keep referring to, Mr. Janvert? I

confess I don't understand at all. I'd taken a liking to
Mr. Peruge and he—"

"Don't spare any of your *liking* for me," Janvert
said. "I don't go for the way you like people. As for
your question, that has a simple answer. The FBI will
be here presently and Alcohol Tax officers. If we think
of any others who want to share in this investigation,
we'll invite them."

"But *you* have no official standing, Mr. Janvert,
is that right?" Hellstrom asked.

Janvert took a moment to reassess Hellstrom.
There had been an edge to that question he did not
like, and he moved unconsciously a pace away from
Saldo.

"Is that correct?" Hellstrom insisted.

Janvert set his jaw belligerently. "You'd better be
damn careful about *my* official standing, Hellstrom.
Your Miss Kalotermi rode a bicycle to Peruge's motel.
That bicycle was the property of one Carlos Depeaux, another of our people we suspect you took a
liking to."

Stalling for time to think about this, Hellstrom
said, "You're going too fast for me. Who is this—oh,
yes, the employee Mr. Peruge was seeking. I don't understand about a bicycle, but—are you trying to tell
me you also work for this fireworks company, Mr.
Janvert?"

"You're going to see more than fireworks around
here in a bit," Janvert said. "Where is Miss Kalotermi?"

Hellstrom's mind was turning over possible responses at top speed. His first reaction was to be
thankful he'd had the foresight to get Fancy out of
sight and to substitute Mimeca. The very worst had
happened. They'd traced that damned bicycle! Still
stalling for time, he said, "I'm afraid I don't know exactly where Miss—"

Mimeca took this moment to step through the
arch from the dining room. The kitchen door could be
heard slapping closed behind her. She had not seen
Peruge before and assumed Janvert was the luncheon
guest.

"There you are," she said. "Lunch is getting cold."

"Well, here she is now," Hellstrom said, flashing a signal for Mimeca to be silent. "Fancy, this is Mr. Janvert. He has brought us sorrowful news. Mr. Peruge is dead under circumstances that sound rather mysterious."

"How awful!" she said, responding to another signal from Hellstrom to speak up.

Hellstrom looked at Janvert, wondering if the substitution would be accepted. Mimeca fitted Fancy's description very closely. Even their voices were similar.

Janvert glared at her and demanded, "Where the hell did you get that bicycle? What kind of dope did you use to kill Peruge?"

Mimeca put a hand to her mouth, startled. The anger mixed with fear that she could actually smell on Janvert, the sharp voice and unexpected questions, all of this confused her.

"Just a minute here!" Hellstrom signaled in Hive-sign to be silent and follow his lead. He faced her squarely, a stern look on his face, and spoke like a demanding parent. "Fancy, I want you to tell me the truth. Did you spend last night with Mr. Peruge at his motel?"

"With—" She shook her head dumbly from side to side. Hellstrom's alarm was a palpable thing and she could see Saldo actually trembling. Nils had said to tell the truth, though, and he reinforced this with a command in Hive-sign.

The silence in the room remained deep and charged while she framed her answer.

"I—of course not!" she said. "You both know that. I was here in the—" She broke off, throat suddenly dry. She'd almost said *Hive*. The extreme tensions in this room carried a deeply disturbing current. She had to get herself under better control.

"She was here in the house last night," Saldo said. "I saw her myself."

"So that's the way you're going to play it," Janvert sneered. He stared at the woman, sensed a deeper disturbance under her mask of confusion, confirming everything Peruge had said before dying. She had been down there at the motel. She had killed him and probably on orders from Hellstrom. It might be one hell of a job proving it, though. They had only Peruge's account and description of the woman. That was a touchy situation.

"There's going to be more law swarming over this place in a couple of hours than you've ever seen," Janvert growled. "They are going to pick her up for questioning." He pointed to Mimeca. "Don't try to hide her or sneak her away. Her fingerprints were all over that bicycle and all over Peruge's room. She's going to have some mighty interesting questions to answer."

"That may be so," Hellstrom said, his voice firming as he saw his preparations providing them with the escape route he'd anticipated. Mimeca's fingerprints were all over *nothing*. "But you, I take it, Mr. Janvert, are not the law. Until the law—"

"I told you to can that bullshit," Janvert said.

"I can understand why you're upset," Hellstrom said, "but I do not care for your tone or your attitude, or for your choice of language in front of this young woman. I am going to have to ask you—"

"What're you trying to pull off?" Janvert demanded. "Choice of language in front of this young woman! She was bedded with Peruge last night and she knew more fucking tricks than he'd ever heard of. Choice of *words!*"

"That's quite enough!" Hellstrom said. He signaled frantically for Mimeca to leave in a huff, but she was too intent on Janvert to notice. And Hellstrom had told her to fight this with her own personal truth.

"Bedded?" she demanded. "I don't even know your Mr. Peruge."

"That won't work, sister," Janvert said. "I promise you, it won't work."

"You don't have to answer any more of his questions, Fancy," Hellstrom said.

She glanced at Hellstrom, assembling her own estimate of the situation. Peruge dead! What had Fancy done?

"That's right," Janvert said. "Shut her up until you get your stories straight. But I promise you, it won't work. The physical evidence—"

"Indeed," Hellstrom interrupted. "The physical evidence." He sighed with elaborate sadness. It was going perfectly. He faced Mimeca. "Fancy, my dear, you don't have to say another thing until the officials get here, if they do indeed choose to come here for such an outrageous—"

"Oh, they'll come," Janvert said. "And when they do, I expect some *very* interesting answers based on the physical evidence."

Saldo, still trying to suppress his Hive-protection conditioning, gestured to catch Hellstrom's attention and said, "Nils! Should I put him off the place?"

"That won't be necessary," Hellstrom said, gesturing for Saldo to control himself. Saldo obviously was in no condition to risk physical contact with Janvert. There'd be another killing.

"You're damned right it won't be necessary," Janvert said. He put a hand in the bulging pocket of his jacket and moved another two paces away from Saldo. "Don't even try it, baby, or I'll fix you permanently."

"Here! Here!" Hellstrom snapped. "That's quite enough of that!" He looked squarely at Saldo. "What you can do, Saldo, is try to get a call through to Deputy Kraft. If what Mr. Janvert says is true, I don't understand why Kraft is not here already. See if you can contact him and ask him to—"

"Kraft is very busy on a telephone call from his Lakeview office," Janvert said. "Your tame deputy is occupied, understand? Nobody is going to come here and rescue you or interfere in any way before the arrival of the FBI."

Hellstrom saw a tight smile appear on Janvert's face, realized abruptly that the Outsider was playing some kind of calculated game. Hellstrom frowned, wondering if Janvert might actually possess police authority. Was it possible he was trying to provoke an incident that would allow him to take charge here until the others arrived? There were many things that had to be done to protect the Hive before the arrival of Outsider police. Would Janvert try to stop anyone from leaving this room?

"Saldo," Hellstrom said, "as lamentable as this situation is, we still have deadlines to meet, work to do. Delays are costly." Hellstrom signaled for Saldo to leave, get about sealing up the Hive for an all-out investigation. "I suggest you get about that work," Hellstrom said. "We'll wait here with—"

"Nobody leaves!" Janvert snapped. He took another step away from Saldo, hand menacing in the jacket pocket. What did these hicks think they were doing? "This is a murder investigation! If you think you can cover—"

"I think if it turns out to be anything at all, it will be considerably less than murder," Hellstrom said. He signaled urgently for Saldo to leave. "I know for a fact that Fancy did not leave the farm last night. Meanwhile, Mr. Saldo is vitally important to the film we're making. That film represents an investment of several hundred thousand dollars already and it's due in Hollywood in little more than a month. He obviously has taken time off from his work to greet you and escort you to—"

"I was taking a walk to settle my dinner after the lunch break," Saldo said, picking up his cue. He glanced at his wristwatch. "My God! I'm late! Ed will be clawing the wall!" He whirled, strode briskly toward the hall and the outer door.

"Just a minute, you!" Janvert shouted.

Saldo ignored him. Hellstrom's command in Hive-sign had been explicit and brooked no disobedience. Janvert obviously carried a weapon, but the situation was desperate. Would he use it? Saldo felt his back muscles crawl, but he continued unswerving toward the door. The Hive required this of him.

"I'm telling you to stop or else!" Janvert yelled. He moved through the archway into the hall, trying to keep his attention on Saldo's retreating back and on the pair in the living room. Saldo had the door open!

Janvert's hand was slippery with sweat on the gun in his pocket. Did he dare shoot? Saldo was going out!

The door closed.

"Mr. Janvert," Hellstrom said.

Janvert turned, glared at Hellstrom. The bastards!

"Mr. Janvert," Hellstrom repeated, his tone reasonable, "as lamentable as this situation is, I would appreciate our not adding to its complications. We were expecting Mr. Peruge for luncheon and it would be a shame to waste that food. I'm sure all of our tempers would improve if we—"

"You think I'd eat anything here?" Janvert asked. Was Hellstrom really that naive?"

Hellstrom shrugged. "Apparently we must wait for the *law* to arrive, and you do not want Fancy or me to leave your presence. I am proposing a reasonable solution to the waiting period. I'm sure there's a simple answer to these disturbing matters and I am only trying to—"

"Sure you are!" Janvert sneered. "And you *like* me!"

"No, Mr. Janvert, I don't particularly care for you. And I'm sure Fancy shares my aversion. My concern simply goes to—"

"Will you knock off the innocent act!"

Janvert felt himself seething with rage and frustration. He should not have let that other character get out of here. He should've shot at the guy's legs, brought him down.

"If you're worried about our food, Mr. Janvert," Mimeca said, "I'd be only too happy to taste everything before you eat it." She glanced worriedly at Hellstrom. Nils had said he counted on the visitor eating their food. This was a different visitor; did that still hold?

"Taste my—" Janvert shook his head. These characters were incredible! How could they continue with this innocent pose when they *knew* he had them cold?

Mimeca glanced at Hellstrom, seeking a sign of what course to take.

"She's only trying to make you comfortable," Hellstrom explained, and, using Hive-sign, he told Mimeca, "Get him to eat with us!" He watched Janvert carefully. That had been close with Saldo. Janvert had almost used the weapon in his pocket. Were the men of this agency really that desperate?

"We've already had our sample of how Miss Fancy makes men comfortable," Janvert said. "Thanks, but no thanks."

"Well, *I* am going to eat my lunch," Hellstrom said. "You may join us or not as you prefer." He crossed to Mimeca, took her arm. "Come along, my dear. We've done our best."

Janvert had no choice except to follow them into the dining room. He noted the four places at the table and wondered who the fourth place signified? Kraft? Saldo?

Hellstrom seated Mimeca with her back to the china cabinet, took the chair at the head of the table with his back to the kitchen door. He indicated the chair opposite Mimeca for Janvert. "At least, you can sit down with us."

Janvert ignored the invitation, strode deliberately around the table, and took the chair beside Mimeca.

"Wherever you wish," Hellstrom said.

Janvert glanced at the woman. She sat with hands folded in her lap, looking down at her plate almost in an attitude of prayer. Look as innocent as you want, honey! Janvert thought. We have you right where we want you. And if *you* try to sneak off the way your friend did, I will really shoot. We'll worry about consequences later. I might not even aim for your legs.

"We're having baked pork chops," Hellstrom said. "Are you sure I can't order a serving for you?"

"Not on your sweet life or mine," Janvert said. "Especially mine." He glanced up alertly, tension appearing in his gun arm, as the kitchen door creaked open. An older, gray-haired woman with dark olive skin and startlingly bright blue eyes came through the door. She had a heavily wrinkled face which creased into a smile as she peered questioningly at Hellstrom.

Janvert jerked his attention to Hellstrom, caught a
strange flicker-fingered gesture, obviously directed at
the older woman. At the same time, a message-loaded
look passed between Hellstrom and the younger woman seated beside him.

"What're you doing there?" Janvert demanded.

Hellstrom noted Janvert's attention on the hand
signal, looked up at the ceiling with a weary expression. Janvert was going to be very difficult unless they
got him to eat. There were so many things that needed
doing and Saldo was too young to be trusted with all
of them. He had older advisers to consult, but there
was a headstrong character developing in Saldo that
Hellstrom knew he had to curb. Saldo might not consult the backup brains in the Hive.

"I asked you a question," Janvert pressed, leaning toward Hellstrom.

"I was trying to enlist my associates in helping
me to calm you down and get you to join us for luncheon," Hellstrom said, his voice weary. Would Janvert
buy that?

"Fat chance!" Janvert said. He looked back at
the older woman. She still stood expectantly behind
Hellstrom, one hand holding the kitchen door open.
Why didn't the old bitch say something? Was she just
going to wait there until someone told her what to do?
Apparently, that was just what she was going to do.

A long silence dragged out while the old tableau
continued.

Have I judged him correctly? Hellstrom wondered. Should I signal for the serving to go ahead as
ordered?

What the hell are they waiting for? Janvert wondered. He recalled Peruge's reference to "silent wom-
en." The excuse had been that they were studying a
difficult accent. The old bitch did not look like an ac-
tress, though. Her eyes remained bright and alert, but
there was pure patience in the set of her shoulders, the
way she held the swinging door open.

We must risk it, Hellstrom thought.

He broke the silence then. "Mrs. Niles, would
you bring us two servings, please, just for Fancy and

me. Mr. Janvert is not eating." At the same time, masking the action by scratching his head, Hellstrom signaled for her to proceed. The words would be non-sense sounds to Mrs. Niles, who was a nonfertile worker trained specially for this job. She read his hand signs, however, nodded, and retreated into the kitchen.

Janvert grew aware of appetizing smells from the kitchen and began to wonder if he'd acted foolishly. Would these people dare try to poison him here? They were weirdos, certainly, but . . . Yes, they might try to poison him. The elaborate setup confused him, though. Hellstrom surely must've known about Pe-ruge's death. Who else could've ordered that? Who had they been expecting for this meal, then? Knowl-edge of Peruge's death could mean they'd prepared this luncheon as an elaborate sham. That might mean they'd prepared nothing but straightforward, whole-some food. God! That smelled good in the kitchen. He loved pork chops.

Hellstrom was staring calmly out the window at the other end of the table, his manner casual, uncon-cerned. "You know, Fancy, I always like it when we eat here. We should do this more often, instead of grabbing a quick lunch on the set."

"Or missing lunch entirely," she said. "Oh, I've noticed how you do sometimes."

He patted his stomach. "Doesn't hurt to miss an occasional meal. I tend to fat, anyway."

"I'm going to remind you about this," she said. "You're going to ruin your stomach if you go on the way you've been."

"We *have* been busy," Hellstrom said.

They were nuts! Janvert thought. Chatting, small talk at a time like this!

Mrs. Niles backed through the swinging door, turned to reveal a plate in each hand. She hesitated a moment beside Hellstrom, then served the young woman first. When both plates were on the table, Hellstrom signaled for her to bring the drinks. He had ordered vat beer. They made a limited amount of it as a reward for superior work and as a mask to convey some of the adjustment chemicals occasionally required for reject specialists who were being sent back to dronedom.

Janvert glanced at the plate in front of the woman beside him. There was steam rising from it. The pork had been covered with gravy in which large mushrooms could be seen. There was spinach and baked potato beside the meat course and a stiff, white serving of sour cream had been spooned onto the potato. The young woman just sat there, though, hands still folded, eyes downcast. Was she praying, for Christ's sake?

Hellstrom startled him then by placing both hands folded together over his own plate and intoning, "Dear Lord, for this food we are about to eat we give our true and heartfelt thanks. May thy divine grace visit us in this sharing of the substance of life. Amen."

The young woman joined him in the *amen*.

The wealth of feeling in Hellstrom's voice confused Janvert. And this dame, the way she joined him at the end. They must do this regularly. The ritual shook Janvert more than he liked to admit, even to himself, and he responded with anger. More of their damned acting!

The aroma from the plate beside Janvert added to his angry frustration. She was reaching for her fork, too. They were going right ahead with the damned meal!

"Are you sure we cannot serve you anything?" Hellstrom asked.

In sudden angry glee, Janvert reached past the young woman, took Hellstrom's own plate, and said, "Certainly. Glad you asked." He placed the plate triumphantly in front of him, taking special delight in the way the captured dish clinked against the service plate. And he thought: There won't be anything wrong with the food Hellstrom was going to eat!

Hellstrom threw his head back and laughed, unable to restrain himself. He felt that the Hive suddenly had come into a new vitality, expressed in his own person and helping him do battle. Janvert had behaved exactly as he'd hoped.

Smiling, Mimeca peered up through her lashes at

Hellstrom. Janvert *was* predictable, but then Outsiders often were. He had behaved precisely as Hellstrom had said he would. She had to confess to herself that she'd harbored doubts when Hellstrom had flashed the plan in Hive-sign. Janvert had the *loaded* serving in front of him, though, and was picking up knife and fork to eat it. He'd be docile enough pretty soon.

Hellstrom wiped laughter tears from his eyes with a corner of his napkin, called out to the kitchen door, "Mrs. Niles! Bring another serving."

The door opened and the older woman peered around its edge.

Hellstrom pointed to the empty place in front of him, signaling for another serving. She nodded, ducked into the kitchen, and reappeared almost immediately with another heaping plate. Probably her own, Hellstrom thought. He hoped there was more. The neutered workers had such enjoyment from an occasional break in the common fare of vat gruel. Idly, he wondered where these chops had come from—probably that young worker who'd been killed in the generator room last night. They looked tender. And he thought as he picked up his knife and fork: Bless this one who joins the eternal flow of life, becoming part of all.

The meat was not only tender, it was juicy, and Janvert displayed obvious relish.

"Eat hearty," Hellstrom said, gesturing with a fork. "We serve nothing but the very finest food here and Mrs. Niles is a superb cook."

She was, too, Hellstrom reminded himself as he took another savory bite. He hoped again that she had saved at least one serving for herself. She deserved a reward.

The words of Trova Hellstrom. The model of the Hive's insertion into those patterns of other life around us is that of the tesseract, a cube projected into four dimensions. Our tesseract is built of mosaic parts that cannot be detached, whose boundaries blend one into another with indissoluble flow. Thus, the model gives us a habitat and a timeline remarkably self-contained, but merging into the larger system of the planet and the universe beyond. Remember always that our tesseract merges with other systems, and it does this in such diverse and complex ways that we cannot remain concealed indefinitely. We consider the physical dimensions of our Hive as a habitat only for a particular stage of our development. We will outgrow this stage. It is of the utmost concern for the managing specialists of the Hive, therefore, that we not restrict our genetic lines of adaptability. We are aimed at other times as well as other habitats.

"That sounded like an interesting conversation, what I could hear on this end," Clovis Carr said.

Lincoln Kraft stared at her across his big flattop desk. He could see a corner of Steens Mountain out the window behind her head. The sounds of afternoon shopping were just beginning to pick up in the big commercial complex one floor down. There was a poster on the wall to his left giving detailed recommendations on how to prevent rustling. Random patrol of fences was the third item down, and his gaze kept returning to that number, seeking some magic in it. It was almost 3:00 P.M. He had received three telephone calls from the office in Lakeview thus far and each time had been told to "sit tight."

Clovis Carr squirmed her tiny, wiry body into a more comfortable position on the hard wooden seat of her chair. Her deceptively young face tended to set into harsh aging lines when she relaxed. She had been with Kraft since shortly before 11:00 A.M., first at the motel where Peruge's death had been reported by a tough-looking runt of a man who had identified himself to Kraft only as "Janvert." Kraft had understood almost immediately that Janvert and this Clovis Carr were associates, and the pieces had begun to fall into place from there. The pair belonged to Peruge's team. Kraft had played it very carefully from that point, for Hellstrom's suspicions about the recent intruders were well known to everyone associated with Hive security.

These two suspected him, Kraft soon realized. This female stuck to him like a burr on a bear.

The third call from Sheriff Lapham at the courthouse in Lakeview had been part of a pattern that had Kraft more nervous than he'd been since the summer the Hive had picked up a runaway toddler and an entire family had fanned out over the range around the farm hunting the lost child. That one had been turned off by a quickly hatched story that a child of the exact description had been seen being picked up by a couple in an old car only a block away from the place where the toddler had been last seen.

Lopham's orders in this last call had been explicit. "You wait in your office until the FBI gets there, you hear, Linc? This is a job for very delicate professional handling. Take my word on it."

Kraft had been at a loss how to respond to this. He could act professionally insulted (and leave a political scar that the sheriff would never forget); he could obey like an obedient public servant; he could act the dumb, western hick for this dame; or he could appear to be knowledgeable and sophisticated. He didn't know which response would give him the best leverage to probe and seek any clue to help the Hive. One way, they might mistakenly underestimate him, although he rather doubted this was possible now. Another way, he might gain valuable insights by what they did not do.

Such as not leaving him alone.

Kraft's long conditioning to protect the Hive at all costs left him irritated and frustrated, all of his fears sharpened by the sense of danger; but the need to maintain his cover dominated every response that occurred to him. In the end, he did nothing except obey Sheriff Lapham—that and sit here like a lump waiting for the FBI.

The Carr female annoyed him. As long as she stayed there, watching, listening, he could not call Hellstrom. She knew he was nervous, too, and seemed to enjoy it. As though he couldn't see how phony she was! Vacationer? That one?

Her skin was badly sunburned, and there was a

hard and direct stare from cold gray eyes, a firm jaw, and a thin, unsmiling mouth. He suspected she was carrying a pistol in that big black canvas handbag in her lap. There was something about her faintly reminiscent of the models on TV commercials: a controlled and purposeful way of moving, a remoteness that no amount of surface glibness could conceal. She was one of those tiny women who would be skinny and energetic until the day they died. She was all fitted out for her western vacation: dungaree slacks, matching blouse, and brass-button jacket. The clothes still had a sheen of newness about them and looked as though they'd been picked by a wardrobe mistress according to a script adviser's list. They didn't suit her style. The blue bandanna over her long dark hair was the final unlikely touch. Her left hand held that black canvas purse in the casual-but-ready manner of a policewoman. Every time he looked at the purse, Kraft felt more certain she carried a gun in it. Although she had avoided showing Kraft her credentials, Sheriff Lapham had known her name on that first call and he'd treated her with the kind of deference that spoke of official clout, highly potent clout at that.

"That was the sheriff again wasn't it?" she asked, nodding at the telephone on Kraft's desk.

Her voice carried unconcealed scorn, Clovis knew but she had decided not to worry about that. She did not like this thick-nosed, beetle-browed deputy and it was a dislike that went deeper than her suspicions about his involvement in the deaths of her fellow agents. He was western and he showed an evident liking for outdoor life. Those two items alone would have done it. She preferred the nightclub circuit, just as Eddie Janvert did, and this was a damned hick assignment. The skin of her cheeks and nose felt tight and painful from sunburn, adding to her irritation.

"It was the sheriff," Kraft admitted. Why deny it? His answers had signaled the questions and those questions could have originated only with the sheriff: "No, sir; the FBI hasn't shown up yet. . . . Yes, sir; I haven't been out of this here office."

Clovis Carr sniffed. "What've they found out

about Peruge's murder? Anything on the autopsy yet?"

Kraft studied her a moment. There had been one closing item from the sheriff that had to be weighed carefully. When the FBI team arrived, the sheriff wanted Kraft to relay a message to the man in charge. The message sounded simple enough. The U.S. attorney still was not ready to deliver a firm opinion "on the legal basis for intervention." Kraft was to tell the FBI, however, that the agents could proceed on the "presumptive assumption" that Hellstrom's activities in interstate commerce would provide such a basis. According to the sheriff, the FBI team was due at Fosterville any minute and the sheriff wanted to know about it the minute they arrived. Rented cars had been sent to the airport and "Janvert's people" were there to give a briefing.

As the sheriff had given this message, Kraft had written "presumptive assumption" on the notepad beside the telephone. He wondered now if it would lull suspicions if he shared the message with the Carr female. He knew he would have to deliver the message intact to the FBI, but that was another matter. Could any advantage be gained from it now?

"They haven't reported on the autopsy yet," Kraft said.

"You wrote 'presumptive assumption' on your notepad," she said. "Is that about the U.S. attorney's opinion?"

Kraft came to a negative decision about Carr. "I'd better let the FBI discuss that with you. Say, you never did tell me what your connection with this is."

"No, I didn't, did I," she said. "You're a very careful man, Mr. Kraft, aren't you?"

He nodded. "Yes." What did that mean?

A malicious smile twitched the corners of her mouth. "And you don't like to be kept on the bench here."

"I don't like it," he agreed. He wondered at her almost open hostility to him. Was it calculated provocation, or did it reflect something even more disastrous —a high-up decision to distrust the local deputy? He guessed it was distrust of him and wondered how to deal with it. Hellstrom and the Security Council had discussed with him contingency plans for such problems, but no plan had assumed a situation as complex as this one.

Clovis glanced over her shoulder out the window behind her chair. The office was hot and the hard wooden seat of the chair irritated her. She longed for an iced drink and a cool, shadowy lounge bar with soft chairs, Janvert beside her, warm and admiring. For a week now, she'd been playing the part of Janvert's sister on this stupid western vacation. That mask had come off with the discovery of Peruge's death. The cover relationship had been touchy at times. Janvert had not gone out of his way to keep things smooth with Nick Myerlie, who'd fronted as their father. And there'd been DT poking his nose in every time they'd turned around. Spying for the brass, no doubt of it. DT was so damned obvious it was ridiculous. Tight quarters in the damned van and an investigation whose pattern none of them liked had worn on them. There were times when they had chosen not to speak rather than risk a fight. All of that stored-up temper was coming out in her now, with Kraft as its focus. She realized this, but didn't care to suppress it.

The cars of housewives doing their afternoon shopping were beginning to fill the parking lot below the window. Clovis scanned the cars, hoping to see the FBI team emerge from one of them. Nothing. She returned her attention to Kraft.

I could tell this stupid deputy that we're prepared to put him six feet under in the most direct and sanitary way, she thought. It was a fantasy game she liked to play about people she disliked. Kraft would be shocked and alarmed, of course. He already showed signs of the twitches. Nobody was going to blast this son of a bitch, of course. Hardly likely. But Kraft was in trouble. The Chief had pulled strings in Washington which had reached out through the state capital to the sheriff in Lakeview. It was like a marionette system. Potent federal power was breathing down Kraft's collar and he could feel it. He still wanted to see her identification, but he hadn't asked straight out to see it in more than an hour. Lucky, too; she had only her cover identification. That said she was Clovis Myerlie and she'd already been introduced as Clovis Carr.

"This has been a very unusual way to handle a missing-persons case," she said, swinging around to stare at the poster on the side wall. Cattle rustling, yet, and how to prevent same!

"An even more unusual way to handle an unexplained death in a motel," Kraft said.

"Murder case," she corrected him.

"I haven't seen that tied down yet," he said.

"You will."

He kept his gaze on Carr's sunburned face. They both knew that nothing about this case was usual. The sheriff's words still rankled in Kraft's memory. "Linc, we are just the country cousins in this case as of now. The governor himself is in the act. This is not routine, got that? Not routine. We will straighten this out between us later, but right now, I want you to lie doggo and let the FBI run the whole show. They can fight it out with the Alcohol Tax boys on who has jurisdiction, but our jurisdiction stops at the edge of the governor's desk, got me? Don't tell me we have rights and responsibilities. I know 'em as well as you do. Neither of us is going to mention them. Is that all clear?"

It had been very clear.

"Where'd you get that sunburn?" Kraft asked, staring at Carr's face.

Sitting out in your goddamned western sunshine with a pair of binoculars, you son of a bitch! she thought. You know where I got it. But she shrugged and kept her voice nonchalant. "Oh, just hiking around your lovely countryside."

Hiking around the Hive, Kraft thought with a pang of deep disquiet. He said, "None of this might've happened if your Mr. Peruge had gone through normal channels. He should've gone to the sheriff over in Lakeview first instead of coming to me or even to the state people. Sheriff Lapham's a good—"

"A good politician," she interrupted. "We thought we'd rather deal directly with someone who enjoyed a closer relationship with Dr. Hellstrom."

Kraft licked his lips, his mouth suddenly dry. He held himself watchfully alert for any more revelations that touched on their suspicions. He didn't like the way Carr cocked her head to one side to return his gaze.

"I don't understand," he said. "What've I to—"

"You understand," she said.

"Damned if I do!"

"And damned if you don't," she said.

Kraft felt himself caught by the unleashed power behind her hostility. She was deliberately trying to provoke him. She really didn't care how she treated him. He blurted, "Oh, I know what you are, all right. You're from one of those secret government agencies. CIA, I'll bet. You think you own the—"

"Thanks for the promotion," she said, but she bent a more watchful gaze upon him. The conversation had taken an awkward turn that she did not like at all. Eddie had said the Chief wanted them to press the deputy, but not to frighten him off.

Kraft fidgeted in his chair. A painful silence settled over the room, deep and charged. He started casting around for excuses to get away to a telephone. He could excuse himself to go to the toilet, but this female would make sure he went to the toilet and there was no telephone there. The desire to call Hellstrom was losing its appeal, too. It could be very dangerous to call. Every line to the farm might carry a tap by now. What had caused them to link him with Hellstrom? There'd been those times he'd been taken sick on Octsider foods and been nursed back to health at the Hive. The cover was that he'd been a great good friend of old Trova (true), but she was long dead and in the vats. Why should that make these government people suspicious?

His mind went on this way for a time, following the trail of its own fears, worrying out bits of the past to wonder about. Was *that* suspicious, or what about *this* event, or the time he'd . . . It was a useless occupation and it made his palms sweaty.

The ringing of the telephone startled him out of

his nervous reverie. He grabbed for the phone, knocked it from its cradle, had to recover it from a dangling position beside the desk. The voice on the line was anxious and loud when he got the receiver to his ear. "Hello? Hello?"

"This is Deputy Kraft," he said.

"Is Clovis Carr there? They said she'd be there."

"She's here. Who is this?"

"Just put her on the line."

"This is an official phone and I'd—"

"Goddamn it, this is an official call! You put her on this line!"

"Yes, well—"

"Do it now!" There was no mistaking the long history of expected obedience behind that barked command. Kraft felt the power in the voice.

He handed the phone across the desk to Carr. "It's for you."

She took the phone with a puzzled frown, spoke into it. "Yes?"

"Clovis?"

She recognized that voice: the Chief himself! For the love of all that was holy, the Chief calling here!

"Clovis here," she said, her mouth dry.

"Do you know who this is?"

"Yes."

"I have you identified from a voiceprint being played this instant. I want you to listen very carefully and do exactly what I tell you to do."

"Yes, sir. What is it?" Something in the tone told her it was big trouble.

"Can that deputy hear this?" the Chief asked.

"I doubt it."

"We'll have to chance it. Now get this: that light aircraft with the FBI men and the Alcohol Tax team crashed somewhere in the Sisters. That's a mountain north of you. All dead. It could have been an accident, but we are acting on the assumption that it was not. I've just been on to the director, and he is taking that same position, especially in view of what I could tell him about the situation. A new FBI team is on its way from Seattle, but it will be sometime before they arrive."

She gulped, glanced worriedly at Kraft. The deputy was leaning back, hands behind his head, staring at the ceiling.

"What do you want me to do?" she asked.

"I've been in radio contact with the other members of your team, all except Janvert. Is he still at the farm?"

"As far as I know, sir."

"All right; no help for that. It might even be a plus. The others are coming down from the mountain to pick you up. You are to take the deputy with you. Use force if necessary. Take him with you, got that?"

"I've got it." Her exploring fingers felt the outline of the revolver in her purse. She slipped her hand into the bag, took a firm grip on the gun. Involuntarily, her glance went to the big pistol in a holster at Kraft's waist. The son of a bitch probably called that thing a hog leg.

"I've instructed DT on what I want done," the Chief said. "You are to move onto that farm and take over there, subdue any opposition. The director concurs. Responsibility will be ours, however. We have been promised extraordinary cooperation by the FBI. Do you understand?"

"I understand."

"I hope you do. You are not to take chances. You are to kill that deputy if he interferes. And anyone else who tries to block you. We will work out a sufficient justification later. I want that farm in our hands within the hour."

"Yes, sir. Is DT to be in charge?"

"No. Until you get to the farm, you are in charge."

"Me?"

"You. When you contact Janvert, he is to take over."

Her mouth was dry as dust. God! She needed a drink and comforting, but she sensed why the Chief was putting her in charge until they reached Eddie. The Chief knew about her and Eddie. The Chief had a snake's mind. He'd say to himself: *She's the one with the best motivation. She'll want to rescue her boyfriend. Give her the reins.*

She sensed there might be something else on the Chief's mind, but she didn't know how to ask. Was it something to do with Kraft? She pressed the phone tightly against her ear, pushed her chair back toward the window.

"Is that all?" she asked.

"No, you'd better know the worst. We stumbled onto something while talking to the sheriff. He gave it to us himself, very casual and unconcerned. It seems your deputy, whenever he gets sick, is in the habit of convalescing at Hellstrom's farm. In our hunt for Hellstrom's Washington connections, we found a congressman about whom we can say the same thing, and we have our suspicions about at least one senator. Got that?"

She nodded. "I see."

"I think you do. This thing spreads wider every time you pry up another layer. Take no chances with that deputy whatsoever."

"I won't," she said. "How bad was it—I mean, at the Sisters?"

"The plane burned. It was a twin Beech, chartered and recently checked out by the FAA. No reason for it to go down. We haven't been able to examine the wreckage yet, but it was the fire that gave it away: it started a forest fire on the east slope, they say. Forest Service boys are there now, local police, and FAA. We'll have a report as soon as possible."

"What a mess," she said and noted that Kraft was staring at her intently now, trying to listen. "Is there any chance at all that it was an accident?"

"Possible, but not likely. The pilot was former Air America from Vietnam, six thousand hours. Draw your own conclusions. Oh, tell Shorty he has Class-G authorization. Do you know what that is?"

"Yes—yes, sir." My God! Kill and burn if necessary!

"I'll get back to you by radio after you've taken

over that farm," the Chief said. "Within the hour. Good-bye and be thorough."

She heard the receiver click, moved her chair closer to the desk, replaced the phone in its cradle. Using the edge of the desk as a cover, she slipped her revolver from the purse.

Kraft watched her, trying to piece together a version of that conversation from the only end he'd heard. His first inkling that things had changed for the worse came when he saw the silencer of Clovis Carr's pistol raise itself like a steel snake over the far edge of the desk.

Clovis's "working personality" was in full charge now and she put aside thoughts of Janvert's arms around her or other desirable things.

"Keep your hands where I can see them," she said. "I will kill you at the slightest provocation. Do not make *any* sudden movements for any reason. Get to your feet carefully, keeping your hands on the desk. Use extreme caution in everything you do, Mr. Kraft. I don't want to shoot you in this office. It would be messy and difficult to explain, but I will do it if you force me."

From the preliminary oral report on the autopsy of Dzule Peruge. The bruised area on the arm gave indications of an inept injection with a hypodermic. We cannot say at this time what may have been injected, but the biopsies are not yet completed. Other indications on the cadaver indicate what we call among ourselves a "motel death." The syndrome is rather common with males past the age of thirty-five where death occurs under the circumstances described here. The immediate cause of death was what you would call a massive heart failure. We'll send along the technical details later. Whether this remains the proximate cause depends on the biopsies. From the other indications, we can say the subject had engaged in sexual intercourse at a time very close to the time of death perhaps no more than four hours earlier. Yes, that's what we mean. It's a very clear pattern: older man, younger woman (presumed from your account), and too much sex. All the evidence is consistent with this diagnosis. Bluntly, he fucked himself to death.

"Mr. Janvert, we have some things to discuss," Hellstrom said. He leaned toward Janvert across the table.

Janvert, having finished his lunch, sat with his right elbow on the table, chin resting on his hand. He felt lost in thought, bemused by the whole situation: the present company, the Agency, the call from the Chief, this assignment, his former fears . . . Vaguely, he felt that he still ought to be alert and *perhaps* concerned about Hellstrom and the woman, but this did not seem worth the effort.

"It's time we discussed our mutual problems," Hellstrom said.

Janvert nodded on his supporting hand, chuckled as his chin started to slip from the hand. Discuss problems. Certainly.

Something about this rustic farm setting, the excellent meal, something about these people at table with him—somewhere in all this was good and sufficient reason for the transformed mood he now felt. He had fought long enough against liking Hellstrom. Perhaps it wasn't wise to place complete trust in Hellstrom yet, but it was all right to like him. There was a difference between trust and liking. Hellstrom could not be held responsible for the trapped life of a nobody named Eddie Janvert.

Watching the transformation, Hellstrom thought: He's taking it quite well. The dosages were relatively large. Janvert's body was now processing numerous identifier chemicals. Very shortly, he would be accepted by any Hive worker as belonging to the Hive. This was double edged: Janvert would accept the Hive workers, too—any of them. His procreative drive had been suppressed, as had much of his critical ability. If the chemical metamorphosis worked, he would become quite tractable presently.

Hellstrom signaled to Mimeca to observe the changes.

She smiled. Janvert's odors were becoming acceptable.

It's this farm, Janvert told himself. He moved only his eyes to stare out the window beyond the foot of the table. The golden afternoon appeared warm and inviting.

He and Clovis had talked about such a place many times. *"Our own place, preferably an old farm. We'll grow a few things, raise some animals. Our kids can help with that when they're old enough."* It was a fantasy they could share before making love. The poignancy of the unattainable made the present ever more sweet.

"Are you ready for a little discussion yet?" Hellstrom asked.

Discussion, yes. "Sure," Janvert said. He sounded relatively alert, but Hellstrom detected the changes of tone.

The subtle chemistry of fellowship was doing its work. It was a dangerous thing because Janvert might walk openly through any area of the Hive now. No worker would challenge him and haul him summarily off to the nearest vat point. But it meant also that Janvert would respond openly to Hellstrom or any other Hive security interrogator.

Provided this technique worked well on an Outsider. That remained to be tested.

"Your law is a little late arriving," Hellstrom said. "Shouldn't you call and try to find out why?"

Late? Janvert looked up at the clock behind Hellstrom. Almost two o'clock. Where had the time gone? He seemed to recall chatting with Hellstrom and the woman—Fancy was her name. Sweet little thing. But someone was late.

"Are you sure you haven't made a mistake about the FBI and the others?" Hellstrom asked. "Are they coming?"

"I don't think I've made a mistake," Janvert said. He sounded sad. The sadness brought a small surge of anger and adrenaline. Nobody made mistakes in this

business! God, what a shitty business. All because
he'd stumbled over that damned Agency file. No—
that had been only a single step. The trap was far
more complex than that. Eddie Janvert had been conditioned to accept everything the Agency represented.
That conditioning had happened much earlier. Without all this, he might not have met Clovis, either.
Lovely Clovis. Much prettier than this little Fancy
person beside him. He felt that there ought to be other
comparisons between Clovis and Fancy, too, but these
eluded him. The Agency—Agency—Agency—Agency.
It was a bad business. He could sense the leering
presence of the hidden oligarchs whose influence could
be felt all through the Agency. That was it! The
Agency was a bad business.

"I was just thinking," Hellstrom said, "that under
other circumstances we might have been very close
friends."

Friends. Janvert nodded and his head almost
slipped from his supporting hand. They *were* friends.
This Hellstrom was really a very nice guy. He served a
good meal. And it was sweet the way he said grace before eating.

The idea of friendship with Hellstrom fanned a
tiny core of worry in Janvert, though. He began to
wonder about his reactions. It was—Peruge! That was
it: Peruge. Old Peruge had said something important
—ohhh, way back there somewhere. He'd said Hellstrom and friends had some kind of—some kind of—
injection! That was it, an injection. It turned a man
into a sex-mad stud. Peruge had said it. Eighteen times
in one night. Janvert smiled happily to himself. When
you thought about it, that was really very friendly. It
was much more friendly than the damned Agency
where they watched like cats to find out who you
cared for—the way he and Clovis cared for each other
—and then used that against you. That's what the
Agency did. With a little reflection, friendship with
Hellstrom became easily explained. The whole blasted
Agency had finally become too much for one Eddie
Janvert. Wait'll he told Clovis about this. Eighteen
times in one night: that was *very* friendly.

Mimeca, taking her cue from Hellstrom, touched Janvert's arm. She had a nice, friendly little hand. "I thought the same thing," she said. "We really should be friends."

Janvert straightened jerkily, patted her hand on his arm. That was the friendly thing to do. Again, he wondered at himself. He felt he could almost trust this pair. Was that natural? Well, why not? They couldn't have put anything in his food. That was an odd thought, he told himself. In his food. He recalled taking Hellstrom's plate. Yes. Hellstrom had relinquished his very own plate of good food. Now, *that* was friendly. You didn't hide unfriendly things in plain actions. Did you? He stared at the woman beside him, wondering idly why his mind was working at such a crawling pace. Peruge! Something in his food was out of the question. No injection, either. He continued to stare at the woman, wondering why he did it. Sex. He was *not* lusting after this pneumatic little woman with the friendly hands and melting eyes. Maybe Peruge had been wrong. Had Peruge lied? The unfriendly bastard was capable of it.

There could be perfectly natural explanations for this whole thing, Janvert told himself. What could he possibly have against Hellstrom except what the Agency dictated that he have against the poor man? He didn't even know what that was! Project 40. Yes—there'd been something about—papers. Project 40. But that was Hellstrom's project. It must be friendly. It wasn't like the damned Agency. *They* just told you to obey orders.

Janvert felt a sudden need to move around. He pushed his chair back, almost fell over backward, but the pretty woman helped him recover his balance. He patted her hand. Windows. He wanted to look out the windows. Weaving very little, Janvert guided himself down the length of the table to the bay windows. A short stretch of water with no visible flow could be seen in the creekbed. The faint afternoon breeze swayed the tree shadows on the water then and provided an illusion of movement. The silence in the dining room carried a similar illusion. Causally, he wondered how his senses reported reality. It was a very friendly scene, friendly place. There *was* movement.

Why did he have this little niggling worry wa-a-ay down inside? That was the only irritating thing left in this whole situation.

Situation. What situation?

Janvert shook his head from side to side like a wounded animal. Everything was so damned confusing.

Leaning back in his chair, Hellstrom frowned. Hive chemistry was not working on Janvert in quite the way it would have on one of their own. Hive humans remained close enough genetically to the Outsiders for interbreeding. The divergence was only about three hundred years old. Chemical affinity was not surprising. It was to be expected, in fact. But Janvert was not responding with full and open friendliness. It was as though he fought a deep inner battle. Chemistry was not enough, then. That was to be expected, too. The human was much more than flesh. Some holdout place in Janvert's intellect retained a concept of Hellstrom as threat.

Mimeca had followed Janvert to the window, stood now just behind him. "We really mean you no harm," she murmured.

He nodded. Of course they meant him no harm. What a thought. Janvert put a hand in his jacket pocket, felt the gun there. He recognized it. A gun was an unfriendly thing.

"Why can't we be friends?" Mimeca asked.

Tears began to flow from Janvert's eyes, rolling slowly down his cheeks. It was so sad. The gun, this place, Clovis, the Agency, Peruge, everything. So sad. He pulled the gun from his pocket, turned to reveal his tear-stained face, handed the gun to Mimeca. She accepted it, held it awkwardly: one of those awful flesh-destroying Outsider weapons.

"Throw it away," Janvert whispered. "Please, throw that damned thing away."

From a news story, dateline Washington, D.C. . . .

and it was noted that Altman's death was not the first such suicide of a highly placed government official. Washington observers immediately recalled the death on May 22, 1949, of Defense Secretary James Forrestal, who shocked family and associates by leaping from a hospital window.

Altman's death also revived the recurrent Washington rumor that he was in fact the chief of a secret and highly sensitive investigative agency operating under the government's executive arm. One of Altman's senior associates, Joseph Merrivale, issued an angry denial of the rumor, demanding, "Is that bloody 'gabble still going around?"

All in all, it had been a highly successful afternoon in spite of the earlier alarms, Hellstrom told himself. He stood in the barn aerie, staring out the louvered windows to the north. Vehicles were stirring up dust in the distance, but he felt no threat from the Outsiders at the moment. Reports from Washington and the nearby town indicated an easing of pressure.

Janvert had answered all of their questions with only the most gentle of persuasion. It saddened Hellstrom to think about this, comparing it with their previous procedure. So much pain could have been spared the other captives. When you thought about it, this technique was so *obvious*. Fancy had done the Hive a truly great service.

Saldo walked up beside Hellstrom with cat-footed grace and said, "Station six says that dust out there is three heavy vehicles approaching our lower road."

"I think Janvert's 'law' is almost here," Hellstrom said. "Are we ready for them?"

"As ready as we can be. Mimeca is down in the farm house prepared to play Fancy to the hilt. Injured innocence, the whole thing. She's never even heard of Depeaux, that agency, a bicycle—nothing."

"Good. Where did you put Janvert?"

"In an empty cell on level forty-two. Everything is on emergency alert."

With renewed misgivings, Hellstrom thought

about what that meant. Emergency alert: time lost from essential supportive tasks; workers detailed to man the system that could block off long sections of the access galleries with solidifying liquid mucilage; masses of hyped-up workers arrayed behind secret exits and armed with stunwands and the few Outsider weapons the Hive could muster.

"They're coming on very fast," Saldo said, nodding toward the dust cloud from the approaching vehicles.

"They're late," Hellstrom said. "Something delayed them and they're trying to make up for lost time. Are we all ready to clear out this aerie?"

"I'd better give the word," Saldo said.

"In a moment," Hellstrom said. "We can delay them at the gate. Were you able to reach Linc?"

"Nobody answers his phone. You know, when this is over, I think we should provide him with a better Outside cover—a *wife*, another phone at his home tied to the office line."

"Good idea," Hellstrom said. He pointed out the window. "Those are big van-campers. Could they be the ones that were on the mountain?"

"They might—Nils, they're moving much too fast. They're almost at the fence. Maybe we should—"

He broke off in shocked alarm as the first of the big vans crashed through the north gate and swerved aside to block off the flat pillbox of the disguised ventilator outlet. Two figures leaped from the van as it skidded to a stop. One of them carried what appeared to be a black satchel. The other vans roared right past the stopped one, coming straight for the house and barn.

"They're attacking!" Saldo yelled.

A shattering explosion at the ventilator outlet punctuated his warning and was followed immediately by a second, louder explosion. The first truck had been blown onto its side and was burning.

Our own explosives for removing the emergency cover on that ventilator! Hellstrom thought.

There were other blasts now, shots, screams, running people. Two of the attackers spilled from a moving truck, ran crashing through the farmhouse door.

"Nils! Nils!" It was Saldo pulling frantically at his arm. "You've got to get out of here."

The wisdom of Harl. A society that cuts across all of the conduct that Outsiders accept can exist only in a constant state of siege.

Mimeca sat in the farmhouse living room waiting for the arrival of Janvert's "law" when the first explosion rocked the building. A piece of metal from the first van ripped through the north wall a foot above her head. It crashed into the opposite wall and stuck there, smoking. Shots, screams, explosions erupted in the yard.

Ducking low, Mimeca sprinted for the kitchen. Mrs. Niles stored a stunwand in there. She crashed through the swinging door, surprising Mrs. Niles, who was using a stunwand to clear the yard between the farmhouse and barn. Mimeca gave the scene only a passing glance. Her own presence to play the part of Fancy was vital to the Hive's survival. She had to save herself. A door behind Mrs. Niles opened onto solidly built old stairs into the original root cellar. Mimeca jerked the door open, thundered down the stairs. There was a crash overhead, shots, breaking glass. She dashed for the fake shelves that concealed a tunnel to the barn, squeezed through. Workers armed with stunwands were pouring toward her from the other end. Mimeca ran panting past them, through the door to the barn basement. The tunnel behind her was already empty of defenders and she could hear the hiss of mucilage filling the area, plugging it.

A short hall stretched in front of Mimeca, open at the far end on a scene that only the Hive-born would recognize as not one of utter confusion. She trotted toward the area. Workers were dashing about, packages were being carried toward the gallery head, a temporary repeater station had been installed against a wall on the left and guardworkers were keeping it clear there.

As Mineca entered this area, the concealed hatch over the emergency stairs opened above her. Saldo and Hellstrom came dashing down followed by armed workers. The opening of the hatch amplified the clamor of battle overhead, but the noise died abruptly. There came one more explosion, another shot. She heard the brain-resonating humming of many stunwarnds.

Silence.

Hellstrom saw Mimeca, signaled her to join him, but continued his course toward the temporary repeater station. At his approach, a senior observer turned, recognized him, and said, "We've accounted for the ones who got this far, but there are still two more down by the fence. They're out of stun-range from this distance. Shall we get them from behind?"

"Wait," Hellstrom said. "Is it safe for us to go back to the aerie?"

"The two by the fence are armed with at least one machine gun."

"I will go back upstairs," Saldo said. "You wait here. Don't risk yourself, Nils."

"We'll both go," Hellstrom said. He motioned for Saldo to lead the way, spoke to Mimeca. "I'm glad you escaped, *Fancy*."

She nodded, beginning to recover her breath.

"Wait here," Hellstrom told her. "We may need you yet." He turned, followed Saldo, who waited with armed workers at the stairhead. The abruptness and savagery of the attack still had Hellstrom in a state of shock. They were really into the fire now, really into it.

The studio area of the barn presented a scene of remarkably little damage except for a hole blasted in the wall to one side of the north door. Some equipment had been scattered and lay in smashed disarray there. Part of the equipment included a small hive of the new guard-bees. The survivors were buzzing around angrily, but were not attacking the Hive's workers—a remarkable test of efficiency in the conditioning process. Hellstrom made a mental note to compliment the directors of that project and to assign additional resources to it.

The studio's main boom had not been damaged. Saldo already was headed for its cage when Hellstrom emerged from the stairwell. Hellstrom swept his gaze around the studio as he followed. Workers' bodies were being removed briskly by scavenger crews. Casualties, casualties, casualties! Damn those bloody murderers! Hellstrom felt himself experiencing a pure Hive reaction of violent outrage. He wanted to wave his arm to summon followers and sweep down upon the two remaining attackers, tear them apart with bare hands no matter the cost. He sensed the matching eagerness of adrenaline-filled workers all around. They would follow him at the slightest gesture. They no longer were camera crews, actors, technicians, specialists in the multiplex tasks by which the Hive collected Outsider energy/money. They were infuriated workers, every last one of them.

Hellstrom forced himself to cross calmly to the cage, joining Saldo there. He took a deep, trembling breath as he hopped up into the cage. The Hive had never been under such great threat and never before had it needed such cool thinking from its leader specialists. "Get a bullhorn," Hellstrom told Saldo as the boom lifted them toward the aerie. "Call to the two remaining attackers that they must surrender or be killed. Try to take them alive."

"If they resist?" It was not Saldo's normal voice, but pure emotion-charged male, primed for attack.

"You must stop hoping they resist," Hellstrom said. "They are to be stunned and taken alive if at all possible. See if you can get under them in the Hive with a stunwand. That might be one way."

The boom cage wafted them gently to the edge of the loft. Hellstrom stepped out, Saldo right behind. The aerie baffle was open, and excited voices could be heard from inside.

"Tell those workers in there to place more reliance on Hive-sign during stress periods," Hellstrom ordered, angry. "It keeps down the hubbub and upset."

"Yes—yes, of course, Nils."

Saldo found himself awed by the cool command Hellstrom displayed. Here was the true mark of a leader specialist: rational assessment overpowering the anger simmering underneath. No doubt Hellstrom was angered by the attack, but he had himself completely under control.

Hellstrom stepped through the short entry to the aerie and barked, "Let's have some order in here! Restore that baffle. Is our telephone still open to the Outside?"

The noise subsided immediately. Workers moved to obey. A security specialist, standing at the end of the curved bench that had supported the repeaters, passed a telephone to Hellstrom.

"Get the equipment back up here," Hellstrom ordered as he took the telephone, "and send an observer down to Project 40. The observer is not to interfere or interrupt in any way, just observe. At the first word of a breakthrough, this observer is to report directly to me. Is that understood?"

"Understood," Saldo said and moved to obey.

Hellstrom put the telephone to his ear, found it dead. He passed it back to the worker who'd given it to him. "Line's dead. See about restoring it."

The worker took the phone and said, "It was working just a minute ago."

"Well, it's dead now."

"Who were you going to call, Nils?"

"I was going to call Washington and try to find out if the time had come to bluff."

From the diary of Trova Hellstrom. A filled life, good things in their own time, knowledge of constructive service to your fellows, and into the vats when you die; that is the meaning of true fellowship. One in life, one in death.

Clovis had assigned herself to the first van, overriding Myerlie's objections that it was "no place for a woman." She had told him where he could stuff that and he'd slowly smiled, a knowing look behind his eyes. "I understand, honey. It may be a bloody time at that farmhouse and you don't want to see your little Shorty-baby get it. If he does, I'll come back and tell you myself."

So he knows! she thought.

And she spat in his face, brought up her left hand for a chopping blow as he made to strike her. Others intervened and DT had cried, "My God! This is no time to fight among ourselves! What're you two doing? Come on; let's get it moving!"

The first opportunity after they left town, they stopped the lead van and bound Kraft securely, gagged him, and dumped him on the bed in the rear. He objected that they were "going to pay for this," but a gesture with the gun in Clovis's hand had silenced him. He permitted himself to be bound then and lay afterward on the bed, eyes wide open, studying everything he could see.

Clovis sat beside DT, who drove. She watched the passing scenery without really seeing it. So this was how it all ended. The people at that farm would kill Eddie at the first sign of attack. She'd had time to think about it now and felt this as a certainty. It was what any good agent would do. You didn't leave danger behind your back. She felt a red rage in front of her eyes; it actually felt as though it were outside her, beckoning her onward. She also began to see possible other motives behind the Chief's choice of her as leader of this attack. He had wanted the leader to be in a blind, killing rage.

It was after four o'clock before they started. A light breeze brushed ripples in the tall yellow range grass beside the dirt road. She saw the grass, focused on it, looked ahead, and realized they had reached the last turn before the fence. DT was pushing the big van to its limit, roaring up the last mile of road.

"You nervous?" DT asked.

She glanced at the hard, youthful face, still dark with the tan he'd developed in Vietnam. DT's green flight cap cast dark shadows over his eyes, accenting the small white scar at the bridge of his nose.

"That's a helluva question," she said, raising her voice over the motor's roar.

"Nothing wrong with being nervous before a fight," he said. "I remember one time in Nam—"

"I don't want to hear about your fucking brawl!" she cut him off.

He shrugged, noticed that her face was almost gray. She was taking this hard. Helluva business for a woman. Myerlie had been right. No sense getting into that scrap, though. If she wanted to be the gung-ho Ms., that was her lookout. Just as long as she knew how to handle the satchel charge. From all reports, she did.

"What do you do when you're not working?" he asked.

"What's it to you, Junior?"

"Christ, you're feisty! I was just making conversation."

"Then make it with yourself!"

I'd rather make it with you, baby, he thought. You've got a nice body. And he wondered how Shorty enjoyed that. Everybody knew about those two, of course. A real *thing*. Bad business in the Agency, not like him and Tymiena—good clean sex. That was why Clovis was taking this so hard, naturally. Shorty was sure as hell going to get it the minute they opened up. And with Shorty dead, she'd wind up running this show!

He glanced at her once more. Did the Agency really trust her to run this sort of thing?

"They're not expecting us," he said. "This could be a piece of cake. We'll walk right through the place. How many people you think they have up there? Twenty? Thirty, maybe?"

"It's going to be a gawdawful mess," she snarled. "Now, shut up!"

Kraft, listening from the rear of the van, felt something akin to pity for them. They were going to run into a wall of stunwands, every one set to maximum. It was going to be slaughter. He had resigned himself to dying with the pair in this van. What would they do if they knew how many workers really were in the Hive? What would they say if they came back and asked him and he told them, *oh, fifty thousand or so, give or take a couple of hundred.*

Clovis found herself becoming bitterly amused by DT's spate of talk. The nervousness was in him, of course. She had gone beyond that to the killing rage the Chief obviously wanted. They were close enough to the fence now that they could see every exterior detail of the squat concrete structure beyond the gate. The afternoon light was beginning to draw its long shadows within the valley beyond. She could see no sign of human activity at the farmhouse or that portion of the barn visible from this vantage. She picked up her microphone from the radio under the dash to report this to the vans following, but the instant she hit the transmit button, the monitor telltale began to squeal. Jammed! Someone was jamming their frequency!

She glanced at DT, whose tense side glances at the transmitter told her he, too, understood.

She replaced the microphone on its hook and said, "Park the van between the farmhouse and the pillbox. You take the satchel. We'll both get out your side. Toss the satchel along the wall to the east side of the pillbox. Get to the other side of it and cover me. I'll set the charge. When it's set, we run like hell for the edge of that hill beyond there."

"The blast will wreck the van," he objected.

"Better it than us. Start revving her up. We can get more speed than this."

"What about our passenger?"

"He takes his own chances. I hope he gets it good!" She grabbed up the little burp gun from the floor, prepared to release her safety harness. DT wedged an elbow against the satchel charge which had been jammed between his seat and the emergency jump door. "Hit it square in the middle!" Clovis shouted. "It's going to—"

Whatever she had been about to say was drowned in the clattering, screeching turmoil of their crash through the gate. There was no time to say anything more after that.

From the diary of Trova Hellstrom. The nature of our Hive's dependence upon the whole planet must be kept under constant review. This is especially true regarding the food chain, and many of our workers do not understand this clearly. They think we can feed upon ourselves eternally. How stupid! Every food chain is based ultimately upon plants. Our independence hangs on the quality and the quantity of our plants. They must always remain *our* plants, grown *by* us, their production balanced to that diet we have learned provides us with such increased health and longevity when compared with the wild Outsiders.

"They refused to answer our hail," Saldo said. He sounded grimly smug about it.

Saldo stood beside Hellstrom in the gloomy north end of the aerie while workers behind them completed restoring the chamber to its former efficiency. Only a shadowy louver stood between Hellstrom and the wrecked van just inside the gate. Flames still crackled in the van and around it. The gas had caught fire, blazing up with a roar, then exploding to set little spot fires in the surrounding grass. There would be a holocaust down there soon if the workers couldn't get to it.

"I heard," Hellstrom said.

"What shall be our response?" Saldo asked with an odd formality. He was trying too hard to be cool, Hellstrom observed.

"Use our own guns. Try a few shots around them. See if you can't herd them down there to the north. That would give us a chance to extinguish the fires. Have you already sent the patrols out to watch the lower road from town?"

"Yes. Do you want me to have them swing back and take this pair from behind?"

"No. How're we doing at getting a stunwand below them?"

"They're not in a good position for that. We could hit some of our own people. You know how a hard charge bounces in dirt and rocks."

"Who's in charge of the outer patrol?"

"Ed."

Hellstrom nodded. Ed was a strong personality. He could control the workers if anyone could. They must not, under any circumstances, kill this pair. He felt this with growing certainty. The Hive needed survivors to question. He had to find out what had prompted the attack. Hellstrom asked if this had been explained to Ed.

"Yes, I did it myself." Saldo sounded puzzled. Hellstrom was acting with a strange reserve.

"Get started herding that pair," Hellstrom said.

Saldo moved back to obey, returned in a minute.

"Never forget," Hellstrom said, "that the Hive is a flyspeck when compared to existing Outsider forces. We need that pair out there—for their information and for possible use in a compromise. Has the telephone been restored yet?"

"No. The break is somewhere near town. They must've cut the line."

"Likely."

"Why would they compromise with us?" Saldo asked. "If they can wipe us out—" He broke off, shuddered at the enormity of this thought. He felt the panicked inclination to disband the Hive, scatter the workers, hope for a few survivors to restart. Surely, all of them would perish if they stayed here. One atomic bomb—well, ten or twelve atomic bombs and—if enough workers got away now . . .

Saldo began trying to express these fearful ideas to Hellstrom.

"We're not quite ready for that," Hellstrom said. "I have taken the necessary steps if the worst should happen. Our records are ready to be destroyed quickly if we—"

"Our records?"

"You know it would have to be done. I've sent the emergency signal to those who've been our eyes and ears Outside. As of now, they have been cut away from us. They may have to live out their lives now, eating mostly Outsider foods, obeying Outsider laws, accepting brief lives and empty Outsider pleasures as the final price of their service to us. They've always known this might happen. But some of them can survive. Any of them could begin a new Hive. No matter what happens here, Saldo, we are not completely lost."

Saldo closed his eyes, shuddering at the thought of such a prospect.

"Have Janvert restored to a more complete awareness," Hellstrom said. "We may need an envoy."

Saldo's eyes snapped open. "Envoy? Janvert?"

"Yes, and see why it's taking so long to gather in that last pair. They've obviously been herded out into the range. I can see workers beginning to fight the fires." He stared out the window. "They'd better be quick about it, too. If we have too much smoke, we could get Outsider fire crews in here." He looked back at the observation stations. "Do we have a phone connection yet?"

"No," one of the observers called.

"Then use radio," Hellstrom said. "Call the district Forest Service office in Lakeview. Tell them we've had a little grass fire here, but our people have it under control. We will not need Outside help."

Saldo turned away to obey his instructions and marveled at the way all the scattered pieces of Hive security were gathered into Hellstrom's consciousness. No one but Hellstrom had thought about the danger of Outside fire fighters. Another observer was calling to Hellstrom as Saldo let himself out of the aerie.

Hellstrom took the call, recognizing a physical-research specialist on the screen. The specialist began talking as soon as Hellstrom came into range of the pickup. "Get your interfering *observer* out of here, Nils!"

"Has the observer caused trouble in the lab?" Hellstrom asked.

"We are no longer in the lab."

"Not in—where are you?"

"We have taken over the main gallery at level fifty, the entire gallery. We must have it cleared for our installation. Your observer insists you told him to stay here."

Hellstrom thought about that gallery—more than a mile long. "Why do you need the entire gallery?" he asked. "We have essential support—"

"Your stupid workers can use the side tunnels!" the specialist snarled. "Get this cretin out of here! He is delaying us."

"The entire gallery," Hellstrom said, "is quite a—"

"Your own information made this necessary," the specialist explained in a tone of weary patience. "The Outsider observations you *so kindly* brought us. The problem is a matter of size. We are going to use the entire gallery. If your observer interferes, you will find him in the vats."

The connection was broken with an angry *blap!*

From the Hive Manual. The most powerful socializing force in the universe is mutual dependence. The fact that our key workers eat an additional diet of leader food should never obscure from them their interdependence with those not chosen for this privilege.

Clovis lay in deep shade beneath a madroña copse about five hundred yards southeast of the gate into Hellstrom's farm. She could see swarms of people fighting the grass fires up by the fence and some of them obviously had guns, not those mysterious humming weapons she'd seen knocking some of her team flat. Christ! There must be hundreds of people up there fighting those fires! Blue gray smoke spiraled upward from the fires and she could smell the alkali bitterness of the smoke as some of it drifted across her position.

She held her pistol in her right hand, resting it over her left forearm to steady it. They would come from that direction, obviously. DT had worked down to the right behind her with the burp gun. She glanced back, trying to spot him. He'd said to give him ten minutes, then move back. He'd cover her.

She thought about the brief battle in the farm-
yard. Holy Jesus! She had never expected anything
even remotely like that experience. Gawdawful, yes,
but not that. Nude men and women carrying odd dou-
ble-tipped weapons. She could hear the strange crackling hum of the damn things even yet. From the way
her team had fallen under that weird barrage, she suspected the things were lethal.

A new kind of weapon: that had to be the answer
to Project 40. Well, they'd expected a weapon, but not
something like this.

Why were the people nude?

She had not yet allowed herself to ask what might
have happened to Eddie Janvert. Her original guess
stood. Dead, and probably by one of those odd weapons. The things had a limited range, however: about
one hundred yards, she made it. Bullets from her pistol had the reach on them. The trick was to keep the
attackers at a distance and look out for the few with
guns.

She glanced at her wristwatch: three minutes before she could move out.

God, it was hot. Dust from the grass tickled her
nose. She stifled a sneeze. Something moved on the
near slope of the hillside above the fence to the left of
the gate. She snapped off two shots, reloaded, heard
another shot from behind her and a call from DT. He
was in place already. Good. To hell with waiting out
the full ten minutes. She got to her knees, turned, and
sprinted out of the tree shadows in a running crouch,
not looking back. That was DT's job, to cover her
back trail. The odd humming sound came from the
hillside behind her, but there was only a faint tingling
sensation along her spine. She wondered if it could be
imagination, but fear added new energy to her muscles
and she increased her speed.

A shot sounded ahead of her on her left; another,
another. DT using the burp gun on single shot to slow
down pursuers. She shifted course slightly to curve
around behind the place where the shots originated.
She still couldn't see DT, but there was an oak tree
down there and some cows running away beyond it in

an awkward, bounding gait. She picked an oak to the left of the cows as her target, ran, and caught the tree with her left arm as she came to it, swung around behind it, the tree and her arc of momentum stopping her. Sweat soaked her body and her chest ached with each panting breath. More shots came from DT's position then, but she still couldn't see him. Six nude figures were sprinting down the open rangeland from the valley, each carrying one of those weird weapons. She drew three deep breaths to steady herself, rested her gun hand against the tree, and spaced off four aimed shots. Two of the sprinters dropped with a jolting sprawl that said they'd been hit. The others dove into the grass.

DT came into sight abruptly, dropping from the tree, and she realized he'd climbed the damn tree. Good man. He landed cat-footed and running, bore to his left, not looking back, not looking across at Clovis. A good teammate would cover for him and he had now accepted Clovis as a good teammate.

Clovis reloaded, watching the grass move where the four survivors of her fusillade had gone to ground. They were crawling, obviously trying to get within range for their weapons. The grass rippled ominously, moving, coming nearer and nearer. She concentrated on gauging distance. At about four hundred feet, she lifted the magnum and began shooting. She took her time, spacing the shots carefully. At her third shot, a figure lurched into view, toppled backward. Three others arose from the grass, charged, pointing their weapons at her. Taking her time—each of the remaining three shots had to count—she sighted on the first figure, a bald woman with face contorted into a fierce grimace. Clovis's first shot stopped her as though she had run into a wall. Her weapon flew through the air as she fell sideways. The others dove for the grass. Clovis used her two remaining shots, putting them into the grass where the attackers had dropped. Without waiting to see the effect, she turned and ran, reloading as she went.

"Over here! Over here!"

It was DT calling from another oak off to her

left. She changed course toward it, guessing he'd called because there were no more trees in the range-land beyond. It was open grassland down there and cropped close by cattle for at least half a mile. DT caught her arm to help stop her.

"You know, that's weird," he said. "See how the cows have eaten the pasture down below us, but not up toward the farm. It's almost as though the cows avoided that area. The ones I scared away from my first stand up there were real spooky, as though they'd been herded up there by something below us. I don't see a sign of anyone down there, though."

She took a moment to catch her breath. "You have any bright ideas how we're going to get out of this?"

"Keep on like we are," he said.

"We've got to get out and report what we've seen," she said. She looked up at him, but he was keeping his attention on their back trail.

"I think you got another one of those creeps that dove into the grass," he said. "Only one of them seems to be moving. You ready to make another run?"

"As ready as I'll ever be. You see anything of the one I missed?"

"He's still crawling, but he's gonna run outa grass pretty soon. Let's separate now. You bear a bit to your left until you hit the road, then try to follow it. I'll hold right. The creek should be over there; you can see the line of trees off that way about a mile. We'll give 'em two targets to chase. If I can reach the creek—"

DT had been scanning the ground toward the farm as he began speaking and, still speaking, he turned to look in the direction they would run. Clovis whirled around at the startled way DT stopped speaking. She let out an involuntary gasp. A solid line of hairless, nude human figures blocked their escape route. The line stood about five hundred yards below them, beginning far off to their left in the scrub oaks of rising ground there and reaching into the distance at the right, even beyond the trees that marked the creekbank where DT had expected to take cover.

"Jeeee-sus!" DT said.

There must be ten thousand of them! Clovis thought.

"I haven't seen that many gooks since Nam," DT husked. "Jeeeee-sus! It's like we stirred up a whole anthill of 'em."

Clovis nodded, thinking: *That's exactly what we've done.* The whole thing fell into place: Hellstrom was a front for some kind of weirdo cult. She noted the pale skins. They must live underground. The farm was just a cover. She stifled a hysterical giggle. No, the farm was only a *lid!* She raised her gun, intending to take as many of that ominous advancing line as possible, but a crackling hum from close behind numbed her body and mind. She heard one shot as she toppled, but could not decide whether it was from her gun or DT's.

From Nils Hellstrom's diary. The concept of a colony planted directly in the midst of an existing human society is not unique. There have been many secret groups and movements in human history. Gypsies provide a crude analogue of our way even today. No, we are not unique in this. But our Hive is as far removed from those others as they are removed from primitive, cave-dwelling humans. We are like the colonial protozoan, *carchesium,* all of us in the Hive attached to a single, branching stem, and that stem concealed in the very ground beneath the other society that believes itself to be the meek who will inherit the earth. Meek! That word originally meant "mute and silent."

It had been a frantic and confused flight from JFK Airport—an hour's layover at O'Hare, the quick transfer to a chartered flight at Portland and the noisy discomfort of a single engine all the way up the Columbia Gorge, and, then, as evening came down over them, the long haul diagonally across Oregon into the southeastern corner. Merrivale was in a violent mood when the plane set him down in Lakeview, and it was a mood amplified by the elation simmering in him.

When he had least expected it, in fact when he had resigned himself to a degrading personal defeat, they had called on him. They—a board whose existence he had known about, but never identified—*they* had chosen Joseph Merrivale as "our best hope to salvage something from this mess."

With both Peruge and the Chief dead, who else did they have? This gave him a sense of personal power which, in turn, fed his anger. Who was *he* to be subjected to such discomfort?

The report passed to him quickly in Portland did little to mollify him. Peruge was exposed as criminally careless—spending the night with a woman like that! *And while on a job!*

The small plane landed in darkness and there was a gray station wagon with only a driver to greet him. The fact that the driver introduced himself as Waverly Gammel, SAIC (FBI-Special Agent in Charge) renewed the worries Merrivale had managed to keep largely suppressed on the flight, and this, too, fed his anger.

They could be throwing me to the wolves, he thought, as he got into the car beside the driver, leaving his luggage for the pilot to dump in the back. This thought had simmered throughout the long trip from Portland. He had looked down at the occasional winking of lights and thought bitterly that people were going about their ordinary business down there—eating, going to movies, watching television, visiting friends. It was a comforting, ordinary life which Merrivale often fantasized should have been his lot. The other side of his fantasy told him, though, that the silent pattern of safety below depended largely upon his efforts to maintain it. They did not know down there what he was doing for them, the sacrifices he made . . .

Even when you followed your orders to the letter, that didn't help protect you one bit. The sudden promotion had not changed this. It was a universal law: the big fed upon the small and there was always a bigger to make one smaller.

Gammel was a man with a young face and iron

gray hair, harshly chiseled planes in his face that suggested American Indian ancestry. The eyes were deeply set and shadowy in the light from the car's dash. His voice was deep and revealed a faint twang. Texas?

"Bring me up to date," Merrivale said as Gammel took the car out of the airport parking lot. The FBI man drove with an easy competence without concern for extending the car's life. They bounced out a rough track from the airport and turned left onto blacktop.

"You know, of course, that there hasn't been a word from the team you sent into the farm," Gammel said.

"They told me in Portland," Merrivale said, forgetting momentarily to impose his superior British accent. He added quickly, "Bloody lash-up!"

Gammel stopped for an arterial sign, turned left onto a wider blacktop, waited for a noisy bus to pass before continuing. "For the moment, we agree with your assessment that the Fosterville deputy is untrustworthy and that there may be other questionables, both in the sheriff's office and in the community itself. Therefore, we are trusting no locals."

"What're you doing about the deputy?"

"He was taken along by your people, you know. He hasn't been heard from, either."

"What're you telling the local authorities?"

"Spy stuff; hush-hush."

"They're willing to stand aside?"

"Not willing, but they've let discretion overcome their valor; the political suggestions we initiated on high have the general tone of absolute commands at this level."

"Quite. Presumably, you've already invested the countryside around the farm."

Gammel took his eyes off the road for a moment. *Invested?* Oh, yes: occupied. He said, "We've only brought in eleven men. It must remain at that for the moment. The Oregon Highway Patrol sent three cars and six men, but we haven't let them fully into the picture. We're mounting a limited operation on the rebuttable presumption that your office's assessment is correct. However, at the slightest sign that you've misjudged the situation, we'll be forced to return to our book of rules. Understood?"

Rebuttable presumption, Merrivale thought. It was his kind of phrase and he savored it, tucking it away for later personal use in other company. He did not, however, like the implications behind the phrase and he said so.

"Surely," Gammel said, "you understand that we're operating well outside conventions. That team you sent in there had no legal standing whatsoever. That was an assault force, pure and simple. You guys make up your own rules as you go along. We can't always do that. My instructions are clear. I'm to do everything in my power to help you with a cover story and/or provide reasonable protection for your people as I am able, but—and this is a mighty large *but*— these instructions hold only for as long as your assessment of the situation is borne out."

Merrivale listened in frozen silence. It looked more and more as though the board had not promoted him, but were throwing him to the wolves. He had been an associate of two people, now dead, whose policies no longer could be defended. The board had sent him out here in the field all alone, saying, "You'll get every assistance from the FBI in the field. If it is consistent with policy, other backup will be sent along as you request it."

Gobbledygook!

He was one clear target if things went any more sour. As though that were possible! He could almost hear the reorganization gears grinding back in Baltimore and Washington. *Well, you knew what kind of a business this was when you got into it, Merrivale.* They'd look professionally sorrowful while they brought up that standard phrase always used for such occasions: *In this business, you take your lumps when that's required of you.*

That was the situation. No doubt of it. If the situation could be salvaged, he'd do that, but first he had to salvage himself. "Bloody hell!" he muttered and meant every syllable of it. "Let's have the rest of it. What've you managed to learn about my people?"

"Nothing."

"Nothing?" Merrivale was outraged. He turned, studied Gammel's face in the light of an oncoming car. The FBI man held his features immobile, a dark piece of stone for all the emotion showing.

"I would like that *nothing* explained, provided you're able to explain it," Merrivale said, his tone distant and acid.

"As per our instructions," Gammel said, "we have been waiting for you."

Just following orders, Merrivale thought.

He could see the implications in that. There was going to be only one responsible target in this situation. That was in Gammel's orders, too. No doubt of it. No bloody doubt of it.

"I find this almost inconceivable," Merrivale said. He turned, looking out at the darkness flashing with vague movements on his right as the car sped toward Fosterville. He could make out that they were passing through open countryside, the road climbing slightly, dim shapes of hills ahead in starlight. Few other cars shared the road. The dark landscape carried a sense of loneliness which rubbed at Merrivale's feelings of abandonment.

"Let's not misunderstand each other," Gammel said. "I came out here alone to pick you up just so we could talk openly." Gammel glanced at Merrivale. The poor sod was in the jaws of the vise, no mistaking that. Was he just now becoming aware of it?

"Then why aren't you talking openly?" Merrivale demanded.

He's more on the attack than the situation requires, Gammel thought. Does that mean he has information that might throw his agency's position into doubt? I wonder . . .

"I'm doing my best within my instructions," Gammel said. "I had less than an hour at Fosterville before they signaled that you'd be coming in at Lakeview. I had to rush like hell to get there. They said you were coming in at Lakeview because it had the nearest field with lights. Was that it, or was there another reason?"

"What do you mean?"

"I'm still wondering about our own casualties—up at the Sisters."

"Oh—yes, of course. That was in the report I had at Portland. There's still nothing conclusive or I'd have mentioned it. The fire played bloody hob with the wreckage. It could've been lightning and a fuel explosion. They said the pilot should've gone up through the Columbia Gorge, but he was trying to save time by flying direct."

"They haven't ruled out sabotage?"

"They have not. High probability if you ask me. Damn stupid kind of coincidence, don't you think?"

"We're acting on that assumption," Gammel said.

"What've you done with your eleven men and the patrol?" Merrivale asked.

"I've dispatched three cars—two men each. One of the Oregon Highway Patrol cars with three officers was sent around to the south. That's going to take a little time. For part of that trip they will be out of range of the radio relay equipment."

"But what are these three cars doing?"

"We've set up a communications base in the motel at Fosterville. The cars are maintaining contact with that base at regular intervals. My cars are deployed between Fosterville and the farm, and they—"

"Two cars between town and the farm?"

"No, three cars. The OHP car is a fourth. My three cars are deployed in a wide surveillance pattern —one on a Forest Service road to the east and the other two spaced along the actual road to the farm. They were instructed to approach no closer than two miles."

"*Two* miles?"

"Correct, and they were told to stay in their cars."

"But two miles—"

"When we're fairly certain of what we're doing and what we're up against, we don't mind taking risks," Gammel said. "But this case appears to be nothing but uncertainties." He spoke in a level voice, trying to hold his temper. Merrivale's carping was becoming insufferable. Didn't he realize he might be wearing Gammel's own handcuffs before another twenty-four hours was out? They might *have* to arrest Merrivale just to save the FBI's neck. What did this bastard expect?

"But two—"

"You've lost how many people in there?" Gammel demanded, not trying to hide his anger now. "Twelve? Fourteen? I'm told there were nine people in that team you sent in today and you lost at least one team before that. Do you take us for morons?"

"Fourteen, counting Dzule Peruge," Merrivale said. "Your ability to count is unimpaired." In the dim green light of the dash, he noted a muscle working along Gammel's jaw and the tense-knuckled way the man gripped the wheel as he drove.

"So we have one certainly dead, thirteen missing, and our own planeload down in the Sisters; that's twenty in all. You dare ask me why I haven't sent my people in there after yours? If I had my way, we'd have a regiment of marines on hand and we'd be doing just that, but I don't have my way. Why don't I have my way? Because this whole thing smells of a lash-up by your people! And if it explodes, we're not going to get burned in the blast. Is that clear enough for you? Is that open enough?"

"Bloody pack of cowards," Merrivale muttered.

Gammel suddenly swerved the car off the road onto the parking strip, skidded to a stop in gravel, set the hand brake with an angry rasping of its latch, and turned off the lights and the motor. He whirled on the seat to face Merrivale. "Look, you! I understand the hot seat you're on; at least, I have a good idea of the bind you're in. But my agency has not been in this from the first, *although it should have been!* Now, if that turns out to be a nest of commies up there, we'll mop it up and have all the help we need. If it turns out to be an arm of a major industry in this country trying to protect a new invention from the vultures you represent, that is an entirely *different* ball game."

"What do you mean—industry—new invention?"

"You know goddamned well what I mean! We

didn't sit around on our asses accepting you people as our only source of information."

If they have the whole story, why're they still helping us? Merrivale wondered.

As though he'd heard the question, Gammel said, "Our position in this is to try to keep the shit from hitting the fan. You rub dirt on your outfit and you rub dirt on the whole government. Now, if you've been sent out here as a patsy, I can sympathize. But there's no sense in our fighting each other. If this thing's ready to blow and you're here to take the rap, you'd better level with me right now. Are you?"

Taken aback by Gammel's sudden stop and attack, Merrivale sputtered a moment; then, "Now, see here! If you—"

"Are you here to take the rap?"

"Of course not!"

"Bullshit!" Gammel shook his head. "You think we don't have our own suspicions about why your boss took the short road to hell?"

"The short road to—"

"Jumped out of that goddamned window! Are you their patsy?"

"I was sent here with the understanding that you would provide full cooperation until we could field new teams," Merrivale said, speaking stiffly. "I don't find your present attitude cooperative in the least."

Still not mollified, Gammel said, "Tell me—yes or no—do you have new information that dramatically alters your original assessment?"

"Of course not!"

"Nothing new to tell me?"

"I will not be cross-examined by you," Merrivale protested. "You know as much about this situation as I do. More! You've at least been on the scene."

"I hope you're telling the truth," Gammel said. "If you aren't, I personally will supervise whatever action we have to take to fry you." He turned, restarted the car, eased back onto the highway. He turned on his lights as he moved and they startled a big black and white cow that had wandered onto the verge. It galumphed ahead of them for several hundred feet before diving off into the open grassland beside the road.

Considerably subdued and now frightened at the position he might be in if he had no cooperation at all from the FBI, Merrivale said, "I'm truly sorry if I've offended you. As you can imagine, I've been under somewhat of a strain. First the Chief's death and then the orders to take over here personally. No sleep really since this all started."

"Have you eaten?"

"On the plane from Chicago."

"We can get you something at our headquarters in the motel." Gammel reached for the microphone under the dash. "I'll have them lay on coffee and sandwiches. What would you—"

"No need for that," Merrivale said, feeling somewhat better. Gammel obviously was trying to get them back on a friendly footing. That made sense. Merrivale cleared his throat. "What sort of action plan have you devised?"

"We do only a minimum in the dark. We wait for morning and reconnoiter in daylight *and* under constant radio contact with base. That's clearly indicated until we find out what the hell has happened up there. We can't trust the local law yet. I've even been told to play it cool with the OHP. Our primary concern is to clarify some of this water that's been badly muddied up to now."

Muddied by our people, of course, Merrivale thought. The FBI were still a bunch of bloody snobs. He said, "Nothing more tonight?"

"It didn't strike me as advisable to run any more risks than absolutely necessary. We'll have more muscle by morning, anyway."

Merrivale brightened. "More people?"

"Two marine choppers coming up from San Francisco."

"You ordered them?"

"We're still covering for you," Gammel said. He turned, grinned. "They are for surveillance and/or transportation only. We stretched our good-will account considerably to get them with no better explanation than we could give at the time."

"Very well," Merrivale said. "Portland told me you had no telephone contact with the farm. Is that situation the same?"

"The line's out," Gammel said. "Probably cut by your people when they went in. We'll have a repair crew out in the morning. Our own people, of course."

"I see. Then I concur with your field decisions, subject, naturally, to review when we reach your headquarters. They may have more recent information."

"They'd have called me," Gammel said. He tapped the radio under the dash, thinking: They've sent a stuffed shirt. He's a patsy for sure and the poor bastard may not even know it.

From the Hive Manual. As a biological mechanism, human reproduction is not terribly efficient. When compared to insects, humans appear grossly inefficient. The insect and all the lower life forms are dedicated to species survival. Survival comes through reproduction, through mating. Males and females of all life forms other than man are drawn together in the direct and singular interest of reproduction. For the wild forms of humankind, however, unless the setting is right, the perfume is right, the music is sweet—and unless at least one partner feels *loved* (a singularly unstable concept) by the other—the reproductive act may never occur. We of the Hive are dedicated, therefore, to freeing our workers from the concept of romance. The act of procreation must occur as simply, as naturally, and as obliviously as eating. Neither beauty, romance, nor love must figure in Hive reproduction —only the demands of survival.

The night-shrouded countryside around the farm appeared asleep to Hellstrom as he scanned it from the aerie. Darkness blotted all of the familiar landscape and there was only the distant glimmer of Fosterville's light on the horizon. The Hive beneath him had never felt more silent, more charged with the tensions of waiting. Although the oral tradition spoke of early confrontations when the whole Colony Movement (as it was called then) faced extinction, the Hive had never faced a greater crisis. The thing had happened in such natural stages that Hellstrom, looking back, experienced a sense of the inevitable. The Hive's population of almost fifty thousand workers depended for their continued existence upon the decisions that Hellstrom and his aides made during the next few hours.

Hellstrom glanced over his shoulder at the swamp-fire glow of cathodes, the screens that watched over the Outsiders who'd come up from Fosterville just after dark. Three unmarked cars were parked out there in the rangeland now, little more than two miles away. A fourth car, identified as from the highway patrol, had been with them at first, but it was laboring its way around to the south of the valley now. The only track open to it there was the old Thimble Mine road and that came no closer than ten miles to the south of the valley unless its occupants took to the open country. Hellstrom suspected the vehicle might have four-wheel drive, but the character of the land to the south was such that the OHP car could not get closer than three miles from the Hive's perimeter at best.

The aerie's workers, sensing the weight of decision on Hellstrom, had lowered their voices and moved softly.

Should I use Janvert as a mediator? he wondered.

But mediation should begin from a position of strength and the Hive had only a bluff. The secret of the stunwand might be something valuable to offer. Janvert had seen it in action. He would know, too, about the Hive's mastery of human chemistry. He had his own reactions to verify that. But Janvert could only become the Hive's enemy if he went out as an envoy. He'd seen too much of the Hive to even consider neutrality.

Hellstrom glanced at the clock behind the arc of surveillance instruments: 11:29 P.M. It was almost *to-*

morrow, and tomorrow was certain to see a show-down. He could sense that in many things, including the watchful waiting of the three cars parked between the Hive and Fosterville. Thinking about the occupants of those cars, Hellstrom felt a need to know what they were doing now. He returned to the observer station and asked a coordinating specialist, whose face looked deathly pale in the green gloom.

"They are remaining inside the cars," the specialist said. "Their reporting schedules are staggered, about ten minutes apart for any given car. We are confident now that there are no more than two Outsiders in each car."

Waiting for daylight, Hellstrom realized. He said as much.

"It's the general opinion here," the specialist said. "That middle car is only about twenty-five yards from one of the hidden exits, the one at the end of level-two gallery."

"You're suggesting we try to bring in the Outsiders?"

"It would give us answers to some questions."

"It also might ignite a general attack. I think we've pushed our luck as far as it will go." Hellstrom rubbed the back of his neck. He felt worn-out, running on nerve. "What about the car that's going around to the south?"

"It's stuck about where the old mine road starts to cross Muddy Bottom, about eight miles from our perimeter and at least twelve miles from the valley."

"Thank you." Hellstrom turned away.

The aerie was quieter now than it had been when he had arrived two hours before. There had been groups of security specialists passing through then, each being briefed for night sweep. All had faded away into the outside darkness now, nothing but signal points on the aerie's instruments, glowing figures on the screens.

For perhaps the tenth time since taking up station in the aerie, Hellstrom thought: I should rest. I'll need all of my senses alert by daylight. They will come upon us in the morning, I'm sure. I more than any should be ready for them. Many of us will probably die tomorrow. If I'm alert, perhaps I can save some.

He thought sadly of Lincoln Kraft, whose charred body (hardly enough left to bother taking to the vats) had been removed from the wreckage of one of the attackers' vans. Kraft's death made the day's loss thirty-one.

Just a beginning.

The aerie had moved to a subdued murmur of questioning earlier. The words *attack* and *prisoners* had been repeated in many contexts. There'd even been a kind of adrenaline-pumped elation in the aerie, references to "the victory."

Again, Hellstrom thought about the three prisoners the Hive now held. It seemed strange to be holding prisoners. Outsider adults seemed naturally to belong to the vats. Only very small children had ever been considered worthy of reshaping for the Hive's uses. Now—now, there were new possibilities.

Janvert, the most puzzling of the three, had a background in law, Hellstrom had learned through careful questioning. Janvert might be ridiculously easy to wean from Outside ways, provided he could be sufficiently tempered to Hive chemistry. The female, Clovis Carr, was a carrier of aggressive characteristics that the Hive might turn to its advantage. The third one, whose identification papers said he was Daniel Thomas Alden, carried himself like a soldier. There could be valuable characteristics in all of them, but Janvert remained the most interesting. He was small, too, which was desirable in the Hive.

Hellstrom turned back to the observer stations, bent low over the second one from the right. "What about our patrol in the creek bottom?" he asked. "Have they anything new to report on the conversation from that car they're watching?"

"The Outsiders are still puzzled, Nils. They call this a 'very strange case' and they refer occasionally to someone named Gammel, who apparently believes the case is a snafu. What's a snafu?"

"A foul-up," Hellstrom translated. "It's military slang: situation normal all fouled up."

"Something that has gone wrong, then?"

"Yes. Tell me if they hear anything new."

Hellstrom straightened, thought of calling Saldo. The younger man had been sent to keep a discreet observation on Project 40, working from one end of the long gallery at level fifty. It was not a good vantage point, because the major work was being conducted toward the middle of the gallery, at least half a mile from the end, but the researchers had shown increasing irascibility after the earlier incident with an "interfering observer." Hellstrom was counting on Saldo's intelligence to manage the situation. It was a matter of desperation for them to know in the aerie if the situation in the lab showed new promise.

We could never get away with a bluff against the Outsiders, Hellstrom told himself. The Hive might gain a little time for itself, might be able to parlay the stunwands to create a temporary belief in a more potent weapon built on the same principle. But the Outsiders would demand a demonstration. And there was always Harl's warning to consider. The threat to use an absolute weapon put the trigger in the hands of an opponent who might say, *so use it!* The weapon must be applicable at less than absolute energies, and that must be demonstrable, unmistakably demonstrable. The Outsiders had a saying that fit the situation aptly. "Don't kid the kidders." A bluff would not work for long. The Hive would be called—and then what?

The wild Outsiders were very strange, really. They tended not to believe in violence until it was inflicted upon them. They had a saying about this, too. "It can't happen here."

Perhaps this was inevitable in a world that based its societies on threat, violence, and illusions of absolute power. How could such people as Janvert be expected to think in more malleable terms, to think of life dependencies and the interlocked relationships of living systems, to think of inserting the human species into the great circle of life? Such concepts would be gibberish to Outsiders, even those who spoke for the new fad—*ecology*.

From Joseph Merrivale's private notes. As per the instructions handed to me at JFK Airport, I arrived late Sunday in Lakeview to establish a preliminary liaison with FBI-SAIC Waverly Gammel, who had set up a base in Fosterville. He took me to Fosterville where we arrived at 2318 hours. Gammel reported having taken no action except minimal surveillance of target area from distance of approximately two miles and involving only four vehicles with nine men. According to Gammel, this was in compliance with his instructions, a statement not in accord with what I was led to believe at the action briefing. Gammel reports no word from any of our team that entered the target area earlier on this date. Gammel evinces doubts that this case involves narcotics. He has seen the preliminary report on the Peruge autopsy. I must protest my dependence on another agency for the manpower to prosecute this case. Divided authority is producing a situation fraught with potential embarrassments and inconveniences. The loose working agreement under which I must perform my duties can only exacerbate present difficulties. Since many actions have already been taken in the field on this case without my knowledge or agreement, I must lodge my formal protest at the earliest opportunity. My capacity in the present contretemps bodes ill for our responsibilities. I must make it clear that none of the conduct in this case has accorded with my own understanding of the decisions required to resolve the situation.

Saldo made record time coming up from the Hive's 5,000-foot level where the researchers had moved their operations. There were fast elevators only in the so-called new galleries below 3,100 feet, but even these became progressively slower the higher he went. The work in the new galleries delayed him slightly at 3,800 feet, but he bulled his way through, making a note to ask Hellstrom if that work could not be put on minimum standby during the present crisis.

He had left a young assistant at the relocated lab, seated at the southeast end of the long gallery with the

secret weapon Saldo had commandeered: the binoculars once used by the Outsider, Depeaux. The binoculars revealed a spate of activity by the researchers
which Saldo interpreted as readiness for a test of the
system. He dared not approach the specialists, though.
Hellstrom's orders had been explicit on that score.
Only Hellstrom might change that now and, knowing
the urgency, Saldo went to argue for a small interruption of the lab work.

It was almost midnight when the boom cage deposited him on the catwalk outside the aerie. A guardworker there passed him with only a casual glance of
recognition. The inner room was dim and oddly
hushed as he passed through the baffle, and he saw
that most of the Hive's leadership cadre had taken
over the night duty with Hellstrom, who stood at the
room's north end, a blocky figure against the dark outline of the louvered window. Saldo found he did not
have the highest regard for the leadership qualities of
most of those present, excepting Hellstrom, and sometimes even Hellstrom. Some of these workers should
be conserving their strength for the morrow. He knew
this inner reaction reflected a pattern bred and conditioned into him, but the knowledge subtracted little
from his assessment of his own personal qualities.
Hellstrom—and at least half of those present—should
be resting now.

Saldo had known he would find Hellstrom here,
though, and he found nothing inconsistent in the recognition that he, too, would have been standing there
at that window to the north were he in Hellstrom's
place.

Hellstrom turned and recognized Saldo making
his way through the green gloom. "Saldo!" he said.
"Is there something to report?"

Saldo moved close to Hellstrom and, speaking in
a low voice, explained why he had left the lab.

"Are you sure they're about to test it?"

"It looks that way. They've been stringing the
power cables for several hours. They didn't bother
with power cables on the other models until they were
about to test."

"How soon?"

"That's difficult to say."

Hellstrom moved back and forth a few paces restlessly, fatigue visible in the controlled precision of his actions. He stopped in front of Saldo. "I don't see how they could be testing it this soon." He rubbed his chin. "They said the new model would have to use the entire gallery."

"They are using the gallery, all of it, and fans and a strange construction of pipes that they are connecting down the entire length of the gallery. They're supporting the pipe on anything they can collect—chairs, benches—it's a very strange thing they're building. They even took a heavy-duty pump from level-forty-two hydroponics. They just went right in, disconnected it, and took it. The hydroponics manager was upset, as you can imagine, but they merely said you'd authorized it. Is that true?"

"In essence," Hellstrom said.

"Nils, do you think it likely they'd behave this way unless they were about to test and were reasonably sure of success?"

Privately, Hellstrom agreed with Saldo, but there were other considerations, and he had not yet dared to let himself hope. The specialists' behavior *might* be a reflection of the upset that had spread throughout the Hive. Hellstrom did not think this likely, but it was possible.

"Shouldn't you go down and make a personal inquiry?" Saldo asked.

Hellstrom sympathized with the impatience that had brought Saldo up from the lab. It was an impatience shared by many in the Hive. Was anything to be served by going down there now himself, though? The specialists might not tell him anything. They were naturally wary of predicting the outcome in any project. They spoke of probabilities when they did speak, or of possible consequences in certain "lines of development." It was understandable. Experiments had been known to turn upon the experimenters. An earlier test model in Project 40 had created an explosive plasma bubble which had killed fifty-three workers, including four researchers, and had spread havoc two hundred feet in a side gallery at level thirty-nine.

"What power-drain figures did they give Generation?" Hellstrom asked. "How much diversion do they require?"

"The generation specialists asked, but were told the computation is not complete. I've posted another observer in Generation, however. Surely, the researchers must *ask* for the diversion."

"Will Generation make an estimate based on the size of the power cables being used?"

"As much as five hundred thousand kilowatts. It could be less, though."

"That much?" Hellstrom took a deep breath. "Researchers are different from the rest of us in many ways, Saldo. They were bred for a rather narrowed vision, a concentration of intellect. We should be prepared for the possibility of a disastrous failure."

"A dis—" Saldo fell into stricken silence.

"Prepare to evacuate the area for at least three levels around the test gallery," Hellstrom said. "You are to post yourself in Generation. Tell the managing specialist not to connect the power cables until I have given permission. When the researchers come to make the power arrangements, call me. Ask them then, if you're able, what range and error factor they are estimating for the project. Get the power figures and, at the same time, order the evacuation of the galleries. We will risk no more workers than necessary."

Saldo stood in subdued awe. He felt depressed, rebounding from his former pride. None of these precautions had entered his mind. He had thought only to argue Hellstrom into one particular course of action. The stratagem of stationing an observer in Generation with the authority to delay the power hookup, however, filled the demands of Saldo's own plan and did far more.

"Perhaps you'd better send somebody with more imagination and ability to Generation," Saldo said. "Maybe Ed—"

"You are the one I want in Generation," Hellstrom said. "Ed is a seasoned specialist with long experience Outside. He can think like an Outsider, which you cannot. He also has had sufficient tempering that he seldom overestimates his own capabilities, nor underestimates them. In a word, he is *balanced*. If we are to survive these next hours, we require this quality above all others. I trust you to carry out my orders carefully and completely. I know you can and will. Now, get back to your station."

Saldo's shoulders came up and he looked at Hellstrom's fatigue-lined features. "Nils, I didn't think—"

Hellstrom interrupted in a softer tone. "In part, it is my fatigue being short and severe with you. This is something you should have taken into consideration. You could have called me on the internal system without leaving your post. A true leader considers many possibilities before acting. If you were ready for leadership, you would have thought to conserve *my* energies, as well as your own. You will grow into this ability, and the delay time between your consideration of many courses and your decision to act correctly will grow shorter and shorter."

"I'm going back to my post at once," Saldo said. He turned, started across the room. As he moved, voices were raised at the observer stations. A garble of sound could be heard coming over one of the communicators. An observer could be heard asking, "Who else is there to take charge?" Another garble erupted from the communicators. "One at a time!" the observer shouted. "Tell them to hold their stations. If too many of us are running around without coordination, we'll just get in each other's way. We'll take charge of the search from here."

The observer, a young female subleader-in-training, whose face appeared an oval mask of shock in the light from her screen, lifted herself half out of her chair to peer across the bank of instruments at Hellstrom. "One of the captives has escaped in the Hive!"

Hellstrom was at her side as soon as he could get there in a thrusting rush across the room. Saldo hesitated at the door.

"Which one?" Hellstrom demanded, bending over the observer.

"The one called Janvert. Shall we dispatch workers to—

"No."

Saldo spoke from the door. "Nils, should I—"

"Get to your station!" Hellstrom called, not moving his gaze from the screen in front of the young observer. A frightened guardworker appeared on the screen, a young male with the shoulder mark of dronedom. "Which level?" Hellstrom demanded.

"Forty-two," the worker on the screen said. "And he has a stunwand. I don't see how he could—he killed two workers, the ones who said they were sent to—to—at your orders to—"

"I understand," Hellstrom interrupted. They were the specialists he had sent down to bring Janvert to sufficient alertness for use as an envoy. Something had gone wrong and Janvert had escaped. Hellstrom straightened, gazing at the workers around him in the aerie. "Awaken your replacements. Janvert has been Hive-marked. No common worker would recognize him as an Outsider. He can move anywhere in the Hive without attracting attention. We have a double problem. We must recapture him and we must not upset the Hive any more than it already is. Make that clear to every searcher. Send your replacements after Janvert with a phyical description. Issue Outsider guns to at least one worker in each search party as long as the guns last. I don't want stunwands used in the Hive under these circumstances."

"You want him dead and in the vats then," a worker behind Hellstrom said.

"No, I do not!"

"But you said—"

"One gun with each party," Hellstrom said. "The gun is to wound him in the legs only if nothing else can be done to stop him. I want him taken alive. Do you all understand that? We need this Outsider alive."

From the Hive Manual. Life must take life for the sake of life, but no worker should enter this great wheel of regeneration with any motive other than the perpetuation of our species. Only in the species are we linked to infinity and this has a different meaning for the species than it does for the mortal cell.

Janvert had taken a long time to realize the strangeness of his position. For a while, he felt he had become two distinctly different people and he remembered both of them clearly. One had studied law, joined the Agency, loved Clovis Carr, and felt trapped in activities that dehumanized him. The other appeared to have awakened as a fully recognizable individual while eating a meal with Nils Hellstrom and a rather doll-like woman named Fancy. This other individual had behaved in a wildly detached manner. This individual remembered walking meekly with Hellstrom into a room where people stood around and asked questions. As this weird *other*, Janvert remembered answering those questions with complete candor. He had answered willingly, searching out details that might expand the answers. He had actually worked very hard to make his answers understood.

There were other strange memories, too—big open tanks in a tremendous room, some of the tanks bubbling and seething; another equally large room crawling with toddlers, little children who bounced and played in odd silence on a screened floor that surged under them in places like a trampoline. He recalled an acid smell in that room, but with a sense of cleanliness about it. He remembered water spurting suddenly from the ceiling onto the toddlers as he passed, and then that other smell, the one he recalled from the whole *other* experience and was around him even now. It was fetid, rank, and warm in the nostrils.

The self he thought of as his original identity appeared to have been dormant all during the *other* experience, but it was aware now. He recognized where he was in both sets of memories. It was a room with rough gray walls, a depression with a hole centered in it in one corner for relieving himself, a waist-high shelf about one foot by three feet near the room's only door, apparently of the same material as the walls. A

black plastic pitcher and glass occupied the shelf.
They held warm water. There had been a food bowl
on the shelf earlier. He recalled that bowl and the
blank-faced nude male who'd brought it—no conversation in that one at all. There were no windows in the
room, just the one door and the toilet depression. He
heard water rushing under the toilet hole occasionally.
There were water jets around the depression, too, and
they had turned on once, cleaning the area. There was
no chair, only the floor to sit on, and he had been
stripped to the skin. He could see nothing in the place
that might make a weapon. The plastic water pitcher
and glass wouldn't break; he'd tried.

His memory presented him with the images of
other visitors, too—a pair of older females who held
him with remarkable ease while they examined him in-
timately, then injected something into his left buttock.
The area of the injection still tingled. The return of his
original awareness had begun soon after that injection,
though. He estimated that had been at least three
hours ago. They'd taken his watch and he felt unsure
of time, but guessing at it made him feel he was doing
something positive.

I have to escape, he told himself.

His weird *other* self, lapsing into a dormancy of its
own now, brought up memories of hordes of nude
people swarming in the tunnels through which he had
been brought to this place. It was a human anthill.
How could he escape through that?

The door opened and a relatively young woman
entered. In the moment she left the door open he
glimpsed an older, tougher looking female outside,
carrying one of those mysterious weapons that looked
like a whip with a double end. The young woman who
came in had a stubble of black hair around the genitals and a similar cap on her head, and there was no
moon-faced vacancy in her features or her movements. She carried in her left hand what appeared to
be an ordinary stethoscope.

Janvert leaped to his feet as she entered, moved
around near the shelf with his back to the wall.

She seemed amused. "Relax. I'm just here to see

how you're taking all this." She clipped the stethoscope around her neck, took up the other end in her left hand.

Janvert groped for the water pitcher without taking his attention from her and his hand knocked the pitcher from the shelf.

"Now, look what you've done," she said, bending to recover the pitcher which lay in a puddle of its own water.

As she stooped, Janvert moved in desperation, brought his right hand down in a vicious chop across her neck. She fell flat and didn't move.

Now, there was the other guard outside. Relax and think, Janvert told himself. Cool green light from a recessed cove around the ceiling washed the room, creating a death pallor in the skin of the woman on the floor. He bent over her, felt for a pulse, found none. Quickly, he recovered her stethoscope, listened for a heartbeat. Nothing. The realization that his one frantic blow had killed her filled him with a chill sense of his own perilous position. Moved by urgency, he dragged the woman's body out of the way to the right of the door, looked back to see if he'd left any sign of struggle. The water pitcher still lay there, but Janvert hesitated. The hesitation saved him.

Once more, the door opened and the older woman poked her head inside with a look of obvious curiosity on her face.

Janvert, leaping from behind the door, grabbed her head, yanked her into the cell, bringing a knee up into her midriff. She grunted, dropping her weapon, and he released her, chopped her as he had the first one, whirled, and slammed the door.

Now, he had both of them and one of their weapons. He examined the odd whiplike object. The thing was black plastic, similar in color and texture to the pitcher and water glass. It was about a yard long with a stubby handle indented for fingers. There was a click-notched dial in the handle base and a yellow stud under the index-finger indentation.

Janvert pointed the double end at the guard he had just knocked down, and he depressed the stud.

The wand went *bap-hummmm,* and he released the stud. The humming stopped. The older woman had jerked as the weapon came alive. Now, the skin along her exposed side began to turn a dark red-purple. He bent, felt for a pulse. Nothing. Two of them dead. He backed away, looked at the door. It opened inward, he knew, and there was a cupped indentation at waist height that he had tried earlier. The door had refused to open then. He wondered now if, in his panic, he had locked himself in. Desperation moving him, he tried the door. It opened immediately with only a faint click and he glimpsed people thronging past the door before he closed it.

"I have to think," he told himself, speaking aloud.

They would expect him to head for the surface, of course. Could they have other ways of leaving, though? What lay below him? He knew there must be at least one lower level. His captors had led him past an open, doorless double-elevator shaft with barebones cars passing upward on one side and downward on the other. He held one of their weapons and he now knew it could kill. Hellstrom's people would search for him. They'd move room by room through their tunnel warren, and they obviously had the manpower to be thorough.

I'll go down.

He had no idea how far underground he might be. They had brought him on elevators and there had been many floors, but his *other* self had not thought to count them.

They'd fed him something to make him docile, of course. That other self was Hellstrom's creation. It might even be the answer to Project 40. The MIT papers could just be a description of something needed to create the chemicals for manipulating humans.

The searchers wouldn't expect him to go downward, though. If there was any other way out of this human anthill, he'd find it by doing the unexpected.

Keep doing the unexpected, he reminded himself.

He still didn't feel in complete command of himself, but he knew he couldn't wait any longer. He held the captive weapon at the ready in his right hand, opened the door, peered out. There was less activity in the tunnel now, but a silent file of naked men and women crossed in front of him from left to right without a single curious glance. Janvert counted nine in the group. A longer line was passing in the other direction of the far side of the tunnel. They, too, ignored him.

As they passed, Janvert slipped out of the cell and fell into step at the end of the line going left. He dropped back at the first elevator, waited for a downcar to appear, stepped up quickly as he saw a lean, blank-faced male doing. They both faced the front of the car, rode silently downward.

The smell of the place began to repel Janvert more and more as he found himself growing increasingly alert. The man with him in the elevator appeared not to notice it. He breathed easily, but Janvert experienced a faint nausea every time he focused on the smell. Best not to think about it then, he warned himself. His partner in the elevator remained a figure of mysterious menace, but something kept the man from taking special notice of Janvert. The man's pubic hair had been shaved or removed in some other way. His head was shiny in its baldness.

The man leaped out as the elevator passed another floor and Janvert now had the car to himself. He counted gray walls and floors, got to ten before wondering how long he should stay with this car. He glanced up at the ceiling. It was as featureless as the floor. Something glistening gray was stuck to the ceiling near the wall on his left. He reached up, touched the substance. Some of it clung to his finger and he brought it back, sniffed it. The smell was that of the gruel in his food bowl. He rubbed it off on his thigh. The significance of food on the ceiling began to demand his attention. That ceiling might become a floor in the elevator's return phase. The cars never seemed to stop. People leaped on and off them through the doorless openings. Everything spoke of an endless chain of cars circling between levels of Hellstrom's anthill.

Abruptly, the car lurched, tipped slightly to his left. It lurched again, tipped more. Janvert knelt against the lower edge, crouched there as the elevator turned flat on its side. Nothing but gray wall showed in the door opening as he walked the side around until the former ceiling became the floor, confirming his guess. The car was going up now. He leaped out at the first opening, found not another person in sight. He was in a tunnel illuminated by dim red light, but there was a brighter yellow glow off in the distance to his right. The tunnel stretched away into red gloom beyond that glow. He glanced left, found a gentle curve to the tunnel's floor which bent it out of sight to the right. He decided to head for the glow, turned right, held himself to a normal walking pace. He had to be just another occupant of this warren going about his normal business. The weapon felt heavy in his right hand, slippery beneath the perspiration in his palm.

He heard the sound of running water before he reached the area of the glow, but he could see by then that the light came from long slits parallel to the floor and the arched ceiling. The slits were eye height, and he had only to turn his head as he passed to look into a wide, low chamber with long tanks spaced through it, water running in them, people working with businesslike concentration around the tanks. Janvert peered at the nearest tank, discerned fish boiling in it, little fish about six inches long. He saw now that the people farther out in the room were scooping fish from a tank into a wheeled carrier.

A fish farm, by God!

Janvert continued past the glowing slits and there was another glow ahead of him now, a distinct cast of pink in it. The light came from floor-to-ceiling doors that revealed a chamber even larger than the first one. This chamber was jammed with waist-high benches, lights low over them and on the benches, lush plants with rich green leaves. Again, he heard the sound of running water, but fainter here. Workers wearing dark glasses moved among the benches, carrying bags slung from their shoulders and harvesting red fruit that Janvert took to be tomatoes. Filled bags were being carried toward openings in the far wall, dumped through there.

He was encountering more people in the tunnel now and there was a humming sound ahead that grew louder as he approached. He realized he'd been hearing that sound for some time now but had been filtering it out of his consciousness.

Thus far, none of the people he had met paid any special attention to him.

He felt it was getting warmer in the tunnel as he neared that irritating humming. The sound was almost painful in its intensity. He came presently to larger slits in the tunnel's left-hand wall, peered through into a gigantic chamber. It went down at least two stories, up an equal distance, and was filled with tall tubular objects that dwarfed the workers moving on the floor far below him. He estimated that the things were at least fifty feet high and probably a hundred feet in diameter. They were the obvious source of the humming and there was a noticeable ozone smell coming through the slits into the tunnel.

Electrical generators, Janvert guessed.

But it was the biggest generator plant he had ever seen. It stretched away at least half a mile to his left and more than that on his right and looked to be at least half a mile wide. If those were generators, he wondered what was driving them.

Janvert answered his own question as he came to the far end of his tunnel. It turned left there with a double ramp. One ramp went down into the lighted room and the other ramp, parallel to the first on the right and separated from it by a thin wall, slanted down into a gloomy area where he could discern the oily rush of water passing beneath dim lights.

Water—was that his escape route?

Janvert went purposefully down the ramp to the water, passed another file of people without a side glance. He emerged onto a black ledge beside the water. It was a damned river! The thing stretched away in the gloom and he could detect moving lights on the far side about a quarter of a mile away.

The ledge beside the river decreased in width as

Janvert moved along it below the generator room. He could hear the water beneath his ledge, the muted humming on his left.

The possible dimensions of this enterprise beneath the earth began to insinuate themselves into Janvert's awareness. It was so large he began to suspect the government must be involved in it somehow. What other answer could there be? It was too big to escape notice. Or—was it?

If the government had a hand in this, why had the Agency known nothing about it? That didn't seem possible. The Chief had been privy to some of the touchiest secrets in the land. That had been made clear on many occasions. Even Merrivale probably would have known about something this big.

In this questioning reverie, Janvert almost collided with a gray-haired man who stood in his path at what appeared to be the end of the ledge. A spidery open stairway climbed upward beyond the man. The gray-haired one lifted his right hand, wiggled the fingers oddly in front of Janvert's face.

Janvert shrugged.

The man wiggled his fingers once more, shook his head from side to side. He was obviously puzzled.

Janvert lifted the weapon, pointed it at the man.

The other stepped backward, shock apparent on his face. His mouth was open, eyes wide and staring, muscles bunched defensively. Once more he held up his hand, wiggled his fingers.

"What do you want?" Janvert asked.

It was as though Janvert had struck him. The man took another step backward, stopped at the edge of the spidery stairs. Still, he didn't answer.

Janvert glanced around. They appeared to be alone on this ledge and he could feel tension mounting. The hand signal obviously was supposed to mean something to him. The fact that it didn't was growing increasingly apparent. With abrupt decision, Janvert flicked the firing stud on his weapon, heard a short *bap-hum,* and the gray-haired man crumpled.

Quickly, Janvert dragged the body into the gloom at the edge of the ledge, hesitated. Should he dump the man into the river? There might be people downstream to see it and come looking for an explanation. He decided against it and went up the stairs.

The stairs ended at a platform that formed the anchor point for a catwalk across the rushing river. Janvert struck out boldly across the catwalk. He felt no particular qualms at having killed another denizen of Hellstrom's warren. The oily movement of water about thirty feet below and the continuing pressure of the fetid odor combined to produce in him a feeling of vertigo, however, and he guided himself with his left hand on the rail beside him.

The catwalk entered a short, narrow tunnel at the far side of the river and there was an open, glowing yellow tube to light his way from above. A door blocked the inner end of the short tunnel. It held a wheeled handle at waist height in its center and there was a green-glowing *A* above the wheel with a stylized symbol beside it which he took to be part of an insect's body, segmented and tapering, but without a head.

Holding the weapon ready, Janvert applied left pressure to the wheel with his left hand. It resisted for a moment, then turned freely to an abrupt stop. He heaved outward on the wheel and it gave abruptly with a soughing sound and he felt a breeze on the back of his neck. Faintly glowing pink light beyond the door revealed another tunnel barely wider than the door. The light came from widely spaced overhead fixtures—small flat discs. The tunnel slanted upward at a gentle angle.

Janvert stepped inside, sealed the door behind him with a spin of a duplicate handle on the inside. He began to climb.

Hive Security Report 7-A: Janvert. Worker whose description agrees with that of Janvert reported on level forty-eight near turbine station six. Although this would indicate fugitive is going down in the Hive instead of up, it is being investigated. Workers who reported the sighting say they thought he was a leader

specialist because of his long hair and possession of a
stunwand. This would tend to confirm the sighting, but
it still seems unusual that he would not try to break
through immediately to the surface.

Janvert estimated he had climbed almost three
hundred feet in the narrow tunnel before he paused
for a rest. The tunnel executed a sharp switchback approximately every thousand paces and he estimated
the slope at about three percent. He guessed that the
tunnel was a ventilator of some kind, but he had seen
no openings thus far, and there was something about
the stillness of the place and the occasional pockets of
dust that spoke of long disuse. Could it be an emergency exit? Perhaps it had been dug for access while
larger tunnels were being excavated. Could it possibly
lead to an emergency exit? He didn't dare let himself
hope for that yet. The tunnel was just taking him upward.

He resumed his climb presently and in five more
switchbacks came to another door with a wheeled handle. He stopped, looked at the door. What was on the
other side? Should he pass it? He had a weapon. The
weapon carried the deciding argument. He worked the
door handle, put a shoulder to the door, and thrust it
open. Air soughed against his face.

Janvert stepped out of the tunnel onto a narrow,
railed platform about halfway up the wall of an im-
mense circular and domed room. It stretched away
from him in bright blue-white light for at least two
hundred yards. The floor of the giant room curved
slightly downward to the center and it was alive with
men and women in a complexity of sexual couplings.

Janvert stared at them, frozen in blank astonish-
ment.

The room was filled with an undercurrent of
grunts and sounds of flesh slapping flesh. Couples
were separating, stumbling to new partners, and just
going on with their amazing sexual activity.

Breeding!

He recalled Peruge's astonished account of the

night with Fancy. She'd called it *breeding*. That was the only word that really fit this amazing scene. It excited no prurient interest in him. It even repelled him slightly. The place carried its own distinctive odor—a wild mixture of perspiration and a musty something that reminded him of saliva, all of it riding on the original stink of this whole warren. He noted now that the floor was damp and it appeared resilient. It was a faint blue gray and it glistened in the few places not occupied by writhing couples. Through the movement of flesh at the center of the room, he detected a wide circle of darker material which appeared to be a drain —it was grilled, by God! There were marks on some of the flesh to show the grill pattern.

What could be more efficient?

Still in a state of semishock, Janvert retreated into the tunnel, sealed the door, resumed his climb. His memory carried the wild image of that room. He didn't think he would ever forget that scene. Nobody would believe him, though. That had to be seen to be believed.

He knew he was working against a background of semihysteria. So that's what they mean by "sexual congress!"

He suspected he could have climbed down from his platform and joined the orgy without anyone the wiser. Just another male breeder.

Janvert passed two more wheel-handled doors before recovering a semblance of mental balance. He looked at each door with revulsion, trying to imagine what he might find on the other side. This was a goddamned human hive! He stopped abruptly, frozen by the full import of that thought.

Hive.

He glanced around at the dimly lighted walls of the tunnel, sensed the faint humming of machinery, the smells, all the signs of teeming life around him. *HIVE!*

Janvert took three deep, shuddering breaths before resuming his climb. His thoughts were in turmoil. It was a human hive. They lived here the way insects lived. How did insects live? They did things no human

wanted to do—some things no human *could* do. They
had drones and workers—and a queen and—they ate
to live. They ate things that the human stomach would
reject if the human consciousness didn't reject it first.
For insects, breeding was just—breeding. The more he
thought about it, the more the pattern fitted. This was
no secret government project! This was a horror, an
abomination, a thing that needed to be burned out!

Hive Security Report 16-A: Janvert. The body of a
turbine specialist killed by stunwand has been found
near the center of the primary watercourse. Janvert's
work for sure. Double guard has been ordered on all
turbine inlets and screens, although no human could
survive a trip through the power system. More likely
he's in the old construction access tunnels that were
converted to emergency ventilation standby. Search
concentrating there.

Janvert stopped at the next door, pressed an ear
to the door's surface, listening. He heard faint,
rhythmic thumpings on the other side—some kind of
machine, he guessed. There was a hiss accompanying
the thumps. He released the wheel latch, opened the
door a crack, and peered in. It was a much smaller
room than the other, but still big. He guessed it to be a
hundred feet on a side. The ceiling was low and the
door opened directly onto the room's floor. The light
was only a dim red glow from tubes across the ceiling,
revealing stubby benches, each with a maze of transparent glass tubing in pillars at both ends. The tubing
pulsed with fluids in brilliant glowing colors and this
distracted him for a moment from what lay between
the pillars on the bench surfaces.
    He stared at the objects, unwilling to believe his
eyes were reporting accurately. Each bench carried
what appeared to be the stump of a human body from
about the waist to the knees. Some were grossly male
and some female. Among the females were a few
whose abdomens bulged as though they were preg-

nant. Beyond waist and knees there was nothing that could be thought of as flesh—only that tubing with its pulsing colors. Could they be real?

Janvert slipped into the room, touched the nearest one, a male stump. The flesh was warm! He jerked his hand away, felt vomit rising in his throat. He backed against the door to the tunnel, unable to take his gaze from the contents of this room. Those were live stumps of human flesh. They had to be!

Movement in the room's far corner caught his attention. He saw people parading along the benches there, bending, studying the stumps, examining the tubing. It was like a caricature of doctors doing their rounds. Janvert slipped back into the tunnel before he was seen, closed the door, and stood there with his forehead pressed against the smooth, cool surface.

Those were human reproductive sections. He could imagine Hellstrom's *hive* keeping those monstrosities alive for breeding purposes. The thought of his own flesh subjected to such indignity sent shudders coursing through him. His back, neck, and shoulders trembled and his knees felt incapable of supporting him. Reproductive stumps!

Somewhere below him there sounded a dull thud and in his ears he felt a change in the tunnel's air pressure. Bare feet could be heard slapping the tunnel floor, running.

They're in here after me!

Terror driving him, he jerked open the door, slid through, sealed the door behind him. The medical procession noticed him this time, but they could only jerk upright in surprise before the stunwand in Janvert's hand sent them tumbling. He plunged through the nightmare room, trying not to look at any of the stumps. An arched passage led from the room into a large gallery thronging with people. Terror still hounding him, he whirled left, shouldered through the throng, pushing people aside, heedless of the disturbance and curiosity he obviously was arousing. Milling turmoil marked his path. There were waving hands behind him, a few inarticulate outcries, and one oddly

piercing female voice calling after him, "Say there!
Say there!"

At the first elevator entrance, he shouldered a
man away from the opening, leaped into an upbound
car, staring down at faces that kept staring upward
with puzzlement and some alarm until the floor of the
car closed off the opening.

Two women and a man shared the car with him.
One of the women looked like an older version of
Fancy, but the younger one had a full head of blonde
hair, one of the few he'd seen like that in the depths of
Hellstrom's hive. The man, completely hairless, with a
narrow, foxy face and brightly alert eyes, reminded
Janvert of Merrivale. All three showed obvious curiosity and the man bent toward him, sniffing. What he
inhaled seemed to puzzle him because he sniffed
again.

In panic, Janvert turned the captured weapon on
him, swept its beam across the women. They slumped
to the floor as the car passed another opening. A
woman with heavy breasts and a round, blank face
tried to enter, but Janvert kicked her in the midriff,
sent her sprawling into the people behind her. The car
passed another opening without incident, another—
another. He dove out at the fourth opening into a
throng of people, plunged through them across the
tunnel and into a smaller side passage that had attracted him because it was unoccupied. Two of the men
he'd sent sprawling behind him leaped to their feet
and started to give chase, but he dropped them with a
burst from the weapon, then fled, skidded around a
corner to the left, another corner, and found himself
back in the main gallery at least a hundred yards from
where he'd left the elevator. A milling crowd could be
seen down there with figures jammed into the side passage and more trying to enter it.

Janvert turned right, holding the weapon upright
in front of him to conceal it from the people behind,
forced himself to assume a slow walking pace while he
tried to bring his heaving lungs under control. As he
moved, he listened carefully for sounds of pursuit. The
sounds of disturbance faded, but he heard no pursuers

and, presently, he dared to cross the tunnel to his left, leaving it by a smaller right-angle passage that slanted upward steeply. This passage opened within a hundred paces into another large cross tunnel with an elevator directly in front of him. He wove his way without incident through passing people, stepped into the first up-bound car. The car picked up speed the instant he entered. He glanced around to see if some operator he'd missed controlled this, but he was alone in the car. Openings flashed past him. He counted nine, wondering if Hellstrom had some secret control of this car and they'd sped it up to trap him. He didn't dare try to leave at this speed.

His panic increasing, Janvert moved to the doorway, searching the sides of the car for controls, but there were none. As he moved, the car came to another opening, slowed. He jumped out, almost collided with two men guiding a long cart piled with what appeared to be yellow fabric thrown loosely into it. They dodged him, grinned and waved, their fingers moving in the same kind of intricate designs he'd seen in the gray-haired man beside the river. Janvert smiled ruefully, shrugged, and the pair accepted this, continuing to trundle their car down the tunnel.

Janvert turned to the right, away from them, saw that the tunnel ended shortly in a wide arch with bright lights and machinery visible in a large room beyond the arch, people busily working there. He felt he didn't dare turn around now, continued into a wide, low room with metal-shaping machinery on floor stands scattered through it. He recognized a lathe, a stamping press of some kind (the ceiling had been opened above it to take the machine's upper part), and there were several drill presses with men and women bent over them, working steadily, ignoring his presence. There was an underlying smell of oil in the place and the biting acridity of hot metal. It could have been any large machine shop except for the nudity. Carts carrying bins of unidentifiable metal objects were being pushed along several of the aisles between the machines.

Janvert tried to act knowledgeably busy, strode

as directly as he could across the room, hoping to find
an exit on the far side. He noted that people were paying a different kind of attention to him now and he
wondered why. One woman actually left a lathe and
came up to sniff at his elbow. Janvert tried his universal shrug, glanced down to see perspiration glistening
on his skin. Had his sweat attracted her, for God's
sake?

The far wall of the room he was crossing showed
no open door and he was beginning to feel trapped
when he saw a wheeled latch in the wall: it alerted
him to one of the doors into the tunnel he'd used earlier. The door was only a faint line in the wall, but it
opened outward when he worked the latch. He moved
through the doorway as though he had every right
there, sealed it behind him. The tunnel sloped up to
his right. He listened for sounds to tell him whether
others shared the tunnel, heard nothing, and set off
upward.

His back and legs ached with fatigue and he wondered how much more of this he could endure. His
stomach was a region of painful hollowness, his mouth
and throat were dry. Desperation drove him, though,
and he knew he would press himself upward until he
dropped. He had to escape from this monstrous place.

From the Hive Manual. Chemical releasers that can
evoke a predetermined response from the individual of
any animal species must be very numerous and may
be infinite within the refined nuances of variation. The
so-called rational mind of consciousness in the human
animal presents no insurmountable obstacle to such a
releasing process, but may be considered only as a
threshold to be overcome. And once consciousness has
been sufficiently depressed, the releaser is freed to do
its work. Here, in this area once considered the exclu-
sive domain of instinct, we of the Hive are sure to develop our greatest unifying forces.

Hellstrom stood in the aerie beneath a Hive-sign

display that translated "Use everything—waste nothing." It was past 3:00 A.M., and he had gone beyond wishing he could get a brief sleep. Now, he only prayed for rest of any kind.

"See those changes in the air pressure," an observer behind him said. "He's into the emergency ventilator system again. How is he doing that? Quick! Send the alarm. Where's the nearest search team?"

"Why aren't we blocking off that system, level by level, or at least every other level?" Hellstrom asked resignedly.

"We only have enough teams to keep a ten-level guard on the system," a male voice to his left said.

Hellstrom peered through the green gloom of the aerie, trying to identify who'd spoken. Had that been Ed? Was he back from checking the Outside patrols already?

Damn that Janvert! The man was diabolical in his ingenuity. Dead and injured workers, behavior disruptions from the disturbance of his passage, the growing turmoil left in the wake of running searchers —everything was conspiring to upset the entire Hive. They would be years finding and clearing up all of the traces of this night. Janvert was terrified, of course, and the chemistry of his terror was spreading through the Hive. As more and more workers read that subtle signal from a human who, according to his other chemical markers, seemed one of them, their fears moved like an outspreading wave. It could damned well provoke a crisis if he wasn't caught soon.

It had been a mistake not to increase his guard as they brought him back to normalcy.

My mistake, Hellstrom told himself bitterly.

The chemistry of fellowship was, indeed, a double-edged blade. It cut both ways. Those guarding him had been lulled by it unconsciously. When had a worker ever attacked his fellows?

He listened to the observer stations coordinating this new turn in the search. Their hunt juices were up and he sensed the excitement in their voices. It was almost as though they didn't want to catch Janvert too soon.

Hellstrom sighed and said, "Get the female captive up here."

Someone off in the gloom said, "She's still unconscious."

That was Ed for sure, Hellstrom told himself. He said, "Well, revive her and get her up here!"

Hive-sign display over the central vat chamber. It is right and holy that we yield up our bodies when we die, that the compounds of our transient lives are not lost to that greater force manifested in our hive.

At the eighth switchback door on his upward flight, Janvert brought himself to a stumbling, panting halt, slumping against the door. He could feel its coolness through his hair as he pressed his head against it, looking down at his bare feet. God, it was hot in the tunnel! And the stink was worse. He felt he could not move another step without rest. His heart was pounding, his chest ached, sweat poured from his body. He wondered if he dared venture back into the main tunnels and search for an elevator. He pressed an ear against the door, listened, could hear no special activity on the other side. This worried him. Were they waiting there for him to emerge?

Only faint sounds of machinery and an omnipresent sense of human movement came to him. An odd sense of almost silence beyond this door, though. Again, he pressed an ear against it, heard nothing he could identify as a direct menace.

There would be more people out there, though, these weird denizens of Hellstrom's hive. How many were there? Ten thousand? Not one of them on the census rolls. He knew this. The whole place conveyed a secretive sense of purposes that cut across everything outside in the sharpest and most outrageous ways. Here were people who lived by rules that denied everything the outside society believed. Did they have a god in here? He recalled Hellstrom saying grace. Sham! Pure sham!

It was a damned crawling, revolting hive.

The last words of Trova Hellstrom. The defeat of the Outsiders is assured by their arrogance. They defy powers greater than themselves. We in the Hive are the true creatures of reason. We will wait patiently in the manner of the insects, with a logic that perhaps no wild Outsider will ever understand, because the insects have taught us that the true winner in the race for survival is the *last* to finish that race.

Janvert guessed he'd waited five minutes before fear overcame his fatigue. He wasn't really rested, but he had to go on. He was breathing easier, but the ache remained in his legs; there was a lancing pain in his side when he took too deep a breath, and the arches of his feet felt as though knives were cutting them, a consequence of running barefoot. He knew his body could take little more of this driving punishment before collapse. He had to go out there and find an elevator. He straightened, intending to open the door, and the corner of his left eye caught a flicker of movement down the tunnel. Pursuers carrying guns rounded the corner below him, but their weapons were not raised as they climbed, and they reacted with a brief moment of shock that saved Janvert. His weapon had been held across his left arm as he reached for the door's wheel latch and he had only to press the stud, which his hand did almost of itself. The figures below him collapsed as the *bap-hum* filled the tunnel.

In falling, one of the pursuers raised a pistol and fired one shot that hit a light fixture below Janvert and sent a searing shard of some shattered material into his cheek. His left hand, clapped reflexively against the wound, came away with the glittering shard and a bright smear of blood.

Janvert had no way of knowing if the weapon in his hand worked through walls, but the deepest panic he'd known thus far dictated his next actions. He lifted the weapon, depressed the stud on it, and fanned it across the door in front of him before opening it.

Six figures lay in a tangled sprawl beyond the door as it opened, and one of them held a nickel-plated .45 automatic with carved ivory grips. Janvert lifted it from relaxed fingers as he stepped into the room. He glanced around, saw what appeared to be a long, narrow barracks with triple-tiered bunks around the walls. The only occupants were the six figures on the floor—all males, all nude, all but one bald, and all of them breathing. So the weapon only knocked people out when a solid barrier attenuated its force. Janvert nodded to himself. He had a weapon in each hand now, and one of them felt reassuringly familiar.

Hive translation from "The Wisdom of the Wild." The path to species extinction begins with the proud belief that in each individual there is a mentalistic being—an *ego* or personality, spirit, anima, character, soul, or mind—and that this separated incarnation is somehow free.

"Now he has a gun," Hellstrom said. "That's great! That's just great. Is he a superman? Less than half an hour ago he was in the central breeder section. I was assured we had him trapped there and now—now I'm told he has knocked out two entire search teams eight levels higher!"

Hellstrom sat almost at the middle of the aerie's observation arc, directly behind the observer at the center position. The chair he occupied was his one concession to a body demanding relief from its mounting fatigue. He had been active now for most of twenty-six hours and the aerie clock showed just past 4:00 A.M.

"What are your orders?" the observer in front of him asked.

Hellstrom stared at the observer's head outlined against the glowing screen. *My orders?*

"What makes anyone believe my orders have changed?" he asked. "You are to capture him!"

"You still want him alive?"

"More than ever! If he's really this resourceful, we need to mingle his blood with ours."

"He's obviously out in the main tunnels again," the observer said.

"Of course! Tell the searchers to concentrate on the elevators. He's had a long climb. He'll be tired. Concentrate every search team in the upper levels along the elevators. Have them scan every car and knock out any doubtfuls. I know—" Hellstrom held up a silencing hand as the observer turned in shocked alarm. "It can't be helped."

"But our own—"

"Better we do it than leave it to him. Look at what he's done. He obviously has his stunward turned to maximum and doesn't know much about it. He's killing workers close up with it. I feel the same outrage as all of you over this, but we must remember that he is panic stricken and he doesn't know what he's doing."

"He knows enough to stay out of our hands!" someone behind Hellstrom muttered.

Hellstrom ignored the sign of discontent and asked, "Where is that female captive? I ordered her brought up here almost an hour ago."

"She had to be revived, Nils. They're bringing her."

"Well, tell them to hurry."

From the Hive Manual. One of our strengths lies in the recognition of the diversity we gain through a unique application of the social behavior of insects as opposed to the social behavior evolved by the wild human animal. With this lesson ever before us, we are, for the first time in the long history of life on this planet, designing our own future.

Janvert stood behind two females and two males

in an upbound elevator. The quartet had shown disturbance at his entry and he had interpreted this as growing out of the wound on his cheek. A peremptory gesture with the gun, however, had quieted them, but he was left with the odd feeling that the gesture, not the gun, had elicited the response. To test this, he tucked the automatic under his right arm when one of the men turned, and he waved a palm at the man. It was as though Janvert had said *turn around and leave me alone*. The man turned, wiggled his fingers at his companions, and all of them ignored Janvert from that point.

He had the hang of the elevators now. You stood to the back in these upper-level cars. The act of stepping forward slowed them at a passing floor. Near the doorway there was a critical area that operated an invisible sensor.

One of the women glanced back at him presently, nodded at the doorway which was passing a blank gray wall. Last stop coming up? Janvert wondered. The others moved forward in a body. Janvert readied himself to join them, lifting the captured wand in his left hand. As he moved, the first thin edge of the opening gaped above him. The car slowed and he saw a cluster of bare legs, two weapons pointing inward at the elevator car.

Janvert depressed the stud on his own weapon, fanned it across the doorway as the opening deepened. He caught his fellow passengers as well as those outside. He leaped over the passengers, spraying his weapon right and left in a humming arc of destruction, and ran down the tunnel to the right, partly on the cold floor, partly on fallen flesh still warm under his feet. As he ran, he heard a gushing crunch behind, glanced back without breaking stride. One of his fellow passengers had fallen with head across the door opening. The upward-surging car had left a head rolling on the floor in a patch of gore.

Janvert turned away, finding it odd that he felt nothing. Nothing at all. That denizen of this hive had been dead already, killed by one of his own kind's weapons. It made no difference what was done to the body after that. No difference at all.

Continuing to depress the firing stud for short bursts of humming, Janvert trotted down the tunnel, clearing a path as he went. In this way, he rounded a corner, caught another group of elevator watchers. They collapsed as he burst upon them, but there was a new group running toward him down the tunnel ahead and Janvert heard the thrumming of their weapons. Obviously they were out of range. He lifted the automatic, emptied it into this group, dodged into the first up-car, and rode it two floors before emerging into another tunnel where the opening had been left unguarded.

Janvert dodged hurrying figures to cross this tunnel, entered another sharply slanted up-ramp which he abandoned at the first doorway on his right. This led into another hydroponics garden full of harvesters. He recognized tomatoes and hurled the empty automatic at a worker who ran toward him protesting the intrusion. He ran, firing the captured weapon ahead and to both sides. Tomatoes splashed on the floor from tumbling harvest sacks, and their red pulp spattered over his feet and legs as he skidded through them. His chest was one big band of flame, throat dry and painful, his body almost ready to quit.

A series of small openings became visible in the far wall of the hydroponics room as he approached. They were about chest height and he could see sacked produce whisking upward—then baskets, bins. He recognized berries, what appeared to be deep green cucumbers, string beans. . .

A dumbwaiter system!

Shoulders sagging, he came to a halt, stared at the wall. There was no door along its entire length—only these openings with produce whipping upward. There were flat shelves on a conveyor; some of them came past him empty. Containers went onto the shelves. The openings were about three feet square and the moving shelves didn't appear to be much larger. Could he get in there onto one of those shelves? They moved upward at frightening speed. He could

hear sounds of tumult growing in the tunnel behind
him. What other chance did he have? He couldn't go
back.

Janvert summoned a small reserve of strength,
backed off several steps, and watched for an empty
carrier. When one appeared, he dove for the opening,
rolling himself around the weapon clutched in his
hands. The instant his head entered the opening, the
carrier slowed and he landed hard. The shelf swayed
under him, but he compressed himself into a fetal ball,
managed to stay aboard. His left shoulder rubbed the
back wall as the carrier gathered speed, and he left a
trail of skin before he could jerk away. He peered up
and around.

The dumbwaiter system operated in a long slot
between gray walls, an area illuminated only by light
from the feeder openings. He could make out many
carriers moving swiftly upward around him and there
was an acrid fruit smell overriding the other stinks. He
passed more openings, glimpsed a startled face at one
—a woman carrying a basket piled high with yellow
fruit that looked like tiny pumpkins. Janvert peered
upward, trying to find out how the system terminated.
Did it disgorge into chopping machinery? Was there a
bloody mincer arrangement up there, a sorting system,
or conveyors?

A wide line of light was becoming visible far
above him and he could hear the increasing roar of
machinery up there. It drowned out the whistling,
clanking, hissing of the conveyor he was riding. The
wide line of light was nearer—nearer—he tensed himself and was caught by surprise as a trip system tipped
his shelf at the top of the lift, dumping him into a bin
piled high with yellow carrots.

Clutching the bin's top with his left hand, Janvert
righted himself, clambered over the edge into a room
of long, waist-high troughs that flowed with bubbling
pulp of many colors. Workers moved all through the
area dumping bins of produce into the troughs.

It was easily six feet to the floor and Janvert
landed with a slippery squishing that sent him lurching
into a female who had come up to the conveyor outlet

with an empty bin on wheels. Janvert's momentum sent her sprawling. He kept her down with a burst from his weapon, charged forward, slipping and skidding. There was pulped tomato on his feet and the floor itself carried a skimming of multicolored debris from the processing that continued all around him.

He passed another group before reaching a doorway, but their food-spattered appearance differed little from his and they paid no attention to him. Janvert plunged through the door, was hit by a cold shock of water spraying from overhead nozzles. He gasped, splashing through the water, and was almost clean when he emerged on the far side through another door into a wide, dimly lighted tunnel. Water was draining off him, off the captured weapon in his hand, collecting in a puddle under him, but there were similar puddles all around.

Janvert glanced left—the long vista of a tunnel down there, but few people and none of them appeared interested in him. He looked to his right, saw a spidery stairway similar to the one at the underground river. The stairs went upward into gloom and that was *his* direction. Janvert turned, slogged toward the stairs, began climbing, drawing himself up by sliding his left hand on the rail and pulling. His mouth was hanging open with fatigue and the aftermath of that shocking shower.

At the fifth rung on the stairs, he saw legs appear at the top. He fired his weapon without pausing, kept it humming as he climbed the remaining steps. Five sprawled figures lay on a platform where the stairs ended. He limped around them, his gaze fastened on a door beyond them. The door had only a bar latch which he lifted. The hinges were on the inside to the right. He pulled the bar. The door creaked open, revealing a dank dirt passage and the upthrusting roots of a tree stump that the door's movement had pushed outward and down. Janvert dragged himself past the stump into starlit darkness, heard the door creaking closed behind him. The stump tipped back into its concealing position with only a faint thump.

Janvert stood shivering in cold night air.

It took him a moment to realize that he had escaped from Hellstrom's madhouse human hive. He peered upward: stars. No doubt of it—he was outside. But where? The starlight gave him few clues to his surroundings. He could see a faint suggestion of trees directly ahead. He groped for the stump that masked the exit. His fingers encountered a hard surface which a fingernail told him was real wood. His eyes were adjusting, though, and escape from the tunnels had tapped a source of energy he hadn't known existed. There was a faint glow in the sky slightly to his left and he guessed that would be Fosterville. He tried to recall the distance. Ten miles? His overworked body would never make that on bare feet. The area in front of him appeared to be a grassy slope with dark spots in it.

Most of the water had dried from his body, but he still trembled with the cold. He knew he couldn't delay any longer. Those bodies behind him would be found. Hellstrom's people would be out here after him all too soon. He had to put distance between himself and that camouflaged exit. No matter how he did it, he had to get back to civilization and tell what he had seen.

Taking the sky glow as his compass point, Janvert set out down the slope. He clutched the captured weapon in his right hand. This thing was his passport to belief when he told his story. A demonstration of this weapon on a convenient animal would silence all doubt.

The rough ground hurt his bare feet, caught his toes with unseen rocks and roots. He stumbled, hobbled, ran full into a low wooden fence, and fell across it into the dust of a narrow road.

Janvert picked himself up, studied what he could see of the road in the starlight. It appeared to angle down to his left in the general direction of what he thought was Fosterville. He turned in that direction, stumbled down the dusty track, panting, not trying to be quiet. He was too worn-out for that. The road dipped into a shallow swale and he lost the sky glow for a moment, but had it again at the next rise.

The dust kicked up by his feet tickled his nose. There was a breeze like a feather touch on his right cheek and down his arm and his bare flank. The track dipped once more and turned gently to the right into a deeper darkness that suggested trees. He missed part of the turn, stubbed the little toe on his left foot against the edge of a rut. He hissed a curse, knelt, and gripped the injured member until the pain eased. As he knelt, he saw a sudden flickering of light in the darkness directly ahead. By reflex, Janvert brought up the captured weapon, pointed it, and fired—a single humming burst.

The light vanished.

He straightened, groped his way forward with his left hand out-stretched, the weapon held close to his right side. His outstretched hand was too high to meet the next obstruction, and he fell across a cold metallic surface, the weapon scraping it with a noisy clatter that froze him for the moment it took to realize he was sprawled half across the hood of a car.

A car!

He eased himself back, skinned his elbow on a hood ornament, then guided himself with his free hand around the left side of the car. At the window, his fingers explored an open crack at the top and he smelled tobacco smoke. He tried to peer through the window, but it was too dark. There was a rhythmic wheezing inside, though. He groped for the door handle, jerked the door open in a startling flash of light from the automatic switch. The light revealed two men in business suits, neat white shirts and ties, slumped unconscious in the front seat. The driver held a smoldering cigarette which was charring a circle in the left leg of his pants. Janvert took the cigarette and dropped it in the dust by his feet, crushed out the burning cloth with one hand.

The man lighting a cigarette—the flicker of light at which he'd fired. This weapon didn't kill from a distance, then. Walls and distance made it less than fatal, and it obviously had a limited range beyond that.

Janvert shook the driver's shoulder, got only a lolling head for response. They were out cold. The movement opened the man's coat, though, revealing a shoulder holster and a snub-nose magnum pistol. Janvert took the gun and then saw the radio beneath the dash.

These weren't Hellstrom's people! These were cops!

What the drone said (Hive axiom). You Outsiders! It's your children we're after, not you! We'll get them, too, over your dead bodies.

"How can he be Outside?" Hellstrom demanded, outrage amplifying the sudden surge of fear that swept over him. He whirled from the dark north end of the gloomy aerie, strode across the room to the female at the observer console who'd called out to him.

"He is," she said. "See! There!" She pointed to the screen glowing with green brilliance in front of her. The screen showed Janvert's figure, its outline shimmering in the scattered radiation of night-vision projection. Janvert was creeping along a dusty road.

"That's the north perimeter," Hellstrom whispered, recognizing the outline of the landscape beyond Janvert. "How did he get out there?" Reluctant admiration for this incredible male warred in Hellstrom with a swelling rage. *Janvert was Outside!*

"We're getting reports of a disturbance at level three," an observer at Hellstrom's left called.

"He's found one of the hidden doors out of level three," Hellstrom said. "How did he get that far? He'll be at that car with its watchers in seconds! The car's right down in those trees." He pointed at the screen. "Have the watchers heard him yet?"

"We have a pursuit team out after him," an observer on the left called. "They'll be a few minutes, though. They were on five and we routed them through the upper exits."

The observer in front of Hellstrom said, "I got an interference flash just before I saw him, as though he'd used his weapon. Could he have knocked out the watchers in that car?"

"Or killed them," Hellstrom said. "Poetic justice if he did. Who's observing that car?"

"The team was pulled back an hour ago to help search for the escaped captive," someone behind him said.

Hellstrom nodded. Of course! He'd given the order himself.

"There hasn't been any conversation in that car for sometime," the observer just to his left said. "I have the pickup on the tree above the car." The observer tapped the shiny ivory plug in her right ear. "I can hear Janvert approaching—the watchers in the car sound unconscious. They're wheezing the way Outsiders always do when you stun them heavily."

"Maybe it's a break for us at last," Hellstrom said. "How far away is the pursuit team?"

"Five minutes at the most," someone behind him said.

"Get backup squads out onto the rangeland between him and the town," Hellstrom said. "Just in case—"

"What about the other watchers?" the observer in front of him asked.

"Tell our workers not to attract attention to themselves! Devil take that Janvert! The Hive needs breeders that resourceful."

How had the man escaped from the Hive?

The observer on his left said, "He's almost at the car."

An observer farther down the arc said, "Here's the report on how he got out." She turned, her face in eerie side light from the screens, and told him briefly what the cleanup teams had found at level three.

He rode a food conveyor! Hellstrom thought. The Outsider took risks no ordinary worker would think of taking. The implications in that would have to be considered more thoroughly—later.

"The captive female," Hellstrom said. "Has she been shown what will happen to her if she fails?"

Someone behind him spoke with obvious distaste, "She's been shown, Nils."

Hellstrom nodded. They didn't like this, of course. He didn't like it himself. But it was necessity and all of them could see that now.

"Bring her in here," Hellstrom said.

They had to drag her into the range of the dim lights at the observation screens and then hold her upright when they stopped.

Hellstrom suppressed his own revulsion, spoke slowly and distinctly as though to a newly hatched child, and all the time he felt that he was sacrificing himself for the Hive.

"Clovis Carr," he said. "That is the name you gave us. Do you still identify with it?"

She stared through the gloom at the greenish death pallor of Hellstrom's skin. This is a nightmare, she told herself. I'll wake up and find out it's all been a nightmare.

Hellstrom saw the recognition that use of her name aroused. "In a moment, Miss Carr, your friend Janvert will come within range of a remote speaker we have out there." He pointed to the screen. "I will attract Mr. Janvert's attention then, and it will be up to you to get him back here if you can. I deeply regret that we must cause you this mental anguish, but you can see the necessity. Will you try?"

She nodded, her face a pale mask of terror in the green light. Try? Sure! Play right along with the nightmare.

"Very good," Hellstrom said. "You must think in a positive way, Miss Carr. You must think success. I believe you can do this."

Again she nodded, but it was as though she had no conscious control over her muscles.

From the Hive Manual. The society itself must be considered as living material. The same ethics and morality that concern us when we interfere with the sacred flesh of an individual cell must concern us equally when we intrude into the processes of the society.

Janvert was reaching for the radio microphone, hardly believing he had that token of civilization within his grasp, when a voice boomed at him from high over his right shoulder.

"Janvert!"

He jerked back, slamming the door to shut off the car's dome light, dodged to the front of the car and crouched there, pointing his weapon up into the darkness.

"Janvert, I know you can hear me."

The voice came from up in the trees, but it was too dark to show any detail to Janvert. He held himself locked in indecision. What a fool he'd been to leave the car's dome light on!

"I am speaking to you through a remote system, Janvert," the voice said. "There is an electronic device in a tree near you. It will pick up your answer and transmit it to me. You must answer me now."

A loudspeaker!

Still, Janvert crouched in silence. It was a trick. They wanted him to speak just to locate him.

"We have someone here who wants to speak to you," the voice said. "Listen carefully, Janvert."

At first, Janvert failed to recognize the new voice issuing from the speaker. There was such a throat-strained quality in the words, as though each required superhuman effort. It was a woman, though, and then she said, "Eddie! It's Clovis. Please answer me!"

Clovis was the only one who called him Eddie. The others all used that hated *Shorty*. He stared up through the darkness. Clovis?

"Eddie," she said, "if you don't come back, they're going to take me down to a—a place where—where they—cut off your legs and the rest—" She was sobbing now. "Your legs and the rest of your body at the waist and—oh, God! Eddie, I'm so frightened. Eddie! Please answer me! Please come back!"

Janvert recalled that room of stumped bodies, the

multicolored tubes, the hideously accentuated sexuality. Abruptly, he experienced a flashing memory: the severed head on the tunnel floor, the gore, his own feet trampling through red fruit, his body spattered with . . .

He doubled over, vomited.

Clovis's voice went on and on, pleading with him.

"Eddie, please, can you hear me? Please! Don't let them do that to me. Oh, God! Why doesn't he answer?"

I can't answer her, Janvert thought.

But he had to respond. He had to do something. The air was full of the nauseating smell of his own vomit and his chest ached, but his head felt cleared. He straightened, supporting himself with a hand on the car's hood.

"Hellstrom!" he called.

"Right here." It was the first voice Janvert had heard.

"How can I trust you?" Janvert asked. He started working his way back to the car's door. He had to get to that radio.

"We will harm neither you nor Miss Carr if you return," Hellstrom said. "We do not lie about such things, Mr. Janvert. You will be placed under necessary restraints, but neither of you will be harmed. We will permit the two of you to associate and have any relationship you wish, but if you do not return to us immediately, we will carry out our threat. We will do so with the deepest regret, but we will do it. Our own attitudes toward a procreative stump are much different from yours, Mr. Janvert. Believe me."

"I believe you," Janvert said. He was at the car's door now, hesitating. If he opened the door and grabbed for the microphone, what would they do up there? They must have searchers out here by now. They had that speaker in the tree. They had some way of knowing what he was doing. He had to take precautions, then. He lifted the captured weapon, intending to spray the area around him randomly before opening the door. He didn't allow himself to think about Clovis. But that room . . . His finger on the firing stud re-

fused to move. That room with the stubs of bodies!
Again, he felt nausea clutching him.

Clovis could still be heard over the speaker. She
was crying somewhere in the background, sobbing and
calling his name. "Eddie—Eddie—Eddie—please help
me. Make it stop—"

Janvert closed his eyes. *What can I do?*

As the thought pulsed in his mind, he felt a tingling on his back and right side, heard a distant humming that followed him all the way down to the dusty
ground beside the car, but he no longer heard it by the
time he was stretched in the dust.

From the Hive Manual. Protective resemblance has
always been a major key to our survival. This is shown
by the oral tradition as well as by the earliest written
records that we have preserved. The mimicry our
ancestors learned from insects helps protect us from
the attacks of the wild Outsiders. Observation of insects tells us, however, that the survival value of this
device remains low unless we perfect it and combine it
with many other techniques, especially new techniques
that we must constantly search out. To spur us on the
way, we must think always of Outsiders as predators.
They will attack if they find us. They are sure to find
us someday and we must prepare for this. Our preparation must include both defensive and offensive characteristics. In offensive weapons, let us always keep
the insect as our model—the weapon must *condition*
any attacker against repeating acts of violence against
us.

The vibration of the Hive began somewhere far
down below the aerie and reached upward and outward with shock waves that would register on seismic
recorders all around the planet. When it stopped,
Hellstrom thought: *Earthquake!* It was a fearful prayer in his mind, however, not a recognition. Let it be an
earthquake and not the destruction of Project 40!

He had just begun to relax from the recapture of

Janvert not twenty minutes ago when the vibration began.

The aerie stopped creaking and there was a moment of abnormal silence, as though all of the workers of the Hive held their breath simultaneously. In that moment, Hellstrom moved through the aerie's gloom, noting that the lights still functioned, the screens still glowed. He said, "Damage reports, please. Somebody get me Saldo." The note of calm command in his own voice surprised him.

Within seconds, they had Saldo on a screen at the right side of the arc. Hellstrom could see a section of a wide gallery behind Saldo, dust settling there.

"They held me!" Saldo greeted him. The younger man looked shocked and just the smallest amount cowed. One of the big symbiotes who attended the researchers moved in behind Saldo then and thrust him aside. The scarred, ebony features of a researcher filled the screen. A pink palm came up in front of the face then and the fingers winked in Hive-sign.

Hellstrom translated aloud for those around him who could not see the screen.

"We do not appreciate the distrust represented by your observer with orders to delay the power connection for our project. Let the alarm you felt be a small sign of our displeasure. We could have warned you to expect it, but your behavior did not deserve such warning. Recall the resonance we all felt in the Hive and rest assured that the effect was of an order many thousands of times greater at the locus of our projected impulse. Project 40, except for some small refinements which may include damping the local feedback, can be judged a complete success."

"Where was the locus of your projection?" Hellstrom asked.

"In the Pacific Ocean near the islands that the Outsiders call Japan. They will observe a new island there shortly."

The big face moved out of the screen's range to be replaced by Saldo.

"They restrained me," Saldo protested. "They held me and ignored my orders. They connected the power and wouldn't let me call you. They disobeyed you, Nils!"

Hellstrom flashed a "calm yourself" sign and, as Saldo fell silent, said, "Complete the loose ends of your observation, Saldo. Assemble a report, including development time for the refinements they mention, then report to me personally in full." He signaled to close the communication, turned away.

The Hive had its defensive-offensive weapon, then, but with it came many other problems. The crisis disturbance that had spread all through the Hive had left its mark on the researchers. Their ordinary irritability had been amplified into a species of revolt. There was damage to the Hive's interdependence system. This might buy them the time to recover, though. Whatever else it needed, the Hive needed long periods of undisturbed time most of all. The big changes devoured great blocks of time. He could see this when he compared himself to the new breed. Hellstrom held few illusions about himself. He really preferred to vocalize, and Hive-sign always represented a strain on him, but for some of the new breed, this pattern was reversed. Hellstrom knew he took an unhealthy enjoyment in the possession of a distinct name and an Outsider-like identity, but most of the Hive's workers were free of this bondage.

I am a transitional form, he told himself, *and someday I will be obsolete.*

From the Hive Manual. Freedom represents a concept that is tied inextricably to the discredited abstract of individualism/ego. We sacrifice none of this *freedom* to gain our more efficient, reliable, and convenient basic human stock.

Merrivale stood on the balcony outside his second-floor motel room waiting for daylight. It was cold, but he had dressed in a Highlands-made gray woolen sweater with a high turtleneck. It was thick enough to protect him even when he leaned against the iron balustrade. He puffed thoughtfully on a cigarette, listening to night sounds. There were distant footsteps out in the parking lot and a murmur of voices from a room down the balcony where a light had come on a few minutes ago.

A door below him opened, sending yellow light in a great splashing fan across the courtyard to the blue edge of the swimming pool. A man strode out into the light, peered upward.

Merrivale, looking down, recognized Gammel and expected the FBI man might have a report on the earth shock. The quake, a distant rumbling that had filled his room with primitive fears, had awakened Merrivale almost forty-five minutes earlier. Gammel already had been awake and in the room downstairs they were using as a command post. Merrivale had him on the house telephone in a few seconds, demanding, "What was that?"

"Felt like an earthquake. We're checking out whether there was any damage. You okay?"

Merrivale had turned on his bedside light. There was power, at least. He glanced around his room. "Yes, I'm fine. Doesn't seem to be any damage here at all."

Some of the motel's other tenants had been on the balcony and in the courtyard when Merrivale went out, but most had returned to their rooms by now.

Gammel, recognizing Merrivale on the balcony, motioned for him to come down. "Hurry it up."

Merrivale stubbed out his cigarette, crushed it underfoot, and headed down the balcony toward the stairs. There was something tensely alarming in Gammel's manner.

Merrivale made it down to the first-floor room in a swift ten seconds, taking the stairs two at a time, not bothering about noise. He plunged through the door Gammel was holding open from the inside, heard the door slam behind him.

It wasn't until he was fully into the room, seeing the three men clustered around a table that held a radio transceiver and a telephone with the receiver off

the hook, that Merrivale began to get a full sense of
how truly wrong things had gone.

There was a bed against the wall behind the table, its covers thrown off and dragged part way into
the room. An ash tray had fallen off the table and lay
ignored in its spilled contents. One of the men around
the table still wore pajamas, although Gammel and the
others were fully dressed. Light came from two floor
lamps pulled close to the table. All of the men, including Gammel, were focused in some way on the telephone with its receiver off. Two of the men were
actually staring at the phone. The man in pajamas
was looking from the phone to Merrivale, back to the
phone, and to Merrivale. Gammel was pointing at the
instrument while he glared at Merrivale.

"Dammit to hell! They knew our number!" Gammel blared.

"What?" Merrivale was taken aback by the accusatory tone.

"We had that phone put in late yesterday," Gammel explained. "It's a private line."

"I don't understand," Merrivale said. He studied
Gammel's rocky face, seeking a clue to this odd conversation.

"It was Hellstrom calling us," Gammel said. "He
says he has one of your people with him—and—do
you have an Eddie Janvert?"

"Shorty? Shorty led the team that—"

Gammel put a hand to lips to shut him off.

Merrivale nodded.

Gammel said, "Hellstrom tells me we'd better listen to your man or they will blow this town and half
the state of Oregon off the planet."

"What?"

"He says that wasn't an earthquake we all felt. It
was some weapon he claims can rip the planet apart.
How trustworthy is your man Janvert?"

Merrivale answered automatically, "Completely!" Immediately, he wished he had not said that. It
had been a thoughtless response to a question that demanded he defend the Agency's capabilities. Janvert
might not be completely trustworthy, or it might be

necessary to show doubt of his actual trustworthiness.
Too late now, though. His answer had trapped him,
reduced the range of possible responses.

"Janvert is on that phone and wants to talk to
you," Gammel said. "He tells me he can verify Hellstrom's threat and that he can explain why one of our
cars is failing to respond on the radio."

Merrivale stalled for time to assess the situation.
"I thought you told me the phone to the farm was out
of order. Are they calling from the farm?"

"As far as we know. One of my men is out right
now trying to work a trace. Hellstrom apparently had
the phone fixed himself, or it—"

"Janvert says our people are merely unconscious,
but he refused to say why or explain. He insisted we
get you first. I told him you might be asleep, but—"
Gammel nodded at the telephone.

Merrivale swallowed in a dry throat. Blow up
half the state? Poppycock! He crossed to the phone
with as much confidence as he could muster, picked it
up, spoke in his best British accent. "Merrivale here."

Gammel moved to a tape recorder spinning away
behind the transceiver, jacked an earphone into it, and
listened, nodding for Merrivale to continue.

That's old Jollyvale all right, Janvert thought as
he heard the voice. Wonder why they sent him?

Clovis stood directly across from Janvert, still
frightened, but no longer sobbing. He found it odd
that her nudity didn't excite him.

Janvert nodded to Hellstrom, who stood a pace
away in the gloomy room above the barn-studio.
Hellstrom's face appeared deathly pale in the green
light that came from banks of what appeared to Janvert as TV screens.

"Tell him," Hellstrom said.

Merrivale's voice was being broadcast to the entire aerie room from a speaker on the control bank.

"Hello, Joe," Janvert said, deliberately using
Merrivale's first name for the first time. "This is Eddie
Janvert. I'm sure you recognize my voice, but I'll
identify myself further if you want. I'm the one you

gave the president's Signal Corps number and code to, remember?"

Damn him! Merrivale thought, resenting that admission as much as the familiar tone and use of his first name. It was Janvert, though. No doubt of it. "Tell me what is going on," Merrivale said.

"Unless you want this whole planet to become one giant morgue, you'd better listen carefully to what I tell you and you'd better believe me," Janvert said.

"Now, see here, Shorty," Merrivale said. "What's all this nonsense they've been telling me about blowing up—"

"You shut up and listen!" Janvert snapped. "You hear me? Hellstrom has a weapon that makes an atom bomb look like a child's popgun. Those guys in the car, those FBI agents your buddy was worried about—they were knocked out by a little hand version of this weapon. That hand-held weapon can kill people at a distance or just knock them out. Believe me, I've seen it. Now, you—"

"Shorty," Merrivale interrupted, "I think you'd better let me come up there and—"

"Oh, you'll come up here all right," Janvert said, "but if you have any doubts, get rid of them. And if you try to attack this place again—well, if I even suspect you *might* do that, I'm going to use that number and code you gave me and I'm going to call the president to give him a full—"

"Now, Shorty! Your government wouldn't—"

"Fuck the government! Hellstrom's weapon is zeroed in right now on the Capitol. They've already demonstrated its effectiveness. Why don't you check *that?*"

"Check what? That little earthquake we—"

"The new island off the coast of Japan," Janvert said. "Hellstrom's people have a tap on the Pentagon's satellite teletype relay. They know about it and there's a seismic sea wave warning all around the Pacific Basin already."

"What in the bloody hell are you talking about, Shorty?" Merrivale demanded. As he spoke, Merrivale bent over the table, clawed a notepad and pencil into position, and scrawled, "Gammel—check that!" Gammel bent to read the note, nodded, and pointed to it for another of the agents to obey, then whispered an explanation.

Janvert was talking again, his voice coming out clear and precise as though he were trying to explain something to a disobedient child. "I warned you to listen carefully," Janvert said. "Hellstrom's hive is just one tiny extrusion from a giant complex of tunnels. Those tunnels spread out to hell and they go down more than five thousand feet. They are lined with a special concrete that Hellstrom says is proof against a fission bomb. I believe him. There are some fifty thousand people living in these tunnels. Believe me— please believe me."

Merrivale found his attention caught in fascination by the spinning reels on Gammel's tape recorder, lifted his gaze to meet a look of shock in the SAIC's eyes.

Merrivale thought: Bloody hell! If Shorty's right, this isn't a job for us, it's a job for the military. Somehow, Shorty was to be believed. It just wasn't possible that a statement so shocking could be false. Merrivale bent to the notepad and wrote, "Call army."

Glancing at the words, Gammel hesitated, then motioned another of his aides to read it and obey. The aide looked at the pad, stared questioningly at Gammel, who nodded vigorously to reinforce the command, then motioned for the man to bend close. Gammel whispered for a moment and the aide's face paled. He dashed out of the room.

"As unbelievable as your story sounds," Merrivale said, "I will take your word for it at the moment. However, you must know what I will have to do in response. This is far too big a situation for me to—"

"You son of a bitch! If you attack, the whole planet's done for!"

Merrivale froze in shock, the phone pressed against his ear, detecting a glint of shared response in Gammel's eyes. That was *not* how one addressed a superior!

In the Hive aerie, Hellstrom leaned close to Janvert and whispered, "Tell him the Hive wishes to negotiate. Temporize. Ask him why he hasn't investigated with the Pentagon about the new island. Tell him we are quite ready to vaporize an area of several hundred square miles around Washington, D.C., if he needs further demonstrations."

Janvert relayed this message.

"Have you seen this weapon?" Merrivale asked.

"Yes!"

"Describe it."

"Are you nuts? They won't let me describe it. But I've seen it and I've seen the little hand version of it."

The first aide Gammel had sent from the room returned, whispered hoarsely in the SAIC's ear. Gammel scribbled on the notepad, "Pentagon confirms. They sending assault team."

Merrivale said, "Shorty, do you really believe they can do this?"

"I've been telling you nothing else, goddammit! Haven't you checked with the Pentagon yet?"

"Shorty, I hate to say this, but it seems to me that several fission bombs, one right on top of the other into—"

"You goddamned idiot! Will you stop making stupid suggestions like that?"

Merrivale glared at the base of the telephone. "Shorty, I must ask that you moderate your tone and your passions. This—this *hive*, as you call it, sounds like the very kind of subversion that we must—"

"I'm calling the president!" Janvert said. "You know I can do it. You gave me the Signal Corps number and code yourself. He'll answer, too. You and the Agency can go plumb straight to—"

"Shorty!" Merrivale was outraged and abruptly fearful. This thing was getting completely out of hand. Janvert's fanciful warnings might have some substance in them—the military would find out about that quickly enough—but a call to the president would have widespread repercussions. Heads would roll. They bloody well would!

"Calm yourself, Shorty," Merrivale said. "Now,

listen to me. What assurance do I have that you're telling me the truth? You describe a pretty desperate situation which I find extremely difficult to believe. If it is anything even remotely resembling what you describe, however, it clearly calls for a military solution and I've no alternative but to—"

"You asshole!" Janvert snapped. "Haven't you understood a single thing I've said? There won't be any *world* for your damned military solution to take place on if you make one wrong move now! There won't be anything! These people can blow the planet apart, or pulverize any piece of it they choose. You couldn't break through to them in time to prevent that. The planet's at stake—the whole planet, do you understand me?"

Gammel reached out, grabbed Merrivale's telephone arm, and shook it to demand attention. Merrivale looked at him.

Gammel held up a sheet of paper on which he had written, "Go along with him. Ask personal inspection visit. Until we're sure, we cannot take chances."

Merrivale pursed his lips in thought. Go along with him? That was madness. Blow up the world, indeed! He said, "Shorty, I'm sure my own profound doubts about this—"

Abruptly, Gammel dropped his earphones, grabbed the telephone out of Merrivale's hand, thrust him aside, and motioned for two of his aides to hold Merrivale.

"Janvert," Gammel said, "this is Waverly Gammel. I spoke to you a few minutes ago when you first called. I'm a senior agent with the FBI. I've been listening to your conversation and I, for one, am ready to go along with—"

"They're just stalling!" Merrivale shouted, struggling with the agents who held him. "They're bluffing, you fool! They can't—"

Gammel put a hand over the receiver and addressed his men. "Take him outside and shut the door." He returned to his conversation with Janvert, explaining, "That was Merrivale. I've had him forcibly removed. Under the circumstances, I suspect he must be insane. I am going to come out to that—that *hive* myself and I am going to look at whatever it is you can show me to substantiate this weird story. I will ask that any action from this end be delayed until I report back, but I will put a time limit on that. Do you understand all of that, Janvert?"

"You sound like somebody with a few smarts, Gammel," Janvert said. "I thank God for that. Just a minute."

Hellstrom bent close to Janvert, spoke in a low voice.

Janvert said, "Hellstrom says you can come out here under those terms and will be permitted to report back in person. It's my opinion that you can trust him."

"That's good enough for me," Gammel said. "Tell me exactly where I report at that farm."

"Just come to the barn," Janvert said. "That's where it all begins."

As Janvert replaced the telephone in its cradle, Hellstrom turned away, wondering why he no longer felt tired. The Hive was going to get its *big block of time.* That seemed obvious. There were a few among the wild Outsiders who could be reasoned with—people such as this Janvert and the agent on the telephone. Such people would understand the implications of the Hive's new *stinger.* They would recognize the need for change. Things were going to change in this world, too. Hellstrom knew what his own course had to be. He would bargain with the Outsider government for conditions under which the Hive could continue its mimic existence unobserved by the wild masses. The secrecy could not last indefinitely, of course. The Hive itself would see to that. They were going to swarm before long and there was nothing the Outsiders could do to prevent that swarming. Swarm would follow swarm thereafter and the wild ones would be assimilated and pushed back into smaller and smaller portions of the planet they shared now with tomorrow's humans.

From Joseph Merrivale's report to the Agency board.

As you know, we are effectively blocked from any further active participation in this matter, a decision the short sightedness of which we all recognize. We are consulted on the problem from time to time, however, and I can give you some idea of how things are proceeding in Washington.

My own private guess at the moment is that Hellstrom will be permitted to continue with his filthy cult, at least for the time being, and he may even be allowed to continue making his subversive films.

The seesaw of the official debate is polarized around the following two opposing viewpoints:

1. Blast them out and damn the consequences. This is a minority viewpoint which I share, but it is losing adherents.
2. Stall for time by making a secret agreement with Hellstrom, thereby keeping knowledge of the Hive from the public, while at the same time mounting a massive research program aimed at the destruction of what is coming to be called in official circles "the Hellstrom horror."

ABOUT THE AUTHOR

FRANK HERBERT was born in Tacoma, Washington, in 1920, and served in the U.S. Navy during World War II. Although known primarily as a science fiction writer, Mr. Herbert has worked as a newspaperman on the West Coast for over twenty years, and his recent novel, *Soul Catcher,* attests to his skills in areas other than science fiction. His reputation as a writer, however, stems from the success of *Dune,* first published in 1965, one of the rare books to capture *both* of science fiction's highest honors—the coveted Hugo and Nebula awards. Because one of his earlier novels won the International Fantasy Award, Frank Herbert has the distinction of being the first writer to win all three honors, the highest in the field. Mr. Herbert's other books include: *Dune Messiah* (the successor to *Dune*); *Dragon in the Sea; The Godmakers; The Green Brain; Destination: Void; The Eyes of Heisenberg; New World or No World; The Santaroga Barrier;* and *Whipping Star.* His latest novel, HELLSTROM'S HIVE, was inspired by the award-winning motion picture, *The Hellstrom Chronicle.* Frank Herbert has worked as a professional photographer, TV cameraman, oyster diver, lay analyst, jungle survival instructor, radio news commentator, and teacher of creative writing. He has done research in such diverse fields as undersea geology, navigation, psychology, jungle botany, and anthropology. Mr. Herbert lives with his wife and three children in Seattle, Washington.

A SELECTED LIST OF SCIENCE FICTION AND FANTASY TITLES AVAILABLE FROM CORGI

While every effort is made to keep prices low, it is sometimes necessary to increase prices at short notice. Corgi Books reserve the right to show and charge new retail prices on covers which may differ from those previously advertised in the text or elsewhere.

The prices shown below were correct at the time of going to press.

☐	11669 6	The Dragon Lensman	David Kyle	£1.25
☐	11151 1	Fantastic Voyage	Isaac Asimov	85p
☐	13869 3	Star Trek 1	James Blish	95p
☐	12731 4	Star Trek 8	James Blish	95p
☐	10746 8	The Cabal	Saul Dunn	75p
☐	10886 3	The Cabal 2 : The Black Moon	Saul Dunn	85p
☐	10694 1	Raven: Swordmistress of Chaos	Richard Kirk	70p
☐	10861 8	Raven 2 : A Time of Ghosts	Richard Kirk	80p
☐	11131 7	Raven 5 : A Time of Dying	Richard Kirk	95p
☐	11313 1	The White Dragon	Anne McCaffrey	£1.95
☐	10965 7	Get Off the Unicorn	Anne McCaffrey	£1.75
☐	10881 2	Dragonsinger : Harper of Pern	Anne McCaffrey	£1.50
☐	10661 5	Dragonsong	Anne McCaffrey	£1.25
☐	10773 5	Dragonflight	Anne McCaffrey	£1.25
☐	11936 9	The Ship Who Sang	Anne McCaffrey	£1.50
☐	11789 7	Decision at Doona	Anne McCaffrey	£1.50
☐	11219 4	The City and the Stars	Arthur C. Clarke	95p
☐	01077 8	Dragonworld	Byron Preiss & J. Michael Reaves	£3.95
☐	11178 3	A Canticle for Leibowitz	Walter M. Miller	£1.25
☐	11194 5	Earth Abides	George R. Stewart	£1.00

All these books are available at your bookshop or newsagent, or can be ordered direct from the publisher. Just tick the titles you want and fill in the form below.

CORGI BOOKS, Cash Sales Department, P.O. Box 11, Falmouth, Cornwall.
Please send cheque or postal order, no currency.
Please allow cost of book(s) plus the following for postage and packing:

U.K. CUSTOMERS. 40p for the first book, 18p for the second book and 13p for each additional book ordered, to a maximum charge of £1.49.

B.F.P.O. & EIRE. Please allow 40p for the first book, 18p for the second book plus 13p per copy for the next three books, thereafter 7p per book.

OVERSEAS CUSTOMERS. Please allow 60p for the first book plus 18p per copy for each additional book.

NAME (Block letters) ....

ADDRESS ....

....